The Keystone Trilogy - I

RETURN

Ian Houston

◆ FriesenPress

One Printers Way
Altona, MB R0G 0B0
Canada

www.friesenpress.com

ISBN
978-1-03-919947-7 (Hardcover)
978-1-03-919946-0 (Paperback)
978-1-03-919948-4 (eBook)

1. YOUNG ADULT FICTION, SUPERHEROES

Distributed to the trade by The Ingram Book Company

For Dan.
For leaving the laces loose.

PROLOGUE

PROLOGUE

Ancient Greece,
approximately 1200 BC

The Temple of Artemis stood on a rocky promontory, overlooking a scalloped bay. The prosperous port town of Aulis clustered around the bay's edge, whitewashed walls gleaming between rows of tile roofs brightly painted red, blue, and green. Below the houses, great wooden piers thrust like spears into the sparkling aquamarine waters, where hundreds of biremes—long, broad wooden ships of shallow draft, with fifty oars to each side—floated in the eerie calm. The work of taking on extra provisions and fresh water was still ongoing. Tiny figures like laden ants passed from the docks to the decks of the ships and back again. Beneath them, the waters of the bay were flat as glass. Each vessel stood upon a reflection of itself. Not a sail among them stirred, despite the salt-laden breeze that blew among the temple's fluted columns atop the cliff.

Agamemnon, king of Mycenae, looked upon the scene below, one foot upon the low stone wall separating the Temple Garden from the cliff's edge. His golden armor, polished to a glossy shine, glowed in the setting sun. A crested helm sat on the wall, next to his sandaled foot. In his hands, he held a letter, sealed with silver wax borrowed

∨

from the temple acolytes. The creamy paper was scuffed and bent; the king continually worried the letter's edge with a thumbnail.

The steep cliffs below the temple were interrupted, here and there, by the gleaming white sands of narrow beaches. Normally, thunderous waves would break against these cliffs, heaving great clouds of spume skyward. The surf would inundate the sunny strands as flocks of gulls darted and dove among the breakers. The wind would roar with the tide, blow stiff and chilly up the temple's skirts. Not so, today. Today, the breeze was a paltry thing in the Temple Garden; it blew not at all down below.

Despite this, a great vessel was approaching the docks of Aulis, akin to the biremes but thrice their size. Double banks of oars, two tiers of a hundred each to either side, drove the great ship through the still waters. Its sails were pristine white and blindingly brilliant in the slanting evening sunlight, and it flew the blue-and-white flags of Mycenae. The sides had been festooned with holly wreathes and garlands of olive and oak branches in celebration of the coming wedding ceremonies. The royal barge of Queen Clytemnestra had at last arrived. Soldiers lining the rails of the smaller boats, tiny from the lofty heights of the Temple Garden, gave voice to a great cheer. With no wind to compete against, the noise carried easily to the king's ears despite the distance.

There came the scuff of sandaled feet on the gravel path behind him. Achilles's resonant voice said, "It is not too late to reconsider, My King."

King Agamemnon straightened. Though he took a deep breath, as if to respond, for a long moment, he did nothing but tap the edge of the letter against his left palm. Then he said, "I have already done so." Stiffly, still staring out over the bay, he held the letter over his shoulder.

Achilles's footsteps sounded eagerly on the path. The letter was plucked from the king's hand. "I will not pause for breath, My

King. It will be there before the ship has finished docking." He hurried away.

The king listened to Achilles's retreating footsteps. He considered the steep descent from the temple, the distance from where he stood to Aulis rolling away in a series of lowering hills, cloaked in vast shady tracts of poplar, oak, and cypress. At this time of year, the sacred groves of Artemis were alive with color: emerald green, golden yellow, fiery orange, burnt umber. On any other day, the turning leaves would be lifted by the ocean breeze to sail across green meadows speckled with wildflowers. But not today. Today, the goddess Artemis, in her wrath, had stilled the winds and calmed the waves.

At length, the king picked up his helm and tucked it under his arm. He followed the garden path to the temple's front portico. Along the way, he passed decorative displays of pale roses, strawberries, and woven branches laden with pistachios. Canvas tents in white and silver, bearing the goddess's crescent moon motif, provided shade for tables laden with fresh bread, sliced fruit, olives, cheeses, and choice cuts of meat. Silver ewers of watered wine glistened with condensation, having only recently been brought forth from the coolness of the temple cellars. The temple acolytes had gone to great lengths to prepare for the wedding ceremony.

It was a shame to waste such bounty. A suitable gift should mollify the high priestess, reflected the king, but it wasn't *her* he needed to please. It was her mistress, the goddess Artemis. Caught up in frowning contemplation of his predicament, the king did not at first see his brother, Menelaus, waiting for him on the temple steps. It was not until Menelaus spoke that the king was pulled from his reverie. His heart plummeted within him; in his hands, Menelaus held the letter. Achilles, seated in his burnished bronze parade armor on the steps nearby, held his head in his hands.

"Aga," said Menelaus. "Lovely evening for a wedding, is it not?"

"No, Menni, it is not. Let Achilles be on his way with the missive. We will find some other solution to this mess."

"This mess *you* have caused." His brother's voice was thick with scorn.

Agamemnon's heavy brows drew down like lowering storm clouds. He regarded his brother through narrowed eyes. Menelaus was unimpressed. Like a shadowy twin to Agamemnon, he was dressed in dark armor, muscular arms crossed over his chest. He matched the king's flinty glare with a stony stare of his own.

The sound of the approaching wedding procession, drums and pipes ringing cheerfully in the still air, drew the king's eyes away from his brother. Even as he watched, Queen Clytemnestra and her escort rounded the final bend in the road and began the last ascent to the temple. Seated next to the queen on the royal palanquin, which was held aloft by eight burly slaves, was the king's eldest daughter, Iphigenia.

Shaded by a silk canopy of royal blue and white, she was elaborately draped in a flowing gown of diaphanous silver layers, adorned all about with gold and sparkling jewels. Her hair was wreathed by a crown of bright meadow flowers. The veil that should have been covering her face was held aside by one graceful hand as Iphigenia gazed wonderingly at her surroundings. The king could see it written plainly on his daughter's face: she hardly dared believe she would wed the renowned hero Achilles in the Great Temple of Artemis at Aulis. There was no more auspicious place for the union in all of Greece! She had such an open and innocent countenance. The king shook his head. *Such a waste.*

Queen Clytemnestra caught sight of the king and his companions waiting, then turned to chide Iphigenia. The girl hastily lowered her veil. It was though a curtain descended on his hopes; Agamemnon felt himself deflate. It was too late. It had been too late the moment he let fly his spear on the hunt three days past. Menelaus was right:

he, Agamemnon, had caused this, and no other. As the hunting party, one by one, had fallen behind, he alone had pursued their quarry into the sacred groves of Artemis. It had been none other than him who slew the great stag, defiling the hallowed bowers of the goddess's groves with sacred blood. None but the king could pay for the crime.

Divining some of his brother's thoughts, Menelaus moved to the king's side and placed a heavy hand on his shoulder. "Aga, what's done is done," he said, tone urgent. "What matters now is what you do next." He paused, then leaned close to confide, "Calchas the Seer has been among the soldiers, telling tales of his vision."

The king jerked as if slapped. "What? The treacherous dog! Now, if I do not do this thing, the soldiers will know me for a coward and a godless heretic! They will rebel!"

He ground his teeth, nostrils flaring. He well recalled the vision Menelaus referred to. After slaying the great stag in the sacred grove, the king had ordered his soldiers to gather the body, then transport it to the camp. Nervously, they complied, not wishing to offend the goddess any further but unwilling to disobey their king and risk harsh discipline. Late that evening, while Agamemnon and his entourage celebrated the king's prowess with a great feast of holy venison, toasting each other liberally and boasting of the deeds they would do in the coming battle, the goddess Artemis had spoken to the seer, Calchas, in a dream. The seer had barged into the king's pavilion in the middle of the night, sweaty and apologetic, but he refused to leave, causing a row until the king had shouted for the soldiers attempting to eject the frantic wizard to stand down.

The seer had then portentously informed the king, in front of all present, that the goddess Artemis was deeply offended. The king must make amends. The king had scoffed and made light of the situation, but Calchas had been adamant about his visions. He warned the king that if he did not do as requested, the goddess would prevent him from pursuing his vendetta against the Kingdom of Troy. The war would go poorly if the king did not take heed!

Agamemnon had ordered the histrionic seer from his sight. He'd warned those gathered to forget the incident, hinting that it would go poorly for any caught noising the story about camp. When the king's temper had cooled, however, Menelaus had come to him, insisting that Calchas had been right. The seer's holy vision must be obeyed. Yes, it was harsh, but the king had slain a sacred stag in the holy precincts of the goddess's grove. The king, alone, must atone . . . but Menelaus had proposed a plan for how to go about it. It had seemed like a good idea at the time. If nothing else, it solved the problem of how to accomplish the task the goddess demanded.

Now, as predicted by the seer, Agamemnon's fleet lay becalmed in the harbor below. The soldiers could not simply row to their destination; they would be too tired to fight! He knew he must capitulate. Ah, but the price . . . it was too high! Would men ever be more than playthings for the petty gods?

"Let it be done quickly, then!" growled the king. He donned his helm, as though preparing for war. Then he turned and mounted the steps, disappearing into the cool interior of the temple.

Achilles sighed. "The gods are cruel," he said, and followed the king inside.

By this time, the lowering sun was trading places with the rising moon. Menelaus lingered a few moments in the gathering twilight to watch the wedding party approach. His sharp eyes picked out the seer, Calchas, huffing along behind the lively procession in his rosy robes. As the seer paused to catch his breath, he noticed Menelaus watching him. They exchanged a brief and guarded nod. When a young acolyte hesitantly touched Menelaus's elbow, the king's brother donned his helm and passed beneath the temple's shady portico.

A few moments later, Iphigenia, flanked by the queen and Calchas, entered the temple. The priestesses of Artemis, silver togas glimmering in the sparse torchlight, lifted their voices and sang The Benediction of the Moon. The song wove echoes among the temple pillars, uplifting the hearts of the soldiers who had escorted the queen and princess to the holy Temple of Artemis. The soldiers spread out, marched the length of the building, and took up ranks on either side, silhouetted in the archways of the temple's open walls.

In the center of the temple stood the naos on a raised platform which supported the massive white marble altar stone, surrounded by delicate pale columns. These divided the space from the temple's outer ring while still leaving it open to the elements. Behind the altar stood the goddess Artemis, three times larger than life, also carved of marble, one hand resting on the head of a dappled fawn, the other upraised and holding a silver crescent moon. Beneath the goddess's impassive gaze, Agamemnon and his brother, Menelaus, flanked the altar stone. Behind the stone at the goddess's feet stood Achilles, looking decidedly grim.

The altar had been draped in blue and white silk. Upon it sat a silver bowl containing apricots, olives, figs, pears, and grapes, a matching ewer of watered wine, a silver knife, and a long cord woven of silver strands. Agamemnon stared at the arrangement of objects, contemplating their symbolic meaning. The bounty of life and its pleasures. The need for self-sacrifice. The way all men were bound in service to other men and to the gods. His eyes lingered on the knife.

Abruptly, the king turned on his heel and descended from the naos, meeting the queen halfway. She passed the promised bride to the king with a warm tilt of her lips. Within the shadows of his helm, the king's eyes were hard. He did not reciprocate her smile. The queen's expression remained fixed, smile held firmly in place, but her eyes searched Agamemnon's face.

Resolutely, he turned away, offering his arm to his daughter. She slipped her hand through the crook of his elbow, briefly laying her head on his shoulder. The king stiffened at that. Iphigenia drew back to regard his profile through her veil. Agamemnon, for his part, stared straight ahead. With a tug on her arm, he bid her forward. Together, they approached the naos, then climbed the three shallow steps to the altar stone. Behind them, the queen, escorted by Calchas, took up her position below the naos to witness proceedings.

Across the altar stone, Achilles stood, hands held out, palms upward, awaiting the warm clasp of his bride. Iphigenia stepped forward and reached for him. As she did so, Menelaus took up the woven silver cord from the altar. It would be used to bind the promised couple's hands together, and the high priestess would say the blessing on the goddess's behalf.

Iphigenia's fingers grazed Achilles's palms. The warrior turned away, jaw tight. He walked stiffly toward the rear of the temple. Startled, Iphigenia stood paralyzed, hands still reaching for the promised husband who was no longer there.

"My daughter," rasped the king, throat closing around his grief. "Know that I will always love you." He nodded to Menelaus. The king's brother stepped forward, looped the silver cord around Iphigenia's wrists, and pulled it tight.

"Aga! What is this madness?" Queen Clytemnestra rushed forward and was checked; Calchas held her tightly. A pair of guards were suddenly between her and the naos, spears crossed to bar her way.

The king and his brother took Iphigenia by the ankles and shoulders and hoisted her onto the altar. A loud clatter echoed among the columns as she was swung into place, knocking the silver bowl and ewer aside. Wine splashed and fruit thudded as it bounced down the steps. The king took up the silver knife from the altar as Menelaus pressed Iphigenia's shoulders back against the cold stone. The priestesses continued to sing, unsurprised by this turn of events. They had known all along what the goddess Artemis had demanded as penance from King Agamemnon.

"Great Goddess Artemis," intoned Calchas, orator's voice ringing among the shadowed pillars of the temple. "Hear your servant! We offer You this sacrifice . . ."

"My lord, *no!*" screamed the queen. Savagely, she shoved Calchas aside. He fell heavily, invocation cut off with a strangled groan. Clytemnestra launched herself at the soldiers, clawing and kicking wildly. Her shrieking curses and the grunting of the soldiers who held her at bay were folded into the rising voices of the temple choir. Chanting their invocations to Artemis, the priestesses moved forward as one and dragged the queen away.

Agamemnon paused as his daughter's struggles suddenly ceased. It was as though Iphigenia's energy had been stolen by the queen's departure. The king watched the realization dawn in her eyes: Achilles had walked away in shame. Without her mother, the girl was alone, stripped of her last defender. No one was coming to save her, now.

Iphigenia lay very still upon the altar, staring quietly at the silver blade poised above her. For a long moment, father and daughter remained frozen, poised on the cusp of an irreversible choice. As the seconds stretched, it almost seemed as if Iphigenia was the one to choose, for she did not weep or cry out. She did not flinch from the death held in her father's hands. She did not plead with her voice or with her eyes. Rather, Iphigenia's eyes *forgave*.

She lifted her chin, baring her throat.

"Oh, my child." And now the king wept openly. "You were always the strongest of us. Please forgive me!"

He brought the blade flashing down.

It was a beautiful day at the pier. A crisp breeze ruffled my wavy blonde hair and chivvied uniformly square white clouds across a brilliant blue sky. Weather drones winked in the sunlight at every cloud-corner, but none of the larger weather platforms were in evidence; their cool, gargantuan shadows slid elsewhere across the City, for the time being. Not far away, skyscrapers marched into hazy distance in all directions, smart-glass faces gleaming. The spaces between were stitched with lines of twinkling hover-traffic lights.

Here, the noise of the City seemed muted, pleasantly distant. True, it was only a little gap in the City's endless ranks, but even a little gap seemed wonderful to me. Over the ever-present babble of voices that formed the constant humming backdrop to my life on the streets, there was only the occasional cry of a gull and the quiet shushing of water as it lapped against the breakwater. It was as close to true peace and quiet as I'd ever come, and I loved it.

Aside from a hundred some-odd jump-suited citizens engaged in work on and around the pier, loading and unloading the boats and hover-trucks with cranes and gravity conveyors—along with a few using telekinesis for the same task—everybody seemed to be here for the same reason I was: to take their leisure. Nattily dressed old folks stood at railings or sat on benches staring out over the water, lost in nostalgic reveries. Fashionable couples in holographic clothes strolled by arm in arm, leaning into each other and sharing snacks purchased from the vendors that lined the pier. Children ran about, exclaiming excitedly over the most mundane things while their parents, having seen it all before, shared knowing smirks or fond smiles. I felt like those children when I came here, like I'd stumbled into something rare and miraculous, something I'd never seen before. A glimpse into the past that so obsessed my father, maybe. A little window into a time when it wasn't all City, everywhere.

I'd found myself coming back here more and more frequently. Something about it brought a rare calm to my mind. Amidst the cheerful babble and purposeful bustle, I felt like I could hear my thoughts more clearly. It helped me to center myself, made practicing my nearly useless Super-power just a little bit easier. For the first time in my seventeen years of life, my ability wasn't spontaneously flaring up—or at least, it wasn't flaring up so often. I was, finally, maybe just possibly, beginning to gain a degree of agency over its expression. No surprise, then, that my occasional visits to the pier had quickly become a daily habit. Hope, painful and raw, had blossomed in my chest. Maybe, just maybe, with enough focus and practice . . .

I shook my head and veered away from that line of thinking. I'd given up on the idea of becoming a Super-hero long ago. It was nice to come here and practice. Maybe, if I could get a handle on my powers, when I was no longer such an aggravation to my long-suffering parents, I could go home again. But that was about all I could really hope for.

Unfortunately, my life was about to take a sudden turn.

It wasn't the first time I'd been beaten up, sad to say, and it wouldn't be the last. I had always attracted bullies. Might have been my nearly uncontrollable Super-power, always reaching out and messing with people. Might have been the fact that I never quite knew when to back down. Might have just had the knack for ending up in the wrong place at the wrong time. I certainly never tried to throw the first punch. Maybe if I had, things might have been different growing up. But probably not. I had a strong sense of justice, and I wasn't usually patient enough to wait for someone else to

step in and make things right. I couldn't help getting myself into
. . . situations.

This particular situation fell into the "wrong place at the wrong
time" category, and it started out like a lot of similar incidents.
Hanging out at the pier, minding my own business, when someone
nearby took an unhealthy interest in what I was doing. Admittedly,
what I was doing *was* pretty weird. I'm a little embarrassed to say
it, but at the time, I was trying to swap a half-eaten sandwich I'd
snagged from a recycler a few blocks from the pier for a new pair of
bootlaces. Predictably, the Merchant Gull I was attempting to make
the trade with wasn't having any of it. Somehow, it knew the sandwich had been in a recycler. Specialized nanos were already at work
on it, breaking down synthesized bread and meat into their component molecules. By the time we finished haggling and the bird
settled down to lunch, the sandwich likely wouldn't be much more
than pinkish-gray molecular goo. Great for turning into practically
anything you might desire, if you had a fabricator, but not terribly
appetizing for a hungry bird. And this gull was cagey. I think it was
holding out so it wouldn't have to trade both laces.

For a moment, I considered using my one remaining lace to snag
the bird by its skinny ankle and truss it up, but I quickly rejected
the idea. Even as my bootlace rose into the air, wavering unsteadily,
I could sense my unreliable control over my Super-power growing
shaky. I might lose my chance to replace my laces if I made a clumsy
strike and the bird took to the air. The gull was already sidling sideways, eyeing the snakelike motions of my bootlace warily. Despite
all its modifications, some remnant genetic instinct told it that anything moving in such a sinuous fashion must be predatory. Its wings
were half-cocked, ready to scoop the air to power it up and away.

Like me, my fraying bootlace slumped, defeated. No way I'd be
quick enough. It was laughable, really. If my powers had been fully
under my command, I could have simply beckoned to the Merchant

Gull's scavenged laces, and they would have readily slithered over to me whether the pesky creature liked it or not. As it was, I was reduced to bargaining my meager supply of found things with an aggravating Anymal in the hopes of replacing my one sad bootlace. Not that I had much choice; it was on the verge of separating into individual strands. I needed a proper set of laces if I was to continue practicing my ability. I really needed to get my powers under control, not because I thought they'd help me become a Super-hero or anything, but just so I wouldn't accidentally tie someone else's laces together as they walked by, making them pitch headlong on the crowded pavement. Unfortunately, stuff like that tended to be pretty common around me.

I sighed and reached into my pocket. I hadn't wanted to do this . . . but it might be my only chance. I slowly withdrew my final bargaining chip. And that's when the Dockside Dragons sat up and took notice.

At one point, getting noticed by a group of Supers was all I'd ever wanted. But this wasn't the sort of group I'd had in mind as a kid. I'd wanted to fight crime, do my bit to help those citizens struggling to put the patchwork politics of the City back into order. But after being rejected by half a dozen groups, my parents had given up on convincing anyone to take me. My power was singularly useless, and I couldn't really control it all that well anyway. It was prone to twisting up strings and wires and cords around me without any effort on my part, and when I *did* want to use it, it was like I didn't have any ability at all. Shame had eventually driven me out of my house and into the City. I guess I just didn't want to be a burden on my parents anymore. But I didn't try out for any more Super-groups after that. Matter of fact, I'd actively avoided other Supers. Too embarrassed, I suppose. And too wary. Outside of the big-name Super-groups, there were plenty of underground clubs and gangs willing to take on disillusioned Supers, but I'd bumped into a few of them before (some of those previous *situations* I mentioned) and I didn't find the lifestyle terribly appealing. I was taking risks with public displays of my power at the pier, but I suppose the feeling of calm I found there had lulled me into a false sense of security. Or maybe a part of me was hoping to be press-ganged. At least, then I would *belong* somewhere. Still, I couldn't imagine, just then, why anyone would want me and my stupid, unreliable power. Besides, the Dragons' attention had less to do with my laces wiggling around than with the golden token in my hand.

I angled it to catch the sun. It glittered enticingly. Embossed on the front was a pair of dice. The reverse showed an elaborate "CC" with a crown. A City Casino access pass. Useless to me; without a suit and tie, an entourage, a fat stack of credits, I'd never be let near the entrance. But the Merchant Gull paused, considering. It knew it could trade the token for any number of things, even if I couldn't. The assumption of anyone I tried to trade it to would be that I had stolen it, and I didn't particularly want to end up in a City Police holding pen. But a Merchant Gull? They stole things all the time, and nobody was going to waste time trying to incarcerate one. It's just how they were; no telling what they'd originally been designed to do. Whoever had dropped the Casino pass must have been losing their mind with frustration. CC passes weren't cheap. And the Dockside Dragons knew it.

Most of the time, the Dockside Dragons didn't bother people who mind their own business. They ran your basic protection racket, sold drugs and weapons, and occasionally robbed a liquor store or a gas station. A couple of them were minor Supers. Their leader called himself Lung, which is an old word meaning "dragon," hence the name of the gang. Like his namesake, Lung could breathe fire. The threat of getting on his bad side was generally enough to keep people in the area polite when the Dragons were around. But the Dragons were smart enough not to step on the wrong toes or draw too much attention to themselves. Like me, they weren't interested in official attention from City Police or any of the Corporations. But a City Casino token? It must have seemed too good to be true. Whoever gave this little treasure to Lung would be handsomely rewarded, no doubt about that. The whole crew would benefit if they could get their hands on it.

One of their number must've had Super-sight or some other enhanced sense. The glitter of the coin caught his eye, and he took a closer look. They'd been lounging over one hundred meters away, but now they were on their feet, ambling over to where I crouched pestering the bird. I was oblivious, still trying to cajole the gull into giving up its laces. All the while, they were spreading out, angling to form a half circle, leaving no easy way out. They'd taken their aesthetic from old histories, apparently: a bunch of predatory punks, all ripped jeans and black leather and dangling chains, fingernails and hair in garish neon colors, wildly spiked; sewn-on patches proclaimed their favorite bands and brands, their views on authority and politics. They made rude comments and crass hand gestures as they approached, laughing and shoving each other as they worked themselves up to violence. My father would've smirked his knowing historian's smirk and said, "Some things never change," but I wasn't in any position to judge.

I was clearly a budding Super, but what little evidence of my powers they could see wasn't particularly intimidating. Not like I was a tele-K or pyro-K or something powerful and flashy like that. I didn't have Super-strength or speed or indestructibility. I was just manipulating bits of string, and doing it poorly, too. Plus, I was alone. Hard to imagine easier prey.

"Hey!" I heard a smoker's rasp, still a dozen meters away, too excited at the prospect of mugging a CC pass off me to wait until I couldn't get away. Not that it mattered: I was so caught up in what I was doing that I didn't fully notice him call out. I guess maybe

I assumed he was talking to somebody else. Next thing I knew a Dragon had kicked my feet out from under me and a knee was digging into my back. The gull made an indignant squawk and snatched up the laces in its beak before taking to the air. My face was pressed hard into the splintery planks of the pier. I heard a *snicking* sound, followed by a menacing low hum. Out of the corner of my eye, I spotted a blue-green flicker: an ion-blade. Just a switchblade-style knife, not a full sword, but still more than capable of cutting me or shocking me badly. My heart surged painfully in my chest.

My assailant leaned close, putting the crackling weapon into my line of sight. "Are you deaf, son?" he growled. "I'm talkin' to you!" His buddies guffawed and egged him on. "Less you wanna get cut, I suggest you answer when a Dragon talks to you. You pickin' up what I'm puttin' down?"

One of his buddies stepped on my hand, twisting his heel hard. Pain lanced up my arm as my bones ground against the pier. The Casino token rolled from my grip. It bounced once before lofting into the air, sailing straight into another Dragon's waiting hand. "Blackjack!" he cried. The other Dragons crowed raucously.

I managed to stammer out something very stupid that sounded a lot like, "Hey, that's mine," which seemed to tickle the bloke on my back—not enough to make him take his knee off my spine, however. He laughed and smacked the back of my head with his free hand. I was having trouble getting my breath. My heart was pounding, and sweat was stinging my eyes. My hand felt like it might be broken. Things had gone from easy-going to eating pier so suddenly, my head felt like it was spinning. This was not how I'd expected to spend my day. I mean, I'd been bullied before, sure. I'd even had the living daylights beaten out of me a time or two. But I had never, ever, been threatened with an ion-knife. I had never had someone so casually imply that my life was next to worthless to him. And now that they had the Casino pass, they didn't seem to be in any hurry to leave off their sport.

Glancing around, I could see that nobody was planning on stepping in. The crowds had thinned out almost completely. Just a few bystanders remained, watching avidly while trying not to look like they were hoping for blood. I caught one man's eye, but he just turned and hurried away, shoulders hunched. He didn't want anything to do with the Dragons either. Can't say I really blamed him.

The angry hum of the ion-blade snapped me back to my precarious circumstances. Encouraged by the other Dragons, the thug on my back was trying to see just how close he could get the knife's aura to my skin without giving me a nasty shock. I was damp with fear sweat, and I was sure the blade would arc from much further away than he expected. I couldn't help it, I cringed away from the awful sound of it. Laughter and hoots of derision answered my cowardice. Somebody guffawed and said, "Good one, mate!" thumping my assailant on the back. It jostled him. Not much, but it was enough. The crackling halo of the ion-blade grazed me just behind my ear. The effect was instantaneous and brutal. My head thrashed on my neck, and my jaw clenched. My limbs drummed the wooden pier spasmodically, and my vision went white with rocketing stars. I gagged on a gasping breath, tasting blood from my own tongue. A low moan escaped me. Over the ringing in my ears, I heard the jerk on my back whooping, "Yeehaw, just like at the rodeo! Who wants the next ride?"

My nerves were blazing ropes of fire, igniting me from within. Every molecule in my body was screaming simultaneous warnings of damage. I definitely did not want another shock. But how was I supposed to escape? I'm not a small guy, but there were so many of them, and I could barely catch my breath. My heart felt like it was about to explode. I wanted to struggle, to fight back, but I was terrified. Fear paralyzed me. I couldn't move, I couldn't even think. I had no idea what to do.

That's when I felt my Super-power building inside me. Experience had taught me to recognize the sensation. It always happened just before my ability self-activated. It was going to do something all on its own if I didn't try to guide it somehow. But what could I do? One bootlace thrashing around uselessly wasn't going to get me out of this. There had to be some way to turn it to my advantage! But how? I was low on options. So, I did the first thing that popped into my head: I bent my leg at the knee to bring my foot closer to my attacker's back. My sad, frazzled bootlace reached up and tapped the Dragon on the shoulder.

Everything happened quickly after that. He glanced back, maybe thinking one of the other Dragons had something to say. The hard plastic end of my bootlace jabbed him in the eye. He squealed and dropped the ion-knife, clapping his hands over his face. I wasn't going to get another chance. I bucked him off and wriggled free. I scrambled to my feet and started running, shouldering my way between two stunned-looking Dragons. They weren't at all certain what had just happened to their comrade and were glancing around as if looking for a sniper. They grunted and gave ground, and I was off, sprinting down the pier like my life depended on it. And maybe it did.

A chorus of shouts erupted behind me. I heard pounding feet. My bootlace had snatched up the fallen ion-knife as I fled, waving it in wild sparking arcs behind me, but the Dragons were not deterred in the slightest. The end of the pier was fast approaching. I didn't have anywhere to go but down once I got there, and I didn't swim very well. I tried to nerve myself to take the leap, but my courage failed me. Skidding to a stop, I found myself staring down into frothing waves as they broke on the rocks below.

An instant later, an arm wrapped around my chest and I was hauled over backward. Patchwork clouds and the stubborn Merchant Gull wheeled overhead. I was thrown to the wooden boards hard enough to knock the wind from my lungs. My world was suddenly walled in by punching fists and kicking feet. I heard someone give a strangled yelp as my bootlace managed to stick the ion-knife into him. Another Dragon's laces suddenly lashed his ankles together and he lurched, off balance. Jostled in the scrum, he tipped over the edge, screaming. I heard a splash, rather than a crunch, then his spluttering expletives. Somehow, I got my feet under me. I fought frantically to rise. Something struck me on the side of the head and the world reeled. I staggered, was shoved, then tripped, flailing, when my feet were kicked out from under me. Once again, I was face down on the splintering planks of the pier. Fists and feet battered my ribs, my legs. Someone stomped on my arm. I rolled away, clutching my forearm as it flared with sickening pain, but it only brought me into range of more stomping feet. It was all I could do to cover my stomach and head as they mobbed me.

The beating continued. I have no idea how long. I distinctly recall seeing a dirty sneaker clip the sizzling ion-blade and send it spinning off the edge of the dock. The greedy Merchant Gull dove after it. Other than that, it was a blur of movement, shouting, and pain. At some point, the pain was so all-encompassing that I stopped feeling individual impacts. I couldn't keep track. I fought wildly, always trying to break out of the circle, gain some distance. I got my second wind, and strength surged through me. It surprised me as much as them. I regained my feet, even managed to knock one of them over. But three more were on me before I could go more than a few steps. It didn't matter what I did; there were simply too many of them.

I must have blacked out. I have a hazy memory of being rolled over onto my back. Someone was holding up a blurry object and asking me how many fingers I saw. I gurgled something past a loose tooth. I felt wretched, but I was too out of it to know how bad it was. I tried to ask if I was dying. The result was little more than incoherent mumbles. My voice buzzed inside my skull, leaving me disoriented. Chances are nothing I said made much sense. Then a picture of the Dragons jostling and shoving to be the first to take a swing at me popped into my head. I had my hands up, remonstrating with them: "Fellas, fellas, please! Be civilized! Form a punchline!"

I sort of sneeze-laughed. The fellow checking me over paused and leaned back on his heels, a look of concern on his face. I wheezed painfully with dizzy hilarity until my aching ribs made me realize I couldn't breathe. My laughter choked off with a hacking sob. I became aware of the stranger's frown. He had open, honest Korean features, but his frown made him look very serious. He looked up at someone standing nearby and said, "He's messed up pretty bad. I can heal him, but it's going to take some time."

I remember my bootlace reaching up and wrapping around the stranger's wrist. He yelped in surprise, but I was only trying to bring his hand closer so I could count his fingers.

The girl with him leaned closer. "A Suh-Super? W-we b-better get . . . get him b-back to puh . . . puh . . . pee-ay." A soft voice, issuing uncertainly from beneath a storm cloud of unruly brown hair. Her eyes glowed neon green. I felt a frisson of something wash over me, like a tingle of static electricity. Waves of little bumps moved across my skin, but it was just a symptom. The feeling had arisen from within. My ears rang with a resonant harmonic sound, like musical chords.

"Sarah?" Even mangled by my swollen mouth, she recognized her own name. She stumbled back, startled.

I blinked, trying to bring her into focus. I felt like I should know her. Were her eyes made of metal? I thought I could hear them whirring and clicking as she looked me over. And what did she mean by *PA?* The thought chased me down into spiraling darkness.

‖

I woke up feeling marvelous, with no idea how long I'd been out. The room I was in was windowless, aside from a tall, narrow pane of glass set in the upper half of one of the two doors, both of which were closed. Judging by the bed and the equipment in the room, I was in some kind of hospital. The room was dark, but the lights were on in the hall beyond the window. I could tell it was a hallway because occasionally the light was momentarily occluded by someone moving past with the purposeful stride of a nurse or orderly.

Not my first visit to a hospital, but something was different. There was a background hum I couldn't identify, a sound almost below hearing. It seemed to thrum through the walls. Setting that aside, I wasn't hooked up to any machinery or monitors. There was no IV drip, no indication that anyone was keeping an eye on my vital signs. Either they weren't particularly concerned about my well-being, or they'd already determined I would live. How long had I been out?

I made to lever myself upright and grunted in pain and surprise. My arm was a mass of bruises that still vaguely resembled a boot print. My fingers looked like sausages. It all came back in a rush, and I remembered hearing the crunch of bones. My stomach flipped over. I took a deep breath and swallowed sudden nausea, feeling light-headed. *A broken arm. Great. Just great.* Moving gingerly, I made my way to the windowless door. *Ah, perfect.* A washroom, as I'd hoped. I took a moment to relieve myself, then splashed water on my face. I left the light off on purpose, not particularly wanting to see the damage that had been done. Now that I was fully awake and moving around, I wasn't feeling quite so marvelous anymore. My body was beginning to protest. I was hurt badly, there was no denying it. My whole body ached and twinged with every movement. The pain was getting worse, and it was everywhere. I was hard pressed to itemize my injuries just then. I gave up and stood outside the washroom, looking at the little rectangle of hallway light, trying to decide if I should get moving or lay back down. I didn't know where I was, or who had brought me here. Evidently, they wanted me to recover, or they wouldn't have taken me to a hospital. I cast my mind back, trying to put the scattered pieces back together.

I remembered . . . glowing green eyes looking down at me . . . a soft, stuttering voice. Had she been pretty? It was hard to remember, but I seemed to think she was, in a mousy librarian kind of way. Maybe I was idealizing my cloudy recollections because she'd saved me from the Dragons. I frowned. Or had it been her Korean friend who had intervened? For some reason, I was sure it had been her who had chased the Dragons away. Hadn't he arrived after? And he'd said something about healing me, too. I tried to flex my fingers, but they felt thick and clumsy. My arm throbbed painfully in response. The ache went deep, and it wasn't just my arm, it was everywhere. If he was planning on healing me, maybe he hadn't started yet.

I blinked. I was still seeing her glowing green eyes, clicking and whirring. Was she even human? In hindsight, it felt as if she'd been looking at me in a way other people couldn't. Looking deeper. But no, that wasn't right. It had been the other way around. As though *I* had been looking into *her*. I was pretty sure she'd been oblivious to the whole thing. She had simply been trying to assess my condition. I grinned. She had been concerned for me; I was sure of it. Why did the idea please me so much?

I set the question aside. If it was true, I was safe enough, I decided. More rest wouldn't hurt. Or at least, it wouldn't hurt as much as forcing myself to stand here outside the washroom. I really wasn't feeling well.

I clambered back into bed and promptly fell into a deep, dreamless sleep.

❧

The nurse woke me, in that peremptory way nurses have: checking my vitals against the data-stream delivered by my nanos; asking me to rate my level of discomfort and pain; offering an analgesic, coffee, a snack; asking me questions. It was all very professional, very routine. For the most part, it didn't matter what I said. He already knew who I was from my nano-log. First thing they'd have checked was my particulars, just to make sure I didn't have any unusual genetic abnormalities, allergies, deficiencies, and so on. Then someone would have recalibrated my medical nanos to prioritize any life-threatening injuries, assuming the millions of tiny machines in my body hadn't already figured out what needed doing. Probably I'd avoided invasive surgery. The Dragons hadn't worked me over that badly, had they?

When he was done, the nurse gathered his equipment and made to leave, but I stopped him at the door with a question.

"Where exactly am I?"

He turned back briefly to say, "Project Arete." He pronounced it *ar-uh-tay.* Seeing no recognition in my eyes, he added, "You'll be safe here. The director will be in to see you soon, and you can ask her all the questions you like. Until then, just rest." The click of the door closing behind him punctuated his command.

I was sore, and I was tired enough that my nanos must be working overtime to accelerate my body's natural healing processes, but I didn't think I'd be able to sleep. My brain whirled with uncertain questions. What was Project Arete? *Where* was it? Would I be free to leave, or had I just been "recruited" whether I liked it or not? And if I was free to leave, what would they want out of me in exchange for fixing me up? Medical tech wasn't cheap.

Despite my misgivings, I managed to worry and fret myself into a fairly deep sleep, so I was a little surprised when a knock on the door brought me round again. I was still struggling to sit up when the director entered the room and flipped on the light. I blinked to clear the spots from my vision. Behind her, fully a dozen assistants clustered in the hall, murmuring quietly among themselves or working busily at various devices. An orderly pushed through the crowd, clearly annoyed, but unwilling to say anything with the director there. He vanished down the hall once he was through the press.

"David North?" Her voice was a rich alto, with a hint of an exotic accent.

"Hi." I couldn't think of what else to say. The crowd of people in the hallway was intimidating. Clearly, this was an important and very busy woman. She stepped inside the room and firmly closed the door behind her. Her aides took the hint and spread themselves out along the hallway, most (though not all) vanishing from sight. A serious-looking older man with a military bearing remained in visual contact on the other side of the door's slim window. He met my eyes and gave me a slow nod, just to let me know he was watching me.

The woman moved over to the foot of the bed and pressed the control to adjust it into a sitting position. I let her, partly because I hadn't realized the bed had been adjustable, and partly because it gave me a chance to look her over. She was of Spanish genetics, medium height, with thick wavy dark-brown hair pulled back in a coiled braid, appraising brown eyes. Her face was unlined—somewhat androgynous and stern-looking—but despite the overall impression of a woman in the prime of her life, I suspected nano-technology of a higher-than-usual quality maintained her appearance of youthful vitality. Her clothing was simple, the cut and quality of the fabrics demonstrating her wealth rather than any overt ostentation, a restrained and effective display of both good taste and subtlety. Tucked under one arm was a thick dossier.

"Who are you?" I asked. I'd always preferred the direct approach over subtlety.

"My name is Mercedes Helena Cantero Ruiz," she said, the name tripping off her tongue so fast I barely caught it. "I'm the director of Operations here at Project Arete. How are you feeling?" She seated herself in a comfortable-looking armchair next to the bed.

"Fine, I guess." She'd flipped open the dossier and was riffling through the pages. Judging from the few glances I got of the contents, the file was all about me. Some of the stuff in there went right back to the very beginning.

She glanced up with an arched brow. "Be more elaborate, please. You're clearly an intelligent young man. Single word answers won't satisfy me." The tone of her voice gave every impression she was used to being obeyed. No, not simply obeyed, *respected.*

"What exactly do you want to know?" I asked. I gestured at the dossier. "I doubt I could tell you anything that isn't already in there."

"This?" She set the dossier aside on a little table. "It's thorough, certainly, but it isn't the full story. It lacks color. It tells me what you are, yes, but not who. So, why not start by telling me how you ended up here?"

"Dumb luck, I suppose. Some of your people found me after the Dragons worked me over." She waited, clearly expecting more details. I sighed. "I had a City Casino token. Maybe they wanted it."

The director pursed her lips and waited. She could look very severe when she wanted to. Despite the urge to confess every stupid mistake I'd ever made, I kept my mouth shut.

"You're a minor telekinetic, yes? With a string fixation?"

"It doesn't sound very impressive when you put it like that." I grinned, but she wasn't laughing. "Look, I've never really thought about it. If you can't control it, tele-K isn't very handy, is it?"

She ignored the pun. "Tell me, David, how does someone we might generously dub a burgeoning Super survive a prolonged physical altercation with a dozen street toughs? And before you answer, I should point out that at least three of them possessed potentially lethal abilities."

The smile fell from my face. "Honor among thieves?" I quipped. "An overabundance of forbearance on their part?" But my heart wasn't in it. They had been trying to kill me.

"Maybe at first, David. They were focused on the coin. But with the prize secured, they decided to make an example out of you. And rather than take your lumps, you poked their leader in the eye with the proverbial stick."

"It was a shoelace," I muttered, but she wasn't done.

"We have drone footage showing how the fight began, and how it proceeded. They weren't playing around, David. You publicly humiliated them."

"So?"

"So, I'll ask again, how did you survive?"

I glared at her. "You're obviously trying to get me to admit something you already know, so why don't you just tell me and save us both the trouble? I don't know what you want me to say! I don't understand where you're going with this!"

She tapped the dossier with a manicured fingernail. "According to this, during the conflict, you activated no less than three distinct and unrelated Super-powers. The eyewitness accounts are rather conflicted, but they tend to agree on that point. It's not something you see every day." Ms. Ruiz leaned toward me. "It's not something you see *ever.*"

I furrowed my brow. What on Earth was she talking about? "Eyewitnesses aren't very reliable. I have one power, and it sucks. I can't even control it, most of the time."

"Will you demonstrate it for me?"

"I'd rather not."

She didn't press me and changed tack. "How long have you known you have a Super-ability?"

I answered her question with one of my own. "Why do you have an interest in my power?"

Her smile held genuine warmth. "The two who found you aren't 'my people,' as you put it. They're not employees; they're students. Project Arete is something of a scientific think tank, with interests in all branches of scientific advancement. Naturally, Super-research and training form a healthy part of what we do."

"Naturally." I may have sounded somewhat acerbic. *Everybody* was interested in Supers. Of course they were: control the Supers, control the power. Not a whole lot different than the Dockside Dragons, really, or any other faction in the City, for that matter. Interesting that the two who found me were both Supers, though.

Ms. Ruiz must have sensed some of my reservations because she said, "I think you'll find we're not quite what you expect." There was amusement in her voice. I couldn't fathom the source of her good humor. Safe to assume she knew something I didn't. I decided to change the subject.

"So, the two who found me . . . what, they go to school here? They're learning to use their abilities?" It was hard not to sound hopeful. First, I didn't have many friends—*any* friends, if I'm being totally honest. Second, my ability had proven to be something of an annoyance to those around me. I'd been unable to control it at all when I was younger, so it had frequently reached out and tangled people's hair, undone belts, tied shoelaces together . . . Let me into your home, you were liable to find your wiring shorting out, your clothing and bedding separated into individual threads. Anything resembling string was a fair target. My Super-power didn't discriminate. The only saving grace was that it tended to latch onto the easy targets first—drawstrings and shoelaces, rather than tightly woven textiles; soft threads over stiff wire—and I'd learned that a constant slow leak of my power prevented a buildup and sudden spontaneous expression. That was why I'd been trying to trade the laces off the Merchant Gull. Wearing long laces and leaving them loose meant my power had an easy target that was always within reach. It was much safer for everyone around me if my laces were always waving around wildly than if I let things build up to the point where they got out of control.

At this point, I realized I'd been speaking out loud. I was pouring out my worries and frustrations to a total stranger while she sat there and made encouraging noises. I stuttered to a stop and stared at her. She looked back at me without any trace of shame or guilt.

I made a rueful face. "Oh, you're good," I said. "What is that, some kind of mind control power?" I found myself tensing, looking around the room. What were the chances I could get through the door and past all her assistants in the hallway? The gruff military-looking guy was still out there, watching our interaction, buzz-cut hair and salt-and-pepper beard only adding to my original impression of him. Given my physical state, odds weren't on my side.

"Believe it or not, David, no. That was nothing more than simple empathy and compassion."

I thought back over the last fifteen minutes and realized she was telling the truth. All she'd done was ask leading questions and look genuinely interested in my answers.

She didn't chide me further. "The young man who brought you here is named Yoon Chang-gi, but he goes by Kevin. He's been looking in on you, using his Super-power to assist your recovery. He has a gift for healing. One silver lining to your situation: it's given him ample opportunity to practice."

I wasn't sure how I felt about being a practice dummy for a novice Super but decided it was best not to quibble. Still, it was hard to keep my misgivings out of my voice. "Good for Kevin, I guess."

Ms. Ruiz stood to leave. "You can thank him yourself when he drops by this evening." The tone of her voice left no room for doubt that she thought I should be grateful. She stood by the bed a moment, giving me a long, appraising look. I began to feel guilty for my surliness, but all she said was, "I hope you'll decide to stay on with us once you've recovered."

I sat there, nonplussed. Was she offering to train me? She seemed so blasted genuine, but I wanted very much to mistrust her. What can I say? It was sort of my default mode.

"I'll think about it," I mumbled.

Ms. Ruiz nodded. "All I ask is that you keep the offer in mind," she began.

I tuned her out. I couldn't believe this busy, influential woman was taking the time to put me at ease; was, in fact, offering to take me in. She couldn't have known it would have the exact opposite effect. I'd developed a healthy paranoia from my time on the streets of the City. But it seemed they liked the personal touch at Project Arete.

". . . an opportunity to enrich yourself, and us thereby," the director finished.

I didn't know how to respond, so I opted to remain silent. She didn't press the issue and let herself out, taking the dossier with her. The military man stared at me through the window a little while longer, then fell in behind the gaggle of assistants who trailed the director down the hallway.

Mercedes Helena Cantero Ruiz (if I'd remembered that correctly) had been both kind and attentive toward the end, but I was feeling incredibly overwhelmed by it all. It had been years since I'd been the center of attention, and let's be honest, back then, the attention I received wasn't exactly positive. Avoiding just this kind of spotlight had become a deeply ingrained habit. All that care and compassion, and with such sincerity, too! I admit it, part of me was greedy for more. But I was also suspicious. She had started out by grilling me.

Why the background check? And why all the personal attention from the very top? *What's the catch?* I wanted to ask. If I were to accept her offer, what would it cost me?

Kevin, when he finally appeared, seemed harried and out of sorts. He shouldered into the room with only a perfunctory knock. He had a backpack slung over his shoulder. A jumble of flimsies, tablets, and genuine paper books were threatening to spill from the half-closed zipper.

"Hey, David, sorry I'm late!" He tossed his bag on the floor, and then he just stood there, suddenly conscious that we hadn't actually met before. Not while I was awake and completely with it, anyway. He was of medium height, with an athletic build and attractive, symmetrical Korean features. He wore gray slacks and a white polo shirt, with a green zip-up sweater over top.

"You must be Kevin," I said. "Just come from class?" For some reason, I wanted to put him at ease. Despite what I'd said to Ms. Ruiz, I *was* grateful. Very much so. He had saved my life, after all.

He lifted a hand to push his straight black hair back from his forehead and grinned. It made his dark, narrow eyes scrunch right up. I liked him immediately. "Yeah. I have a very busy schedule this term. Between all the usual school stuff, I spend a lot of time in the Greenhouse." He started ticking off subjects and rapidly ran out of fingers. "Martial arts, music, phys. ed., biology, math, history, archery, yoga, chemistry, philosophy, physics, botany, dance . . ." He trailed off at the look on my face. "What?"

I was laughing. "Last I checked, there were only twenty-four hours in a day. Where do you find the time?"

He moved over to the chair the director had vacated a few hours earlier and plopped himself down. "Well, it's less like a school and more like a lifestyle. Learning is just . . . all the time, you know?"

Kind of like being on the streets: you adapt, or you get paved over, as one acquaintance had put it. The City could just swallow you up, like it had almost swallowed me up.

He must have noted the look on my face. "Everything okay?" Kevin asked. "How are you feeling?"

"Honestly, not so hot. It's been a long day, and I feel like I only just woke up."

"No surprise, David. You were hurt pretty bad. It's a good thing Sarah found you when she did."

He was watching me carefully. I stared at him blankly. "Sarah?" The name didn't ring a bell.

"Oh. I thought . . ." He rubbed the back of his neck, started over. "Yeah, Sarah. She's a Super training here at PA. Absolutely *loaded* with powers. She's the one who scattered the Dragons and then called me."

One girl against a dozen gangbangers? Some of them had danger-ous powers, too. It couldn't have been easy. She must have some serious talent.

"I'd like to meet her," I said. "Say thanks."

Kevin looked nonplussed. "Uh, yeah. Yeah, sure."

A lukewarm response, at best. Why wouldn't he want me to meet her? I filed it away for later.

"How bad have I been hurt, exactly?"

More items to tick off on his fingers: "Severe concussion . . . you were out for almost three days, and the swelling in your brain was pretty bad. You're also richer by forty-seven stitches: thirteen in the scalp, twenty-nine on your left cheek, five to fix your lower right eyelid. You had a fairly serious break of the right radius and some broken fingers . . . three broken ribs. And I'm guessing one of the Dragons was wearing steel-toed boots because you had a bruised kidney that was on the verge of rupturing." His voice lost the clinical tone and he said, in all seriousness, "I wasn't sure I'd be able to sort you out, to be honest. But between me and the medical staff, you're through the worst of it. You'll probably be pretty tender for a while, but your nanos will continue to patch you up. I imagine you'll be good to go after today's session." He was suddenly bashful. "That is, if you'll consent . . . I mean, if you're okay with me . . ."

Healing me? "Yeah! Yeah, of course."

He lost his uncertainty the moment he focused on his power. His face grew serious, and his gaze turned inward. Slowly, he reached out and put a hand on the blanket over my knee. At first, nothing happened. Then, as if I were an empty vessel held under a faucet, I felt myself filling with warmth. A golden tingle spread from his hand, down through my toes, and up into my stomach. From there, a sense of ease seemed to settle and spread, reaching slowly through my body, until even my throbbing, swollen fingers were bathed in a sense of wholeness and well-being.

I'm not sure how long it lasted, but when he was done, he lifted his hand and gave me a somewhat dreamy smile. It took a moment for his eyes to focus. Experimentally, I flexed my arm, then curled and uncurled my fingers. There was an unsteadiness to my movements, a sort of shaky weakness, like after a good workout. Everything seemed to function, but my body was clearly low on resources, and it was going to be a while before I was one hundred percent. Still, if I wasn't exactly fixed, I wasn't quite so broken anymore, either.

The silence had stretched out, and Kevin was watching me expectantly. "That's amazing," I said at last.

"I haven't been tested for potential, yet," Kevin admitted, "but there's a good chance with practice, I'll be able to get better at it. Honestly, plants are so much easier. Simpler structures. Right now, I'm mostly guiding your body to do what it already knows how to do, smoothing out the process a little, tweaking things here and there to maximize efficiency. I also accelerate things a bit, so you'll probably be pretty hungry in a few moments. Best thing to do is eat, eat, eat. You have to fuel the furnace."

Come to think of it, I was pretty hungry. "Food would be good."

He produced a sling and helped me get my broken arm into a comfortable position. "You'll need that for a little while yet. Bones are challenging for me." Then he gestured at the wall opposite the washroom. "Fabricator is over there. Just tell it what you want." He pointed to another device on the counter next to the sink. "You have a beverage machine for drinks of all kinds and smaller treats when you don't feel like a full meal. Pretty much anything you like, and if you find something the machine doesn't know how to make, we can probably figure out a way to program it." Finally, indicating a hatch in the wall, he added, "Just dump anything you don't eat into the recycler, plate and utensils and all. It all gets broken down and reused somewhere in the facility, in one form or another."

"Thanks, Kevin."

"You're welcome. I'll drop in when I can, see how you're doing. Anything I can bring you? Something to read, maybe? Any hobbies you enjoy?"

I rolled my wrist and wiggled my fingers. "Maybe . . . a guitar?"

I expected him to tell me I was being overly optimistic. Instead, he responded with enthusiasm. "Sure!" He jumped up and scooped his bag off the floor. "See you later, then!"

The door didn't have time to finish closing before he'd poked his head back into the room. "I almost forgot. They want you to have this." He tossed something on the foot of the bed. "It's called a Map. It's made of percipient plastic, and it's an invaluable resource. Direct access to PANet. Quite possibly the most useful tool anyone at Project Arete gets issued. Some free advice? Call up current events in the City. Take a quick glance through faction politics and area control maps. Get a feel for the neighborhoods you're walking through *before* you walk through them. What you just went through was entirely avoidable, David." He paused long enough to see his words sink in. The speech had the feel of something practiced, or something he was repeating from when he'd been introduced to PA himself. He grinned to take the sting from the rebuke. "Educate yourself! You'll be glad you did!" He vanished back into the corridor.

I picked up the Map. Stuck to the back of it was an informational pamphlet about Project Arete: mission statement, methods, members, current projects, etcetera. I peeled it free and dropped it on the side table for later perusal. The device itself was a thin tablet of lightweight black plastic, about as bulky as five or six stacked playing cards, and it powered on the moment I touched it. A screen appeared on the otherwise blank surface. It read, *"Keying . . . please wait."* After a moment, it went blank again.

Huh. Some kind of smart device. I turned it over, looking for buttons, instructions, anything. It was entirely smooth and blank. Must be smart-glass, then. I tapped it gently with a fingertip. Nothing. It didn't flex or twist when I applied pressure either. "Power on," I said. Still nothing. I frowned. Normally, smart-glass devices responded to voice commands or touch. Maybe it was out of battery? Wouldn't be very useful if I couldn't figure out how to make it go. Well, whatever. I was hungry, and I wanted to go back to sleep. I moved to toss the device on the side table with the PA pamphlet.

The Map lit up with a melodic *ping!* and vibrated slightly, making me jump. A message on the screen said, *"Great! The Map is keyed to you alone now, and nobody else will have access to it. It's powered by your body's electrical field, so as long as you're touching it or carrying it in a pocket, it'll recharge. I've never seen one run out of battery. Percipient plastic is pretty nifty stuff."*

Percipient plastic? I thought, and was stunned to see my question printed on the screen. I dropped the device in shock.

The screen remained lit by the response: "*Yeah, that's what the geeks call it. Alien tech. Leverages your nano-network, somehow. You'd have to ask Francis. I'm more into biology.*"

My head spun. PA made use of *Cupid* tech? What on Earth had I stumbled into?

With a shaking hand, I picked up the Map. Messages had continued to appear. The Map made it clear they were coming from Kevin. He was thinking at his own Map as he made his way across the Project Arete facility, and I was receiving his thoughts here, on my Map. Unbelievable.

"*There're all sorts of cool things in the facility,*" Kevin was saying. "*You'll have plenty of time to explore, ask questions, and make discoveries. For now, you should focus on food, then sleep. I bet you're starving by now. That healing was pretty major.*"

I was famished, actually.

"*Do all the devices at PA work like this?*" I asked. In my mind! The thought appeared on the screen anyway.

"*No, it's mostly smart-glass and AI interfaces. Nothing special. But most of it won't work unless you have a Map or a visitor's pass. Security made easy. Nobody can go anywhere or do anything if they're not invited.*"

"*Glad you remembered to leave the Map, then. I feel like I could eat my boots.*"

"*Which reminds me, use the fabricator to make some new clothes. Your gear was pretty worn out. It's in the corner if you want to toss it in the recycler and have it remade good as new.*"

I glanced over. So it was. A pair of grubby, beat-up combat boots with only one frayed bootlace between them, filthy blue jeans, an old gray T-shirt, and my battered orange hoodie—pretty much all I owned.

"*Thanks. Will do.*" I had no idea how it knew which thoughts to transmit and which thoughts to keep private, but I was glad the Map didn't transmit feelings. I wanted to freak out; run screaming from the room. I wanted to weep with relief and jump for joy. I couldn't figure out quite how I felt about it all. It just seemed too good to be true. And more than a little scary, too. Alien tech! Were there Cupids here, in the Project Arete facility? I swallowed nervously and looked around. How would I know if there were? There could be one in the room right now, and I wouldn't be aware of it unless it chose to reveal itself.

Kevin, of course, was oblivious to my misgivings. *No problem,* he sent. *See you tomorrow!*

The Map went dark.

Inert Map in hand, I shuffled across the room in my hospital gown. On my way by the door to the hall, I tapped the window and was rewarded with a menu panel. A few moments later, the glass was completely opaque. From a few paces away, it looked no different than the rest of the door.

Next, I turned to inspect the fabricator. Top of the line model from the looks of it. As Kevin had mentioned, it had an AI interface. This one was named Theodore, according to the face plate. After a moment, the unit spoke up. "Something I can help you with, sir?" Theodore had taken note of my scrutiny.

"Uh, yeah. Can I call you Theo?"

"Certainly, sir, a very efficient alternative. And how shall I address you?"

"Call me David, please."

Not much different than the device my parents had used for general household needs before I ran away. A little politer, perhaps. I could still hear my dad arguing with Oscar. The AI had always seemed to irk him, for some reason. He called it the Grouch, and Oscar seemed to resent it. I smiled at the memory, then spoke to the fabricator.

"Theo, I'm really hungry, and I'm recovering from some serious injuries."

"I'm sorry to hear that, David."

"Appreciate the sympathy. But what I'm really after is some solid nutrition. Recovery food, you know?"

"I know just the thing! Any flavor preferences?"

"A lot."

Theo chuckled warmly. "Understood, David."

While Theo worked, I limped over to the corner to gather my things. It made for a rather pitiful armful. I trudged over to the recycler and opened the hatch, then hesitated. Did I really want to do this? Just dispose of my old life, just like that? I wasn't entirely sure I wanted to stay here, and yet . . . was living on the streets any better? How could Project Arete possibly be worse? A part of me had already decided, I knew. But standing there with that sad bundle of dirty clothing in my arms, I found I had to nerve myself up to it. I shook my head. *Foolish sentimentality*, I chided myself. I'd be getting it all back.

In it went. I may have pushed the hatch shut a little more firmly than necessary.

"Theo, after the meal, can you remake all the stuff I just tossed in the recycler, minus the dirt?"

"The task is well within my functional parameters. It will be my pleasure."

"Thanks." But something was bothering me. I thought about it for a moment. "Except . . . the orange hoodie. Clean it up, but maybe leave the wear and tear alone . . . the frayed cuffs, the loose threads, all that."

"An interesting stipulation. Do I detect a bit of an emotional attachment, David?"

"Yeah, maybe a little. It was a gift from my mom, the last time I saw her."

"Not too long ago, I hope."

"Over a year ago," I admitted.

"Do you want to talk about it?" Theo's concern was disarmingly authentic.

I stopped. Was I seriously unburdening myself on an AI? Cripes. I'd obviously been living on my own too long if machines were more like people to me than actual people were. Earlier I'd had not one, but *two* living, breathing, *caring* human beings I could have talked to. I'd hardly told either of them anything. Maybe I should stay on at PA, if only for my sanity's sake.

Theo had been programmed with too much respect to pry any further, but I couldn't help but wonder if he was required to report his observations on my mental state to the people in charge. Brooding, I hardly tasted my meal. The first plateful, anyway. By the time I was finished, my hunger had become a living thing with a mind of its own. Kevin hadn't been kidding when he'd said the accelerated use of my body's resources would demand fuel. Theo cheerfully provided a second heaping plate of food, which I washed down with a mug of strong black coffee. Then I went back to bed, thinking I'd play around with the Map some more. What else could it do? But not even the coffee was enough to keep me awake.

Despite my vague uncertainty about my new circumstances, after two more days in recovery, it appeared I would get things entirely my way. Project Arete would be thrilled (claimed Ms. Ruiz) if I decided to hang around for a while and get to know some of the other students. She encouraged me to explore and meet the faculty. If I liked what I saw, I could stay on. If not, I was free to leave at any time. The Map was a gift, and may it serve me well. Ms. Ruiz didn't even put a proviso on my departure, some ominous statement like, "If you leave, you may never come back!" Quite the opposite, in fact.

"Please remember," said the director, "if you decide to leave, our doors are always open. Until next time, I wish you the very best of luck."

With that, I was left on my own to ruminate. But I'd never been much for sitting still. Instead, I hopped out of bed and changed into my newly reconstituted clothes. I pulled on fresh underwear and socks, then slid into my jeans. A perfect recreation: they fit me like I'd been wearing them for months. Next came the gray T-shirt, which smelled fresh and clean.

I picked up the orange hoodie and looked it over. As requested, Theo had left the wear and tear alone. It looked just like what it was: a much-loved, oversized, and very comfortable pullover sweatshirt with a hood—what my mother had called a bunny hug. Bunny was an old word for Hopper or Flop-ear, she'd told me. Wearing the hoodie did feel like snuggling something warm and soft. I was glad I'd left it alone; it felt reassuringly familiar. That meant more than I could express, considering my life was potentially about to change completely. I dragged the hoodie over my head and settled it over my torso with a deep sense of satisfaction.

Finally, I stepped into my new running shoes. I'd decided to abandon the beat-up old combat boots for something more practical and comfortable. Earthy orange, like my hoodie, they were perfectly fitted to my feet, thanks to a quick body scan by Theo. The laces were new, too, made of highly durable synthetic cord, nearly indestructible. But they were meant for the boots. Once my new shoes were laced up, I had nearly a meter of loose laces on either side of both feet. I concentrated, and almost without effort, they began to wriggle freely.

I decided that not having to fight with my Super-power was a good sign. Allowing my ability to imbue the laces with a life of their own, I stepped out into the hall and went exploring.

Kevin hadn't been able to visit again, except to drop off the guitar I'd asked for, but he'd messaged a few times via Map to check in on me. He did so again when I was only a little way down the hall. I pulled the Map from my pocket.

"Hey, David. Feeling okay?"

This section of PA, as expected, resembled most modern hospitals I was familiar with. Though a little higher tech, a little more maintained, it was just as bustling with people passing to and fro on various errands. The feeling in the air was that time was of the essence here, and I couldn't help feeling like I was in the way. The sooner I exited the hospital area and found my way into the Project Arete facility proper, the happier I'd be. I still wasn't entirely sure they were going to let me simply walk out of here.

"Like a brand-new man!" I replied.

The truth was, I felt like I'd been run over by a hover bus. My whole body ached, and I'd had an almost constant headache since I woke up. But it seemed churlish to tell Kevin that. He'd done his best for me. Besides, I was honestly thrilled to have befriended someone my own age. Even without miraculous healing powers,

Kevin seemed like he'd be a good friend to have. He was genuinely concerned about me. So why alienate him? I'd probably feel a whole lot worse if it hadn't been for him.

"Glad to hear it. Listen, don't be angry, but . . ."

Uh-oh. That didn't bode well. I rounded a corner, smiling apologetically as I dodged around a woman in surgical scrubs. A quick tweak of my power snatched my errant laces from her path at the last moment. Relieved that my ability was still responding to my commands, I hurried on.

"I took the liberty of putting your name down for the next AV test," Kevin finished.

"AV test?" He'd mentioned that his Super-powers hadn't been tested yet. He must be referring to the Super-power test.

Kevin confirmed it. *"Yes, it tells you the potential of your powers. They run a group through the test periodically, and I thought maybe you might be interested. There's nowhere else in the City that I've ever heard of with the technology or the expertise to map a Super's potential. Project Arete is probably unique in that."*

An intriguing possibility. I stopped walking and looked down at my shoelaces. They writhed and patted the ground around me, wove weird little arabesques through the air. A few people so far had given me strange looks, but I was used to that. Unlike being out in the City, nobody here seemed particularly surprised or concerned that I was a Super.

"David? You're not mad, are you?"

I sighed. *"Nah, Kevin. It's fine. If I decide I'm not interested, I won't attend."*

"Totally understandable. It's just . . . well, you asked about Sarah, but she's . . . I don't know how to put it. She's shy. Painfully shy. The thought of meeting you makes her nervous."

"Why would that be?"

"Don't take it personally. Everybody makes her nervous. I just thought this would be a good way for you to meet her without her feeling singled out. She'll be in the same group, along with her best friend. And I'll be there, too."

Ah, that explained why he'd been hesitant when I'd asked to meet her: he felt protective toward her. Ironic, if she really was as powerful as Kevin claimed. I'd have to remember to be careful. A girl with that much ability could make her displeasure known in no uncertain terms. If she was as shy as he said she was, she might not like any extra attention from a stranger. It was probably best to let Kevin take the lead, which meant I was going to this meeting. In my mind, her green eyes glowed brightly. I realized I had a big dopey grin on my face and quickly glanced down at the Map to be sure I hadn't accidentally shared that last chain of thought. I hadn't.

"Look, I don't see much point in testing my power. It's pretty lame." The Map helpfully translated my mental shrug: *"But I guess it can't hurt."* I paused to consider that and realized it was a fairly accurate assessment of my attitude. If nothing else, it would at least help lay to rest Ms. Ruiz's ridiculous suspicions about what I could do. Multiple unrelated powers, she'd said. I rolled my eyes at the sheer lunacy of it, then turned my attention back to the Map.

"Anyway, you're right. I would like to meet her, if only to thank her for her help."

I *had* to meet her. I had to know if she felt the same way I did. I grimaced and scratched the back of my head as a new thought occurred to me. What if she didn't feel the same? What if this sense of connection was entirely one way? I was going to feel really stupid, wasn't I?

Kevin: *"Oh, good. I thought I'd stepped over the line."*

"Well, maybe, but . . . I trust you, I guess." It came as something of a surprise to realize that I actually did. I hadn't had much cause to trust people over the past few years. The City could be cruel. I took

a deep breath and plowed ahead, despite my misgivings. *"I have to level with you, Kevin, I'm not entirely convinced PA has my best intentions at heart. I'm a Super, and everybody in the City uses Supers to help secure their power. Even a relatively innocuous ability like mine could be put to use doing parlor tricks to lure in new recruits."*

"That's not what we're about," he began.

"I know. I can see that. But that doesn't mean I have the full picture. You probably don't either."

My Map remained silent.

"I guess I'm just not used to letting people push me into things. In my experience, it usually isn't for my own good. My life up until now hasn't been . . ." I paused. Did I really want to go there? I trusted him, true. He'd helped save my life. After experiencing his healing power, I found it hard to picture him ever intentionally hurting anyone. But how well did I know him, really? It had only been a couple days. *"Well, never mind all that. Thanks for thinking of me."*

"If it makes you feel any better," Kevin replied, *"nobody is going to force you to go through with it. If you decide it's not for you, just don't get tested. But at least join us for the information session. Then you can make an informed choice."*

"Sure. Knowledge is power and all that."

"That's the spirit!" Then, after a moment: *"I think."*

"Listen, I'm going to sign off. I'm standing in the hall like an idiot. You caught me in the middle of exploring."

He was only too happy to change the subject. *"Oh, great! Have fun! If you get a chance, swing by the Greenhouse and say hi. If not, I'll forward the details of the AV test and see you at the preliminary meeting."*

"Sounds good."

I slipped the Map back into my pocket, and my explorations began in earnest. To my delight, the Map was also a key card, and it let me into every door I tried. At first, I worried I was being foolish to go swiping the Map at access terminals: advertising my movements, no doubt. It probably tracked every step I took, listened in on every conversation I had. Likewise, a transcript of my messages with Kevin had probably been logged somewhere, for later scrutiny. But I quickly lost my trepidation, along with my bearings. The place was *huge*. Cold, clinical corridors gave way to opulent, beautifully furnished living spaces. Central hubs—complete with restaurants and shops of all kinds and full of relaxed and chatting people of every description—gave access to a dizzying maze of elevators, escalators, utility corridors, laboratories humming with inscrutable machinery, and classrooms full of students of all ages. Atriums bursting with the heady perfumes of synthetic jungle plants echoed to the calls of colorful customized birds and small, nervously inquisitive Chamonkleons. The strange little Anymals vacillated between cautious camouflage—shifting their color and pattern to blend in with their surroundings—and brazen territorial outbursts of screeching and bared fangs. If they'd been any longer than my hand, I might have been more worried. But the little scamps tended to vanish abruptly after announcing themselves.

By this point, it was obvious the facility was almost entirely underground. That humming sound I hadn't been able to place back in my hospital room was from the ventilation system. Moreover, the ceilings in every open area I came to, the jungle park areas included, seemed to lay beneath a bright blue sky, full of warm sunshine, but it didn't quite feel right. The sky wasn't quite high enough; the weather was too random and natural to be the actual weather of the City outside, with its weather drones and meteorological platforms like levitated mountains. Try as I might, I couldn't tell how the sunlight was generated. Clever mirrored tunnels? Some sort of screen or hologram to create the illusion of being outside? I shook my head in wonder and carried on.

Everywhere I went, the people I met were surprisingly affable. There's an edge to most of the City's denizens, a wary suspicion if nothing else, and most of these people didn't have it. They were safe, provided for, gainfully employed. There was no need for them to make hard choices or scrabble for resources. When I stumbled into the middle of business meetings, philosophical debates, or classroom lectures, people paused and offered a smile, made introductions, or asked how they could be of assistance. In one lab, a short frizzy-haired old woman with watery eyes made gigantic by thick lensed glasses (how old-fashioned!) blinked at me peevishly and said, "Don't gawk so, boy. Makes you look the victim of a botched eye transplant. Hand me that black glass rod there, will you?"

I obeyed and watched as she used it to prod something into place in the back of a glowing chamber that crackled with electrical discharge. Her already frazzled hair stood up on end while she did so, and her eyebrows bristled. She muttered something to herself, jabbing aggressively. Finally satisfied, she withdrew the glass rod from the chamber. It was a good thirty centimeters shorter than it had been. She frowned at it in ominous silence. I retreated while she was distracted. But she was the only person I met who didn't seem pleased to see me.

On and on, I went, through endless halls spread across numerous levels. I was thoroughly lost and thoroughly fascinated. I couldn't begin to decide what half of these people were doing. At one point, I wandered through what seemed to be a museum. It was given over to displays of bizarre off-world creatures. Were they real, or very realistic props? An hour later, I was moving cautiously among what appeared to be a trio of half-built spacecraft while busy mechanics worked steadily at piecing them together. One fellow grunted a greeting as I passed; another gave me a cheery wave and a grin. Sparks flew from welding torches.

All of this wandering eventually made me very hungry and thirsty, and I timidly approached a heavy-set man with red-brown skin and close-cropped black hair. He squinted at me for a moment when I asked for directions to the closest cafeteria.

"Lose your Map, son?" He pulled a little rectangle of plastic from his pocket and showed me the display. The corridor I was in would intersect with a hub in another fifty yards, and from there, an escalator would take me up to a dining mezzanine. As I turned away, he called after me, "Have 'em ping your Map! This place makes a lot more sense with it than without!"

A few minutes later, I was seated at a restaurant with a steaming mug of hot chocolate and a piece of apple pie. It was a pleasant little café, overlooking a spacious garden plaza with a tinkling fountain. There were only three other people there, all at the same table across the way, talking quietly with their heads together. They had a chart of some kind rolled out on the table between them. While I watched, they argued in a friendly and animated way, pointing frequently at their diagram and pausing to rub their chins in thought.

Satisfied that I was more or less alone, I pulled out my Map and looked at it closely for what felt like the first time. Up until now, I'd only used it to message Kevin. What else could it do? The man in the hall had used it to show me an actual map of the facility, and given the bewildering size of the place and the City that surrounded it, it made sense the word Map was used to refer to the device itself. Showing people where they were and how to get where they were going was probably its primary function. What had Kevin called it? Percipient plastic? What the heck did that mean, exactly?

The screen, already glowing softly at my touch, suddenly flickered to life with an answer to my unvoiced thought:

per·cip·i·ent/
pər'sipēənt/
<u>*adjective*</u>
perceiving or capable of perceiving

having perception; discerning; discriminating
<u>*noun*</u>
a person or thing that perceives

Following the definition, a little glowing link offered pronunciation advice. Similar words like *astute* and *discerning* were listed, along with opposites, such as *obtuse,* or *stupid.*

So, it was smart. I'd already established that. But this confirmed it: the Map actually read my thoughts. *Wild.* I placed it on the table and took my hands off it. My heart had sped up at the reminder that I was carrying around alien technology. I really had no idea what I was getting into. But everything I had seen made me want to be a part of . . . whatever *this* was. Mind-reading Maps? Spaceship repair? Crazy science experiments? Historical research? This place was bizarre and magical, and like a dream come true. The more I wandered around, the more questions I had. I knew the Map could answer a lot of them, but before I dug into that, I needed to know more about what Project Arete was all about, how it was funded, and who guided their choices and policies. That likely meant digging into Mercedes Helena Cantero Ruiz.

The Map rapidly revealed more information on Project Arete than I could possibly hope to read without dedicating months of my life to learning their history. The various short versions I found all tended to agree with what Director Ruiz had said: PA was all about the advancement of humanity through science. The word "arete" is an old Greek word—more of a concept, really—that refers to the intrinsic quality and excellence of things. Project Arete was all about bringing out that excellence and enhancing it. That explained why it wasn't their MO to press-gang or coerce people into joining; excellence in ethics, education, and enlightenment—in principle—precluded any activities the general populace might label amoral. This went a long way to reassuring me that I'd be safe to choose whether I wanted to stay without having to deal with a hoard of cultish mind-slaves moaning, "Joooooiiiinn uussss," and dragging me back against my will. So far, so good.

I know what you're thinking: of *course* it all looked copacetic. I was using a Map provided by PA to access PANet to look up information on PA. But that was one of the first things I checked. PANet was little more than a hub. Like any other access node, it relied on nano-communications to reach out into the City and pull information from both public and private sources. It had its own proprietary security, of course, but what really surprised me was just how many of those private sources were available to Project Arete. Clearly, they were in good standing with the vast majority of the power players in the City, and that meant they must actively work at keeping good relations.

I thought back to my brief meeting with Mercedes Helena Cantero Ruiz. *Yeah, that tracks.* The director's primary function was very likely playing politics. If nothing else, she'd impressed me as someone who was very thorough, very capable, and very influential. If Project Arete was her brainchild, then no doubt she was constantly working to keep it comfortably positioned within the ever-changing landscape of City politics.

A brief glance through the Project Arete pamphlet I'd stuffed into my pocket didn't illuminate much else. It added another layer to the word "arete," translating it as *virtue,* and alluded to the same philosophy of excellence and self-improvement. The ancient Greeks would apply this word to almost anything: personal brilliance, physical achievement, moral stature, even the aesthetic design of a building. This was where the word "aristocrat" came from, according to some linguists, and arete had apparently been a keystone in the philosophical arch of a great many ancient thinkers, such as Plato and Aristotle. But this was obviously propaganda produced in-house. Did Project Arete really follow these ideals in its daily work?

Mercedes Helena Cantero Ruiz, it turned out, was an open book. The problem I had: there was *too much* information, just like with Project Arete itself. The Map produced an epic biography that began with her birth and reported, moment by moment, almost everything she had ever said or done. Every burp, every fart, every giggle. I found it hard to believe so much information had actually been collected on her. How could anyone know she would be worth reporting on before she became wealthy and influential?

Even asking the Map to condense her life history into a brief synopsis gave me a thousand pages of tedious detail. I had to wonder, after nearly an hour of wading through this deepening mire, if there was an easier way. The tone of her file was mostly dry and emotionless, but there was a hint of hero worship, too. Whoever compiled all this evidently thought very highly of her, but that alone didn't tell me much.

Picking out paragraphs at random, I got the impression of a brilliant woman who had become an activist very early on. Born in 2215 (I was right, nearly one hundred years old!), just a little over two decades into the world-wide convulsions that began with the One World Treaty of 2193. Her childhood included early Tier fundraisers for the sake of amputee children. After that, nano-drives in her teens to supply basic daily health benefits to those without the tiny helper robots swimming in their bloodstreams. At that time, nano-technology wasn't ubiquitous, and only the wealthiest could afford it. She went on to organize rallies in protest of weather control experiments in her early twenties (one of her few notable failures: weather control technology, despite its shaky start, was here to stay). This paved the way for a lot of environmental activism throughout her adult life. It all eventually petered out in the late 2200s, when it became evident nobody really cared anymore. Synthetics were the future. Animals, plants, nature? They had become Anymals, FastGro, the City. Other brands abound, of course, but she could see which way the artificial wind was blowing. No real lasting change would be accomplished through activism. A fundamental shift in the human mindset had failed to occur; therefore, technology would simply have to keep pace with our headlong rush for disaster. She would have to shift focus if she was hoping to stave off the inevitable decline of our species.

I can't say I agreed with her there. We seemed to be doing just fine. Technology was outpacing us, if anything. We'd reached a point, thanks to the arrival of the Cupids, where almost anything we could imagine could be fabricated, and with very little cost in energy, material, or waste. True, there was little left that was original or natural, but I hadn't grown up with any of that stuff. Hard to miss what you've never known.

I skipped ahead. Despite all the other work she'd done, Ms. Ruiz's primary concern for most of her life seemed to be assisting refugees displaced by war and environmental disasters. Not a surprise, given the era she was born in. Worldwide conflicts, disastrous weather control experiments—how could they fail to shape a person's outlook? Especially someone like Ms. Ruiz, who seemed to be driven and passionate about creating positive changes for the maximum number of people possible.

Decades of her adult life had been devoted to establishing programs to facilitate border crossings (even as those borders broke down), supply effective representation for immigration and naturalization cases (even as the concept of "country" grew increasingly murky), and to work toward freeing people unjustly persecuted or incarcerated in foreign countries (even as countries collapsed entirely, dividing into dozens of miniature versions of themselves, often with conflicting ideologies). Despite all the complications, she was tireless in her pursuit of personal liberties and freedom of movement across the growing City for all who desired it.

On the surface, she seemed like something of an avenging angel, both compassionate and righteous. As her networks grew, so, too, did her wealth and influence, along with her ability to reach further afield, deeper into the darkest places. Even her detractors seemed to label her as an overwhelming force for good in a corrupt world. Their issues with her seemed largely centered around her personal aggrandizement. Someone so wealthy should give more, they implied, should do more. But from what I could tell, almost all of her extremely vast empire was tied up in charities, missions, outreach programs, and investments geared toward the advancement of universal education, scientific achievement, exploration, technology, and, more recently, with the understanding of Super-powers and how the sudden evolution of *human* into *Super-human* was changing the status quo.

I could spend days reading this stuff and still not really know what made her tick, but it certainly made for an impressive resume. She definitely seemed like the sort of person I would want to work for. She was actively accomplishing some good in the world, that much was undeniable. And she, or someone she employed, could likely help me better understand my Super-powers. I wondered if Kevin was right. Did Project Arete hold the key to unlocking my potential? What if I *could* do more than make my laces wiggle around on their own? What else might I be capable of? If I wanted to find out, it seemed fate had been kind and delivered me into the arms of the very people I needed to talk to.

Still, something felt weird about it all. Despite all the obvious bustle and purpose in the Project Arete facility, I had this insistent feeling that it was all just a cover. The real work was something else entirely. I couldn't quite figure out why I thought so. But in my guts, I knew it was true. Maybe it was this Map. Percipient plastic seemed . . . too futuristic. I had never heard of *anything* like this before. This kind of technology was unbelievably advanced. The things you could do with a material powered by personal electrical fields that could read minds or predict the user's needs . . . it was mind-boggling. More than a little scary. And here they were just handing the stuff out to any stranger who happened to drop by! Obviously, PA was in bed with Cupids, but I couldn't imagine how that relationship might work. I'd never heard of anyone cozying up to the strange aliens before.

I looked over at the trio across the café, still busily debating their design. They seemed comfortable, familiar with the surroundings. Maybe they had been here at PA for a while. They could probably answer a few of my questions. Resolved to find out more, I got up and walked over to them.

At that moment, one of the men was holding forth to his two colleagues. He looked thirty-something, a bookish type, with short black hair and a very insistent tone when speaking. His skin was that slightly darker color between olive and brown that could belong to any number of genetic heritages. Next to him was a woman of mostly Caucasian genetics in her mid-twenties, wearing a dark-blue skirt and white blouse, with straight blonde hair cut to her shoulders, eyebrows immaculately crafted over warm brown eyes, and finger-nails trimmed short and brightly multi-colored. The third member of the party was an indeterminately older gentleman, also primar-ily Caucasian, though his hooked nose hinted at mixed genetics. Like me, he was comfortably attired in a hoodie and jeans. He was sipping an espresso and absently pushing his loose gray curls back from his face. His bright blue eyes swiveled to me as I approached. The bookish man, whose back was to me, was saying something about needing a better conduit to avoid power surges and complete bricking, whatever that meant. He trailed off as the older gentleman looked over.

"Uh, hi," I ventured. I realized my shoelaces were untied and gave them a mental nudge to start lacing up properly. First impressions, right? Only the older man seemed to notice my laces wiggling around all by themselves. He raised an eyebrow; then his eyes lifted to rove over the injuries on my face, but he didn't comment. I realized my laces were way too long for my shoes and gave it up as a bad job. Probably better not to lose control of my power in front of three strangers anyway. I took a deep breath and forged ahead.

"I'm David, and um . . . well, I've been invited to join the team here at Project Arete. Am I saying that right? Ar-uh-tay? Uh . . ."

The young woman smiled and pushed a spare chair out with a sandaled foot. Her toenails were as bright and colorful as her fingernails. "Relax, David. Have a seat. I'm Dawn. This is Miguel"—she airily waved toward bookish with black hair—"and this is Francis." The older gentleman nodded and gave me an easy smile, offering his hand for a firm shake. Briefly, I wondered if this was the same Francis Kevin had mentioned in connection with how Maps made use of internal nano-networks. The younger two didn't follow suit with a handshake, but they adjusted themselves in a subtle way, reorienting their bodies toward me, and I suddenly felt included.

"I don't suppose you know anything about power transfer conduits?" asked Dawn in a hopeful tone. "We're not getting anywhere with this design; keep overloading the junctions and fusing the whole mess into total glass. Miguel insists we just need heavier cables, but the numbers *work*. It should be fine as it is, well within tolerance, and it just *isn't*."

"Is this your design?" I asked, looking down at the blueprint on the table. It was a mess of black and red squiggles and interconnected blue and green lines. Various shapes in various colors were scattered throughout. I couldn't tell what I was looking at.

"Yes," replied Miguel. He tapped the green line nearest him. "Power transfer conduits. Supplies the device through several relays to rapidly transfer power where it needs to go. But this"—he tapped a small black square in the middle of the chart—"keeps soaking up excess power that shouldn't even be getting to it. Fries it every time we fire up for a test, so we can't even be sure our theory is correct. Can't even run the test! Think ice cream under a hot lamp. Not pretty. Anyway, we can't just keep replacing the thing. It's a pain to program and wire in—unbelievably tiny!—never mind the small fortune we burn every time."

But I wasn't listening. I was staring at the chart. It was like looking at a pile of strings that had been dropped and kicked around until they were hopelessly tangled, like a particularly complicated weaving made from four different threads. But the green line was . . . more *ornate* than useful. I could see a couple of places that didn't need to be looped like they were. You could still reach all the same places with the green lines without the extra wiggles. Without thinking, I said so, pointing out the places I meant.

Miguel was irked. He immediately began protesting, stabbing a finger at the chart, and citing numerous examples of why this or that green line was necessary, none of which made much sense to me. Dawn ignored him, leaning over to trace the green lines with an elegant finger. Her pretty face was a picture of intense concentration. Francis smiled, his eyes gazing thoughtfully at the design. It was a slow smile, like the sun rising, until his whole face was lit up. Clapping me on the shoulder, he rolled up the chart and stood up so abruptly, his chair tipped over backward. Instinctively, I made his shoelace grab the chair leg and pull it back down before it went over entirely. Francis must have felt a tug on his foot because he glanced down. His shoelace rapidly retied itself.

He looked up at his coworkers. "I have a sneaking suspicion that strings are David's thing," he announced, then marched away. Dawn and Miguel were on their feet, too, still arguing about whether it would work, how to test it. Francis was already on the escalator by the time they ran after him.

Flabbergasted, I watched them go. So bizarre! They had simply taken me at my word and assumed I had a right to be there. They'd even taken it for granted I might have something valuable to contribute. I wasn't used to people asking my opinion on anything, never mind actually listening to the answer. More than just listen—they had rushed off in a tizzy to go test my theory! I could have told them it wasn't a theory. Somehow, I knew I was right about my assessment of the lines on the chart. I just didn't know what they were *for.*

Well, so much for asking them about Mercedes Ruiz. With a sigh, I went back to my table and ordered another hot chocolate. My strange encounter with the three engineers left me feeling out of my depth. I'd lost my appetite for exploration. There was simply too much stuff going on here, and it seemed like every corner I turned, I tripped over another question. I wasn't sure what to do. While pondering my next move, it occurred to me that I had been at the Project Arete facility for over half a week, recovering from my concussion and bruised kidney. My busted arm was sore, but the sling helped a bit. I flexed my elbow experimentally. It felt a lot better, actually.

I considered taking the sling off, but then thought better of it. The first time I'd broken my arm, falling off a balcony when I was eight, I had doffed the sling the first chance I got. The fabric of the sling, coiled and trailing after me, was less of a nuisance as a play pal than it was binding my arm to my chest. But I had paid for the freedom when I took a tumble the next day, making the fracture considerably worse and slowing down my recovery time by a large margin. I could clearly remember my parents sitting me down to explain the necessity of the sling and the need for patience while I healed. I was like most boys at that age: overly rambunctious, and always getting banged up. My parents had always worried I'd break my skull, running headfirst at life, before I learned to slow down.

I frowned. My parents . . .

I pulled out the Map. The softly glowing rectangle lit up with my parents' names and address, followed by a question mark. It knew I was thinking about calling home, and it also knew that I wasn't sure if I wanted to tell my parents everything that was going on. This freaky thing was going to take some getting used to. I stared at it for a long time, chewing on my lip. No. What would I say? *Hey, Mom and Dad, got beat up again. But don't worry about that. I'm calling from an alien computer, and they just want to run a few tests before I leave . . .*

Tomorrow. Tomorrow, I would call them . . . after I found out if my powers would ever amount to anything. Maybe it was childish, but I was hoping to have good news, something they could be proud of.

With nowhere else to go, I used the Map to make my way back to the hospital room. Everything was exactly as I'd left it. I ate a hearty meal, then spent the rest of the night strumming the guitar Kevin had left me. It was a synthetic maple acoustic with a very warm tone, and I liked how smooth the action was. I let my fingers explore how I was feeling. The longer I played, the less I thought about the test and the more my mind calmed. Yet, try as I might, I couldn't get my power to cooperate when I tried to play without my hands. After half a dozen trips to the recycler, I told Theo not to bother replacing the latest batch of broken strings and left the guitar three short. I went to bed frustrated and stared at the ceiling for a long time. Thoughts of Sarah kept running through my head. I knew I was obsessing, but I couldn't figure out why, or what else I could do about it except go and meet her.

Sleep, when it finally came, was a relief.

IV

The following morning, Theo put together an impressive breakfast, which I inhaled with hardly a pause for breath. I'd always had a big appetite, but the accelerated healing Kevin had set in motion was burning through the calories. I was back for seconds so fast, the AI replicator was surprised into making a comment.

"Slow down and try to enjoy your meal, sir! At this rate, PA will run out of food for the rest of the facility!"

I laughed and dug in. While I shoveled up pancakes, bacon, scrambled eggs, and hash browns, all smothered in sweet and sticky syrup, I used the Map to get a better feel for the facility's layout. By the time I finished eating, I felt fairly confident I'd be able to find my way to Mr. Gold's classroom. According to Kevin, that was where the meeting would take place.

My stomach was tied in knots, and not from the meal. Every single person going to this meeting was a Super. I spent a lot longer than I normally would in the washroom, trying to make myself presentable. I didn't know how many people would be attending, but it was a bit intimidating to know that in less than an hour, I'd be in a room full of people with powers, all of whom, like Sarah, would probably outclass me by a large margin. To make matters worse, I kept seeing Sarah's glowing green eyes. I felt like I'd dreamed those eyes all night. I couldn't decide what made me more nervous: getting tested for my potential or meeting her. I wasn't even sure why I'd become so fixated on the idea of meeting this girl. I kept telling myself that I owed Sarah my thanks for interrupting my untimely demise, but it was something more than that. It was as if I knew her already. Sounds crazy, now that I'm saying it, but it's true. The moment her glowing green eyes met mine on the pier that day, it was like she was looking into my soul. Some part of me had latched onto her like I was a drowning man, and she was the only thing keeping me afloat. I knew it was stupid, but it felt like fate. Dockside Dragons and my dizzied state notwithstanding, I'd been in the right place at the right time. It was hard to shake the sense of certainty. I was *supposed* to meet her.

I rolled my eyes at myself. *Yeah, right. More likely, you just got kicked in the head one too many times.* I huffed out a breath and walked away from the washroom mirror. In the end, the bruising and stitches weren't something I could easily cover up. I looked frightful, and nothing short of wearing a mask was going to change that. It was interesting that Dawn, Miguel, and Francis hadn't commented on my appearance yesterday. But maybe they'd been too caught up in their design problem to worry about it. The sling on my arm had clearly signaled I'd been hurt in some way. Maybe people here didn't pry unless invited. Francis had raised an eyebrow, but at the time, I'd assumed it was because of my shoelaces. *Ah well.* I shrugged. Not worth worrying about now.

The classroom, when I finally found it, didn't look as you might expect: there were no immersive learning suites for accessing a shared virtual space here. Instead, the room featured one big desk in the corner, fairly cluttered and disorganized; smart-glass screens and advertising flimsies on the walls; overflowing shelves and filing cabinets; those old uncomfortable desks with hard plastic chairs attached by a metal bar; even a chalkboard, with actual chalk and dusty brushes. Mr. Gold, as it turned out, was fond of anachronisms and collected old and out-of-date things. He used them in preference to modern technology. When he couldn't do that, he had his modern tech disguised as old tech. His laser pointer, for example, projected a hologram that made it look like an old yard stick, with measurement intervals marked off along its length in black. He'd patterned the whole classroom off a school room from the early 2000s, right down to tile floors in a checkerboard pattern of pale brown and sky blue. No windows, though, because like every other part of PA, the classroom was underground. I had gathered, by this point, that the facility was rather unremarkable up at ground level, some sort of strip mall that hardly anybody ever visited, but there were over fifty levels below.

I looked around the room, surprised. It felt like I'd stepped through a portal into the past. I half expected to find asbestos in the walls if I went digging. My dad had told me all about how ancient humans had once built with the craziest, most dangerous, and unstable materials. He would have loved this guy.

I had arrived early enough that only Kevin and one other person were there. He was sitting near the front with a Korean girl a couple years younger. She had warm brown eyes in a heart-shaped face. Her dark hair was worn in a short feathery bob. Like Kevin, she'd chosen slacks and a button-down shirt with a zip-up sweater over top, though she'd chosen black and bright pink over his more somber gray and green. I didn't want to interrupt their silent conversation, which was flowing rapidly back in forth in sign language, so I gave her what I hoped was a friendly smile and offered him a serious nod. Then I took a seat in the back of the room.

It wasn't long before the two joined me. The girl smiled hugely and waved, even though she was standing right next to me.

"David, this is my little sister, Yoon Seul-gi. Everyone calls her Susie. Susie, meet David North." He positioned himself so that he was mostly facing her, and he punctuated his words with rapid hand signs. Her big brown eyes flickered back and forth between his gestures and me, and then she gave me a solemn little bow. I was utterly charmed.

"Hi, Susie. It's nice to meet you." Kevin dutifully translated with signs, but she watched my mouth as I spoke and clearly had no trouble understanding me. "Are you a Super, too?" I asked.

She nodded and made a hand gesture I didn't recognize.

"Languages," translated Kevin.

I wasn't sure what to make of that, so I just made an impressed face. The two of them took seats nearby, while I did something impulsive and more than a little bit crazy. Pulling out my Map, I concentrated my thoughts.

"*Yes,*" my Map informed me, "*the idea is feasible.*" No comment on whether it was a *good* idea, I noticed, but I went ahead and did it anyway.

I turned to Susie. "*Check this out,*" I signed. Her eyes flew wide with shock.

"*You know sign!*" She swatted Kevin on the arm, and he turned to find me making my response with hand gestures.

"*Not a word of it. But there are plenty of sign databases out there, so I had my Map find an up-to-date version and download it. I'm basically thinking what I want to say to my Map, and it's causing my nanos to coordinate the appropriate muscles. Feels pretty weird, actually. Kind of like pins and needles.*"

"*David, that's . . . Why would you . . . ?*" Susie was stunned. Her hands fluttered uncertainly.

Kevin was a little more concerned. "*I'm not sure that's safe,*" he warned me. "*And how are you understanding us when we sign to you?*"

I grinned. "*Alien tech!*" Nanos in my eyes were sending copies of incoming visual information to my Map so it could interpret for me. Signals sent from my Map to the nano-machines in my inner ear stimulated my eardrum directly. A neat little workaround of my brain, which didn't have a clue how to interpret or perform sign language. I heard what Kevin and Susie signed as if they were speaking; in Kevin's case, in his own voice; in Susie's case, in the child-like voice of a popular syndicated cartoon character called Pororo, who had been enjoying a recent revival on the syndicated entertainment networks. It only served to make Susie seem more adorable. Still, probably best not to tell her that she now sounded like an animated bird.

The three of us chatted amiably while we waited for the others to arrive. Heeding Kevin's advice, I spoke out loud rather than giving the Map continued control of my hands, but I allowed it to continue translating their signs for me. It seemed harmless enough, and it *was* awfully convenient. Doubtless there were a million other things the Map could do, if people simply thought outside the box a little bit. I was surprised nobody else had experimented with it in this way before.

There was a blur of movement and loose papers erupted into the air. A pair of identical blonde jock types were suddenly sitting next to us, grinning. Susie yelped and pressed a hand to her chest. Kevin twitched but didn't otherwise react. Me? I fell out of my chair. The twins burst out laughing. One punched the other in the shoulder with a movement so fast, it was nearly invisible. The impact sent a thunderclap of sound through the room. The other took the blow without flinching, as if he were made of stone.

I forced a smile and tried for a hearty chuckle. "Ha, good one!" Super-strength. Super-speed. Super-endurance. These two were potentially *deadly.* Probably best to stay on their good side.

The one on the left had the grace to look a little abashed. He reached down with one hand and hauled me to my feet without apparent effort. I'm not a small guy, but I suddenly felt like a toddler. I settled back into my seat as he said, "Sorry, dude. Can't help ourselves sometimes."

"Alan Frøsaker," put in his brother, thumbing his own broad chest. "That's Jake."

"Hey," I greeted them. "You can bet I won't be forgetting the two of you any time soon. Probably have nightmares!"

Alan chuckled, pleased. Jake offered a sheepish grin. Blonde, blue-eyed, and ruddy faced, they were both tall and broad with thick arms and legs. They were dressed nearly identically, in smart black slacks and blue shirts, but where Alan had chosen a sleeveless tank top that revealed his muscular arms and shoulders, Jake was wearing a full-sleeved dress shirt and black tie. They struck me as a little rustic, for some reason, which isn't to say they weren't City boys—there's really no such thing as rural anymore—but they both behaved as I imagined a couple of old-time farm boys might: polite and forthright, respectful, but liable to blow off steam with physical outbursts like their startling entrance. They were friendly with Kevin, and treated Susie as their own little sister. They teased her gently, while she was unfailingly sweet in response. The way they poked fun at her made me feel like they'd also protect her against anyone more aggressive. After a bit of conversation, my impression was that Alan was the leader and Jake was the follower. If I didn't miss my guess, Alan was also the prankster, while Jake was the conscience who patched things up after Alan's pranks went sideways. Still, they seemed decent.

A glance at my Map showed me that the meeting should have begun already. As though summoned by the thought, our host appeared in the doorway, juggling a battered briefcase and an armload of old books. He shuffled to the desk and deposited his burden with a thump and then stood, rubbing his lower back.

As I already mentioned, his name was Mr. Gold ("Call me Henry!"). He looked like one of those long-faced, mopey Hunting Fetches: wrinkles; drooping cheeks; big bruised saggy pouches under his watery eyes; downturned mouth with thin lips; patchy gray stubble on his cheeks and chin. Even his ears were large and a bit floppy, and his jaw length fringe of limp gray hair only exaggerated the effect. Overall, he looked about one hundred years old and terribly morose, but he could have been twenty the way he was dressed: faded black hoodie worn at the cuffs and collar, with one of those heavy metal band logos that's so ornate it's totally unreadable splashed across the front in blood red. I think it said "Catoblepas" or something like that. He wore ragged jeans, which seemed to be authentically torn from actual wear, not simply fabricated that way. Floppy, dirty white sneakers with broken laces knotted at the sides completed his ensemble.

That made me smirk. No tying the teacher's shoelaces together, like the last time I'd been in a classroom. Not that it had been my fault. He'd just walked too close to me, and my power had reached out and done its thing. I looked down at my own shoes. My laces drooped lazily along the floor. One had twined partway up a leg of my chair but was otherwise still. My power seemed quiescent for now, and it made me nervous. Much better if it was constantly leaking out. I didn't want to have an incident during the meeting.

"Well!" said Mr. Gold, and he clapped his hands together loudly. I glanced up to see him walking toward our little group with a friendly smile. "Hello, Jake. Hello, Alan. Glad to see you both. You guys get a Powerball team sorted out yet?" He took a perch on an empty desk, his feet up on the seat.

"Working on it," said Alan. "Just need a couple more players."

Mr. Gold nodded around the circle. "Kevin, I know. You must be Susie?" She smiled and waved, the same enthusiastic greeting she'd given me. Clumsily, Mr. Gold signed, "*A pleasure to meet you, Ms. Yoon.*" It was fairly obvious he wasn't well versed in this mode of communication, but he was making the effort anyway. Susie's smile got even bigger. Out loud, he said, "And who's this, then?"

"This is David North," said Kevin.

Mr. Gold inspected my face with a critical eye. "Ah, that's right. The incident at the docks. I'm sorry you had to go through that."

I shrugged noncommittally.

"Well!" He looked around the mostly empty room. "Still a couple more to join us. Amuse yourselves quietly for a bit. I'm sure they'll be here soon." He pulled out a Map but didn't move from his perch on the desk. Kevin, Susie, Jake, and Alan all began conversing animatedly, as if Mr. Gold wasn't there. I sat quietly, letting the conversation flow around me. My focus had turned inward.

I could *feel* her—Sarah—coming down the hall. Each step she took brought her closer. How was that even possible? I began counting under my breath. *Three, two, one.* Right on cue, she appeared in the doorway.

She wasn't short, but she was thin, and her shoulders were stooped, like she was trying to look small. She wore a simple knee-length skirt in dark green and a loose sweater the color of autumn leaves. Black tights and sensible black flats completed the outfit. Her frizzy brown hair had been corralled under a green-and-gold head scarf. Her face was a little long, with a narrow chin, sharp nose, and prominent cheekbones. I guessed her to be about a year younger than me, but it was hard to tell. To be honest, she was plain and unremarkable, except for her eyes. I met her neon green gaze from across the room, and she halted, eyes wide like an Anymal caught in a bright light. Did she zoom in, scrutinize the damage to my face? Was she able to flick between visual modes to build a composite picture, compare what she saw with a facial recognition database? I tried to hold her eyes, but she dropped her gaze immediately. A gentle nudge from a taller girl in the hall behind her broke the spell. It was like I'd caught her unprepared and unguarded. She folded up in an instant, turning inward. Her pale face was suddenly suffused with a rosy hue. She scurried to the far corner and sat with a hunched shoulder toward the rest of us. The posture made me think she was trying to hide behind her hair, but, of course, she'd tied it back.

Sarah's regal friend followed her into the room and sat next to her, positioning herself like a shield between Sarah and the rest of us.

She was a tall, brown-skinned girl of strong Indian genetics. Long black hair worn in a thick braid fell past her waist. She was flawlessly gorgeous, with an exotic beauty all her own. No patterning herself after others, for this girl; she could easily be an archetype that others would try to mimic. Her clothing was practical and utilitarian: well-fitted black cargos with numerous pockets; a crimson blouse with long sleeves rolled up to the elbow; a multi-pocketed sleeveless black vest over top. Chin high, her dark eyes flashed over us, assessing and categorizing everyone present before finally settling on me, the one unknown in the room. I saw no sign of sympathy for my injuries in her eyes.

"Well!" Mr. Gold leapt to his feet, suddenly animated. Kevin also rose to his feet. "Well!" Mr. Gold said again, and clapped his hands. "Looks like we're all here! Sarah, Amyati, I'm glad you could make it." He strode to the front of the room and turned to face everyone, rubbing his hands. Kevin took up a position next to him, facing Susie, translating Mr. Gold's words into sign. "Is everyone excited to find out their potential today?"

There were murmurs of agreement. I held my tongue, watching Sarah from the corner of my eye. She fidgeted, her eyes on the desk in front of her.

Mr. Gold launched into his lecture. He may have looked like a corpse, but his attitude was sprightly. The way he moved around the room, practically bouncing from place to place, it was like he'd just been into the sugar. He waved his arms excitedly when he talked, and he spoke with conviction. I found myself warming to him, *because* of his weirdness rather than in spite of it. I mean, in a world where appearance was highly customizable, like most everything else, you had to be a little bit mad to choose to look like he did. But there was no denying his enthusiasm.

The topic of his speech was what's called the Abeyant Vector. I sat up and leaned toward him. This must be the "AV" Kevin had mentioned. Basically (said Mr. Gold), this was a scale that measured our potential Super-powers. "Abeyant" means dormant or hidden. The measurement would give us an idea of how much power we might eventually access if we were to train diligently. Training, apparently, could take the form of meditation, experimentation, guided application of known abilities, and so on. It was a finicky process that had to be custom tailored to each Super. But, once you knew your potential, it was possible to work outward, from what was known, toward what could be discovered.

I was surprised to learn that uncontrolled, spontaneous manifestation of powers wasn't particularly uncommon. I'd always thought I was unique in developing an aberrant, uncontrollable power. In fact, most people realized they had a Super-power only when it suddenly acted up, either very early in life, as in my case, or around puberty. However, in most cases, Supers instinctively knew how to control their powers. After the first flare-up, which was usually pretty sketchy, things settled down and the process of discovering just what you were capable of began. More rarely, powers continued firing off on their own. I'd had some experience with this, myself. But Mr. Gold's lecture made me realize the normal course of events *was* happening for me, albeit slowly. I *had* gained some small degree of control when I discovered that letting my power "leak" prevented it from lashing out so often. In a way, I'd been fortunate. I only had the ability to be a minor nuisance. With some of the powers out there, it could get pretty ugly if a method of control wasn't discovered quickly.

Anyway, as Mr. Gold explained it, they had some kind of quantum computer at the Project Arete facility that could measure our hidden potential, or Abeyant Vector. They used the term "vector" because it implied not just magnitude (how *much* power we have) but direction (what *kind* of power we have). That's right—they could *predict* what sort of powers we might develop based on what we already had.

It was news to me, but Super-powers generally developed along lines of ("somewhat fuzzy," Mr. Gold admitted) logic. While they didn't necessarily follow courses that would make sense to you or me, there was supposedly some overarching logic to the way the powers were organized and the way they manifested. Using this logic (and probably a great deal of trial and error), the people at Project Arete had *mapped* the various Super-powers—or the ones that had so far been discovered, at any rate—and figured out a way to predict ("with a very reasonable degree of accuracy!" enthused Mr. Gold) who could do what.

For example, a guy who gets knocked on the head at the pool as a kid and falls unconscious into the water but somehow doesn't drown (despite the lifeguard looking the other way) isn't likely to develop the ability to fly. His powers probably have to do with water, or perhaps the preservation of life. See? Logic, of a sort. Thus, the development of his powers leads him along that vector: first discovering his ability to breathe underwater, then learning to swim with the speed and grace of a Killfish, and then being able to resist the water pressure at greater depths (or whatever). This process goes on until he's reached his limit of power—either he eventually becomes the Human Submarine, or his development stops somewhere short of that goal.

His powers might take another track, but each power that develops will be related in some way to the power that manifested before it. And before you say it, I know: he *could*, in fact, wind up being able to fly. Maybe he survived underwater because his power allowed him to produce air in his own lungs while he held his breath, rather than actually breathe water. In which case, his Abeyant Vector might lead him down a path of different air-related powers.

As Mr. Gold had said at the beginning, it wasn't an exact science, and it was best not to assume we knew everything. The point of determining our Abeyant Vector was to figure out just how much more work was left to do to unlock our full potential and, if possible, to guide that development along safe and ethical channels. Some powers can kill the person who manifests them if he or she isn't careful. More crucially, some powers can kill others.

I sat back, considering all he'd said. Did I want to get tested? I admit it, I wasn't terribly excited to find out my AV. At that point in my life, all I could do was manipulate bits of string, sometimes wires, sometimes as far away as three meters. Whoop-de-freaking-do. Such incredible *potential.* Better watch your step, villainous scum, or I'll show you my sliding knot trick. Maybe knit you a scarf. Or a blanket! Because you'll need one. I hear it gets awfully chilly in prison. *Yeah, right.*

So, that was the gist of it. After the presentation, if we were interested, we could take an orientation tour, meet some of the faculty, and even take a spin in the quantum computer to see what's what. All seven of us were there because we had demonstrated Super-abilities of one kind or another. But it was up to us to pursue our potential, our personal *arete.*

I was a little taken aback that I could get tested *today.* I'd thought this was just an information session, and we'd be given some time to think it over. Kevin had neglected to mention that the meeting would segue directly into the actual test. I wasn't given time to stew on that, however. Mr. Gold opened the floor to questions.

Amyati immediately spoke up. Her voice was strong and certain, slightly accented. She must come from a distant part of the City, I thought. "This test will tell me exactly what powers I have yet to access?"

Jake and Alan were clearly endowed with Super-strength, speed, and endurance. They made no effort to hide it. Kevin was a healer. Susie's power had to do with languages, apparently. I wiggled string, but only because I didn't have much choice in the matter. Sarah had robot eyes, which must have had all sorts of applications, but what

Ian Houston

else could she do? Kevin had said she was loaded with abilities. You couldn't tell just by looking at her. There was no obvious indication what Amyati was capable of either.

"Well!" said Mr. Gold. "It isn't going to tell us *every*thing we might want to know, but it *does* give us a particularly accurate idea of where your particular power node is positioned on the overall map." Mr. Gold was referring to a sort of 3D chart they had, a connected network of known Super-powers and their relationships to each other. "More importantly, it gives us an idea of the *scale* of your power—that is, the radius on the map from your individual node, which encompasses all the different powers you might one day attain. Bearing in mind, of course, that you won't reach them all. That has to do with your Abeyant Vector. Someone scoring an AV of fifty is going to have a larger radius on the map, be able to go further along the path from their starting point, and will probably have more branches in their developing tree of abilities than someone who rates, say, a twenty, or a one."

Mr. Gold cleared his throat and took a sip of water. Looking around, I saw that all of us were paying close attention. Kevin's hands had fallen still, and Susie's wide brown eyes were now fixed on the eccentric old man. Sarah and Amyati were looking thoughtful, considering all we'd been told. We were all curious about the powers we might possess. Even I had begun to realize, despite my ingrained reticence, that there was no reason not to go through with the test. The only one who didn't really seem to be listening was the scrawny kid on the far side of the room, maybe thirteen or fourteen years old, doodling with a finger on a smart-glass data-pad as if he'd heard the speech a dozen times before.

I frowned and glanced around. Where had he come from? I did a quick head count. Kevin, Susie, Jake, Alan, Sarah, Amyati. Six, plus me. But now there was this eighth kid. I stared, perplexed.

Sensing my regard, he stopped drawing and looked over at me. For an instant, our eyes met. He had surprisingly clear gray eyes in a pale oval face, thin dark eyebrows, and a narrow nose. His face was very mobile and expressive, and right now, it was expressing total surprise. I felt a physical shock as our eyes met, like wires snapping taut between us, humming like a strummed power chord. He inhaled sharply . . . and then he simply wasn't there. The feeling of guitar strings vibrating persisted for a moment, a sound below hearing, more in my bones than in my ears, like . . . like a fading mental echo. It left my head feeling like an empty concert hall.

What the heck just happened? Did I imagine . . . there was someone? Did something . . . ? But it was gone. Whatever had just happened, I couldn't recall it at all. Like a dream, it had simply slipped away. I wouldn't, in truth, recall this moment until a little later, when that connection was re-established and reinforced. Instead, worried I had been caught daydreaming, I made a quick survey of the room. Nobody seemed to have noticed anything untoward. Except for a flash of neon green from Sarah, giving me a furtive sideways glance, everyone was looking at Mr. Gold.

"All that means," Mr. Gold was saying, making gestures to illustrate his speech, "is that the variety and overall impact"—he punched the air—"of the things you will be able to do will increase as you follow the path." He walked two fingers past us, a little Super intent on his personal journey. "Some of you may, in fact, develop multiple related powers." His hands, in an attitude of prayer, went in opposite directions, palms upward. "When this happens, one can usually pursue both pathways to the limit of one's Abeyant Vector. This sort of branching of the way is rather common above 25 AV, and it's not unusual to see the path loop back to familiar ground and explore channels that were previously passed over.

"However,"—and here his tone became deadly serious—"it is incumbent upon me to be clear, and I cannot stress this enough, your AV *is what it is!*" Fierce jabs of the index finger punctuated his point. "If you rate an Abeyant Vector of five," he continued, "no amount of wishing is going to change that number. Work hard, and you will be able to unlock all your abilities. Once you reach that point, you will have to carry on with life knowing that you have achieved your full potential, at least as far as Super-powers go. Your Abeyant Vector is the absolute limit!" He made a flat handed gesture of negation.

"But take heart! Super-powers are not the be all and end all. They are simply an inherent quality of a particular individual's makeup, and you will or won't have them—or rather, the *potential* for them . . . the *chance* to discover them and develop them *if* you apply yourself!" Mr. Gold paused, arms folded. His long face scrutinized each of us in turn. Then he smiled and was abruptly jovial again.

"Well, since I'm sure you're all curious by now, my Abeyant Vector—are you ready for this?—is zero." Mr. Gold chuckled and raised a hand to forestall any response. "I'm quite all right with that. I happen to have a knack for teaching. And that means, anyone I help reach their full potential is an extension of my influence in the world. So, in that sense, I might be more powerful than any of you! Any last questions?"

There were, of course. I sat silently as the others piped up. Frankly, that last bit was disappointing. AV was set in stone? It couldn't be improved? If that were true, and I scored low, there would be no way to get better. Wouldn't matter if I worked hard, I wouldn't develop epic Super-powers. *Like Sarah supposedly has.* I snuck a glance at her, but she wasn't paying any attention to me. From the sounds of it, I was stuck with the one crummy power I had. What if my AV was only seven or eight, and I never got better than I was? What if it was only two or three, and I was lucky to have unlocked as much as I had? It couldn't be that simple, could it?

My perspective suddenly shifted. Super-powers were a relatively new thing, in historical terms. But if it was a case of have or have not, the world was already well on its way to a major class divide. It put my useless little ability into a new light, in a way. I'd had a taste of what it was like to possess a Super-power, even if it was unreliable. But I'd been clinging to the hope that I was something special, that I could do some good in the world—that I could eventually help change things for the better. It was disappointing to be told there might be a very finite limit on what I could do. But . . . even if all I could do was tie people's shoelaces together, wasn't I still one of the lucky ones? The vast majority of people didn't have any abilities at all. Sure, my power wasn't going to stop a Super-villain. It hadn't even been enough to stop a bunch of street punks from nearly killing me. But it was better than nothing. Didn't I owe it to myself to find out all I could about it, learn to make the most of it? Who knows, maybe with some clever, out-of-the-box thinking, I could find a way to make it useful.

I looked up to find Sarah's neon green eyes regarding me curiously. She blushed and glanced away, but I was left with the impression she was just as intrigued by me as I was by her. No time like the present, right? Now that the info session was winding to a close, it was time to get Kevin to introduce me. He'd resumed his seat next to Susie, and I turned to get his attention.

Mr. Gold interrupted us with a loud clap of his hands. "Well!" he exclaimed. "I suppose you're all eager to get to it! Right, then! I'd better warn the geeks we're coming." He loped from the room, Map in hand, forgetting his overstuffed briefcase and stack of books. One by one, we all filed into the hall after him.

O ut in the hall, Mr. Gold had vanished. The others were milling about, talking quietly. I joined Kevin and Susie to wait for further instructions.

"*So exciting!*" Susie signed. I gave her a thumbs up. It was sign language I knew that didn't require the Map to use me like a puppet.

Mr. Gold had said the AV scale went up to a somewhat ambiguous and theoretical one hundred, and they'd never tested anyone higher than a ninety-one. He didn't say who it had been, but he had dropped hints. I suspected it was the Golden Knight. His powers had been so potent, he had moved off-world to Luna Base. He was capable, in theory, of calling down a controlled solar flare. Not exactly something you want to happen inside an atmosphere. The Golden Knight had all the trademarks of Project Arete training: all that idealism and morality. He was practically a saint, and Mr. Gold's comment about influencing the future of the world through those he educated had me wondering if the Golden Knight maybe took his name from an erstwhile mentor. Sure made me think of Mr. Gold in a different light. More powerful than any of us, indeed!

In the larger scheme of things, even a massively potent Abeyant Vector of seventy-five was exponentially weaker than the kind of power the Golden Knight could call on. I had dreamed of that kind of Super-power my whole life, but the odds were frankly slim. Ever since my power had made itself known, it had never shown any signs of being more than a very limited tele-K. I simply wasn't Super-hero material.

RETUЯN

Alan's loud voice dominated the discussion in the hall. He made the rounds, introducing himself, asking everyone about their powers and how high they expected to rate on the AV scale. Amyati loftily asserted that she would rate extremely high. She expected to use certification of her potential to gain access to a university of her choice on a Super-scholarship. I hadn't even known there was such a thing. Could people really leverage the promise of their powers that way? It made me wonder what part of the world she was from. Around here, universities and colleges had typically been converted to ad-hoc parliament buildings, corporate headquarters, or fortified bases. Places of learning—such as Project Arete appeared to be—weren't in high demand. The City around here was too unstable for that, divided into a patchwork of competing agendas.

I suddenly realized I was assuming I'd woken up in the same part of the City I'd passed out in, but I hadn't actually gone to the surface to make sure. Other than Mr. Gold's comment about the unfortunate business at the docks, which implied he had a familiarity with the area where I was attacked, there was little else to indicate I was in the same part of the City. The unexpected sense of dislocation was so alarming, I pulled out my Map and double-checked on the spot. Yes, I was in familiar territory. Well, a good distance beneath it anyway. The relief I felt was intense.

Dismissed by Amyati, Alan had moved on to chat up Sarah and was explaining to the shy brunette that he and Jake had Super-strength and Super-speed, but they weren't sure which of them was faster or stronger. From the sounds of things, the two of them had been squabbling in a good-natured way their whole lives, trying to prove which one of them was more powerful. The AV test was sure to sort it out once and for all.

For her part, Sarah just blushed furiously while the competitive duo talked over each other, clutching her Map to her chest like a tiny shield. She seemed paralyzed by their attention. It was like watching a pair of Kongs chat up a Chamonkleon. They towered over her, both of them imposingly bulky. Sarah, while only slightly below average height and weight, appeared thin and frail next to the twins. If she could have blended into the walls, she probably would have.

Kevin was using rapid sign language to explain something to his sister, Susie, pausing occasionally to brush his straight black hair back from his forehead. She absorbed whatever he was telling her in silence, eyes wide and attentive. I glimpsed enough of the signs to gather it had something to do with the upcoming test.

I found it interesting that Susie was deaf. Like Sarah's mechanical eyes, it was an oddity. Nano-machines could have repaired anything but a serious neurological disorder, so there couldn't actually be anything wrong with her ears. Something just wasn't connecting in her brain. Unlike Kevin, who was medium height and sturdily built, she was quite small, very pale. Maybe a birth-glitch? Mech-wombs were almost perfectly reliable, but she might have been the one in a million.

I leaned against the wall, watching Sarah try to hide in plain sight, wondering how to approach her. Now that I had the opportunity, I felt almost as shy as she was. With the big, boisterous twins taking up so much space around her, I felt unusually intimidated. It wasn't a feeling I was used to. My parents had often told me I had more confidence than good sense, but just then I wasn't sure how to proceed toward my goal. I only knew I had to find some way to have a quiet conversation with Sarah. It was important that I meet her, to thank her, at least.

I was nerving myself up to join the one-sided conversation, if only to save her from Alan's blustering attention, when my Map chimed softly.

"*Ask Mr. Gold if two people have ever been tested for AV simultaneously,*" said the display.

"*Who is this?*" I shot back. There was no name on the display.

"Later. Ask. Please!"

None of the others seemed to be looking my way or using their Maps for anything obvious. Then again, with percipient plastic, it would be easy to touch a Map while it was hidden in a pocket. A quick thought command, and a message would wing its way to me. Assuming the Map offered a way to mask identity, it could have been any of them.

Mr. Gold stepped back into the hall from a cross corridor to lead us to our next destination. I opened my mouth to ask him a question. And stopped. I couldn't recall what I had been about to ask. My Map vibrated. Distracted, I looked down at it.

The screen said, *"AV of two people at the same time ASK, ASK, ASK!"*

"Uh, Mr. Gold?"

He turned to look at me, walking backward down the hall as our motley group fell into step with him. "Hm?"

"Uh, this machine, this . . . this quantum computer. Have you ever used it to . . . ?" I trailed off, losing my train of thought. At another tingle in my fingers, I glanced down at the Map.

"Two at once!"

I hurriedly blurted out the question. "Have you ever tested two people at the same time before? For their Abeyant Vector, I mean." No sooner had I said it, I wondered why I'd even asked. What on Earth was going on?

"Interesting question, David." Mr. Gold considered for a moment as he pivoted to face front.

We were heading to an atrium on the third floor, where we'd be introduced to the Quantum Crew, the team responsible for the quantum computer. Along with Mr. Gold and several others, they were part of the larger Super-Power Research Group, just one of the many pies Project Arete had its fingers in. Aside from maintenance and upgrades of the quantum computer, the Quantum Crew's job was determining Abeyant Vectors, as well as mapping the various Super-powers and their connections.

Mapping. Map, map, map. My brain spun uselessly around the idea. Why did it make me feel like I was forgetting something?

"I can't recall that we've ever tried that particular experiment before," Mr. Gold was saying. "We have, of course, tested almost everyone on the faculty, most of the contractors and employees, and a great many students. I suppose it could be done, but I wonder if it would provide any useful information. If you received a proper reading, which might not happen, the results might be a combination or even multiplication of the AV of the people in the chamber. It would be impossible to tell how much of the total AV belonged to who." He paused, considering. "But you never know. Could be worth pursuing! I'll mention it to the Quantum Crew."

He looked over his shoulder to smile his jowly smile at me, but I wasn't looking. Wasn't even listening. I didn't realize he was responding to a question I had asked. I was trying to figure out why my Map was saying, "*Thank you.*"

The Quantum Crew, as they were called, turned out to be three of the most stereotypical lab geeks I'd ever seen. All men over forty, in white lab coats, carrying official-looking clipboards, pockets bristling with pens and other tools of uncertain function. All three of them had multi-phase scanners dangling around their necks, basically removable versions of Sarah's mechanical eyes. The trio also sported similar medium-length gray hair, in various states of dishevelment. About the only way to tell them apart was the name tags they wore, which read Ralph, Moses, and Gavin. I half suspected the name tags were for their benefit as much as ours. Ralph wore brown slip-on loafers, while Moses and Gavin wore comfortable-looking white sneakers. Moses was sporting laces with a skull and crossbones motif. Gavin's laces were frayed and coming undone. I risked applying my power long enough to fix them up while introductions were made, and then Ralph invited us to follow along to the lab.

A spacious freight elevator delivered us to the precincts of the quantum computer and the surrounding laboratories. It wasn't the usual way in, apparently, but it was the most conveniently located. Large pieces of machinery were frequently going in and out of the labs here; as we descended, workers in dark-blue coveralls rode down with us, pushing trolleys laden with heavy crates.

Inside the Quantum Lab, a brightly lit white tiled hallway took us toward the main computer control room. Peeking into doorways on either side of the hall as we passed, I caught tantalizing glimpses of cutting-edge science and tech research in progress. Most of the rooms were dark, with projects in progress left lying on tables and work benches. There was surprisingly little security in evidence.

The primary control room for the quantum computer was walled with glass on three sides and looked out over a large open bay. While Moses and Ralph fired up the control consoles, Gavin entered the bay through a sliding panel in the glass wall to our left and threw several heavy levers. They echoed loudly in the open space, and one by one, banks of bright white overhead lights came on with a hum, illuminating the quantum computer bay.

It was much larger than I would have guessed, easily big enough to park a hover-bus or three. In the center, a raised circular platform supported a cube that was maybe three meters to a side. The cube was glossy black, and as Moses and Ralph flipped switches and turned dials in the control room, lines of soft blue light began to etch across its surface. The glowing lines turned frequently at ninety-degree angles, slowly twining around the cube on all sides until it was covered in branching geometric paths of light. A single thick bar of yellow light split the cube horizontally around the middle, perfectly dividing the top from the bottom.

Thick cables, like armored black shoelaces meant for a giant, protruded from the base of the cube platform. They coiled across the floor, climbed the walls, and disappeared into crevices and pipes. Thinner wires in blue, purple, and orange hung from the ceiling and connected to the top of the cube, where a long hydraulic arm suddenly hissed and began to raise the upper half. The lower section slid down into the platform, folding out of sight. White fog rolled from the gaps in the floor as it did so, spilling off the platform and creeping across the bay. All of us were impressed and a little intimidated. We stood silently, staring, as the machine came to life.

Gavin came back into the control room. "Gets 'em every time," he chuckled. He fist-bumped Moses.

"Told ya it would be worth installing special effects," said Moses with an impish grin.

Ralph rolled his eyes at his compatriots. "I got the panel," he said. "Wrangle the kids into the box."

Mr. Gold turned to the group, now clustered together nervously. He smiled disarmingly. "Don't worry about the machine's ominous aspect. I would have warned you about the theatrics, but the Quantum Crew enjoy the big reveal too much for me to spoil their fun," he explained.

He gestured toward the bay. "What you're looking at is the device that tests your Abeyant Vector. Other than a couple hundred million teeny-tiny quantum flux sensors that stud the interior of the box, there are no other detection devices of any kind. No audio, no video, no radiation-measuring devices—nothing. When you stand on the platform and the box is sealed around you, you become an unknown factor. Potentially, you could be in just about any state. Until we look at you with our own eyes, we will have no way of knowing if you are standing, sitting, running in circles, or doing jumping jacks. The only thing those little flux sensors do is detect quantum flux— that is to say, *possibilities*.

"How to explain when I don't quite understand it myself? Think of it like this: any possible action you could take is another path, like a fork in the road. Those roads lead into other quantum states, or realities, if you prefer. So, in this reality, maybe you pick your nose." Mr. Gold smiled around at the chuckles this comment elicited.

"Meanwhile," he continued, "in another reality, you might have chosen to *scratch* your nose instead. In a similar fashion, while you're in that box, you could be tap dancing, belting out a power ballad at the top of your lungs, taking a nap, or doing almost any other thing, including activating your Super-powers. Because nobody out here will know, to us, you'll be in a state of quantum flux. That is to say, you'll have the *potential* to be doing *any* of those things, as far as those of us on the outside are concerned. You'll know what you're up to in there, but we won't.

"More importantly, the computer won't know either. The only way it can observe what's in the box is through those flux sensors. So, while you're in this state of quantum uncertainty, the computer will get a feel for your potential by measuring *all* of your possible states. Those little flux sensors see the possibilities, all the different things you could be doing, and count them.

"In other words, if any action you might conceivably take *actually happens,* and each occurs in its own concrete reality, and if all of those possible realities happen *at the same time,* then you are theoretically doing everything possible all at once. Only one of those things manifests here, in this reality, but the rest are going on, out there, in parallel dimensions." He gestured vaguely around, then paused to let this sink in. "Still with me?" he asked.

Jake and Alan were looking a little lost. Sarah and Amyati had clearly followed every word avidly, possibly leaping to their own conclusions. They both seemed whip smart. It was impossible to get a read on Kevin and Susie; their faces were currently devoid of any expression. It was evident that they were listening, though. Well,

Kevin was. His hands were moving rapidly in sign-language, relaying everything Mr. Gold had said to his sister. She watched her brother's hands intently.

"To sum up," said Mr. Gold, "in some of these potential realities, you would have activated your powers. The computer watches these near-infinite realities and counts how many likely involved Super-powers. Then it gives us a number. This number is a percentage, an estimate of how many possible realities involved your Super-powers activating.

"It is essentially impossible to score one hundred, for a couple reasons. First, one hundred would mean your powers would be in a constant state of expression, active in every conceivable reality, impossible for you to turn off. That's not a sustainable situation, so it never really happens. Second, there simply aren't enough quantum flux sensors to monitor every single possibility.

"Yes, that means some of those possible realities will escape our notice. The sensors are small, but there just isn't enough space for an infinite number of them in the box. We got pretty darn close, though, and the more you have, the smaller your margin of error. We've reached a point where the margin is vanishingly small: typically, less than one tenth of one percent, assuming our math is correct."

"Part of this is due to a simple fact: cause leads to effect. As a result, our potential options at any given moment are constrained but what just came before. A simple example of what I mean is jumping as high as you can. While you're in the air, you simply can't jump again. Physics doesn't allow it. The potential realities that branch from that moment are limited by what is already happening. Until you land, jumping higher, among other things, isn't a path that will branch from your current reality."

"But what if we can fly?" asked Jake. Everyone snickered, but I got the feeling he really wanted to know. If he jumped, and that meant he couldn't jump again because his feet were already in the air, flying would obviously open up the possibility of continuing upward. He had missed the point, but it was easy to miss.

I leaned over and said, "If you're flying, you're not swimming or climbing or running. See what I mean?"

Jake furrowed his brow, nodding slowly.

"You can rely on the results," Mr. Gold asserted. "In fact, I daresay that if you fail to achieve your full potential, it isn't because the computer was wrong about how far you can go. It's because it doesn't measure your grit and determination. Keep that in mind when you get your rating! This number is a target to shoot for, not a guarantee of your future abilities. You're still going to have to put in the work!"

The group was getting restless after Mr. Gold's extended explanation. Jake and Alan were interrogating Sarah in low voices, asking for further clarification. She was rescued from her stuttering (and possibly hopeless) attempt to dumb it down for them by Amyati, who whispered rather fiercely, "Stand in the box; get measured. Who cares how it works? The point is that it *does*." The twins seemed satisfied by this and subsided.

Mr. Gold cleared his throat and held up a hand until we fell still. "My apologies if my explanation was either too technical or not technical enough. I'm not a quantum physicist, I'm afraid. These three fellows"—he waved a hand at Ralph, Gavin, and Moses—"might be computer geniuses and eminently qualified to make this fancy contraption go, but they probably can't explain it fully either. A lot of the technical details are handled by consultants of various disciplines.

"If you have some free time later, ask your Map about Schrödinger and his cat. A very old story, now, but perhaps it will illuminate. Or lead you further down the rabbit hole." He chuckled at himself, then realized we hadn't followed his train of thought. "A reference to another very old story. In any case"—and here he smiled brightly at Amyati—"stand in the box; get measured! Who's game?"

Nobody volunteered. There was a nervous giggle from Sarah as the twins gave each other a shove and started scuffling, trying to push each other to the front. Kevin and Susie remained impassive, watching the rest of us. Waiting to see what would happen to the first to go in the box, just like me. Annoyed by the twins and their antics, or perhaps by our sudden collective uncertainty, Amyati took a deep breath and stepped forward. I had to give the girl credit. She had guts.

Moses and Gavin escorted her down the ramp into the bay. A few moments later, Amyati had been positioned beneath the upper half of the cube. Ralph, in the control room at a computer panel positioned by one of the windows that overlooked the bay, adopted his best flight attendant voice. "Welcome to flight Quantum One. My name is Ralph, and I'll be your host this morning. Please ensure your seat tray is in an upright and locked position and your arms and legs remain inside the vehicle at all times."

As the cube folded up around her, Amyati stuck out her tongue. Ralph's eyes twinkled. He turned and gave an odd two-fingers-down salute to Gavin and Moses on the bay floor.

The cube sealed with a whirr of hydraulics. Blue lights raced across the cube's surface, a quick flicker that followed the strange geometric channels twining from one face to another, and that was it. One rapid strobe of light, a heartbeat of silence, and the roof of the cube was rising, the lower walls folding down into the floor. In all, it took maybe two or three seconds. Even with the hissing of the fog machine, it was anti-climactic.

Amyati strode forth, looking triumphant. As she entered the control room, everyone clustered around her, peppering her with questions.

"How was it?"

"Did it hurt?"

"Was it weird?"

Amyati shushed us. "It was like floating in a bubble of night sky. All those sensors light up like stars. Very pretty, but there isn't much to it." This last seemed to be directed at Sarah, by way of reassurance.

Her poetic description opened the door for the others to paint a picture of the experience with their words. The twins each took a turn in the box, then bounded exuberantly back into the control room, each competing to tell the wildest tale of what the experience had been like.

"It was like being stretched in all directions at once!" cried Alan, eyes wide.

"No, it was more like being smashed into tiny pieces," argued Jake, "and each piece is another version of you!"

So, they *had* understood some of Mr. Gold's explanation. Maybe they weren't as dense as they acted.

Then it was Sarah's turn. The box closed around her with a hydraulic *shush*, then a rapid play of lights. A few seconds passed, but the box remained closed. The three quantum technicians conferred unhurriedly in low whispers, flicked switches, turned dials, and referred to readouts. Mr. Gold looked on, unconcerned. He caught my worried look and gave me a thumbs up. When the cube finally opened, the sudden noise was unexpectedly loud in the uncertain silence. I jumped. Sarah emerged, pale and shaking.

"I . . . I d-don't . . . fffeel vuh-vuh . . ." She couldn't finish the thought. Her voice was barely a squeak.

Mr. Gold halted proceedings. He and the trio of computer technicians sat her down and checked her over to be sure she was okay. The rest of us stood around, a cluster of suddenly uncertain teenagers, while the adults briskly and efficiently assessed Sarah's condition. Eventually, they managed to coax out of her that she'd had a panic attack.

"Claustrophobia," said Gavin. The geeks nodded back and forth.

"We've seen it before, running other groups through the cube," Ralph elaborated. "Could happen to anybody, really. Rarely ever does, though."

"Bird poop," said Gavin matter-of-factly.

"What?" Alan, Kevin, and I asked simultaneously.

Ralph rolled his eyes. "Old Chinese superstition. Getting pooped on by a bird is considered good luck because it rarely happens. Used to be, when it did, people would immediately go and gamble." He smiled kindly at Sarah. "Lucky you, eh?"

"Just chalk it up to nerves," advised Moses, and he gave her shoulder a friendly squeeze.

Sarah's anxiety was already passing. The silly banter of the techs seemed to have helped. "I j-just need a muh . . . a moment."

Moses nodded and spoke quietly to Mr. Gold.

"Okay, folks!" said Mr. Gold, clapping his hands to get our attention as he turned to us. He gestured at the trio of techs, who were already busily fiddling with their computer. "These fine gentlemen are going to run through a quick safety checklist, just to be sure there are no serious anomalies. These things don't happen often, but when they do, we have another opportunity to determine the cause. Could be a setting is slightly off, and Sarah is sensitive to the spooky action of quantum particles. In the meantime, who wants a little tour?"

I moved to join the group as Mr. Gold led them out of the room. Glancing over my shoulder, I saw Sarah had remained where she was, hunched on a bench against the wall. Her arms were crossed over her stomach, and she was looking at the floor between her feet. I hesitated, glancing over at Ralph. He was absorbed in the readouts flickering rapidly across his screen. Down below in the bay, Gavin and Moses had crawled beneath the cube platform, muffled voices calling back and forth.

"Moe, the Chamonkleon's out of his cage."

"On it, Vinny. Pass me that banana, will ya? Just gotta coax the little scamp back into place." I saw a hand emerge and grope among their scattered tools. The "banana" was an oddly curved yellow wrench that would likely allow Moses to reach into the guts of the machine to make adjustments without having to remove pieces in the way.

"Is the Spikeface overheated again?" Referring to a bulky radiator, if I didn't miss my guess.

"No, sir. Plenty of water. Fed him yesterday afternoon."

And so on. I felt like I was in some sort of menagerie listening to a couple of zookeepers. It would have been amusing if it weren't for the fact that they were very seriously checking over an extremely complicated piece of technology to be sure Sarah hadn't been zapped with some kind of weird quantum energy.

"Excuse me."

I stepped out of the doorway to allow Ralph to exit. He descended to the bay, on his way to inspect the cube itself. In the far corner, Mr. Gold was gesturing at bundles of conduits in his animated way, explaining to the rest of the group some aspect of the machine's design.

I stood in the doorway, watching. I was very aware of Sarah, sitting nearby. Was it me, or were we both trying very hard not to look at each other? I took a deep breath. I wasn't going to get a better chance than this. I resisted the urge to go and sit next to her. Kevin had said she was painfully shy, and I'd seen some evidence of that. I didn't want to spook her.

"Sarah, I . . ." Why was this so difficult? I swallowed. "My name is David," I finished lamely.

"Hh . . . hi, duh . . . D-david." It was barely a whisper. A quick glance showed her staring a hole in the floor. Her face was bright red.

"I just wanted to say thanks. For the other day." No need to tell her what I meant. "Kevin said it was you who bailed me out."

No response. I watched as Ralph inspected the cube itself, inside and out, using his scanners. He frequently reached up to adjust dials on the vision-enhancing goggles, switching scanning modes and zooming in or out. He meticulously replaced two tiny sensors, then announced a clean bill of health. Nobody was paying any attention to him. He huffed and put his hands on his hips, then saw me watching. I gave him a thumbs up, and he grinned.

"You're welcome." It was barely audible, but she'd nerved herself up to say it and had managed it without stuttering. I smiled but didn't turn around. The others were on their way back to the control booth. I was almost out of time.

I blurted it out. "Sarah, since that day on the pier, it's like . . ."

I couldn't find the words. My heart was pounding, and my armpits were sweaty. My hands felt clammy. The others had started up the ramp. I started babbling, all in a rush. "It's like I know you, like I was supposed to meet you. I know it sounds crazy, but I feel like we're connected, somehow." There, I'd said it. I could feel her, holding her breath behind me.

"Yuh . . . you knew . . . knew muh . . . my n-name," she whispered.

I finally turned to face her. She was bright pink, but she wasn't looking at me. She was looking inward, recalling the moment we'd met. I could *feel* it. And she could, too. A beatific smile spread across her face. For a moment, she was transformed: radiant, angelic.

It lasted less than a second. She shook herself and came back to the present. For a moment, our eyes locked. Then she looked away, embarrassed. The movement of her eyes left glowing afterimages streaked across my vision. I decided to risk it and walked over to sit next to her. She turned slightly away and froze but didn't leap up and run. I lowered my voice and strove for sincerity. I dared to hope she might feel it through the strange bond we shared. "I owe you my life,

Sarah. You will *always* be safe with me. I promise." I reached over and squeezed her hand.

This surprised her, enough to make her glance up at me, but the tentative brush of her gaze was gone as quickly as it arrived. Footsteps and raised voices announced the others' return. Sarah snatched her hand away, twisting her fingers in her lap. Jake and Alan had wedged themselves in the door, both trying to pass through it at the same time. I laughed out loud as I stood up. What a couple of clowns! They burst through, scuffling, playing it up.

Amyati entered next, rolling her eyes. "Always a circus with you two," she said, her words echoing my thoughts.

I moved over to the window as she seated herself on the bench next to Sarah. It would have been impossible for her to miss the rosy color of Sarah's face. I could almost feel Amyati's piercing gaze drilling into my back. I ignored it. Down in the bay, Gavin and Moses were making their final adjustments to the Quantum Cube as Ralph loped up the ramp toward the control room.

"Ready for the final tests," he announced. He resumed his position at the computer.

Below, Kevin had mounted the platform. The cube unfolded, and fog rolled past his feet. Watching it, I began to feel strangely uneasy. Kevin stepped into the box, and it sealed around him. A whirl of blue light, and he was done. As he emerged, he flashed a hand sign to Susie, and she took his place in the box.

My feeling of uneasiness intensified. I looked around the room, but Jake and Alan were bantering with Amyati. Ralph was flicking switches and turning dials, grazing smart-glass screens with his fingertips, intent on his job.

The cube was sealed. One second, two seconds. The now familiar hiss of fog heralded the box's unfolding. Waiting on the platform, Kevin offered his sister a hand in stepping down from the box. She saw me watching and waved up at me with her beaming smile. After a moment, Moses collected them and ushered them toward the control booth.

That left only me. Nobody else had disintegrated in the cube. Despite Sarah's momentary upset, she seemed to be drawing strength from Amyati's fierce presence. No lasting harm had been done. The incident likely had more to do with Sarah's own anxieties than any fault of the quantum device; the Abeyant Vector assessment process itself seemed harmless enough, and the diagnostic had confirmed as much. So, why wasn't I reassured? Despite all my reasoning, I still felt a persistent little thread of doubt. I couldn't seem to pluck it free. Getting into that cube, I felt sure, would trigger a chain of events that could easily spiral out of my control. I had no idea where my certainty was coming from. Then again, I'd felt certain about talking to Sarah, and look where that had gone. She'd said, what, maybe eight words to me?

I looked down at my laces. *You have loose ends,* they seemed to say. I sighed. I *always* had loose ends. But my laces were right, of course. I couldn't just walk away, leave without knowing. Some part of me would always wonder.

"No loose ends," I muttered. But even that phrase was making me hesitate. *No loose ends.* Why did that make me feel like I was forgetting something?

Irritated, I gave my head an angry shake. *You're being irrational!* I berated myself. *Quit stalling and get in the bloody box!* Slowly, I entered the hangar and mounted the platform. Fog swirled past my legs. I stood there, watching it roil. I felt like I was looking at the fog of my own feelings, whirling in little eddies in all directions. I glanced back up at the booth. Kevin gave me a thumbs up. Alan pulled a face, and Jake slugged him. Susie waved happily. It was all a great big adventure for her, apparently. Amyati simply stared. But it was Sarah's eyes I was looking for. Two little points of neon green light, watching me steadily from the back of the group.

RETUЯN

Resolutely, I shoved down my misgivings. Sarah had done it; so could I. Turning my back on the control booth, I stepped into the Quantum Cube. With a hiss, the machine sealed around me.

VI

Someone was in the box with me.

I caught a glimpse of clear gray eyes just as everything went black. The moment I did, I knew exactly who it was. It all came back in a rush: the kid I'd seen earlier that morning, during Mr. Gold's talk, who had been doodling on a data-pad when I first spotted him; the same one who hadn't been there for most of the information session, then had appeared like magic without anybody noticing a thing, only to vanish, taking all memory of his fleeting presence with him—that strange sense of connection ringing in my ears. The moment I saw his eyes in the box, I felt it again—*snap!*—a humming wire pulled taut between us.

I had forgotten him almost instantly, the first time I'd seen him. Then, out in the hallway after class, I almost recalled him. But even as he pinged my Map and hassled me to ask Mr. Gold about testing two people in the quantum computer simultaneously, I'd only barely managed to keep the thought in my head long enough to ask. Not even that long: it had taken me three tries to get the question out! I'd forgotten so quickly that I hadn't even listened to Mr. Gold's reply. Now here he was again, a finger over his lips, invoking silence even as the cube sealed shut around us.

Darkness. And in that darkness, as if standing between mirrors, was me, over and over again, stretching away into infinity in all directions, vanishing into the limitless distance. An ocean of me. Were these . . . other dimensions? Parallel worlds, like Mr. Gold had mentioned?

"Hello?"

My voice echoed in emptiness. I cocked my head, thinking I'd heard a response, or the echo of one. But I'd forgotten it before the echoes died away. I was alone. I raised my hand, watched as the action was repeated down the lines of myself in an infinite series. The nearer versions of me made almost precisely the same gesture. The further down the line I looked, the more divergent the action. Beyond the extreme limit of my sight, where shadowy Davids lifted both hands—or none, instead of one—there were probably Davids making completely different motions, walking, running, sitting . . . Activating powers? Of course. Some of them must be. Possibly even powers I wasn't aware I possessed. It was almost exactly as Mr. Gold had described. Was that because this was how it actually was? Or was this simply what I was expecting?

A movement caught my attention. Out in the crowd of myself, I noticed someone else. I furrowed my brow. He looked . . . awfully familiar.

Looking around, I saw him repeated, over and over again, scattered randomly throughout the infinite repetitions of me. He wasn't everywhere, like I was, but he was there often enough that I was surprised I hadn't noticed him before that moment. There were a thousand—a million—versions of him. I spun in a circle, dizzied by the scale of the vision. All around me, I watched him laugh, talk, and roughhouse with other versions of me. I watched him scream in frustration and anger, point accusatory fingers, swing his fists; I watched him begging me to look at him, to please just look. To *see* him.

Sudden knowledge hit me like a grav-train. I staggered, head splitting. I clutched at my skull, feeling as if my mind were leaking out between my fingers. A multitude of memories throbbed behind my eyes. Cory, I remembered. Cory Sullivan. I'd known him forever. We'd met on the streets, looked out for each other. He'd been so young, and his abilities had been useful for getting us out of trouble. He made people forget!

I struggled back to my feet. His power had affected me, I realized. I'd forgotten that I knew him. But as I watched him interacting with me, it dawned on me that that wasn't exactly true. Yes, I knew him elsewhere. Out there, in other realities. Some of those memories were flowing through me now, pushing back the fog of forgetfulness. But I'd never known him *here*, had I? Not in this world. I'd never actually met him before today. That electric moment in Mr. Gold's classroom, when I'd first noticed him, that had been the first time, and then he'd immediately fogged my memory.

What had changed? Something was allowing me to fight through it, to shrug it off. What was different about me now that helped me remember? The answer flashed through my mind: *a physical shock as our eyes met, like wires snapping taut between us, humming like a strummed power chord.* That moment in the classroom, so like the moment with Sarah at the pier. I hadn't chosen to connect to either of them, it had simply happened.

Slowly, it dawned on me. He was just like me: he couldn't control his power. It wasn't always on, exactly, but it reached out, instinctively, and did whatever it wanted. But in his case, that meant messing with people's memories. It made him utterly, completely forgettable. He might as well be invisible.

I turned my attention inward. I didn't know what I was looking for, but some instinct was guiding me. There was a sound that wasn't really a sound—a hum I could orient on, like turning my head to hear a voice. There was a string, running from me to him, and it vibrated. It was almost as if he were shaking it furiously from the other end, trying to get my attention, except . . . it was *my* string. It was *my* power that connected us. I was feeling his frustration, his panic, his desperation. I don't think he was aware of what he was projecting.

Cautiously—like flexing an inexplicable third arm—I reached out and gave the cord a tug. He was suddenly standing right next to me. His clear gray eyes were brimming with a frantic loneliness, searching for some sign of recognition. Had he been right here the entire time? How many times had I forgotten only to remember and forget again?

The whole situation piled up on me, and I sank to my knees, astounded. He had done the impossible: he had made someone remember. Here, where he was always forgotten, somebody now remembered. *Me.* By getting into the Quantum Cube with me, he had forced into being the one version of reality in which he was no longer alone. I suspected I had seen too many iterations of him to completely forget him now. I might lose track of many, if not most, versions of him, but I could no longer forget him entirely. Some part of me would always remember some part of him. It was enough, but only because of who *I* was.

I didn't fully grasp it then, but on some intuitive level, I was beginning to understand. Meeting Sarah had begun some kind of awakening of my abilities. Meeting Cory was a direct result of that. Or maybe it had been the fight at the docks, getting knocked around. Maybe in my fear and frantic attempts to escape I'd accessed some deeper level. Hadn't Mercedes Ruiz said something about eye-witnesses claiming I'd activated a bunch of different powers? Could that be connected, too?

It was too much to process, and it was happening too fast. I tried to concentrate on what I could be sure of. Seeing all those versions of myself had opened a floodgate. Some of me were further along in their self-discovery than I was, perhaps. It was enough to give me a glimpse of the truth: my power wasn't just about tying shoelaces together; it was about . . . making *connections*. And Cory had just taken advantage of that. What I couldn't understand was how he had known to choose me. How had he known to interfere with *my* AV test? Was it just a lucky guess, based on the fact that I had seen him in Mr. Gold's classroom when nobody else had remembered him long enough to pay any attention? And now that we were connected, would our connection—how had Mr. Gold put it?—*constrain* our future choices? Looking out into the infinite vastness all around me, I knew without doubt that in some of those realities, I would discover the answer, and I might not like what I found. Would this reality be one of them?

This was the beginning, I realized. This was the premonition I had felt. The thing I had dreaded. This was why I hadn't wanted to get into the box. This was what started the chain of events that I might not be able to control. I put my head in my hands and shuddered as chills ran over me. All I could think was: *What have we done?*

I don't know how long I crouched there. The test only lasted a few seconds, objectively. Inside the box, though, with reality unfolding in every direction, time didn't seem to have much meaning. At some point, I felt a tentative hand on my shoulder. Cory was still there, waiting for some sign I recalled who he was. This probably wasn't the reaction he'd been hoping for. He must have been wondering if he'd been forgotten again.

I unfolded and stood. Had I forgotten? Already? I couldn't be sure. Maybe. But only for a moment. And I would try not to forget again. I turned to him and opened my arms. There simply weren't any words. Cory threw himself into my embrace and sobbed with relief.

They told me afterward that my test had taken a few extra seconds, just like Sarah's. Outwardly, it appeared no different than any of the others, save for the duration. In Sarah's case, the somewhat delayed opening of the box was due to her potential. Her Abeyant Vector turned out to be quite astounding, and the computer, when it gets readings over seventy-five, is programmed to double-check. No surprise she caused a delay.

In my case, the computer had no idea what to make of me. Of *us*. The readings went crazy, and the Quantum geeks were in a spin. They'd never seen anything like it. When the Quantum Cube opened, I found all three of them waiting for me eagerly, along with Mr. Gold. The rest of the group looked down from the control booth, wondering what was going on.

I was still holding Cory tightly. His slight body shook with the force of his tears. I knew I couldn't let him go until he was done, so I just stood there with my arms around him. *Don't mind us,* I thought. *Just having a bit of a moment.* But I kept my mouth shut.

Mr. Gold looked at me quizzically. "David, is everything all right?" He stepped back, startled. "Who is . . . ?!"

His voice galvanized Cory, who jumped back as if he'd been burned. As I let him go, I felt the wave of forgetfulness roll past me. I staggered, suddenly dizzy. Mr. Gold blinked and cleared his throat. "How was it? Not so bad, am I right?" He smiled warmly. Cory was standing right there, and Mr. Gold simply ignored him. The trio of quantum techs were already returning to the control booth, discussing the latest set of tests.

"Uh, Cory?" I whispered. "What did you just do?"

Cory dragged his sleeve across his eyes. "I can't help it," he said. "You know I can't. He's fuzzed. They're all fuzzed."

Mr. Gold gently took hold of my arm, still paying no attention to Cory. "You okay, David? You seem a bit out of sorts." *Me?* I almost laughed at the absurdity of it. He coaxed me out of the box, guiding me back up the ramp to the control room. I cast a panicked glance over my shoulder at Cory. "How long will I remember you for?" I called.

He hiccupped and swiped angrily at his nose. The cube hissed and began to close. He yelped and dodged between the lower panels as they rose from the floor. "I-I don't know. I don't know!" He hurried to catch up, grabbing at my sleeve. "You have to remember me, you have to!"

"I will!" I promised him, not at all sure if it was true. "Stay close!"

Mr. Gold was frowning, clearly perplexed, but he seemed to have already forgotten that I was talking to someone who wasn't, apparently, there.

The group exchanged puzzled looks as I entered the room. I offered them a guilty shrug and said, "Heh . . . twice in one set of tests, what are the odds?"

As I'd hoped, this got Gavin, Moses, and Ralph babbling about the claustrophobia effect. They started going over readouts, calling up diagnostics of Sarah's run to compare to mine. I didn't have the heart to tell them the box was *way* bigger inside than out. Infinitely bigger. Claustrophobia wasn't what I was feeling. It was more like agoraphobia. But even that couldn't begin to describe it. My whole world had just been tipped on its ear. Nothing worked like I thought it did. Not my power. Not reality. Not anything.

I looked around and found Cory; made sure he saw me see him. He bit his trembling lip and tried hard not to burst into tears. I still knew he was there. It was working. It was going to work! It had to. I couldn't let this kid be completely forgotten again. I couldn't imagine what it must have been like for him. How could I turn away from him now? If I was the only one he had, then I had to be there for him, whatever it took.

"Well," said Mr. Gold, some of his customary energy returning. He scratched his head, then raised his open palms. "Who wants to see the results?"

There was a chorus of agreement.

"Great. Let's break for lunch, then reconvene in, say, one hour?"

I followed the rest of the group to the cargo elevator. Cory remained glued to my side, but he was quiet and watchful. I think he realized the two of us talking openly would only serve to make me look crazy. I had the impression anyone taking note of his presence would cause his power to fire, and the less that happened, the better. I had no idea what the long-term effects on people's minds might be. As it was, he was more or less constantly fogging their brains just by being in the midst of the group. There was a Cory-sized hole in everyone's memory but mine. I watched, fascinated, as they talked over and around him. Frequently, they stumbled to a halt mid-sentence, or forgot what they were doing when a glimpse of Cory caused a brief stutter in their train of thought. Every time, they simply looked around, realized where they were and what they were doing, and picked up where they'd left off as if nothing had happened. Cory might not be in control of his abilities, but he was powerful—there was no doubt about that.

The cargo elevator reached the atrium, and we spilled out amidst the exotic synthetic plants. A light misty rain was falling to either side of the railed walkway, and colorful customized birds flitted past, trilling and screeching. I watched a rotund little black-and-gray critter with a mobile nose go snuffling through the soil beneath the leaves and, once again, found myself wondering what I'd stumbled into. The Project Arete facility was incredible. I couldn't believe it had been buried beneath the City all this time and I'd never known about it.

The group dispersed to find a quick bite to eat. Kevin and Susie went with the twins, searching for sushi. Sarah paused beside me for a moment, as if she was about to say something. Her fingers worried the hem of her shirt, and she tapped the toe of her right shoe on the ground behind her. Her face was flushed, but all she did was open and close her mouth a few times. I could sense her anxiety through our link and knew without having to be told that she'd felt some of what had happened in the cube. Just how much had she sensed, though? She was ignoring Cory, just like everybody else, and it didn't seem like an act. She really didn't remember he was there. Before she could say anything, however, Amyati was there, tugging her along. The pair hurried off to find a meal, Sarah casting one last worried look over her shoulder before they vanished down an escalator.

I leaned against the rail and watched Mr. Gold disappear deeper into the facility. I took a moment to calm my breathing, trying to slow my racing heart. When he'd been gone for a few minutes, I turned to Cory.

"You hungry?"

He nodded eagerly. "Yeah." He was watching me avidly. I'd meant hungry for food, but I could see he was starved for human contact. His power pushed at me insistently, trying to shove him out of my thoughts. It was making my head ache, just paying attention to him.

I pinched the bridge of my nose. "I know a place. Let's go." We had to do something to reinforce our bond before I lost him again.

VII

I t took all my concentration to keep Cory in mind until we reached the same quiet café where I'd met Dawn, Francis, and Miguel. As before, most of the tables were empty. We took a seat on the lower level, near the fountain, where tall ferns and flower-laden hedges afforded a measure of privacy. I ordered enough for three, to the amusement of the server, who naturally assumed I was dining alone, and let Cory help himself to lasagna and scampi while I loaded my plate with a salad of crunchy PA-grown leaves mixed with colorful nutrient cubes. A mess of spaghetti and meatballs swimming in marinara sauce joined the salad.

I was barely two bites in when a wave of vertigo left me clutching the edge of the table. I felt like my eyes were crossing. I marshaled my thoughts and refocused on my new friend. "Talk to me, Cory. Help me remember."

The halting conversation that ensued doubled back on itself numerous times. The effect he had on memory was unusual, to say the least, and more than a little frustrating. Fortunately, Cory seemed to have developed a sort of long-suffering patience. He'd been repeating himself to people, to no avail, since he was about five or six years old. At least with me, there was a reasonable chance of recalling what had been said. For now, anyway.

More importantly, I found I could usually recall Cory himself: who he was and what he did to my mind. This helped, insofar as it reminded me of why I had to struggle to focus on him. Every time I did, different details would come to the fore. I was constantly having to connect the dots, fill in the gaps. It made me feel like I was forever behind the eight ball, but in hindsight, I'm certain hanging out with Cory trained my Super-powers more than anything else I did during my time with Project Arete. If my powers are about making connections (and that did seem to be the vague theme of my Super-ability's "fuzzy logic" by that point), then I was getting non-stop practice whenever he was around. *Bonus.*

Cory's power was insistent, and only an extreme effort allowed me to fix my attention on him. It was like wading against a constant current. I'm filling in the gaps in my recollection from things I remembered or learned later, but our conversation began with discussing how he'd spent his time prior to meeting me. I gathered Cory had been in the habit of crashing at the Restoration Point Church across the street from the ground-level strip mall that masked Project Arete's activities. The church never locked its doors, and there was a well-stocked kitchen he could take advantage of when he was hungry. He had never felt right, stealing from a church, so he would steal from other places to replace whatever he pilfered, and he always cleaned up after himself. As far as he knew, nobody at the church was any the wiser about his presence. He could fall asleep amidst the hustle and bustle of the soup kitchen, and people would step over and around him without remembering they had avoided him. Occasionally, he would wake up to find some kind soul had noticed him long enough to drape a warm blanket over him, but even then, he was just another anonymous homeless kid to them.

People-watching is more than a hobby, for a kid like Cory—it's a lifeline. It was the closest he could get to connecting, most of the time. He would sit for hours on the front steps of the Restoration Point Church, daydreaming about the people who passed on the street, making up stories about their lives. While I was hanging out in libraries or coffee shops, begging for food at the back of restaurants or laying in a park shaded by synthetic maples and oaks, staring up at the grid of clouds and daydreaming about being a Super-hero,

Cory daydreamed of Normalcy, imagining the sort of life he could never have.

A couple walking by might become his mother and father, for a brief time. The laughing child, whose hands they held between them, could be a brother or sister. He could, if he chose, walk with them, hold their hands, and talk to them. But he only did that a few times. They forgot him so rapidly, it only ended up making him feel lonelier than before. No one ever talked to him directly. Everything he received from people, any warmth or contact that came his way, was always meant for someone else. So, he sat, or he wandered, and he watched and played pretend. He learned not to try making his fantasies a reality. The disappointing failures only crushed his hopes.

I was beginning to appreciate the nature of our connection: the rarity of it, yes, but also the importance of it. There was no one else for him. It was a massive responsibility, considering I'd never been responsible for anyone but myself, but it only reinforced my desire to be there for him. And perhaps my need to help him was a little selfish, too. After all, I'd been kicking around on the streets for a few years. I'd arrived at PA without any friends, and now, within days, I'd forged a connection to Cory—and possibly Sarah, too. The problem was, l didn't quite fathom how my connections to Cory and Sarah had been made. With Sarah, it had been pure instinct. If it was an aspect of my Super-power, I wasn't at all sure how I'd activated it or whether I'd be able to trigger it again. With Cory, somehow passing through the Quantum Cube with him had allowed me to maintain an awareness of other potential realities. There were Davids who hung out with Corys who remembered each other just fine. Maybe in other realities Cory had a better handle on his abilities. It was reasonable to assume most of the other Davids I'd seen would have gone through a similar experience in the Quantum Cube. Perhaps I was connected to them. Perhaps they were actually the ones remembering Cory here in this reality, not me. I don't know. It hurt my brain to think about it, and it hurt my heart even more. Before I met Cory, I used to think I knew what loneliness was. Now, I couldn't imagine anyone lonelier than him.

I had to ask, "Does anyone else remember you at all?"

Cory said, "The Cupids, I guess. But it's not the same."

Mind officially blown. *Cory* talked to *Cupids?* What? Where? When? How? I pelted him with questions.

"Woah, David, slow down!" Cory laughed. I think he was chuffed to have something he could string me along with. Maybe part of him was still worried I would forget him if he didn't keep me interested.

"Seriously, Cory, Cupids! That's incredible! Tell me!" Kevin had put me in mind of Cupids when he'd chucked the Map at me, but I hadn't seriously believed there were any aliens in the PA facility. I badgered Cory relentlessly until he agreed to tell me how he'd met a Cupid.

The strip mall above the Project Arete facility is called Sycamore Grove, following the ancient North American tradition of honoring what had been bulldozed to build it. Cory, watching from the Restoration Point Church, regularly saw freight being delivered to the stores there. He began to wonder where all the deliveries went; much more was being delivered than was ever purchased, he felt sure. Not a lot of people visited Sycamore Grove anymore.

Cory stole a smart-glass tablet and began taking notes. He counted delivery vehicles, made a record of company logos, and tallied how many were unmarked. He came to recognize a number of repeat delivery drivers, and they weren't always driving for the same company. He counted shoppers, estimated the volume of their purchases, and compared that with the stuff going in. The disparity was immense.

He began hanging around the mall itself. Soon, he noticed a lot of the people coming and going didn't shop at all. They might eat at the food court, then grab some clothes at a boutique shop and step into a change room, only to emerge hours or even days later. While they were gone, the clothes they had supposedly gone to the change room to try on found their way back to the store displays.

These people didn't always emerge from the same store they went into either. Cory could never be sure if he was missing someone coming or going, but he became reasonably confident that there were at least three different entrances into some kind of hidden base below the mall. He didn't know what all the secrecy was about, and he was a little afraid to find out—it was all very cloak and dagger— but there was one thing he was sure of: he wasn't going to be noticed walking in.

It took him a few days to nerve himself up to it. Before he did, he inspected a few of the deliveries at close range, ascertaining that it was mostly computer equipment, tools, educational materials, and a great deal of foodstuff. Occasionally, an Anymal or two. He freed a couple, tried to make pets of them, but they simply forgot him, too. In any case, nothing that seemed dangerous was being delivered by this route. He was relieved, but he maintained a healthy sense of caution as he followed his favorite mystery visitor to a hidden elevator and stepped inside with her.

She was a pleasant-faced, matronly type, the sort he imagined might be a good mother. He stood close to her as the elevator descended, leaning his head against her shoulder. Putting his arms around her. She absent-mindedly rubbed his arm in stutter-stop fashion while he reveled in the clean citrusy smell and nearness of her. She glanced down at the crown of his head quizzically a time or two, wondering who he was, but she immediately forgot she had seen anyone and looked away before registering he was still in front of her eyes. Then she would suddenly become aware of the feel of his shoulder beneath her hand, give herself a shake, and glance down again in surprise.

The elevator interrupted the moment when it said, "Ding!" then chuckled at its impersonation of itself. The woman sarcastically replied that it never got old, and the elevator solemnly apologized for bringing her down. She did laugh at that. Then she was walking away across the marble floors of a grand lobby, entirely oblivious to Cory's presence. He swallowed a lump in his throat, struggling—and failing—not to cry. Security guards had arrived to greet the elevator, having seen him on their surveillance cameras, but when the doors opened, he walked right past them while they discussed last night's Powerball game. They made no move to confront him nor to comfort him in his grief. If anyone reviewed the camera footage later, they forgot about him before they logged his presence.

The scope of Cory's power was hard for me to wrap my mind around. If what he was saying was true, even *images* of him were sometimes enough to make people forget. How could that be possible? But Cory couldn't explain it any more than I could.

Being forgotten wasn't anything new. He had always been alone. He decided he might as well see what this strange new place had to offer him, and he'd been exploring the Project Arete facility ever since. Something close to a year, at my best guess. As days wore on, he went back to the Restoration Point Church less and less. At some point, he secured an unclaimed Map from a box left unattended in a storage room. He had actually taken his first Map from a serious-looking fellow's business suit pocket, only to discover the man could get anyone else with a Map to locate the one he'd misplaced. This led to a series of encounters with the man in the suit, whose anger somehow allowed him to remember Cory for varying lengths of time, frequently chasing him as a Map thief, only to lose track of him. Perhaps the man didn't remember Cory so much as the fact that he was upset about his missing Map. Cory, standing in front of him with the Map in question, was forgotten, but the strangely mobile Map was not.

Baffled, the man began sending security to recover the mysteriously roving Map, and Cory was forced to abandon it lest he be remembered long enough to end up trapped in a cell somewhere. It had been pointless to carry it around, anyway. The Map's security encryption had keyed to the serious fellow's specific electrical aura and brain waves. Cory had never managed to use the device. Instead, when he found the box of unclaimed Maps, the first one he fished from the case keyed itself to him. From that point forward, it was Cory's Map. If anyone reported the theft, if anyone in Project Arete Security wondered about the stolen device, they never remembered long enough to pursue it.

Eventually, Cory had noticed that the deeper one went into Project Arete, the less security there seemed to be. It was as though they relied on the outer layers of security to filter out those who were unwelcome. In this way, those who lived and worked further in wouldn't be inconvenienced by checkpoints or passcodes. I'd noticed this, too, on the way down to the Quantum Lab. The Maps served as a very useful and effective security system. You couldn't get anywhere or do much of anything within the facility without one, and you couldn't steal someone else's. If, like Cory, you did manage to get ahold of an unkeyed Map, it keyed to you. It didn't take much effort to figure out from the constant stream of metrics collected by a Map who an individual was. In less than an hour, a Map would know almost everything there is to know about you. Undesirables without an ability like Cory's wouldn't be able to hang around for long without being caught.

But Maps didn't allow access to the deepest sections of Project Arete. Cory was vague on the details; I got the impression he was a little bit ashamed to admit he'd been engaged in illicit activities. Plus, he seemed to have an ingrained habit of secrecy. Never being able to connect with anyone hadn't taught him to build trust. I didn't push for details. I figured as we got to know each other, I could demonstrate by my actions that I was reliable, someone he could confide in. In any case, he'd found a way into a top-secret section of the facility, and he'd gone exploring.

In a dim tunnel with glass walls and ceilings, barely lit by weak blue lights set in strips close to the floor, after walking what felt like kilometers, Cory had noticed a faint grayish light ahead. A few hundred meters on, he turned and pressed his face against the glass, using his hands to minimize reflections. Thirty meters directly ahead, and slightly above him, a hazy man-like figure was descending through dark water. *Have I walked so far?* Cory wondered. Had the tunnel left the shores of Restoration Point? Was he standing under the bay?

Attenuated light filtered down from above: sun, on an overcast day, struggling to penetrate to a depth of perhaps fifty meters. The faint grayish light he had seen emanated from the figure in the water. Cory squinted, but he couldn't see it clearly. It was like a tall, skinny man seen through dense fog. Its own glow lit the fog around it from within, giving the suggestion of form, but it wasn't really suspended in mist; rather, its edges were diffuse and blurry.

The being touched down in the rock and sand of the seabed and drifted away, following the general direction of the tunnel: deeper into the water. It didn't walk. It simply allowed its legs and arms to dangle as it slid effortlessly along the bottom of the bay. Cory could see gentle eddies of sand spiraling lazily and settling in its wake.

Though his legs ached, Cory's curiosity drew him on. Cautiously, he trailed after the weird phantasm; hanging back a little when he realized it would drift right through the wall of the tunnel if it kept on its present course. This it did, simply passing through the wall as if it weren't there. It was a pale, fuzzy distortion, like the ripple of summer heat on a highway when the sun is allowed to shine full force, a haze in the air in which one can imagine the mirage of a man.

Cory halted, suddenly afraid. There was nothing but kilometers of tunnel behind him. Ahead, the ephemeral being had halted its lazy drifting. It had noticed his presence. It hung in place, partially filling the tunnel ahead. Cory had the impression it had turned to face him, less from any indication given by its form or orientation and more from the weight of its regard. He could *feel* it looking at him. It *saw* him! Then it spoke.

<predators marking their territory>
<overpowering urge to flee>

Cory ran faster and further than he'd ever run in his life. The alien thoughts assaulted him as he fled.

<aggressive avian territorial displays>
<apologetic necessity and regret>

"Wait," I said. "That doesn't make any sense. It what?"

Cory rubbed his face. "I really don't know," he admitted. "It was like thoughts just bubbled up in my head. Pictures. Hundreds of images, all jumbled up, but they were almost the same."

"Like they had a theme?" I suggested.

"Yeah! Only that wasn't all of it. There were feelings, too. Really strong. Like during a dream. It was like it came from inside me, but way more than I'd normally feel things. I couldn't tell what was being sent to me by the Cupid and what was really mine. But it didn't matter. The fear was too much. I just had to run like mad."

"Wow," I said. I hadn't considered what it would be like to actually *talk* to a Cupid before. But, of course, it would be weird. They were *aliens*. They'd just been around long enough that people had sort of accepted they were there. Most people never met one, never mind interacted with one.

So, there were Cupids *here*, at Project Arete? That . . . explained a lot: percipient plastic, the quantum computer, the spaceships they were building, the Super-power research, the funding and freedom PA seemed to enjoy. The good relations with other factions in the City, too. Nobody messed with Cupids anymore. Humanity had learned that lesson the hard way.

"Was that the only time you spoke to a Cupid?" I asked. Cory was picking his nose, and I grinned. It was easy to forget he was just a kid. He'd been through a lot and had been forced to grow up quickly. Without thinking about it, I gave him a friendly swat to make him stop. Startled, his power flared.

I finished my meal in peace, glad of the chance to collect my thoughts. It had been a long day, already, and it was barely past noon. I was more than a little annoyed by my ridiculous conversation with Sarah, brief as it had been. *"You will always be safe with me"*? Please. The girl was a dynamo! She must've scored at least a 75 AV if the Quantum Cube had paused to check again. If anyone was in danger, it would be *her* doing the protecting, not the other way around. Matter of fact, that's exactly how it had played out at the docks. She'd swooped in and rescued *me*. Who had I been trying to fool?

I rubbed at my temples. What was with this headache today? Must be serious if my nanos weren't dealing with it. I sighed. Probably the concussion. Getting kicked in the head will do that to you.

Feeling irritable, I ordered a root beer float to go. Time to go find out how I'd scored.

VIII

Amyati made her announcement, looking smug. Like a haughty princess, she received the congratulations of the group as no less than her due. And rightly so: an Abeyant Vector of sixty-eight was nothing to sniff at! It was every bit as impressive as she had claimed it would be. She was guaranteed her pick of the most prestigious universities, if there really were places in the City that offered scholarships on the strength of one's Super-powers. She was plainly an ambitious and driven person, and judging from her protectiveness of Sarah, there might even be a good heart beneath her prickly exterior. No doubt, she'd be a credit to any establishment that took her in.

She took her seat next to Sarah, and the two whispered excitedly together. I watched from the back of the room, wondering at how easily Amyati seemed to pull the nervous girl from her shell. Sarah seemed to feel safe with Amyati. Well, *safer*, at any rate. She still stuttered and blushed often. Amyati did most of the talking. But it was nice to know Sarah wasn't a complete social pariah. I was a little wistful, to be totally candid. I wanted it to be me, sitting with my head next to Sarah's, whispering back and forth.

It was mid-afternoon. Less than two hours had passed since I'd connected to Cory in the Quantum Cube. I wasn't quite sure where he had gone, and that worried me a little, but I was sure he would turn up again. I still remembered him. Surely, that meant I would notice him if he were there, right?

We were back in Mr. Gold's classroom for our Abeyant Vector test results. And we were in for more surprises. Jake and Alan's scores came up almost identical: twenty-seven and twenty-eight. Respectable power, and the possibilities for development were wide open for both. Earlier in the day, Mr. Gold had mentioned those of us with ratings over twenty-five might find their powers "branching out" along different paths. The twins both had Super-strength and Super-speed, definitely Super-endurance as well, but over time, they had the potential to develop entirely new abilities. No reason to believe those new powers would develop along similar lines either.

Unsurprisingly, they fell to squabbling over which one of them had scored higher. Mr. Gold denied the possibility of a mix-up in the results, and Alan was smugly satisfied. The quantum computer had proven it: he was, in fact, slightly better than Jake.

"Only at some things," scoffed Jake.

Alan grudgingly admitted he'd never been much good at school. But then he brightened. "I'm faster, stronger, tougher, *and* better looking. And I don't get tongue-tied talking to girls, so everything is right with the world!"

Jake looked at me and shrugged as if to say, "*You see what I have to deal with?*" I didn't get the impression he was truly offended; more like he realized further argument would only encourage his brother. He leaned over to me and confided, "If he makes team captain, I'll never hear the end of it."

Team captain? Oh, right. Powerball. Mr. Gold had asked them about it earlier, and it had come up a few times when the group had been chatting between AV tests. Kevin, to my surprise, had agreed to join them for a game. The twins seemed excited about that. Project Arete had a partial team, an arena, and all the necessary gear, but involvement in the game had languished since a couple of the local star players had left to join one of the bigger syndicated leagues.

I could see Alan dreamed of becoming a big Powerball star. Jake, though? It didn't fit. He seemed more thoughtful than his brother. Whatever his goals were, they weren't so simple. Or maybe they were. I knew better than to make assumptions, but it was hard not to with these two. They both played the big dumb jock a little too well, sometimes. Idly, I considered Powerball for myself. *Who knows? Maybe they'll need someone to make sure their laces are snug before they hit the field.*

Ah, who was I kidding? I was pointedly avoiding thinking about everything that had happened that morning. Something big was going on, and I was smack dab in the middle of it. Lace-snugger for the next great Powerball team was not in my future. But just then, I was trying my hardest to pretend like everything was Normal. I didn't want to think about Cory. I didn't want to think about when he might make his next appearance. I didn't want to think about the fact that I'd just seen a billion different versions of myself in a magic science box. I most definitely did not want to think about the possible implications. What I wanted was to rate a moderately high AV, figure out some nifty Super-power tricks, and maybe use them to do some good in the world. Possibly make a few friends along the way. Maybe even a girlfriend! I glanced over at Sarah. But no . . . I was getting *way* ahead of myself. I sighed and looked away. One thing was certain, though: I definitely did *not* want to get dragged into anything with the potential to make my life more complicated than it already was.

Kevin was taking his turn approaching Mr. Gold's desk. I set my worries aside, smiled, and applauded along with the others when he read out his results: 18 AV. Unlike his sister, Kevin wasn't prone to public displays of emotion, but he was grinning ear to ear as he returned to his seat. Alan gave him a fist bump, and Jake leaned over to give his shoulder a friendly squeeze. Susie bounced out of her seat to throw her arms around him, and Kevin laughed, struggling in her embrace with mock embarrassment.

Mr. Gold beckoned her to the front of the class next. She left off mauling Kevin to accept the envelope. Like everyone else, she read the results while standing at the front of the class. After a moment, she picked up a piece of chalk and wrote the number forty-four on the chalkboard before resuming her seat next to Kevin. There were murmurs of appreciation all around, everyone holding up a peace sign or a thumbs up or reaching out for a fist bump, which she returned enthusiastically with an adorable grin. Kevin's gestures said, "*I'm so happy for you. You'll be accepted by the CSS for sure.*"

I looked it up with my Map. The CSS was the Center for Semiotic Studies, a language institute at Luna Base. They were responsible, in large part, for the working relationship humanity had with the Cupids. "As combination telepaths/empaths, Cupids are notoriously difficult to understand," read the blurb on their information site. I thought back to Cory's description of his encounter with the Cupid below PA. Telepathic *and* empathic. That made sense. They projected both thoughts and feelings. Susie must be hoping to go to the moon to assist in the ongoing efforts to improve communications. I didn't know anything about her Super-power, beyond the fact that it had something to do with languages, but it must be of benefit somehow. Was I seriously witnessing the beginning of a new era in human-alien relations? Would I be able to look back one day and say I had been there when Susie Yoon had taken the first steps on her path to the moon? Crazy.

Up until this point, everyone had freely shared their results, and the general mood of easy camaraderie felt natural, comfortable. I was beginning to wonder if Project Arete put small groups together for their AV tests this way on purpose, to begin a sort of bonding process through shared tension and excitement. It wasn't as though we had been through a major trial together, but it was interesting that we were all around the same age. We all seemed to have blown the AV test into a big thing in our own minds. How much of that was our own natural anxiety, and how much was what we'd been told about the test? I was fairly new to PA, but the others had been there awhile. Maybe they'd been primed to think of the AV test as a sort of coming of age for Supers, and I'd picked up on the vibe. Certainly, now that it was behind us, we were all acting like we had known each other forever, even though most of us hardly knew a thing about any of the others.

Sarah broke the mood, however. Envelope in hand, she scurried back to her desk, quietly read the contents. Then she put the results back in the envelope and tucked it away in her pocket. There were voices raised in query. She blushed furiously and shook her head. After some cajoling, it was clear she would remain mute on the subject.

Only I knew what her results were. Cory stood behind her, reading over her shoulder, and he held up first eight fingers, then five. I quickly looked away, wondering why it annoyed me so much. Yes, I was curious, but it wasn't for me to know if she didn't want to share, was it? I felt a little like I'd unexpectedly walked in on her naked. I found myself quietly seething. What was Cory thinking, snooping like that? I ground my teeth furiously, promising myself I'd have stern words with him the next time I managed to corner him. What kind of kid was he, abusing his powers like that? With a sinking heart, I realized I had no idea. Not really. Caught up in the moment in the Quantum Cube, I'd felt like I knew everything about him. But how could I be sure any of what I'd felt was true?

Too late, now. We were connected, whether I liked it or not.

A hush fell over the room as Mr. Gold stood and walked over to me, handing me the final envelope. Unusual enough that I hadn't been called to the front of the class like everyone else, but when he just stood there, arms folded, waiting and watching, a sort of tension electrified the room. Everyone was curious to see why the new kid was being singled out for special attention.

Fingers trembling, I tore open the envelope and pulled out the assessment. My eyes scanned the contents automatically, but when

I reached the end, I felt like I'd misread it. My heart skipped a beat, and I had to stop and begin again.

The test had come up inconclusive. The number that had been generated by the quantum computer wasn't fixed, instead fluctuating rapidly between fifty-five and 158. Most definitely not a normal reading. The only logical conclusion, according to the Quantum Crew, was that the quantum computer would need to be fully recalibrated, a much lengthier process than the basic once-over Moses, Ralph, and Gavin had given the system after Sarah's bout of claustrophobia. Unfortunately, that meant I wouldn't be able to determine my AV until they ran another group through on the following day. Fortunately, the note informed me, there *was* a second group scheduled to go through the cube. If I was still interested in determining my AV, I would have to stay the night in the Project Arete facility, report to Mr. Gold's classroom tomorrow, and take part with them.

I suppose I shouldn't have been surprised. The moment Cory made his appearance, I'd known things were going to go sideways. Matter of fact, I'd known it *before* I met Cory. I hadn't been able to shake the premonition of disaster prompting me not to get in the box; I'd simply ignored it. Still, after all day agonizing over my AV, worrying about how low it might be, to get something uncertain like this was a huge disappointment. And yet . . . the *low end* was fifty-five! Higher than everyone here except Sarah and Amyati! There was no denying I'd recently gained access to something more than the minor telekinesis required to wiggle my shoelaces. Did I dare hope?

I bit my lip, uncertain what to think. Eventually, I responded to the curious pestering of the others. "Faulty test, I guess. Have to go back tomorrow." I shrugged, feigning a carelessness I didn't feel.

There was a chorus of sympathy. I sat in silence, not taking part as everyone grouped up around me, chatting and laughing. One by one, they began to drift off. Amyati paused at the door and raised one eloquent black brow, catching Sarah's eye. Sarah gathered her things and stood to go. For a moment, I thought she would say something as she paused next to my desk—her mechanical eyes didn't quite meet my gaze—but she blushed and hurried after Amyati without a word. Kevin had been right. It was painful, how shy she was. But it left me wondering what she might have wanted to say.

Kevin and Susie departed without much in the way of goodbyes, signing rapidly back and forth. I glimpsed enough of it to hear Susie's cartoon voice burbling happily in my ear. Their dreams were both set to come true, and the pair of them were discussing next steps excitedly. Jake and Alan weren't far behind, calling after Kevin, trying to nail him down for a Powerball practice time. That left me alone with Mr. Gold.

I looked down at the assessment again. At the bottom, Mr. Gold had written a note: "*I'd be interested to hear about your experience inside the box. Hang around after the results if you feel like sharing.*"

His frank appraisal, when I met his eyes, made me nervous. He didn't seem to be in a hurry. I pondered: how much might he know? I glanced around the room. Would I even know if Cory was still around? I thought I would, but I couldn't be sure. I could be staring at him right now, forgetting he was right in front of me. The thought made me shiver.

I took a deep breath and lied to Mr. Gold. "Nothing particularly exciting to report, sir. It was dark. The sensors lit up for a moment. The box opened." I lifted my shoulders, hoping the gesture seemed more casual than it felt.

He pursed his lips. "I find that fascinating, David."

I swallowed. "You do?"

"Hadn't you been asking about testing two people at once?" He furrowed his brows as he asked this, as though he wasn't entirely sure, as though he was ransacking a stack of dusty boxes in an attic somewhere, searching for a memento he knew should be there. "Is it coincidence that these numbers could, in theory, be the result of the machine trying to decide between two separate scores?"

"But I was in the box alone," I pointed out, hoping he remembered it the same way.

Mr. Gold blew out a breath and looked at me for a long while. Then he said, "I can't account for it any other way. The machine has never given a result like this before. But perhaps there's something we missed in our initial review."

There is definitely something you're missing, I thought, but I kept my mouth shut. I wasn't about to throw Cory in front of the hover-bus without good reason. And my instincts were telling me to keep his existence to myself, for the time being.

"Well," said Mr. Gold at last. "Tomorrow, then. There's a number the quantum computer kept settling on, then veering sharply away from. Quite simply one of the highest ratings ever to be tested at Project Arete, barring a few notable exceptions. It will be interesting to see if it turns out to be accurate, especially in light of how little you're currently able to do."

I was stunned. Did he truly think I would rate so high?

"Seriously?" I blurted. Or begged, more like. I wanted to believe him so bad it made my guts ache.

Mr. Gold smiled, knowing full well his bait had lured me in. "Tomorrow will confirm or deny my educated guess," he said. "All you have to do is attend." He considered for a moment, then added, "But I'm inclined to agree with the director. There *is* something special about you."

I didn't know what to say to that. He watched me leave, a thoughtful frown on his face. His guesses, if guesses they were, had been entirely too close for comfort.

I spent that evening in a different room from where I had spent the past few days recovering from my injuries. My Map pinged as I was leaving Mr. Gold's classroom to inform me that my things had been moved to make room for other patients. Experimenting, I found I could augment my reality in much the same way I had when I'd "mastered" sign language in an instant. Rather than follow a diagram, I had the Map trigger visual cues using the nanos in my eyes to let me know where to turn. Colored lights led me to my new quarters unerringly, with a minor detour for dinner and a few snacks. I could have had the corridors marked with hovering labels indicating where they led, with expanding details immediately available with a brief thought, but I wasn't interested in being bombarded with more information. If anything, I needed a tinfoil hat. There were too many incoming signals at the moment, and I was having trouble keeping up with it all. Outlining the path I needed with a gentle halo was good enough.

The area I ended up in felt less like a hospital and more like a luxury resort, and since it was conveniently located to both Mr. Gold's classroom and the freight elevator to the Quantum Computing Lab, I didn't see any reason not to stay. I let myself in with a swipe of my Map, then kicked off my shoes. The foyer gave onto a spacious living room, comfortably appointed with a plush burgundy couch and two matching armchairs. The coffee table was a gorgeous synthetic cherrywood. A corner desk in a similar style provided a workstation for PA-related activities, and a smart-glass screen was inset in one wall. Like my hospital room, this one was equipped with an AI recycler and replicator linked to a beverage and snack machine, and a washroom. Through an open door, I spied a cozy bedroom and storage closet.

I flopped on the couch, not bothering to explore beyond the living room. My arm was aching, so I took off the sling and worked my elbow for a while, flexing my fingers and rolling my wrist. It was healing, but it might be a few days yet. Impressive how quickly I was recovering from the fracture, now that I thought about it. Kevin's healing had worked wonders, but Project Arete must also have access to some nifty medical tech. Quality nano-machines at the very least. Had they upgraded me? Wouldn't have surprised me, if they had. The nano-tricks I'd been pulling with the help of the Map probably wouldn't have worked with my old nanos. The existence of my Map, made from percipient plastic, hinted at a wealth of advanced gadgets Project Arete were keeping mostly to themselves. These Map things definitely weren't in use around the City. It made me wonder what else might be hidden in the PA facility.

After a quick shower, I spent some time in front of the mirror, parting my unruly hair, looking at the wound on my scalp, my split eyelid, my slashed cheek. I had more or less been able to forget about being attacked, since I wasn't constantly being reminded by twinges of pain. All the stuff that had been going on during the day had helped distract me, too. But anyone looking at me could see I'd been beaten up recently.

I poked and prodded for a while. Kevin, or nanos, or both, had sealed everything neatly, and the swelling was mostly gone. Might be a while before the marks faded, though. Concentrating, I tried to remove the stitches without touching them. At first, nothing happened. Then I heard an unsteady thudding out in the living room. I paused. I didn't need to look to know my shoes were now trotting around the apartment, propelled by their extra-long laces. I could feel the lengths of synthetic cord clearly, as if I were holding them in my hands. Slowly, watching myself in the mirror, I lifted my hands and moved them apart, as if I were pulling the laces taut. My power responded, if a little reluctantly. My shoes tumbled to a halt.

Concentrating furiously, I made little pinching motions with my fingers. One by one, the stitches pulled loose from my face, jumping free and crawling themselves into an untidy knot on the sink. I gathered them up, breathing heavily; that had been a lot more effort than I'd expected. I tossed the soiled threads in the recycler. A quick rinse of my face and a pat down with a soft towel followed. Then I just looked at myself for a while: shaggy, dirty-blonde waves; straight thick brows; dark blue eyes; slightly crooked nose; broad forehead, cheeks, and jaw. I realized I was hunched up, a habitual slouch from always expecting to get picked on. With an effort, I straightened up and pulled my shoulders back.

Genetically, I was built to be blocky. Not nearly as big as Jake and Alan, but I had the frame for wide shoulders, big arms, and sturdy legs. I'd just never really worked out much. My physical activity was mostly walking around everywhere and climbing things. It left me looking trimmed down, spare. Even so, it was a blunt-looking sort of fellow who stared back at me from the mirror. *He might look blunter still if he filled out a bit*, I thought. With the long pink seam crossing my left cheek from temple to upper lip, the split and swollen eyelid, I seemed rough and ready.

Ready for what, though? I smirked. I probably wouldn't even have scars once the nanos had done their work. Or I could go see Kevin for a little more healing. Then I'd look just as soft and slouchy as before.

Feeling refreshed, I returned to the living room and turned on the broadcasts, but I couldn't focus. The news was the usual depressing flood of negativity: crime, violence, political upheaval, corporate terrorism, Super-villains. It all seemed so far away. I had woken up in another world a few days ago, and everything out there—above ground—seemed like a fantasy. Everything down here, this was where things were real.

I switched off, stretched out on the couch, and stared at the ceiling. I had been alone and disconnected from other people for a long time. Just another loner kid, wandering around the City. Then wham, all at once, no rhyme or reason, I found myself caring about total strangers in a way I hadn't cared about anyone since I was a little kid.

Sarah's face was easy to summon in my mind's eye. What was going on there? It was evident some aspect of my Super-power had reached out and connected me to her, but I couldn't imagine how I had done it, nor could I fathom what good it would do either of us. Unless I got a handle on my powers, it would likely remain a mystery. Still, I didn't feel entirely disappointed in the day. I had held out my hand in friendship, and she hadn't slapped it away. I just had to wait for her to take it. She was so ill at ease and nervous, but I felt like she was trying hard to reach back. Maybe things hadn't gone quite as I'd hoped, but I hadn't ruined my chances. Not yet, anyway.

What about Cory? What was I supposed to make of him? Like it or lump it, we were connected now, too. I'd inadvertently become his lifeline. I thought I could be okay with that, but it was going to take some adjustment, for both of us. He couldn't keep acting like he was alone against the world anymore, and quite frankly, neither could I. Whatever was going on with my powers, whatever had connected us, we were in it together now, for better or for worse. And was that really such a bad thing? If I could save this one kid from himself, wouldn't that qualify me as a sort of Super-hero?

I thought about Mr. Gold and the Quantum Crew—the banter, the easy camaraderie. Everywhere I'd visited in the complex since I arrived, the people had been warm and welcoming. Whatever else Project Arete might be, they'd built a culture of acceptance and inclusiveness. I wanted to be a part of that. I had a family, though, and I hadn't been thinking about them at all. Did I deserve to belong to a group like this if I didn't give any thought for my own parents? It had been a while since I talked to them. As far as they knew, I was still living on the streets, an aimless young man of no fixed address. I knew my mom understood why I had left, but my dad had never appreciated my reasoning. It stung because he had always been the one to get most annoyed when my power acted up and ruined something. He wasn't a Super, so he didn't understand why I couldn't just *apply myself* or *show a little self-control*. But maybe he could look past all that if I told him I was safe; I'd found a place to live, and I was beginning to gain control of things. More to the point: it wouldn't be under his roof that I made my mistakes while trying to master my gift. That ought to make him happy, right? It was somebody else's problem now. *Mine.* And I would figure it out.

I couldn't believe how things had turned out. I was looking at more potential power than anybody would have ever guessed I possessed, more than I ever would have believed I had, despite all my hopes and dreams. I wanted to call my parents, share the good news—give them a reason to be proud of me—but it seemed premature. The preliminary AV test had been inconclusive. Then again, Mr. Gold's hints hadn't exactly been subtle. If I waited until I had something concrete to report, I might not reach out at all. There would always be some excuse for why it wasn't a good time.

I picked up my Map. *No time like the present. Call my mom,* I thought. I heard ringing; then the call clicked over to her message service.

My mom's voice said, "Hey! So sorry to miss your call, but you'll *never* believe it! Gordon and I won a sweepstakes and right now we're in *Tahiti*! We'll be here for a *month* toasting our little buns in the sun and enjoying traditional French Polynesian hospitality! Leave a message, but don't expect a call back!"

The message ended with my father's deep voice growling something in the background. He did something that made her drop the phone. There was a brief clattering and indistinct laughter before the tone.

"Uh, hi, Mom. Hope you guys are having fun." I found my throat closing up around all the things I wanted to say. I forced myself to continue, struggling to sound calm and collected. "Um . . . I don't know why I'm calling, really. I'm safe, I guess. Thought you should know. And . . . I might have found a place to stay, something productive to do with my time. Seems like my powers are not quite what I thought they were, but there are people here who might be able to help me figure it out."

What would that sound like to her? Had I wound up in an institution somewhere? Had I been recruited by a Super-villain's cultish following? I babbled on, hoping to reassure her. "Not that I couldn't figure it out on my own, of course. Just, you know, looking at all my options. I'm free to leave whenever I want." Oof. Yeah, that didn't sound good. "Seriously, though, things are good. Maybe I'll see you around sometime."

Hang up, I thought, and the Map obliged. *Ugh*. I could be such a dork sometimes.

I was feeling dejected now. I felt like I was at war with myself. The street savvy part of me was telling me, *Don't get in too deep. Hold your cards close to your chest. Be ready to cut and run.* But Project Arete was everything I wanted to be a part of. I had been daydreaming my whole life about unlocking my potential and discovering amazing gifts within myself that would let me do some good in the world. Becoming a Super-hero! Project Arete *produced* Super-heroes *as a side project*! Even without their quantum computer, Abeyant Vectors, and studies of Super-powers, PA wielded enough power and influence to be a Super-hero in its own right. They had the technology, the expertise, the staff, and above all, the moral fiber to make a real difference in the world. Everything pointed at them being one of the good guys.

As far as I could see, the only reason they hadn't guided humanity into a new-age utopia by now was that the world, over the past century, had become severely fractured. The City was divided along so many arbitrary lines that nobody, no matter how well intentioned, could put it back together again. It was like a twenty-five-billion-piece puzzle with a bunch of the pieces missing, and every single piece was a different person with a different perspective. They all saw a different image emerging as the pieces were slowly put back together. Nobody could agree on what was right for the future anymore.

Still, I doubted I could find a better outfit to lend my services to.

At length, I found my way to the bedroom. By slow stages, I managed to drift off to sleep. I slept restlessly, however, waking up numerous times during the night. I couldn't shake the feeling that I was being watched. Yet every time I got up and switched on a light, there was nothing to be found. My Map sat on the bedside table, and for a moment, I wondered if I was being monitored. It drew power from my electrical field, but Kevin said it could store quite a lot of energy. I didn't need to be touching it for it to be on. I stared at the Map for a while, but I couldn't imagine a scenario where they would gather anything useful from watching me that way. And even while staring at the Map, I still felt like there was someone else in the room with me. It made my skin crawl.

Sometime around three in the morning, after I'd been lying awake for fifteen or twenty minutes, thinking about it, I said out loud, "Cory?"

He hadn't been there until I spoke. Or if he had, I didn't remember it. Now he was sitting in the armchair on the other side of the room. His legs were curled up, and he had his arms wrapped around his knees; he was the picture of lonely misery. His eyes were wide and damp, and very, very scared.

I propped myself on my elbow to glare at him, feeling unreasonably irritated that he'd been lurking in my room and ruining my sleep, then winced when my busted arm shot a jolt of pain up into my shoulder. I sat up, facing him across the room. Pain throbbed from my wrist up to my shoulder, a constant angry pulsing.

"Where the heck have you been?" I demanded. I was exasperated that he'd simply disappeared, and I couldn't keep it out of my voice. But it wasn't just him. All night, I'd been wrestling with my demons: hope that I might finally make something of myself warred with the certainty that my Super-power was weak and ridiculous; thoughts of Sarah spun in endless circles; now Cory's presence only served to make me realize that maybe I was failing to uphold my end of the bargain. I'd promised to remember him. But how was I supposed to do that if his power kept driving him out of my head? *Why couldn't he just apply a little self-control?* It didn't help that I knew I was thinking like my dad. I hated myself for it.

Cory had curled up smaller, hiding his clear gray eyes against his knees. He mumbled something too muffled to hear. Annoyed, I snapped at him. "What? C'mon, man, speak up. Are you talking to me or your legs?" Blame the lack of sleep, I guess. Not my proudest moment.

"I said, I don't want to be alone anymore!" he screamed. He was on his feet and halfway across the room. I couldn't remember him jumping up. His face was contorted with the agony of his emotions, tears and snot running freely down his face. A lifetime of being forgotten and alone had been brought to a sudden and unexpected end when I arrived—hope, painful and bright, stabbing a light into the dark—only to have me forget and wander off, snatching away his chance for a normal life. Crushing him. His breath sawed in and out in great, gasping heaves. He was shaking with anger, totally forlorn.

"Hey. *Hey,*" I said. I stood up and reached out. He slapped my hands away. "Hey, man! Cory. Cory, *stop!* Listen to me." He scrubbed his face furiously with the back of his arm, then hugged himself as if he might fly apart.

I took another step and got a grip on his shoulders. His face was turned resolutely aside, ashamed of his outburst, maybe, terrified I might snap at him again and push him away. Or worse, forget. Simply forget, and leave him stranded. What must it be like? Forever outcast. Forever forgotten. He couldn't be more than thirteen or fourteen. How had he survived this long once his powers activated?

I pulled him in. He fought me, at first, trying to push away, but I held onto him and pulled him close. I hugged him tightly. "You're not alone anymore," I whispered fiercely.

And, I realized, neither was I. Like a floodgate opening, my own loneliness poured out: the isolation of being removed from school so young; all the years of being bullied; all the failed attempts to connect with people who pushed me away because I was too much of a nuisance; fighting with my father until I just couldn't stand it anymore; living on the street, always looking over my shoulder. I sobbed, uncontrollably, and buried my face in his hair. Cory clung to me; his cheek pressed hard into my chest. He wept, whole body shaking. Overwhelmed by his emotions as they poured down the link between us, all I could do was stand there and let them flow through me. I knew that my own feelings were flooding him, too.

Wordlessly, we clung to each other. We stayed that way for a long time. We cried until our tears stopped coming. Eventually, when I climbed back into bed, I pulled him with me. I put my arm around him as he pressed up against my side, his head on my shoulder. Now that the barriers between us were broken, it was like there had never been any. I lay there for a long time, feeling drained, but also feeling a bit of the weight on my heart lifting. Until that moment, I hadn't realized just how heavy it had been.

Soon, Cory's breathing was coming slow and even with the peace of sleep. I listened to his gentle snoring, and I thought about all the different realities in which he and I had been connected. I thought about how he had made that same connection with me, here, in this reality, against all odds. I thought about how the connection probably wouldn't have worked with anybody else. Only me, because of the nature of my burgeoning Super-power.

Connections. It seemed to suggest, whatever else might be going on, that I was in the right place at the right time. To be here, now. For him.

My eyes felt heavy, and still my thoughts spun in circles. I thought about how, in so many of those other realities I had seen so briefly, it had been chains of hate that bound us, not bonds of love. Anger and accusations and flying fists. I thought about that for a long time. I thought about how annoyed I had been when I first saw him in my room, how I had started by lashing out . . . how close I had come to pushing him away, maybe pushing him right over the edge. I wondered if it still might happen, somewhere down the road, if he might one day become hateful, angry, or vengeful because of something I did, or failed to do. I thought about the foreboding feeling I'd had before I'd stepped into the Quantum Cube, like I had been about to trigger an avalanche. That it might sweep away all I knew and loved.

No. I couldn't allow that to happen. I wouldn't.

I spoke out loud in the dark. "Not here," I promised him. "Not in this reality."

As I finally drifted off to sleep, too exhausted to sustain my nagging thoughts any longer, a final doubt assailed me: *connections.* That meant Sarah was wrapped up in this, too. Who else would be dragged in before it was all over? What, exactly, was the avalanche? And how had I sensed it coming?

IX

Breakfast is a strange affair when you have trouble recalling you're not eating alone.

The following morning, refreshed and eager to get on with the day, I rose early, tripped over Cory as I got out of bed, and nearly broke my other arm. Thinking it must have been the tangle of blankets that had snagged my ankle, I carried on, barely giving it further thought. *Must've had a restless night.*

Even so, I felt surprisingly well rested. After fifteen minutes of light calisthenics, I had a quick rinse in the shower, then went into the kitchen to prepare breakfast. The replicator recommended milk and orange juice, eggs and bacon, oatmeal and yogurt, and a side of fruit. I modified the list to include greasy hash browns smothered in ketchup. I had the replicator make enough for three, served two portions to myself, and set the remainder at a second place at the table. Then I sat down and stared at the other plate, wondering why I had made breakfast for two.

I promptly forgot why I was wondering, thought instead about the day ahead while I ate. Halfway through the meal, I abruptly realized the other plate was half empty. Cory was apparently enjoying it. I poured him some orange juice, set it down in front of myself, and drank most of it before realizing I had meant to give it to him. I poured another glass, concentrating hard, and placed it next to his plate.

"Dude, can't you suppress that mind-wipe thing at all?" I felt like I was talking to empty air. But, no, he was right there. I remembered him walking into the room, sleepy-eyed, then sitting down in front of breakfast still half asleep.

Cory shrugged. "Haven't figured it out yet. It comes and goes like . . . I dunno . . . waves, I guess. It kind of surges sometimes. I can't help it."

"But I'm aware of you right now," I pointed out. "I can remember this conversation." I shoveled in another mouthful of food and talked around it. "So far, anyway. What are you doing differently right now that you weren't doing five minutes ago while you ate?"

He took another bite of hash browns and chewed thoughtfully. Within moments, I had forgotten what I'd asked him. I was staring right at him, and yet it was like he wasn't there. I couldn't hold a memory of him sitting right in front of me long enough to be aware of him. It wasn't until he stabbed my hand with his fork that I realized I had blanked again.

"Sorry," he said. I had been reaching for his plate to clear up the breakfast dishes. I rubbed my hand, chagrined.

"You seem totally normal when you're talking to me—when you *want* to be seen and heard. But when you're distracted, the power slips out and steals my memories. Maybe it's just a concentration thing. Maybe you need to practice making it a choice, instead of just operating on instinct all the time."

"What do you mean?" he asked. He finished the last few bites and handed me the plate.

Gathering the rest of the dishes, I carried them to the recycler. Cory followed me into the living area. Maybe it was the sound of his feet scuffing across the floor that kept me aware of him. Maybe he was trying to focus on being present. Somehow, I managed to get my train of thought under way before it stalled at the station.

"How did you get a Map?" I asked, forgetting that he'd already told me the day before. "Did someone give you one?" Cory was caught off guard by the change of subject. I was pushing buttons

on the beverage machine, trying to get it to exceed the recommended per cup dose of caffeine, when he reminded me he was there
by answering.

"I stole one."

"Cory! Man, don't sneak up on me like that!" I glared at him.

"Ha-ha, David. Very funny."

I stared blankly for a moment before finally catching up with
him. "Sorry, what did you steal?"

Cory rubbed his face. "A *Map*, David. You asked me how I got
one. *Again*. I had to take one. Nobody could remember I was here
long enough to give me one. I figured out what they were by watching people around the facility. People consult them all the time for
all sorts of things. I thought maybe I could talk to people that way
because the Map would have messages on it that you could look at
when you forgot, like a memory outside your own brain or something electronic that I can't wipe by accident. But it doesn't work.
People have to remember to look at the messages, and half the time,
they never do. Even when they *do* notice a message, they either delete
it because they assume it wasn't meant for them or they forget what
they were looking at while trying to figure out who sent it. Think! I
barely managed to reach *you* through the Map!"

I had a vague recollection of that. I also knew I had asked him
about the Map for a reason . . .

"To get you off balance!" I blurted out.

"What?"

"I switched topics like that because I'd already guessed you had
to steal one. Or I remembered. Anyway, I wanted to see what would
happen when you got defensive. Look, I know you're a good kid.
I don't know how, but I know you don't feel good about stealing,
even when you have to do it to survive. The moment I asked, you
got ashamed, and I instantly forgot about you. I felt it through our

link. It's like it's a defense mechanism! I had a theory it might be something like that, but I needed to test it."

Cory pursed his lips and gave me a dubious look.

"Sorry, but I don't think it would've worked the same if I had explained it first." I ran a hand through my hair and huffed out a breath. "Heck, I'm just glad I remembered what I was doing."

Cory was looking thoughtful. I focused on his face and started counting his freckles. They were almost as pale as his skin, but he had quite a few scattered across his cheeks and over the bridge of his nose. Maybe if I just concentrated hard enough, I'd be able to remember he was there.

"Anyway, listen," I said. "I think you should shadow me today . . . everywhere I go. I might not be able to remember you're there all the time, but try to remind me whenever I seem to forget. Maybe with a little practice, it'll get easier. For both of us."

He agreed. Before the fog could steal him away again, I remembered to tell him what I had been thinking before we had fallen asleep.

"Cory?"

"Yeah?"

"You're my little brother now. Okay? I'm going to do my best to look out for you. But I'm going to need your help. Your power is really whacked. But I think we can figure it out if we work together."

I was alone in the kitchen. I thought I heard someone crying, but there was nobody there.

I grabbed my Map and took a moment to set up a reminder program. As with other things I'd attempted, the Map made it easy. Then I stepped into my runners, leaving the laces loose.

It was time to find out if I was a Super-hero.

The second time through the Quantum Cube was nothing like the first: a brief moment of darkness, and for a fraction of a second, a sensation of unfolding, like I was one paper doll in a chain, spanning the darkness in all directions. I can't think of any other way to describe it. To be honest, I closed my eyes the moment the box closed around me, and I refused to open them until I heard the lid being lifted away and the fog machines hissing. It left me feeling dizzied, but otherwise unfazed. It was nowhere near as disconcerting as the weirdly dilated few seconds I'd spent in the cube with Cory just the day before. Relieved, I made my way back to the control room.

I didn't know any of the others taking the test, except for Moses. He looked glum and admitted he wasn't interested in getting tested. He wouldn't be on the wrong side of the computer at all, in fact, if Project Arete hadn't insisted on a policy of testing all staff members at some point or another.

"You ask me," grumped Moses, "it's just an excuse to pile more responsibilities on my plate. Thank you, no."

Most of the others were in their thirties, at a guess. One by one, they took their places in the box. There were few signs of nerves. None professed any concerns over the process—chalk it up to age and experience, I guess—and the computer performed optimally throughout. It was all over far quicker than expected. Before I knew it, we had an hour for lunch while the Quantum Crew put together their reports on the results. Gavin and Ralph, that is. Moses wasn't allowed to peek.

After lunch, we reconvened in Mr. Gold's classroom. Ralph and Gavin attended, as a show of support for Moses. He didn't seem thrilled by the attention. They teased him mercilessly, concocting ever more far-fetched duties to shackle him with when he proved to be a Super off the AV scale.

"I still don't see why I couldn't just get the results back in the lab," Moses griped, arms folded across his chest. "I could have been back to work by now."

"Relax, Moe," said Ralph. "You'll be promoted out of the quantum cave for sure. Gavin and I will just have to figure out a way to continue without you."

"As if. I carry this team."

"Oh-ho, he admits it! Super-strength! I knew it!" crowed Gavin.

Mr. Gold took pity and handed Moses his envelope first. He couldn't get at the results fast enough.

"Ha! Zero! Perfect!" He wadded up the report and tossed it at his chortling cronies.

The remaining results were lackluster. The group was a motley collection of fourteen individuals, most of whom had been working for PA for some time. Few had shown signs of any abilities, so they hadn't been prioritized for the test. Nobody was terribly surprised when most scored between zero and one. Only five of them scored an AV over four, and of those, only two had ratings of any significance: a ten and a seventeen. They were floored to discover they had any power at all, so imagine their surprise when they found out the teenager in their midst had scored an eighty-three.

That's right, 83 AV. I read the results out loud, feeling dazed. I had to read them a second time just to be sure I hadn't accidentally crossed my eyes and gotten the number backward. But even thirty-eight would've been astounding. Yeah, okay, my powers had been behaving oddly lately, but eighty-three? How could I possibly explain *that*? It felt weird, accepting everyone's congratulations and good wishes. Unreal. Like I was just pretending to have powers. Hoping nobody asked me to demonstrate them.

Oddly, the computer was entirely unable to place my potential suite of abilities anywhere on the chart used by Project Arete as a guide to Super-power development. This, more than the rating itself, made the Quantum Crew ecstatic, Moses included. They took pains to assure me their facilities would be entirely at my disposal. To them, I was an opportunity to fill in some major gaps in their charts. I have to admit, the charts were an impressive development in Super-science. If I could contribute to their growing body of knowledge, it would be something to be proud of. But still . . . eighty-three? *How?* What could I *do?* I'm not talking about one or two tricks that I might be able to figure out, here. Eighty-three meant possibly dozens of ways my powers might diverge.

That, more than anything else, sealed the deal. I had to stay on at Project Arete, if only to learn more about my abilities. I couldn't think of anywhere else in the City where I could do so safely. Sure, I might have drawn a couple likely conclusions about my powers, but I really had no idea what I was capable of. It was eye-opening to be grouped up with so many people who had barely rated. On the one hand, it made me realize just how common Super-powers really were. Almost everyone had rated over zero, meaning the potential was there, encoded in their genes. And half of them had rated high enough to actually be able to display some sort of power, however minor. On the other hand, it also impressed upon me just how rare the more powerful Abeyant Vectors must be. Thinking back on it, my original group of eight (if I counted Cory!) were an unusually gifted bunch.

I resolved to track them all down and try to become better friends with them. Chances were good they would all need the same support I desperately craved just then.

Under normal circumstances, a potential Super shows evidence of one power or another, marking potential starting points in the vast array of discovered abilities. Enough research had been done on the correlation between the various Super-powers that a fairly reliable set of developmental paths could be determined, with most, if not all, of the potential branches and connections known. Jake and Alan, for example, both had Super-strength and Super-speed. Almost without exception, Supers who develop those powers also developed Super-endurance. The twins had already shown evidence of this. Their bodies simply couldn't handle the extra force and speed without it.

Super-speed, on the other hand, often leads to extreme physical agility, enhanced reaction times, and even relativistic time-ratio powers, where the Super's *mind* speeds up for brief durations. When this happens, the Super experiences two, three, even four seconds for every second experienced by a Normal. From the Super's point of view, everyone else has slowed down. At 27 and 28 AV, this was highly unlikely for Jake and Alan, but they were high enough on the scale that their powers might diverge and develop along different paths. They might go any number of directions. There were clearly defined connections, though, and some powers were far more likely to develop than others.

All well and good, but in my case, the Quantum Crew hadn't even come up with a starting point. Whatever I was doing when I made my shoelaces wiggle around, it wasn't your typical telekinesis or gravity adjustment. There were elements of known Super-powers there, but it seemed to be a byproduct of the underlying power forming the backbone of my abilities. Whatever I could do, it wasn't anything so obvious. I had some ideas, though. My mostly sleepless night hadn't been entirely unproductive. Lying awake and turning recent events over in my mind had solidified what I'd already begun to suspect: my powers had to do with making connections. After much consideration, I felt I had an inkling of what that might mean.

First, I suspected the speed with which my broken arm was healing must be part of it. Even with newer, more effective nano-machines supporting my recovery, it had only been four days. I had no way to quantify how much Kevin's healing had affected my recovery, but even he had said that bones would take a while. I felt sure my power must have influenced the break for the better; checking my Map satisfied me that I was correct in this guess.

There's a lot that goes on when a bone breaks. It involves a lot of specialized cells, but I discovered one of them is called an osteocyte. If you look at a picture of an osteocyte, you'll see a weird little cell with multiple strings branching off it. Those strings reach out and connect to other osteocytes, forming a lattice, kind of like scaffolding. That's what makes bones so good at supporting bodies. More importantly, this network of connections allows the osteocytes to detect how the bones are being stressed by daily activity. Osteocytes can then guide bone formation to the areas that need it most. To me, the image of osteocytes strung together by bony ropes was something of a revelation: all those little strings forming connections, tying things together, and creating a structure that was far more solid than any individual piece. *Of course*, I would heal broken bones faster than normal; at eighty-three, my power was "on" almost all the time. It was probably seeking out and reinforcing those tiny little connections without me having to think about it.

Would it assist in the healing of other injuries, though? I didn't have much background in biology, but I could make an educated guess. Protein chains, DNA . . . the whole body is basically a living network of connections. I was almost afraid to think about it too much. I didn't want to inadvertently activate my power and wreck an important connection, accidentally damaging myself without knowing how to fix it. Then again, it hadn't happened yet, so I had to assume there was some self-preservation instinct at work. In much the same way, a Super with endurance powerful enough to make him immune to toxins, viruses, and diseases would also be immune to bacteria. Such a power would have to be highly selective; we need bacteria to live. On some subconscious level, the endurance ability detects harm to the body and nixes the culprits but leaves those living in harmony alone. My power was likely the same. I might regenerate faster, but I wouldn't grow cancers unchecked. At least, I didn't think I would . . . only time would tell.

Well then, my bones would heal faster, at the very least. Good to know. So, what else? Solving Dawn, Francis, and Miguel's wiring problem at a glance had to be a part of it, I felt sure. Whatever it was they had been working on, I was certain I had cut their Gordian knot, so to speak. They would take the alterations I had suggested, and they would make progress. The certainty I felt was like closing my eyes and knowing exactly where to put my finger to touch the tip of my nose. It had felt obvious and right, when I'd pointed out the necessary changes. I hesitated to think of it as fate or destiny, but there had been a distinct sense of knowing how things were meant to be, at least as far as their diagram was concerned. And I'd be lying if I said the idea of fate hadn't occurred to me already, where my connection to Sarah was concerned.

Fated or not, I had made a connection, and it was more than just connecting the lines on their schematics. I had connected Dawn and her team to a solution. Potentially, I had connected their project to its future reality and made it possible for them to proceed and accomplish their goals, actually build whatever it was they were building. I know it seems arrogant to claim I was responsible for their later success, yet they themselves would eventually lay their breakthrough at my feet. But I'll get to that.

Now, if that particular connection was a little more esoteric than the simple knitting of my bones, this last consideration took it another step further: I had actually experienced other realities inside the Quantum Cube with Cory. At least, that was how it seemed to me at the time. All those versions of myself, all those versions of him—I knew things about him I had no other way of knowing. Knowledge of who I am bubbled up inside Cory, too. Our interactions began somewhere in the middle, and rippled out from there, as if we'd already known each other for years. Connections to memories that belonged to other versions of myself? I had no way to know.

There was still so much I didn't know about my Super-powers. But I couldn't deny that I was connected to Cory, and I had a vague and ticklish sense of Sarah, too. It was safe to assume with practice, I would be able to bring it into greater focus. What I couldn't begin to guess was what that connection might allow me to do.

There was only one way forward now: experimentation and training. I knew I couldn't safely pursue this on my own. Not with an AV of eighty-three. There was too much room for error. Too much chance of disaster. I needed Project Arete, their expertise and experience. I didn't know where to begin without them. I took a deep breath and turned to discuss my options with Mr. Gold.

During that conversation, Mercedes Helena Cantero Ruiz herself came to the classroom to congratulate me, attended, as before, by a gaggle of assistants and special aides. She and Mr. Gold were both pleased that I had opted to stay. Like the Quantum Crew, they promised to put all of Project Arete's considerable Super-power research and training division at my disposal.

One of Ms. Ruiz's assistants, a wispy blonde fellow with almost no personality, efficiently quizzed me on my interests and aspirations. He teased out a number of ideas I'd had about my future, many of which I hadn't thought about since I was a little kid. I assumed some kind of Super-power was at play, telepathy or empathy or something like that, but at no point did I feel like I was under unusual scrutiny. I did my best to answer honestly, even so. I wasn't used to sharing so much with a stranger, but if he could read my mind, even partially, then it wouldn't do me any good trying to hide anything. Besides, if PA was going to be my new home for the foreseeable future, I'd best get used to the idea of being around other Supers fast. I was going to be spending a lot of my time with them from now on.

Finished, the director's assistant briskly informed me that a schedule would be sent to my Map within a few days. In the meantime, I should try to get familiar with the layout of the facility, move into a proper dormitory, and visit the commissary for any supplies I thought I might need. A list would be included with my schedule if there were any specialty items I might require for my classes.

PA expected me to devote myself to my new educational schedule in exchange for the benefit of their assistance in teasing out my Super-powers, with the understanding that any skills or expertise I developed through their tutelage would be made available to them at need. Outside of my curriculum, however, I was free to pursue whatever caught my interest. I was strongly encouraged to take full advantage of their superior educational facilities. Courses were offered on almost every conceivable subject, and if there was anything I wished to try that they didn't currently have someone on staff to teach, they would find someone with the expertise. In all likelihood, others within the Project Arete community would also be interested.

All this left me wondering what they might eventually ask of me, but I dismissed the thought as unworthy. They were providing room and board, free education, and access to all manner of equipment and facilities, never mind the Super-power stuff. Just then, if they'd asked me to shoot down the moon, I think I would have seriously considered how to go about it. I had an AV of eighty-three! I still couldn't really believe it. But I suspected they wouldn't be asking me to do anything nefarious. Whatever I might eventually be capable of, it behooved them to be my benefactors, educators, and guides. It's human nature to reciprocate; they knew if I could somehow give back in the future, I very likely would. Especially if my training occupied several years. I was bound to form several intimate bonds with others here during that time—all of which would tie me tighter and tighter to Project Arete.

Part of me worried that my own Super-powers would only amplify that aspect of my involvement with them. Connections, after all. But . . . I gave a mental shrug. *Whatever.* There was nothing I could do about it. I needed what PA could offer if I was planning to explore my abilities. I would just have to do my best to avoid trouble.

The morning after discovering my Abeyant Vector, I followed the visual location information offered by my Map and eventually managed to work my way through Project Arete's labyrinthine corridors to the surface. I needed to prove to myself that I was truly free to leave if I wanted to.

There were quite a few exits into the City, and while most of them were hidden or disguised in some way, none seemed to be kept secret from those working within. The egress I found passed through a security checkpoint, manned by men and women in dark-blue body armor complete with kinetic shielding, exoskeletal strength and speed enhancements, and fully integrated AI targeting assistance. They were armed with non-lethal neural pulse rifles known as Hazers. A weapon rack inside their booth held firearms of a deadlier nature, though I'd heard it said a bullet would be preferable to a Hazer daze. A man with a patch that read, "PASec—Baldwin," asked me to pass my Map over a reader mounted on his desk, and then I was stepping into an elevator. The trip was brief, and I was alone in the lift. As it slowed to a halt, the elevator politely reminded me to follow PASec protocol by re-entering the facility through another access point.

I stepped from the lift into organized chaos. The sudden shift from quiet, cool white corridors to the steamy hurly burly of a busy kitchen in full swing was jarring. The kitchen staff nodded politely but didn't otherwise take note of my presence. The breakfast rush demanded all their attention, and they didn't have the time to make chitchat. A strapping older man in a black chef's jacket was coming through the back door as I made to exit. He grunted in surprise, and we danced around each other for a moment. In a gruff voice, he said, "Make yourself useful and pack that bin out to the recycler, would ya?"

I obliged, hefting a heavy plastic container in both arms, and backed out through the door to find myself in a narrow alley between towering skyscrapers. I was pleased to find the pain in my busted arm was minimal, even with the extra effort. The recycler was set in the wall not far from the kitchen's exit. Not knowing what to do with the bin once it was empty, I set it down by the door and continued on my way.

Alleyways were generally pretty clean, in the City, thanks to the constant work of nano-swarms seeking out and breaking down rubbish for repurposing as raw material. The endless ranks of build-ings were in constant need of repair. With nothing to trip over, I was free to crane my neck and get a feel for what part of the City I'd emerged into. People brushed past me in a constant flow. I hadn't realized how much I'd missed being out on the streets until I was pushing through the crosscurrents of pedestrian traffic again. PA probably had tens of thousands of people living and working below—or pursuing an education—but even the busiest corridors didn't compare to being out in the thick of things. This narrow alley alone had three levels of air traffic passing overhead. Bridges and tube ways leapt between neighboring buildings at regular intervals. Some of the buildings had dedicated Skyway terminals on their rooftops. The noise was a constant background roar of voices and engines. AI advertisements lit up smart-glass windows. Holographic ambas-sadors called out to passersby, offering services on behalf of nearby businesses. Recruiters moved through the crowd, selling a thousand brands of safety and security for citizens willing to join their causes. Occasionally, a Super would flash past, weaving at speed through the crowds or simply whipping overhead, dodging through hover-traffic in a brazen display of power. Mercenary enforcers—hired by various competing interests—moved in formations of heavily armed and armored individuals, giving each other wary and respectful nods whenever two groups passed. Wherever they appeared, citizens parted to flow around them, as blithely unconcerned as a river flowing past an island. It was hard not to feel insignificant in the midst of it all. This vibrant, wild, thrumming City was alive; I was nothing more than another drop of blood moving through its pulsing veins.

I exited the alley and hooked around the corner, pausing on the main thoroughfare to give my hammering heart a chance to slow its pace. There was no denying it, the City was an exciting place, but my heightened pulse had more to do with the idea that someone from PA might have followed me outside. Might, in fact, try to stop me from getting very far. Minutes passed while I scanned the crowds clogging the sidewalk. Street-level vehicle traffic was a blurring river of movement channeled through a towering canyon of concrete, plastic, glass, and steel. Far above, a narrow gap between buildings showed a ribbon of sky striped white and blue with uniform bands of cloud cover. Flashes of silver winked at me whenever a shuttle, jet, or high-flying hover-car passed from cloud into sun and back again.

I lowered my gaze and let my eyes rove the crowd, as if I were looking for someone I was supposed to meet. Nobody stood out or behaved in any way that I might have deemed suspicious. The truth was, I could have waited there all day and never known if PA was tailing me or not. Likely they were simply tracking me through my Map. For a moment, I considered leaving it behind, just to see what they might do, but I was reluctant to part with it. For starters, it still worked, even out here, offering a perpetual flow of information superimposed on my field of view. Second, I might need it to contact someone—either at PA or elsewhere—if there was an emergency. Besides, it was my ticket back in. I wasn't really thinking about disappearing back into the City; I just wanted to know if I could. PA was welcome to follow me around if they really wanted to. I wasn't planning on doing anything worth watching, anyway. I just wanted to go back to where it all began; see if I could jog my memory a bit. What Director Ruiz had said about me activating multiple unrelated Super-powers during the fight had stuck with me. I hadn't really believed her at the time—I still didn't—but rating an 83 AV had turned my perception of myself inside out. I no longer had any clear idea of what I was capable of. My recall of the altercation didn't support her assertions; I mostly remembered getting knocked around. Like, a *lot*. But maybe, if I went back there . . .

Refusing to think about what would happen if the Dragons were there, if they happened to recognize me, I shouldered my way back into the press.

Reaching the pier didn't take long. My Map provided the quickest walking route to a taxi stand. From there, it was mere moments before an AI cab had alighted and asked my destination. By this point, I'd already confirmed with a quick mental query that the Map would transfer the necessary funds for the ride. Apparently, Project Arete members enjoyed a generous allowance. I'd suspected as much, since the various shops and restaurants scattered throughout PA never asked for payment. But to actually use someone else's funds, out in the City, felt distinctly larcenous. I hadn't yet done anything to earn the trust or the credits, yet there I was, spending Ms. Ruiz's money. No doubt whatever account had been attached to my Map and my name was monitored somehow. Any egregious or suspicious charges were bound to be flagged, if not denied outright. But the cab accepted the fare when I waved the Map over its payment device, so I shrugged and climbed aboard. The director could probably afford it.

The taxi launched immediately for a mid-level hover lane, pressing me back into my seat almost before I was settled. Other vehicles parted to make way—the taxi darted like a needle through the fabric of traffic, passing through tiny gaps barely wide enough for it to pass—and before I knew it, we had veered off the main artery and were accelerating rapidly. We left barely a ripple of passage in our wake. The margins of error for AI traffic networks are much narrower than for humans.

Glittering buildings flashed by, divided by regular shafts of slanting sunlight; a rapid strobing effect dazzled my eyes. The cab dimmed the smart-glass windows without having to be asked. For a time, I simply stared out the window, letting it all blur into a flickering wall of motion. There was less AI traffic here, compressed into a narrower band of altitudes, with the lower levels given over to human controlled vehicles and the upper airways reserved for larger passenger shuttles. Occasionally, a Sky-Pod zipped by, arcing toward the next transit ring that would send it hurtling on its way. I looked out across the City and marveled at the order and efficiency of the district. Project Arete's influence was obvious now that I was aware of their presence. Can't do secret science in peace below the City if the streets above you are a war zone.

I hadn't forgotten Kevin's advice and pulled out my Map. It provided me with a diagram of the local area, then helpfully delineated the limits of PA's authority and control. A patchwork quilt of colors, according to the legend, indicated the presence of more than two dozen mega-corporations, syndicates, para-military groups, and gangs that enjoyed some level of governance over the surrounding districts. The pier was still nominally under the control of the dockworkers' unions, but they were forced to pay protection money to the Dockside Dragons for their so-called "peace keeping" efforts in the area. Still, I was pleased to find no notice of any ongoing incidents or events involving rival outfits in the area. A relatively quiet day at the pier, then—I aimed to keep it that way.

I caught only the briefest glimpse of the harbor and pier before the taxi began its descent. Hemmed in by buildings on all sides, the highways and thoroughfares of the City around the pier were made of water rather than concrete. Otherwise, it wasn't much different from the rest of the City. It made me wonder why I'd enjoyed it so much. The sensation of discovering an oasis in the middle of the City was revealed as nothing more than an illusion when seen from this vantage.

The cab slowed drastically and eased its way into ground-level traffic. It evinced an almost comical amount of caution, considering it was a machine that could rapidly calculate responses to emergency situations faster than most humans would even notice they were in trouble. I chuckled as I suddenly recalled that AI transportation was rumored to refer to human-piloted vehicles as meat missiles. I opened my mouth to ask the taxi if it was true, but then thought better of it. If it wasn't, I didn't want to give it the idea. With my luck, this would be the one cab in the City with a demented sense of humor and a habit of gossiping with other passenger vehicles it met. I held my tongue until it let me out on the verge of a large circular plaza where half a dozen roads converged. A trio of businessmen were pushing past me into the cab even as I exited. Within seconds, they were long gone.

Easing my way through the crowds milling about the plaza, I retraced my steps of a week ago, senses alert for any sign of the Dragons. I was reassured by the Map's confidence that today was a good day to visit, but I wasn't about to be lulled into a false sense of security. This was the City, after all. The dockworkers' unions took a dim view of violence in the area because it put employees at risk, but that wouldn't necessarily stop the Dragons if they had a good reason to start trouble. All it would take was a member of a rival gang showing up, and all bets would be off.

All around me, people were suddenly donning jackets and patting pockets in search of rain shields. The faint humming of personal kinetic barriers shimmering into being above people's heads presaged the arrival of a fleet of weather drones. They took up a spiraling formation above the plaza before streaking away in all directions. The clouds began to coalesce immediately, thickening into a woolly gray blanket. The City grew dimmer, and the temperature dropped noticeably. I pulled the light jacket I'd fabricated that morning from my hoodie pocket and shook it out. It was just a thin shell, but it would keep the worst of the rain off. I hadn't thought to grab a rain shield before leaving PA; the area wasn't scheduled for heavy precipitation, nor would it last long.

By the time I'd crossed the wide plaza and descended a series of staircases between tiered ranks of apartments, a steady drizzle was falling, darkening the pavement and slicking the buildings with cascading waterfalls. Those caught without protection from the elements hurried their pace. Otherwise, nobody paid any mind. The rain sizzled and hissed where it bounced against force umbrellas. My footsteps thumped hollowly as I strode out onto the wooden pier. The first time I'd come here, I'd wondered if it was real or synthetic, but of course, it couldn't be natural. The docks were far too extensive to be made of real wood.

The crowds had thinned out slightly, thanks to the rain. I paused to buy a flavored nutrient shake from a vendor when I heard a familiar voice behind me say, "Well, if it isn't Mr. Eighty-Three."

I turned, startled, to find Amyati behind me, wearing a predatory grin. She was dressed in a black-and-gold racing jumpsuit and had a hover-dart helmet tucked under one arm. Over her other shoulder, an odd-looking laser rifle was slung from a black nylon strap. Her long black hair was woven into a thick braid. The glossy strands glistened from the rain; she hadn't bothered with a coat or rain shield. I looked around but couldn't see a hover-dart anywhere. Had she parked it and followed me on foot?

"Fancy meeting you here," I said, hoping I sounded bantering and friendly. Of all the people I'd met at PA, Amyati was the only one who'd made no effort to be friendly. She hadn't said much of anything to me, now that I thought about it, but I'd been left with the distinct impression that she didn't like me much. To be fair, it might not have been personal. She didn't seem to like anyone, except for Sarah. But if she'd been following me, why would she reveal herself now? She'd approached me openly, so I was prepared to give her the benefit of the doubt.

"What's with the rifle?" I asked.

"My aunt asked me to pick it up for her on my way back to PA. It was delivered to a research lab near here this morning. Some kind of advanced prototype."

"No case?" I raised an eyebrow. "Odd way to care for cutting-edge technology."

"Alien tech doesn't typically come gift wrapped. You have to take it."

"I'm sorry, what?" Was she saying she'd stolen a piece of alien tech from a lab somewhere in the City? Just this morning? At her *aunt's* behest?

"You heard me." She grinned in a way that said she didn't really care if I'd heard her or not.

"Aren't you worried about reprisal?"

"From whom?" Her disdain was answer enough.

"Well, the Dragons, for one." I swept my nutrient shake in a wide arc. "This is their stomping ground."

"You would know."

I winced, then took a sip of nutrients to cover it up. It didn't taste quite like vanilla, but it was pretty close.

Amyati hadn't moved. She was watching me with a predatory look in her eye. I cocked my head. "Waiting for me to slap your wrist? If you think I'm going to quibble over what you do with your time, you haven't done your homework."

"No moral compass," she asked sweetly, "or no guts?"

I met her gaze squarely. "You tell me." My heart was suddenly hammering in my chest. She was 68 AV, and I didn't have a clue what she could do; didn't know what I could do either. But she didn't need to know that. The way she'd greeted me made it clear she knew I'd scored higher than her.

A long moment passed while her narrowed eyes searched my face. I took a casual sip of my nutrients, trying hard to project an aura of careless confidence. She rolled her eyes as she turned away and began striding down the pier. I breathed a secret sigh of relief and fell into step behind her, finding I had to work slightly to keep pace with the tall girl's purposeful gait. The laser rifle made me nervous; I didn't want to let it out of my sight until I knew what she intended to do with it.

"You should be careful not to let all the talk go to your head," she advised me over her shoulder. "I watched the footage, and if you ask me, it's hardly conclusive."

The abrupt shift of topic left me wrong-footed. "What are you talking about?" I stopped suddenly, raised my voice to call after her. "Wait, you mean the fight? Here, at the docks?"

She pivoted to walk backward as she answered, "Yes. I wanted to see for myself if you really were the savant they seem to think you are." She shrugged and faced front again. "Can't say I'm impressed."

I'd almost missed that last part in the babble of voices around me. People had turned to stare at us curiously. I hurried to catch up, pitching my voice lower. "What do you mean?" And why had she been keeping tabs on me?

"There's plenty of footage available from drones and citizens who were in the area at the time," Amyati informed me. "I've watched the fight from numerous angles, but the director's assumption that you're some kind of phenom seems unfounded. There is, at one point, a flash of fire. There's a quick blast of something that could be kinetic energy, maybe sonic. One of the Dragons falls upward, momentarily. Could be a gravity control thing, but that's pretty rare, so probably just more tele-K."

We'd reached the open end of the pier. A sizeable barge a few hundred meters out was in the process of being loaded with heavy cargo containers. The barge was painted a uniform matte black. It was conspicuous in its complete lack of identifying marks—no obvious company logos adorned the hull; no faction flags flew proudly from the conning tower—which meant they were either very confident in their safety, because of who was backing them, or else they were unaffiliated and were hoping others would *think* they were confident. Amyati leaned against the rail to one side and eyed the activity on the ship's deck. A handful of people were laboriously moving larger containers with deck-mounted cranes, trying to balance the load. A few workers on gravity lifts shuttled smaller boxes and crates from shore.

"The thing is," Amyati continued without looking at me, "none of the footage really shows it's you causing the flashy effects. Too many bodies in the way. You do appear to experience an uncanny surge of strength toward the end, but that could have just been adrenaline. Nanos sometimes amplify the fight-or-flight response. Whatever causes you to rally, it doesn't last long."

"Why are you telling me all this? How did you even find out about the director's theory?"

"Call it professional curiosity. I like to keep tabs on potential rivals."

I nearly choked on my nutrients. "*Rivals?* Amyati, I barely know you!"

"Your point? You scored much higher on the AV test than expected, but there's a big question mark when it comes to what gives you that kind of potential." She sneered. "It sure has heck isn't the shoelace thing."

So, now she was fishing for what I could do. Probably best if she didn't realize I had no idea either.

"How do you even know what I scored? Mr. Gold and the geeks wouldn't have told you."

"The second group you tested with was all very impressed by the Super-powered teen in their midst." She raised an eloquent shoulder. "People talk."

I sighed, but it was no less than I'd expected. It bothered me, though: Had she seriously followed me down here with a laser rifle to intimidate me? I didn't want to believe she was that ruthless, but what else could it be? Was it a calculated attempt at scaring information out of me or simply an opportunistic thing? She'd said she was here anyway, picking up the gun for her aunt (*Stealing it!* I reminded myself sternly). Maybe she'd spotted me and seen a chance to get some questions answered. It was getting harder and harder to give her the benefit of the doubt, though.

I seriously doubted anything I might say would satisfy her curiosity. I tried anyway. "For what it's worth, I agree that the director's out to lunch. It was probably Sarah. She chased off the Dragons, according to Kevin. I bet it's all stuff she can fire off at range."

"Most of it could be," Amyati agreed, "but the timing doesn't add up. You can find footage of her making her way across the City and arriving on the scene *after* you've had the stuffing kicked out of you. All she really does is show up at the last second and bowl them over with a massive telekinetic blast. Half of them cartwheel into the water. The other half pick themselves up, only to be confronted by Sarah wreathed in fire and lightning. They quickly think better of tangling with her and run off."

A fearsome description of Sarah's powers. *Where is she now?* I wondered. I turned away from Amyati to stare at the barge, nutrient shake forgotten in my hand. Try as I might, I couldn't feel Sarah at the other end of our link. Did it even exist anymore? I shook my head. The real question, I thought, was how had Amyati known about the director's theory? And how had she gained access to the footage to see for herself? Some of it could be public, traffic cams and so on, but most would be encrypted by AI, owned by whichever news syndicate or local authority group had had drones in the area to take the images in the first place. You would need some influence to broker a deal and get ahold of it. I eyed her sidelong. How wealthy was she? She certainly acted like the rest of us were commoners.

A new thought struck me: Who was her *aunt?* What kind of woman casually asks her niece to drop by a lab that is presumably well guarded to pilfer alien tech? And what kind of girl would be so cavalier about it? Their moral compasses must be at least a little skewed, but how far would they be willing to go to get what they wanted? Could Amyati or her aunt have hacked PA's databanks? Why would they bother? My powers were hardly important. Even if they thought my high AV score might eventually cause me to become a threat to . . . whatever their business was . . . I clearly wasn't a threat yet. So, why antagonize me?

I gave up trying to figure it out and simply asked her, point-blank. "What's your game, Amyati?" I didn't attempt to keep the disgust from my voice.

Her reply wasn't reassuring: "Who says I'm playing?" The look in her eyes would have made a glacier shiver.

An uneasy silence fell between us. It was time to walk away. Whatever this was, I didn't want anything to do with it. My spine itched at the thought of turning my back on Amyati and the laser rifle, but there was nothing I could do about it. Or was there? Would my power obey if I needed it? I eyed her sidelong, but her attention was back on the barge. "Tell me something, Amyati . . . since you're feeling so talkative."

She smirked. I took it as an invitation to continue.

"Why was Kevin here the day I was attacked by the Dragons?" I'd said it to distract her, more than anything else, but as soon as the question was out, I realized I wanted to know. I hadn't asked Kevin because I hadn't wanted to sound suspicious; I knew I had a tendency to be a little paranoid. I didn't want him to think I was ungrateful. But it did seem mighty convenient he'd been on hand to summon Sarah and apply his healing powers.

Amyati was only too happy to show off her superior knowledge of recent events. "Kevin was here to collect a shipment of seed samples to take back to the Greenhouse. A dockworker slipped and fell. Hit his head on the rocks on his way into the water. Kevin didn't hesitate to assist, but he called in to report the incident." Her tone suggested he was weak for seeking support. "PA agreed with Kevin's assessment of the situation: they didn't want him on his own down here, even if all he was doing was helping. It's Dragon territory; they'd kill to get a healer on their payroll."

"So, they sent Sarah as backup. Wouldn't a fully trained Super have been better?" The strap of the laser rifle looked pretty sturdy. I could probably prevent her from taking aim, if not completely bind her arms, assuming my power didn't have its own ideas.

Amyati moved her head, something between a nod and a negation. "Few Supers at PA have Sarah's wattage. Besides, she's reached a point where field training is the best way forward. It must have seemed like a good opportunity for PA. The Dragons are relatively minor Supers for the most part, nothing compared to Sarah. And since Kevin was aiding a dockworker, it was unlikely to devolve into a conflict unless the Dragons tried to keep him here when he was done. Sarah was simply insurance."

I must have walked right by him, oblivious. Kevin's benevolent attempt at healing a stranger *had* devolved into a conflict, but not because of him.

"So you see," continued Amyati, "Kevin was at the other end of the pier when your little scuffle went down. Things had already escalated, and the anomalous abilities had already been fired by the time Sarah arrived. Kevin didn't get involved until after she'd cleared the scene. So, who activated those powers?"

I cocked my head at her. We were back to this again, were we? She was like a Fetch with a stick. "It must have been the Dragons. Maybe they were trying to blast me and got each other by mistake."

She nodded. "Reasonable assumption, except it's easy to pair facial recognition with PANet databases to identify everyone involved from the footage. None of them have the appropriate powers, except for a minor tele-K, who, incidentally, was the one you stabbed with the ion-knife."

Whom my power had stabbed without my consent, actually, but why split hairs? So, here she was, prodding me to reveal my abilities because the footage hadn't reassured her. Like she'd said, I was a big question mark. But she would have to learn to live with the mystery. I didn't have any answers for her, and there was no point standing here denying knowledge of my own powers. I could protest until I was blue in the face; she wasn't going to believe me. Besides, I didn't see any reason to enlighten her about my own ignorance.

Amyati had opened her mouth to say something more, but I interrupted her. "Hey, is that guy on the barge waving at us?" I pointed.

She glanced back at the barge, then stood up straight. To my surprise, it was a signal she'd been waiting for. She unslung the laser rifle, holding it aloft. Within moments, it had left her grip and was sailing serenely across the open water toward the barge. A man dressed all in black was standing by the forward rail, ready to receive it. I looked back and forth between them but couldn't tell which one of them was levitating the weapon. Her eyes were locked on the rifle's progress, but so were his. Neither of them wanted it to fall in the drink.

I handed her my nutrient shake. "Hold this." I'd hardly touched it. Amyati took it with distaste and set it aside on the rail. The laser rifle continued sedately on its way, not even a wobble of distracted concentration. *Darn. Not her, then.* It would have been satisfying to see the weapon disappear beneath the waves.

Still, I felt a lot better about my situation. She'd voluntarily disarmed herself, completing the delivery of the stolen weapon to her aunt's people. She didn't seem concerned that I knew what she'd done, so I didn't expect her to try to silence me. If anything, her brazenness indicated she was proud of her involvement and she wanted people to know it. And why not? Outside of this district, who would care? When it came right down to it, the Dockside Dragons were little more than lizards with a grandiose name. They didn't have any allies with real clout. Conversely, it was safe to assume Amyati's aunt was a power to be reckoned with in the City. She had an effective information network capable of reaching into districts controlled by other factions, and she was confident enough to run her delivery barge through territory she didn't directly control without flying her colors. Was Amyati just an errand girl, or did it go deeper than that? Made me wonder who the Dragons had stolen the rifle from in the first place, but it was probably better that I didn't know.

Amyati was giving me a long, dark look that I didn't much care for. "Are we done here?" I asked.

"For now." She stared at me awhile longer, but I refused to show her that I was intimidated. Whatever she was playing at, it had nothing to do with me. Whatever she read in my face, she nodded to herself, seemingly satisfied. Without another word, she turned on her heel and walked away.

I watched her go, wondering. The aggressive Indian girl was friends with Sarah. I didn't know how I felt about that, but warm and fuzzy wasn't it. I didn't much care to admit it, even to myself, but despite my posturing in front of Amyati, I *was* intimidated. She knew a lot more than she should, and she wasn't afraid to step on toes to get what she wanted. She also appeared to have few qualms about questions of right and wrong. Either she believed might made right, or she was completely devoted to her aunt's criminal enterprise. Ah, but even the word "criminal" implied that there were rigid laws for them to break. The City was a patchwork of competing groups struggling to enforce their own sets of rules, and all any of it really proved was that Amyati's aunt wielded enough power to trample roughshod over the rules set by others. That made her the one setting the rules, didn't it? Everyone *else* were criminals.

Before long, Amyati was lost in the crowd. I kept watching, my mind turning our conversation over and over, wondering if there had been something I missed. A few moments later, a sleek black and gold hover-dart lifted off from the plaza. The rain had eased, and the rider's gold-trimmed black jumpsuit glinted in the watery sunlight. She shot away between tall buildings and was instantly lost to sight.

What a day. And it wasn't even noon, yet! But Amyati had been an unpleasant surprise; she wasn't why I had come here. Turning about, I clambered down off the end of the dock, searching blindly for footing on the rocks below while I hung from the splintery boards. My questing shoelaces found the nearest boulder, then guided my foot to a ledge of rock. I swung forward to shift my weight and dropped beneath the pier. My landing was awkward. I pinwheeled my arms, recovered my balance on the rain-slicked boulder, and crouched low. The water slapping the rocks a little further down echoed from the wood overhead. I leaned against the thick pylon supporting the docks and caught my breath. Now, where would it be? Was the tide too high? Had it been washed away? I began hunting among the boulders.

When I finally spotted it, I gave a little whoop of triumph and squatted to retrieve it. The ion-blade looked a little battered, but overall showed remarkably few signs of ill use. It was wedged deep between two large boulders. Dark water filled the gap just below where the knife had jammed. Lying on my side, I reached out, but it was just a few inches beyond my fingertips. I sat up and pulled off one of my shoes. Holding it by one lace, I lowered it into the gap between the rocks, hunching low to keep an eye on my target and concentrating furiously. Eventually, my dangling shoelace was coaxed to make a loop and snare the handle. I sat up, grinning, and hauled on my shoelace until the weapon popped free with a reluctant scrape of metal on stone.

"Ha!" I was inordinately pleased to finally have it in hand.

There was no sign of the Merchant Gull that had gone after it. Stupid bird had probably been zapped and washed away by the next tide, if a nano-swarm hadn't found it first. The blade, on the other hand, had simply shorted out. It was slightly corroded, perhaps, but there were no obvious signs of damage. It could probably be refurbished with a quick trip through the recycler back at PA.

I stuffed my foot back in my shoe and levered to my feet. Assuming PA had a pattern on file for an ion-blade, it could be done, I thought. Would they? These things were pretty dangerous. If they did have a blueprint, it might be off-limits to most of the staff and students, with any attempts to fabricate one flagged for follow up by PASec. I looked at the blade, turning it this way and that. I didn't really care if it worked or not, I decided. It was a souvenir of my unfortunate encounter with the Dragons. I felt unreasonably cheered by locating it.

I began hopping from rock to rock, making my way back along the pier. The blade put me in mind of a Super, in a way: it looked like a normal, everyday knife, until it was ionized; then it crackled with energy. I tried to picture Sarah, wreathed in lightning. Throwing fire. I couldn't do it. She was too introverted. That kind of bombastic power seemed more appropriate for someone like Alan, or Jake, not shy little Sarah. I just didn't understand how she and Amyati had become friends.

It took me some time to work my way along the rocks until I reached a point where I could easily climb back onto the pier. When I did, I scanned the length of the boardwalk for Amyati, or any of her aunt's cronies, not that I really knew what I was looking for. People dressed all in black and looking sinister, maybe? I'd seen her leave, true, but that didn't mean she couldn't circle around and come back.

There was nothing suspicious that I could see, however, not even with my overactive imagination. Not entirely reassured, I folded up the ion-blade and stuffed it in my back pocket. Then I left the Dragon's docks and made my way back to PA.

XI

My schedule, when it arrived, turned out to be a tightly organized collection of meetings with tutors, support counsellors, peer groups, and physical trainers, intermixed with an eclectic selection of classes aimed at digging into the science and mechanics of Super-powers. While a lot of this stuff was rigidly fixed, the timing of a surprising amount of it shifted fluidly depending on the needs of the people involved, the priorities of Project Arete leadership, and our own inclinations. Everyone's Maps were updated in real time, keeping us abreast of schedule changes, but it made for some frantic moments when I occasionally realized something had been moved around and I was nowhere near where I needed to be.

The weeks quickly became a blur of activity. I drove myself crazy trying to be in three places at once until I realized PA's faculty was well compensated to be as accommodating as possible. Missed classes and training sessions could quickly and easily be rescheduled, thanks to the Maps that everyone carried. This go-with-the-flow approach to education was sometimes maddening, but Project Arete managed to pack a lot of stuff into any given day with minimum hiccups. Of course, the onus was on me to be ready to adjust on the fly. PA assumed its members were invested in self-improvement and the betterment of humankind as a whole, and thus would make every effort to fulfill our itineraries. Slackers would quickly find themselves overwhelmed and falling by the wayside. I found myself wishing for something more structured, sometimes, but it was adapt or be left behind, so I adapted. Despite this, the hectic schedule was neatly balanced with time for socializing, exploration of individual interests, and sporadic moments of time allotted to do nothing at all.

Empty time is an aspect of human need that few people pay much attention to, and I admit, I tended to fill up my spare time as much as possible in an effort to avoid being alone with my thoughts. My Super-power involved making connections, that much seemed certain, and it was proving to be almost too good at it. Because I wasn't entirely in control of it, a frustrating and often challenging side effect was that I tended to make chains of logic out of things that weren't truly connected at all. My power wanted to link things together, and if I didn't actively seek to make the connections myself, it wouldn't always wait for my permission. I didn't like the way my mind so easily spiraled into a loop of pessimistic trouble-seeking. Soaring mental skyscrapers—complete with a population of sinister phantoms—were constantly being built from the scrapheap of my stray thoughts. While there was a part of me that fervently believed something bigger *was* going on below the surface of Project Arete, most of the time I tried very hard to tread water and avoid diving too deep.

My nagging uncertainties aside, I was slowly settling into the swing of things. I found myself with ample opportunity to experiment, following the suggestions of my various teachers. I played around with numerous approaches to guiding and directing my power. All too often, it was an exercise in frustration; despite diligent practice, little I did seemed to improve my control. Still, few and far between as they were, even the smallest of breakthroughs felt like a major victory and fueled my desire to continue.

The time and effort required to focus on my practice was beneficial in calming my mind and my natural inclination toward suspicion, but it was still difficult not to see conspiracies looming behind everything we did. It required concerted effort not to sabotage my good fortune. Most days, I was simply thankful that I was aware of this problematic aspect of my powers and could work to counteract it. With a little mental effort, I could usually set aside my unruly ideas as so much hokum. But then . . . why all the secrecy surrounding Project Arete?

Sigh. *Leave it alone, David.*

As the days went by, I looked for any opportunity to talk to Sarah. The bond that had formed when we first met had faded, but it was impossible to forget what it had felt like. It had been so much more than simply knowing her name: I had known *her,* inside and out. She plainly remembered the surprising intimacy of that moment just as well as I did. If anything, she was avoiding me because of it. I wanted to renew our connection, explore it; I felt sure it must be an aspect of my abilities. If I could only spend some time with her, I was certain I would gain some insight into what I could do. But it was difficult to get past her severe social anxiety. Often, she found it impossible to respond to direct attention at all. She stuttered uncontrollably, and always, always, she blushed so much it made me embarrassed, too. I felt like a great clumsy lout around her. The last thing I wanted was for her or anyone else to think I was trying to bully her into anything. I kept waiting and hoping that she would warm up to me. Maybe, I thought, she'd had a glimpse of my inner landscape during our brief joining. I could only hope she'd liked what she'd seen. Perhaps she was still turning it over in her mind, trying to decide if she could trust her intuition. I knew I couldn't push her. It was hard to be patient, though. Living on the streets had taught me to follow my instincts, to make snap decisions. When things got rough, time to think things through was a luxury. Hesitation could be disastrous. So, in a way, the crazy schedule was good. It kept me occupied while I waited, hoping.

Cory was a sporadic presence during my early days at Project Arete. Sometimes I struggled to keep him in mind; other times, it was impossible to get rid of him. He would pester me with endless questions and demands for attention. It was awkward when others were around, but his power seemed to selectively snip the idea of him from a person's mind without seriously impacting other thoughts. There was confusion, certainly, and there was plenty of head-scratching as people tried to recall just what they'd been doing or saying. Invariably, some bridge between the moment just past and the moment to come would form. They'd fill in the gap with whatever made the most sense to them. If any of them ever got together to compare their fuzzy memories over coffee and found discrepancies, I never heard of it.

Unlike my connection to Sarah, my link to Cory seemed to be stabilizing. He may have been gaining a small measure of control, at least where I was concerned, but I didn't think that could account for my persistent memory of him. Not entirely. I still felt the constant pressure of his power, looking for a way in. He *was* wiping my mind of his presence, all the time. However, I'd noticed my shoelaces weren't moving so freely on their own anymore. It seemed the more I was around Cory, the more my power was turned toward keeping me tied to all the other versions of myself I'd seen in the Quantum Cube, anchoring me to memories of him that he couldn't reach. It was a tenuous theory, at best, but I hadn't yet been able to come up with a better one. At least it also explained why my power was acting up less. It was something to be thankful for, even if it was an incidental sort of self-control.

My education in the district school system where I'd grown up had ended early thanks to my willful Super-power. My parents had attempted to continue my learning by homeschooling, with mixed results. I enjoyed discovering new things, but my father and I were both stubborn to a fault, and he found it difficult to cope with my Super-powered outbursts. Besides, when he had a commission from the Sunset Archaeological Society, he had little time for me. His passion for restoring ancient history would consume him completely.

My mother would step in, then, and while her patience was bound-less, I hated knowing I was inconveniencing her. It took me years to work up the courage, but I eventually struck out on my own. It was better than being a constant thorn in their side. Now, Project Arete was offering me the opportunity to make up for lost time. I didn't want my association with them to end the same way.

They had the tools and the people to teach me everything I had failed to take in through formal schooling, but I was way behind the others in my classes. In order to learn more about my powers, I needed to master concepts in biology, genetics, mathematics, and computer science. Super abilities were a manifestation of inheritable traits, the result of the ongoing evolution of our biological processes and humanity's improving mental and emotional integration with reality. It was pretty esoteric, a lot of it, but the upshot was compara-tively simple: my continuing failure to fully understand and actively control my powers was a symptom of not knowing enough about them. Since all the meditation and time spent attempting to use my power wasn't consistently helping, it seemed to me that only further improving my education would ultimately solve the problem.

Somewhere, I felt sure, I would stumble over some tidbit of infor-mation that would prove to be the key to unlocking my self-control. So, while I enrolled in all the usual Super-control classes that were beneficial to others—meditation and mindfulness, visualization practice, and endless repetitive attempts at activating and deactivat-ing abilities—I also pursued courses in nano-technology and pro-gramming. Human evolution—in particular, the evolution of the Super—was directly linked to the Cupids, after all. Their perfection of humanity's early attempts at nano-tech, the mechanical womb, and their deep understanding of our DNA were critical elements driving the growth of the burgeoning population of Supers.

Added to this were PA's mandatory classes in neuroscience (which I found fascinating), philosophy (which was largely concerned with

the ethics of the use and abuse of Super-powers), and last, but definitely not least: physical education. Centuries of science had made
the benefits of physical fitness crystal clear, but for me, it was also the
most promising path toward control. I often found exercise better
than all the meditation in the world when it came to clearing my
head and getting a handle on my abilities.

In sum, it was an awful lot to find piled on my plate. It hadn't
been that long ago when there had been little to concern me beyond
where my next meal might come from or where I was going to sleep.
Now I fell into bed most nights feeling like a sponge that had soaked
up more water than it could hold. Squeeze me, half of what I'd
learned might splash right back out. I was mentally exhausted and
bone weary, too. Martial arts, Power Ball, and wall climbing formed
the backbone of my physical training, but I ran, biked, kayaked,
and regularly went to the Gym for weight-training—all of which
led to physiotherapy more often than I care to admit. But I'd be
hard pressed to think of a time in my life when I was happier or
more satisfied. The days were packed, I was learning and growing
in new and exciting ways, and there was no end in sight. Sarah
might be avoiding me, but still, life was good—even if my hard-won
gains in controlling my unreliable abilities were rarer than moments
with Sarah.

More than a month into this new life, my Map pinged.

"*David! Have a few minutes to spare? That little conduit problem
. . . don't know how you did it, but it was a tremendous breakthrough.
We've been working around the clock since then and we've had spectacular success. Wondering if you might like to see the results? I want to thank
you in person. The whole team does.*"

It was from Dawn. The Map displayed the location of her team's
lab. It was labeled "Computer Sciences Division." Huh . . . so that
wiring diagram they had been working on was for some kind of
computer. I wondered if it was connected to the Quantum Cube in

some way. I found it gratifying that she attributed their success to my insight. Here, at least, was a connection I had made successfully.

I didn't have to think it over long: I could use a win for a change. What little time I had managed to find to have a quiet word with Sarah was never private. If not Amyati, then classmates, PA staff . . . someone was always around. Sarah was simply too shy. She could never sufficiently relax her guard enough to speak comfortably in those moments, not about anything serious, anyway. The brief and tentative connections felt worse than not being able to make a connection at all.

To make matters worse, the Super-Power Research and Training Division hadn't yet figured out what to do with me. As far as they could tell, I didn't actually fall into any part of their Super-power chart, which hinted that my particular array of powers was something never before encountered. There were elements to what I did that suggested connections to other, known abilities, like tele-K, but we had quickly discovered it wasn't enough to guide our experiments. For over a month, it had been like stabbing blindly in the dark, hoping to strike an invisible target. If we could just make contact, we could determine the general shape of things and begin to draw an outline of what we were facing. So, while it was true that I could make shoelaces wiggle around all on their own within a limited range, that aspect of my abilities was severely restricted in scope. I couldn't manipulate staples, for example, or paper clips, or zippers. Arguably they were all connectors of some kind, but they ignored me just like Amyati did. Even my ability to manipulate shoelaces, ropes, and wires wouldn't rate much more than a two or a three on the AV scale, all by itself. So how had I scored eighty-three?

Surprisingly, there was an argument to be made for some kind of precognitive abilities. Not that I could see the future, exactly, but the thing with the wiring chart had been one "aha!" moment that had been almost supernatural: an intuitive leap, my power instantly connecting the dots and guiding me along an invisible string through a branching labyrinth of possibilities. My insight into Miguel's power transfer conduit design had happened so naturally, so easily, I'd hardly thought of it as amazing at the time. What had been unusual about it, when I considered the implications later, was that I'd felt so certain I had made the difference in their efforts. I'd *known* exactly what to do to put them on their best path to success and never doubted it would work. Now, here was a message from Dawn as proof, staring me in the face.

Even this couldn't account for an 83 AV, though. Taken together, a little precognition and telekinesis were like a match held up to the sun. Locked up somewhere inside me was a maelstrom of potential, and we had no idea what it was for. Believe me, it was terrifying to contemplate, especially when considered in the context of my powers spontaneously expressing themselves ever since I was a little kid. We all knew I was doing *something*. We just didn't know *what*. Dawn had just offered me the chance to see the results of my power activating. It was a no brainer, really. Maybe it would give me some insight.

I dropped the rest of the afternoon's classes to pay Dawn and her team a visit. I needed the sense of accomplishment it might bring. It took very little time for my Map to rearrange my schedule. Helpfully, it also marked restaurants along the route, as my stomach growled. I had to laugh. Smart tech, indeed! Following my hunger, I made my way to the Computer Sciences Division.

When I arrived at the CSD labs, I was greeted by an effervescent intern in her early twenties with a shock of spiky blue hair, unnaturally bright blue eyes, and a pugnacious little upturned nose. Her name tag read "Elm." With her very bubbly assistance, I found my way to Dawn's lab. The door was closed, but it buzzed at my approach and a little green light lit up beside the Map scanner. The click of the lock disengaging was invitation enough, so I stepped inside.

Dawn and Miguel were standing at a computer terminal mounted in an alcove in the far wall, animatedly discussing what was on the screen. They were dressed casually in dark slacks and blue blazers. To my right, leaning back in a high-end leather chair with his feet up on a heavy synthetic oak desk, was Francis, wearing blue jeans and a lab coat. His eyes were closed. He appeared to be fast asleep.

The rest of the room was a cluttered jumble of computer towers, cables, shelves overflowing with books and flimsies, loose stacks of paper, plastic tablets, smart-glass interfaces, discarded pens, pointers, and cola cans. Charts and diagrams plastered the walls three layers thick. Holographic representations of complicated mechanical components in exploded view hung about the room like the ghosts of ancient machines. The only thing missing from this mad scientist's laboratory were the bubbling alchemical vials and tubes. A large double-sided smart-glass screen on a wheeled frame, mounted on a pivot so it could be flipped over, stood out at an angle from the left wall, blocking my view of that side of the room. It, too, was displaying devices, equations, and notes. A soft blue glow emanated from behind it.

Hearing me enter, Dawn and Miguel broke off their discussion. "David, hi! Come in!" called Dawn. Miguel raised a hand in greeting. His grin was warm and welcoming.

I navigated the precarious path between stacked computer equipment and tottering bookshelves and met them in the center of the room. Dawn surprised me with a hug, then stepped back, holding my shoulders and beaming at me. Miguel smirked when I cleared my throat uncomfortably.

Dawn apologized and let her hands drop. "I'm just so excited! And we really owe this breakthrough to you. Miguel's design was the perfect foundation, but you're the one who streamlined it."

Miguel nodded. "It only required a few changes to realize how efficiently you had modified it. That's when we realized the same ideas could be applied to other areas of the power relay system."

"And not just there!" enthused Dawn. "Once we had the solution, it seemed obvious: everything had been designed on the same principles. Power flow, fluid dispersion, nano-paths, crystal lattices, optics, everything. We were able to feed the new parameters into the computer and the nano-builders did the rest."

"And then we flipped the switch. *And it worked.*" Miguel's voice was hushed, almost awed.

"Come and meet Simantha," said Dawn.

"Fair warning," put in Miguel hastily, "there still seem to be some weird power cascades in the circuitry, so we're keeping it behind a protective field for now. But if the kinks settle out, we'll probably let it out for a walk. Maybe you'd like to be the one to show it around?"

Stepping around the larger smart-glass screen after Dawn and Miguel, I saw the entire left wall was a force-field. The blue glow came from this. The naked girl sitting on a padded bench in the cell behind the force-field was perhaps eighteen years old and was astonishingly beautiful, even by customizable modern standards. Though seated, I could see she was tall, with an athletic build and a self-possessed, erect posture. Strong, slim hands rested comfortably on well-muscled thighs. She stared straight ahead, chin slightly raised. Her hair was flaming red and fell in glorious ringlets about her shoulders, just long enough to hide her bare breasts. Her stomach was flat, slightly chiseled.

Seeing me, she stood gracefully and stepped toward the glowing barrier, making no effort to cover herself. Embarrassed, I looked away from her nudity, but not before I noticed the tattoo that partially circled her belly button. It was a silver crescent moon, but unlike any tattoo I had ever seen before. The ink shimmered with silvery opalescence.

"Greetings, David," she said. Her voice was like warm honey. "I am told you had a pivotal role to play in my reconstruction. Please accept my sincerest gratitude." She made a strange gesture, like a benediction.

I mumbled something toward the ceiling. Belatedly divining the reason for my distress, Dawn snatched up a spare lab coat from a nearby pile of gadgetry and stuffed it into a hatch next to the force-field. Once the hatch on our side had clicked shut, Simantha opened a matching hatch inside the enclosure to retrieve the coat. She wrapped it around herself unselfconsciously. Even with the lab coat on, Simantha's long bare legs were a revelation to me. I had to force myself to keep my eyes raised.

She turned her aristocratic face toward me and stared at me with frank curiosity. Her eyes were opalescent silver, shimmering with reflected light like her tattoo. "You do not speak, David. I am distressed by this. I feel I am accustomed to being answered."

I stammered out an apology, floundered to find something to say. I was rescued by Dawn. "Simantha was found in pieces at the bottom of the bay," she explained, "along with parts from numerous other very human-looking bio-mechanical creations."

"It was the only one that was more or less intact," added Miguel. "Most of its parts could be accounted for."

Simantha watched me with an eerie calm as they explained her restoration.

Dawn was almost gushing. "A Cupid oversaw the retrieval—can you believe that? The translators believe they may have had a hand in creating her!"

"It's astonishingly sophisticated. Unbelievably advanced AI, self-repairing nano-molecular networks, percipient plastic skin . . ." Miguel trailed off, shaking his head. "Just incredible."

I finally found my voice. "Why Simantha?"

Simantha herself responded. "Dawn was inspired by the idea that I am a simulated human. She offered 'Sim' names, so that we could speak with more familiarity." It felt like she pitched her voice just for me. I shivered.

"Simantha stuck." Dawn grinned.

"I much prefer it to Simone or Simiya," Simantha agreed.

"So . . . you were just laying down there? Under the water?" I glanced from Simantha to Dawn and Miguel, then back again. "Why? For how long?"

She turned away, looking pensive. "I am uncertain."

Miguel piped up, excited. "Its nano-machines are ancient. They're constantly self-replicating, breaking down old and worn-out nanos, repurposing themselves. Every generation a little counter ticks over. The network is over three thousand years old. Somewhere along the line, a massive energy surge fried most of them and reset the rest. Then they were encased in some kind of alien glass. The remnants have been puttering away ever since, completely cut off from what they required to rebuild."

Dawn nodded. "We chipped her from the ice, so to speak, then offered her some fresh building material."

"What began as a tiny scattering of apparent dust was soon a living network of machinery. We pieced the body back together, and the nanos moved back in. We assumed they would finish repairs." Miguel paused in his recounting and frowned.

"And?" I encouraged.

"And nothing." Miguel shrugged.

"Nothing?"

"Progress stalled. The network was fully operational, but it had no schematics to work with."

Dawn sighed. "We were forced to salvage parts from the remains of the other simulant humans found with Simantha and reverse engineer instructions. We spent the better part of a year cobbling together an approach to simulant design and programming. In theory, all we needed to do was start the process. Once they had something to work with, Simantha's nanos would learn rapidly and take over. The core of her intelligence and awareness are relatively undamaged. We assumed she would be able to guide the process once a new foundation was created."

"Impossible to say just how much of its original sentience or personality remains," Miguel contradicted. "A lot of its behavior is likely just mimicry."

Dawn rolled her eyes. She and the simulant girl shared a secret smile.

"But isn't it a little precipitous to . . ." I trailed off, looking at Simantha uneasily. I had been about to question the prudence of the project right in front of the results. She stood near the force-field, a knowing half-smile still on her lips. Her behavior was remarkably human.

"Despite what Miguel thinks," she offered ruefully, "I am as fully myself as I know how to be. I am not a threat to you or anyone else."

"So why the cage?" When Simantha only lifted her shoulders in response, I turned to Dawn and Miguel, arms folded.

"Well, she is a bit of an unknown still," hedged Dawn. She smiled apologetically at Simantha.

"It's downright unpredictable," Miguel asserted, speaking over his coworker. "We may have designed most of the new operating instructions ourselves, but once it took over . . ." He spread his hands. "We have no idea what its original purpose was. Dawn's assumption is that Cupids built a bunch of these things and turned them loose to observe and report on humanity when they first arrived, then axed the project when it was no longer necessary. But if I were a fully aware AI and that had been done to me? I'd be choked." He turned his grim countenance on Dawn. "So yeah, a little caution is in order."

This felt like familiar ground, something they'd hashed over many times before, with Simantha included, apparently. She spoke up in her own defense. "I cannot think of any further safety protocols that might satisfy you, Miguel. I consented to the installation of the kill switch. What more assurance do you need?"

Miguel scowled and turned away. The mood had shifted quite suddenly, and I was uncertain why I was being included in this conversation.

Dawn supplied the answer. "That's part of why we invited you down here, David. We can't just leave Simantha in the cage, but we can't just let her roam freely either."

"I still think it's too soon," warned Miguel. "But have it your way." He walked away, shaking his head.

Dawn raised an eyebrow at Simantha, and the simulant girl nodded and turned to me. "There is a fail-safe in place that will instantly stop all neural traffic through my nano-network, effectively rendering me comatose by paralyzing my nano-machines and preventing them from sending signals." She gave me a moment to digest this. I stared at her, entirely unsure of what I was supposed to say. "Knowing this," she continued, "would you consent to chaperone me through the Project Arete facility?"

"Wait, you want *me* to babysit?" I was simultaneously thrilled and horrified at the thought of spending time alone with this very attractive and clearly intelligent young woman who could probably twist my head off faster than anyone could activate the kill switch. "Why me?"

"Call it a hunch," suggested Dawn. "Francis sometimes foresees the right decision before all the facts are in, and he has a good feeling about you."

I pursed my lips, looked over at the man still dozing at his desk. A Precog? What, exactly, had he seen or sensed about me? "Dawn . . ." I began.

"David, please." She put her hand on my arm. "Just think about it, okay?"

If they really didn't know what Simantha had been designed for, then I certainly didn't have a clue. While she appeared to be a Normal human, she was in truth a very sophisticated facsimile with nano-enhanced biological and mechanical systems. As such, it was highly likely Simantha possessed above-average (even Super-level) agility, speed, strength, and accuracy, along with extremely rapid reaction times. Shouldn't a Super like Alan or Jake—who might have a chance of keeping up with her if she went haywire—be the one to play caretaker? I may have scored eighty-three on my AV test, but that alone wasn't enough to justify trusting me with something like this.

"If it helps," said Dawn into my frowning silence, "there's no evidence of weapon systems of any kind. Not in Simantha, or in any of the other simulant remains. It's like I said, they were probably just observers."

In which case, the kill switch seemed extreme. I said as much.

"I don't disagree," Dawn sympathized. "But it's better to play it safe."

Ultimately, though, it had been Simantha who had decided. She had volunteered to have the kill switch installed, in order to mollify Miguel and Francis. No wonder Dawn scoffed at the idea that Simantha was dangerous. It was hard to think of a more telling demonstration of her good intentions.

I turned to Simantha. "Don't you know what your purpose was?" I asked.

Simantha bit her lip and shook her head. "There are gaps in my memories. Of one thing I am certain: I am very curious . . . about you, in particular, because Francis implies you will have some positive influence on me . . . about Project Arete, in general, but also, about the new world I find myself in." She smiled warmly, for all the world like one of my peers expressing a keen interest in a particular branch of science or the arts.

What had led to Simantha's eventual demise and centuries-long rest at the bottom of the bay was anybody's guess. There could be hundreds of explanations. I watched her carefully for any sign of disingenuousness, but she was comfortingly forthright. My instincts urged me to trust her. My paranoid worries were remarkably quiet, for a change. Something about her seemed . . . I don't know . . . very natural despite all evidence to the contrary. Except for her eyes, she was hardly inhuman. And it wasn't like I could hold that against her. Sarah's eyes were even more unusual than Simantha's, yet I could have easily lost myself in them if Sarah would only give me the chance. I felt a guilty twinge at that. I couldn't deny physical attraction to Simantha, but my feelings for Sarah had nothing to do with her body. Something about the introverted girl drew out my power, and I wanted to connect to her in that way again. If anything, our bodies would only get in the way. I felt our *souls* had made contact, however briefly.

I dragged my thoughts back to the present and looked at Simantha with new eyes. *Do you have a soul?* I wondered. *Would I be able to connect to you in the same way I linked with Sarah and Cory?* Her silver gaze held mine steadily. I couldn't help shivering a little.

Thinking about Cory made me curious: Had the tunnel where he'd encountered the Cupid been built for salvage teams to gain access to the seafloor in and around the simulants' graves? A secret tunnel neatly avoided the inevitable media attention of a major shore-based salvage operation employing boats, cranes, and submersibles. Divers could quickly and quietly retrieve all the most obvious remnants, and the tunnel, when it was completed, would provide access for a much slower and more careful exploration to follow. It explained some of Project Arete's need for secrecy, anyway. Fully sentient AI still hadn't been achieved by man-made machines, and if repairing an AI originally built by aliens eventually led to a working knowledge of advanced AI design, PA would want to keep a lid on it until they had secured appropriate leverage over the devices and their uses. Not to mention the debate over the potential dangers of artificial intelligence had raged unabated for centuries. Knowledge of Simantha's origins would only fan the flames.

And, of course, there were Cupids who actually spent time within the Project Arete facility! Cory bumping into one was one thing. Overseeing the recovery of simulant humans apparently discarded by them millennia ago was quite another—one more very good reason to maintain a veil of secrecy. There were a number of xeno-phobic human-supremacist groups out there who didn't appreciate the Cupids meddling with our evolution. The past four decades had been marred by sporadic attempts to assassinate Cupids, bomb Cupid-led facilities, and otherwise interfere with the aliens and their grand design. Entirely futile, of course, but that didn't stop the crazies from trying. I wasn't too sure how I felt about it, myself. I might have decided differently about sticking around if I had known Project Arete was so closely involved with the weird aliens. Super-power training was all well and good, but I didn't like the idea of the facility being targeted by extremist violence. More to the point, I didn't like the notion PA might be under direct alien command. If a Cupid had directed PA's salvage of the simulant pieces, what else might they order PA to get involved with? Interacting with a Cupid was safe enough, through the medium of computers and interpret-ers, but face-to-face? One of them could pop up just about anywhere in the facility without warning! I found the idea disturbing, to say the least.

Simantha's lovely face had slowly clouded while I stood, brows drawn down by the weight of my whirling thoughts. Now she was frowning with every sign of human anxiety. "I do not wish to pres-sure you, David," she said, "but your prolonged consideration of my request has me feeling worried. Please say you will agree." Her expression conveyed stark need.

In the end, it was Miguel's attitude that decided me. It was the first time I had encountered the deeply ingrained prejudice many people held toward artificial intelligences. The second, actually. The fact that Simantha hadn't even been given clothing until her nakedness made *me* uncomfortable would have been the first.

I met her glimmering silver eyes and resolutely set aside my concerns. "Simantha, I would be honored." I was surprised by just how much I meant it.

Simantha's face cleared abruptly, and she smiled, but her response was not what I was expecting. "Hello!" she said. "I am called Simantha. Who are you?" Her enchanting silver eyes were looking past me.

I turned to find Cory standing behind me, staring at the statuesque redhead in fascination. Startled at being addressed directly, he replied without thinking. "I'm Cory. You . . . you can remember me?"

"Certainly," said Simantha. "You are a very handsome young man. It is pleasant to look upon you. Do others not find it so?"

I could feel the pressure of his power trying to drive him from my mind, the way it had already erased him from Dawn, Miguel, and Francis's thoughts. Why wasn't she affected?

Cory swallowed. He knew a compliment when he heard one. But when had anyone given him a compliment so matter-of-factly? No one had ever truly *looked upon him*, as Simantha put it. He opted to change the subject. "Why are you behind a force-field?"

Of course! Her nano-network! It would act as a force-field, in a sense, deflecting his power. Not literally, but either she didn't have a simple meat-mind that Cory could fuzz, or if she did, the nano-net laced throughout didn't store memories the way a normal mind did, didn't *forget* the same way. Hers was a much deeper intertwining of biology and technology than the comparatively simple nanos swimming in my bloodstream, tweaking my natural processes.

My mind raced. I looked from Cory to Simantha with renewed wonder. Had I brought this about? By setting Dawn's team on the right track to rebuild Simantha, then by connecting with Cory in the Quantum Cube, I'd made it possible for him to follow me down here and discover her. Was I like him? Was my power always on, and I just didn't know it? Was I making connections all the time, influencing everyone around me? Was this happening because my power had reached out and nudged the pieces into place? I suddenly felt faint and slightly sick.

Simantha's voice brought me back to the moment. "Because," she answered, neatly paraphrasing Miguel's concerns, "I am an unknown quantity and, therefore, potentially unsafe. When it is determined that I am no threat to others, I will be released." She smiled warmly at me. "It will be soon, now, I think."

I found it hard to believe the decision might pivot on my choice, but the die had been cast. I held my peace, thoughts spinning, watching quietly as Cory approached Simantha's holding cell. The expression on his face was one of disbelief, mixed with awful hope. Was this my doing? I shifted my gaze, wondering. Had Francis foreseen this, too?

Dawn and Miguel, meanwhile, had hustled over to the computer on the far wall when Simantha began speaking to Cory, doubtless checking for malfunctions. Neither appeared to be aware of his presence. To them, it must seem she had suddenly begun talking to herself or some imaginary presence—not reassuring behavior, in an artificial intelligence. Or in regular people, come to think of it.

"Simantha," I said in a low voice, questioning the wisdom of it even as I said it, "Cory isn't easily noticed by others. His . . . abilities . . . make most people forget him within moments. If you want to speak to him directly, it would be best to do it when no one else is around or they might think you're malfunctioning, and then they might not let you out right away. But . . ." I hesitated, then plowed ahead. "Well, you seem to be working just fine, except for the missing memories. I quite like you, actually. There's something very genuine about you. And Cory really could use another friend." *So could I*, I didn't say.

Her silver eyes glinted as she shifted her attention to Dawn and Miguel, consulting their computer analysis. She nodded. "Thank you for your advice, David." And to Cory: "Please come and visit me again. I, too, have been forgotten for a long time."

Turning gracefully, Simantha walked back to the bench and resumed her seat. I pulled my unwilling gaze away from her long, slender legs and the enticing shadows beneath the lab coat, face burning. Cory stepped hastily out of the way as Dawn and Miguel hurried over.

"Uh, she said something about running an internal test of some kind," I hazarded.

Dawn's eyes lit up. "Self-diagnostics! I wondered. Well, we can't necessarily trust her results just yet, but we can build on that." She began to herd me toward the door. Cory followed, warily slipping past us into the hall. "Thanks for coming, David. I'm glad you agreed to show her around, but we've got a lot on our plate all of a sudden. These readings won't interpret themselves. I'll ping your Map as things develop, okay?"

In other words, I thought, *please leave now*.

As I exited the lab, I noticed Francis was awake. He was still seated at the desk, watching me in that same quiet, astute way he had when we first met. He didn't say anything, but I had the distinct feeling he'd seen and heard a great deal more than he let on.

The door closed behind me with a sense of finality, locking Simantha and the lab away from me just as surely as my choices were now locked in the past. Feeling queasy, I made my way down the hall, not at all certain what my role in all this truly was. Searching within, I couldn't detect any sign of my powers being active. Wild, paranoid theories aside, I really wasn't any closer to knowing what my powers could do.

XII

It was impossible to feel dejected for long. Cory was ecstatic. Eyes shining, he repeated over and over: "She can see me! She can actually *see* me!"

"She thinks you're handsome," I teased, and tousled his hair. He slugged me in the arm, but he was grinning. His enthusiasm was infectious. I decided my ill-conceived matchmaking attempt might turn out to be for the best, if it made Cory so happy, and I set my worries aside.

The two of us went to find dinner. We spent the evening watching syndicated crime dramas, then stayed up late comparing musical tastes and talking about girls. It quickly became obvious that Cory was madly in love with Simantha, and no surprise. She was the first girl who had ever paid any direct attention to him—a heady feeling, judging from the way he carried on about her. Not that I had a leg to stand on. I kept seeing her standing there in the cell in all her naked glory, without evincing even a shred of embarrassment. Such a departure from Sarah's awkward and mumbling introversion! I will admit a twinge of guilt over that. I wasn't sure what my feelings for Sarah were, precisely, but they weren't the intense physical attraction I'd felt at first glimpse of Simantha. For a little while, Sarah and I had connected on an entirely different level, one less physical and more . . . metaphysical.

Cory was barely into his teens, and it was easy to put his feelings down to a harmless infatuation. In the long run, I figured it would do him some good to have someone he could talk to who wouldn't simply forget him. Despite my best efforts, even I couldn't guarantee him that. It wasn't until much later, lying awake in bed while Cory snored softly against my side, that I realized I had fallen in love too. My spinning thoughts revolved endlessly around images of Simantha, her body, her hair, her incredible eyes, her mesmerizing voice . . . her self-possession and poise. I had never known a girl so perfect—but *of course* she was perfect—she was *designed* that way.

I struggled with the idea of loving an artificial person, a robot intelligence. She had seemed so *real!* So *human!* A little bit lost and scared. I could relate to that. Idly, I toyed with the idea of somehow becoming her hero, finding a way to help her recover her memories. Could Cory's power restore lost memories or only take them way? Would he ever gain enough mastery over his abilities to find out?

I fell asleep debating the philosophical and ethical quandaries of robot-human relationships with myself. Was it possible to build something in such a way that it developed a soul? How human did she have to be before she was truly human? How intelligent or emotionally aware did something have to be before it could be considered sentient? The world's greatest thinkers had never solved these dilemmas to anyone's lasting satisfaction. I wasn't going to either, arguing with myself in a late-night anxiety spiral. Half of the things I considered didn't even make sense. I was half asleep and dreaming, my spinning thoughts twining with my fantasies to weave a confused tapestry of formless dread and self-conscious teenage desire.

In the darkness, Simantha is leaning over me. The softness of her lips brushes my ear and sends sparks of pleasure shooting through me. She whispers, "Do you love me?"

"Yes. Yes!" I breathe deep, swimming in the heady scent of her glorious hair.

Simantha laughs and draws away, shakes her head. I grow frantic, reach for her. Her cool plastic skin slips from my grasp. She doesn't believe me. How could she? She isn't even human. She's only a robot; she has no feelings. How could I possibly convince her?

"Please," I beg. "Don't go." Her edges grow indistinct as she drifts away like smoke. Like a Cupid. "I love you!"

"No, David." The faint threnody of her voice drifts from the perfumed darkness. "How could you? You're only human."

✑

Groggy from lack of sleep, I dragged myself through the following day. Coffee, usually just the thing to perk me up in the morning, did me no good at all. I felt muddled and depressed. Worse, I knew it was just a remnant of the indistinct dreams that had kept me tossing and turning all night. Like most dreams, they had drifted away, leaving nothing except vague uneasiness. But even knowing the source of my ennui did nothing to help me shake it. The third time I yawned hugely in his class, Mr. Gold asked if he was boring me. I shrugged, chagrined, and tried once again to find my focus.

Most of the day passed in the same manner. Everyone could see my head wasn't in the game. My mind kept racing in circles around Simantha. Then, with a spasm of my guilty conscience, I would deliberately bend my thoughts toward Sarah. I still wanted to break through her impossible shyness, reconnect with her. I wanted to get to know her better and explore how the two of us might benefit from that connection. But my thoughts were like a flock of customized birds flying by in a distracting display of exotic color and shape; I couldn't help tracking their flight. And they kept flying back toward the simulant girl.

In between my frustrated daydreams, I spent a lot of the day berating myself for an idiot. In my more lucid moments, I knew fantasizing about Simantha was a useless infatuation. She was, what, three thousand years old? Made of synthetic meat and alien plastic and who knew what else. But it mattered little. My best efforts at self-control were like shooting a single bird from the flock; no matter how many I brought down, there were always more. I just couldn't figure out how to shift my thoughts onto another flightpath. Eventually, I gave it up for a lost cause and decided to go work out. I hadn't been to PA's largest fitness center yet, despite Jake and Alan urging me to join them. Might as well go check it out. Maybe I could lose myself in sweat and exertion, shut my mind off for a while.

The Gymnasium, more properly called the Department of Health and Exercise Science, was immense. The PA Hospital was located within its halls, along with the psychiatric facilities, rehab centers, and Zen retreats for rest and recovery. This was where my first room at PA had been located, while recouping from my injuries. I had since moved into a student dorm nearer the Super-studies labs.

Like much of the Project Arete facility, a large portion of the Gymnasium was given over to classrooms, resource libraries, and laboratories where various studies were always in progress. The people employed there engaged in a huge variety of research: kinesiology, sports medicine, exercise physiology, nutrition, and a wide variety of health and wellness related disciplines like massage, chiropractic, acupuncture and acupressure, aromatherapy, yoga, meditation, neuroscience; this list is by no means exhaustive. It seemed Mercedes Helena Cantero Ruiz was determined to pour her fortune into every scientific discipline known to humanity, pseudo-sciences included. Leaping strides weren't her goal; they were her expectation.

Because of the Gymnasium's central location within the Project Arete facility, it was a major hub of activity. Almost every department was most conveniently accessed from here, in one way or another. This was intentional in PA's design: rather than provide convenient access to health and wellness resources, recreational facilities, and spaces for socializing and team building, PA had designed them to be in the way. This put them at the forefront of awareness and minimized opportunities for making excuses to avoid physical exercise, taking advantage of the very human tendency toward laziness. It would have been *more* work to avoid them. Once there, we were encouraged to hit the Gym on the way to or from our usual workspaces; and most people did. It wasn't a perfect system, but a lot of work went into convincing PA members and their affiliates to take advantage. As a result, most people working in and around PA were relatively fit, healthy, and energetic. Did I mention that the Department of Motivational Psychology is located in the Gymnasium, too?

The main reason I hadn't started regularly using the Gymnasium before then was because I had been caught up in finding my stride in the hectic whirl of classes that was my new life. On top of that, I had been working hard at solidifying my bond with Cory. Doing that with any reasonable degree of success required solitude if I didn't want to be committed to a psychiatric ward. Besides which, I couldn't focus on him properly with too many distractions demanding my attention. Talking to Cory in front of Alan and Jake was one thing; talking to him in a crowded place like the Gymnasium was quite another.

I had briefly considered trying to find some way to help Cory through official channels, but in the end, I'd decided talking to PA about his existence wouldn't do him much good, since nobody would be able to remember him long enough to find a solution. Now that I knew an AI could freely interact with Cory, it might be worth re-examining that option. Then again, I got the distinct impression he didn't *want* me to alert PA to his presence. Now that the initial shock and uncertainty of finding me had passed, he seemed content, most of the time. And sometimes even my inconsistent attention seemed to make him uncomfortable. He had been completely alone for so long, even one person focusing on him must have seemed overwhelming on occasion. I guess I figured he would eventually get used to me, and then he'd start to want some variety. Thinking about it, it did seem to be playing out that way. He'd met Simantha now and was overflowing with his feelings for her. I fully expected him to start visiting her regularly if he could get away with it. I wouldn't mind seeing her again myself.

I sighed. *Sarah. Not Simantha. Sarah.*

I grimaced and pushed into the crowd on the Gymnasium plaza. I needed to burn off my frustration and take my mind off things. Time to find a weight room or a climbing gym, maybe hit someone up for some racquetball.

In the end, I wound up meeting up with Jake and Alan. They convinced me to take part in an impromptu game of Powerball. I was shocked to discover PA had a full-size stadium right in the middle of their facility. Kevin was already there, fully armored and ready to play. His sister sat quietly in the stands with Sarah and Amyati; Susie gave me a bright smile and a friendly wave when she saw me. Sarah offered a brief lift of her fingers, then lapsed back into withdrawn stillness. It was a relief to see her there, even if she didn't look terribly enthused. Maybe I would be able to have a quiet word with her after the game. Amyati, on the other hand, pretended she hadn't noticed me, but I hardly cared. She was someone I was more than happy to avoid.

What I had taken for a friendly pickup game seemed to be something of an event. There were a couple hundred people in the stands already and more arriving every moment. It was a little intimidating, but I did my best to ignore the rising babble of noise, focusing instead on gearing up. I hadn't played since I was a little kid in district school, and I really didn't want to get mauled in front of Sarah. I snuck a glance in her direction a few times while I climbed into the suit and checked over its systems, wondering what had brought her out. She'd been pretty withdrawn lately. More so than usual, that is. The moment we'd shared at the docks had begun to seem like nothing more than my imagination, likewise our brief conversation after our first AV test. She'd definitely turned inward since then. She had always been awkward, it seemed, but her recent isolation seemed extreme, even for her. I couldn't figure it out. Either she was actively avoiding me, or she simply hadn't decided yet how she felt about . . . whatever it was we had shared.

I shifted my eyes to Amyati. Could she have something to do with it? She seemed to be Sarah's only real friend. But from my point of view, the forceful Indian girl seemed to dictate the terms of their relationship. Sarah simply went along with it meekly, because it was easier than trying to deny her. After my run in with Amyati at the pier, I wouldn't put it past her to poison Sarah against me. The problem was, I couldn't figure out why she would want to. What did she have against me? True, I had some idea of her dubious extracurricular activities, but only because she'd made a point of involving me. It's not like I'd gone digging for dirt, and what little knowledge I'd gained hardly compromised her. Who would I tell? What could anyone do about it?

PA might be hoping to extend its influence around the globe, eventually, but until they controlled a larger swath of the City, what happened outside the bounds of their district was only their business insofar as it might undermine their sovereignty. Somehow, I doubted the theft of an unusual laser rifle would be of much threat to them. They were too well established for one teenage girl to topple what they'd built. Was it nothing more than simple jealousy, then? The new guy shows up, shows an interest in her best friend, then scores a higher AV . . . but Sarah didn't strike me as the type to be impressed by a power rating. Or the type to turn her back on a friend just because another option came along.

Alan came over to check on my gear, interrupting my thoughts.

"You good?"

"Yeah. Just being thorough. It's been a while."

"Fair enough. Don't expect us to go easy on you, though." He grinned and thumped me on the shoulder, hard enough to make me stagger even inside the power-armor. *Yikes. I'd better get my head in the game.*

Powerball is extremely straightforward, with few rules. The rules it does have are derived from an ancient Mayan game, or so I've been told. They basically cover how you're allowed to make contact with the ball: right side of the body only. Each team tries to keep the ball in motion, bumping it between team members without letting it touch the ground. Teams are two to six players to a side. Twelve-player games usually turn into a brutal melee, so three or four to a side is most common.

Other than that, everything else is merely formality or local customs. The real trick of the game is in the shape of the field. Fields vary in length, but they're never shorter than 250 meters. They're longer than they are wide, and they're narrower down the center run, like an hourglass. The corridor down the center of the field is walled in, sometimes with vertical walls, sometimes with sloping walls. Powerballers call it the Gauntlet. Close confines in the Gauntlet force players to battle their way through the other team to reach the goal zone. At the mid-point of the Gauntlet, two big metal rings are set into the walls, one on each side, perpendicular to both the wall and the ground.

Teams start at either end of the field. Whichever team has the ball puts it into play and starts bouncing it toward their opponents' end. If they manage to get through the Gauntlet and dump the ball onto the ground at the opposite end, they get a point. They earn bonus points if the ball passes through one of the Gauntlet rings on the way, with no limit on the bonus points they can earn, provided they switch rings each time. Some teams will simply stay in the Gauntlet, knocking the ball back and forth through the rings, trying to rack up points before a final push for the goal zone, but it's risky. The bonus points aren't given to the team that earned them; they're given to the next team to score. It isn't uncommon to see the ball switch sides half a dozen times in the Gauntlet, with both sides earning bonus points the whole time, until one team or the other finally manages to win through the scrum and score it all. This all-or-nothing, high-risk, high-reward aspect of the game is part of what makes it so exciting. Games can swing drastically from moment to moment, and there's no way to predict how a game will end.

Another thing that makes it exciting is the lack of formal rules. Beyond governing how the ball is kept in play and how points are scored, pretty much anything goes. There are as many variations on the game as there are teams that play it. As a result, I had no clear idea of what I was in for. *Business as usual,* I thought, and smiled ruefully.

I caught up with Alan in the middle of the field, where the rest of the players were gathered. There were eight of us in total. Unsurprisingly, Jake and Alan were nominated team captains immediately. The coin toss went to Jake, so Alan got to pick first, as defender.

"Kevin, you're with me." That surprised me. The slim Korean was athletic, but not particularly imposing. Everyone present was both taller and heavier. The power-suits made broad-shouldered, heroic figures of us all, but the difference was obvious.

For his first choice, Jake called over a burly fellow named Oscar. Judging by his relaxed and easy stance, he was a veteran of the game. He gave Alan a feral grin as he brushed past him to stand by Jake, seemingly excited by the prospect of squaring off against the "better" twin. Alan nominated Tanis as his second pick, a heavy-set girl with blunt features and short-cropped dirty-blonde hair. She gnashed her teeth at Oscar, who blew her a kiss. Then Eddy went to Jake's team, another sturdy ogre like Oscar. He rolled his shoulders and cracked his neck, a look of grim determination on his face. He gave Oscar a fist bump as he joined the attacking side. A guy named Griffin rounded out Alan's team. He looked lean, strong, and fast. His eyes glinted dangerously as he sized up his opponents one by one.

Finally—and perhaps unsurprisingly—I was picked last. I had the least experience of any of them, and it showed. I trudged over to Jake and the others, clearly awkward in my power-suit. I was starting to feel like I was getting in over my head. But whatever. If this didn't help me drive Simantha from my mind, nothing would. Except maybe a coma.

The teams moved to opposite ends of the field. The stands were really filling up, now, reinforcing my initial impression that there must be some kind of event going on. What had I gotten myself into? There were enough spectators that it couldn't all be members of PA. They must have opened the doors to citizens topside. I wondered about the security implications for a moment. Was there direct access to the stadium for the purpose of staging events and earning revenues without anyone being the wiser that a massive laboratory complex was all around them?

Jake smacked my shoulder to get my attention. "Quit daydreaming," he said. "The people up there aren't what you have to worry about." I blew out a breath, and the four of us gathered into a huddle. "All right, look. From a defensive point of view, they have a couple options. They can interfere with us physically and make us drop the ball before we get to the goal zone. Or they can try to intercept the ball and bounce it back to the other end." I had the distinct impression he was dumbing it down for my sake.

"They're welcome to try," growled Eddy. Oscar grunted in agreement.

"Don't get cocky," said Jake. "A lot of upsets happen in the goal zone. Fighting through the Gauntlet is exhausting. If we make it, there's every chance one of them will be hot on our heels to intercept. We don't want to get there just to race back again."

"Why not?" asked Oscar in an innocent tone. "More opportunities to beat the snot out of them."

"You guys haven't faced Kevin on the field before, have you?"

"That little twerp? No. Why?"

"Guaranteed they'll take a lance. You'll find out soon enough."

That was ominous. PA Powerball custom dictated defenders could opt for a weapon. If they did, we'd be given the same opportunity. We could refuse, and that would be that. They'd only get one. But if we chose to take one, too, then they'd get the option to take a second. This would continue until we refused to let it go any further. Because of this rule, some games were played with nobody armed, and some games, everybody was waving a force-lance. Most often, one player on each side ended up armed, and everybody else focused on playing the ball while their enforcer tried to wreak havoc on the opposing team. This frequently led to duels between enforcers. The fights could draw massive crowds in syndicated leagues that followed similar customs. With a good swing, a force-lance can toss the 250 some-odd kilos of a fully armored player nearly thirty meters. In games where a full dozen players take the field, it's not uncommon to see two or even three enforcers per team. Those matches are insane, and I wouldn't want to get involved. Bodies fly through the rings as often as the ball.

Jake raised his voice and called across the field. "Enforcer?" His power-armor enhanced his voice, and it echoed around the arena.

At the other end of the field, Alan raised an arm. Someone ran a force-lance out to him. He passed it to Kevin. Jake sighed and muttered, "Told you." He already looked defeated. But I wasn't given much time to worry. He raised an eyebrow at Oscar and Eddy. They nodded. When he turned to me, I simply shrugged. Jake raised an arm. "Yeah, we'll take a lance."

The weapon was trotted out to us. Jake put it in my hands. I looked at him blankly.

"Oz and Ed are mean screens. They'll do a good job keeping you clear. All you gotta do is stick to my butt and keep Kevin away from me. Nothin' to it." There was a note of false heartiness in his voice.

For the second time in as many minutes, I found myself having serious doubts. But then the ref flew over the field and the growing crowd went wild. Glancing up, I saw who it was.

Jetman? He floated serenely ten meters above centerfield, the barest hint of his power keeping him aloft. For a man capable of hitting flight speeds of Mach 6, it was a remarkable display of control. The glaring stadium lights flashed on white teeth and pale palms—made all the brighter by contrast to his dark skin—as he grinned and waved at the gathered crowd. I had to do a double take. *The* Jetman. *Here.* Reffing a pickup game of Powerball! I couldn't believe it. I'd seen him on the news so many times as a kid, I would have recognized him no matter how he was dressed, but his comfortable jumpsuit had been designed as a credible imitation of the high-tech flight suit he usually wore while fighting crime. I stared, completely unable to comprehend his presence. In the stands nearby, Susie laughed out loud, a lovely liquid giggle that carried clearly over the noise of the crowd. She made a helpful *close your mouth* gesture at me.

Well, now I understood why Amyati and Sarah had come out. It wasn't every day you got a chance to see a real-life Super-hero. I swallowed. Dare I hope they might see another Super-hero in the making before the game was through? *Ha! Yeah, right.*

Bravely, I went to meet my doom.

Modern Powerball was played using speed and strength enhancing exoskeletons under impact deflecting kinetic armor. The exact speed and strength these suits offered could be adjusted, allowing teams to handicap Supers like Alan and Jake, who enjoyed an unfair advantage because of their abilities, or enhancing smaller players like Kevin up to their level. Usually it's a combination of both, since the suits could offer about the equivalent of 15 AV. Anything beyond that, players unused to moving so quickly with such force didn't tend to react fast enough and it turned into a mess. Jake and Alan were fighting against the suits, working harder than the rest of us for the same output. They didn't mind; they liked the workout. Half the reason they played Powerball was to train their Super-powers. Both had enhanced endurance. They could handle the extra workload.

Aside from improving speed and strength, the armored Powerball suits protected vital organs with heavy padding, provided a framework to support skeletal structures so excess forces didn't simply crush players into a pulp, and deflected impacts with kinetic shielding. The kinetic shields also gave a little extra oomph to the ball when we gave it a nudge, so the game could get pretty frantic. Typical Powerball armor came equipped with cooling units and an onboard AI nano-medic, too. The suit would provide fluids, anti-inflammatories, painkillers, and stimulant cocktails on the fly. It went a long way toward enhancing a Normal player's endurance for long games, known as Grinders, or the always popular Riots, a series of shorter back-to-back games where the rules might change between matches to keep things interesting.

Floating above us, Jetman called the players to their starting lines. His voice was deep and resonant. The crowd instantly grew hushed. I heard the hum of Kevin's force-lance as he powered it on. Swallowing the lump in my throat, I followed suit. Like holding a hive of angry hornets, it buzzed menacingly in my hand, outlines blurring. Without further ceremony, Jetman dropped the ball toward Jake and the game was on.

Alan and his crew raced to beat us to center field. Kevin was quick on his feet, and he took point for their team, force-lance held high and behind, over his right shoulder. Oscar and Eddy weren't quite as fast, but they lumbered steadily ahead, a wall of exoskeleton-enhanced muscle. I was close on their heels, ready to dart past them if I needed to cut a path for Jake. Ostensibly, Oscar and Eddy's job was to screen me, so I could stick to Jake and use the force-lance to play defense if Kevin or anyone else got close to him, but it immediately became clear that our opponents' game plan was simply to sic Kevin on us. Tanis and Griffin didn't even try to screen Kevin so he could get a clear shot at Jake. Instead, they hung back with Alan, waiting for their opportunity to steal the ball.

Three on one, it seemed as though they'd thrown Kevin headfirst into hover traffic. There was no way he stood a chance. Oscar and Eddy were big, and they weren't afraid of a little guy like Kevin, even if he did have a force-lance. They'd taken their share of knocks, and they knew they could handle it. It was a foregone conclusion: those two ogres were going to rip Kevin apart, and there wouldn't be much left for me to mop up.

I barely had time to wonder why Alan thought Kevin could take our team apart single-handedly before he was on us. He ran straight at our defensive screen. With simultaneous shouts, Oscar and Eddy lunged. At full sprint right behind them, I had a front-row seat to the carnage: Kevin pivoted, then whipped the lance across his body from high to low in a tight spiral. The point grazed Oscar, coming in high, striking him in the shoulder. He tottered to the left even as the lance made solid contact with Eddy, sweeping low, blasting his legs out from under him and cartwheeling him onto his head.

Apparently, Kevin was a deft hand with a force-lance. Which is just a nice way of saying he had transformed from a kind, considerate young man into a terrifying, gleeful savage the moment the battle lines came together. There was no way I was going to be able to stop him, not when Oscar and Eddy were nothing more than bowling pins before his onslaught.

I leapt to avoid colliding with Eddy, raising my own force-lance in preparation to strike, and watched in utter amazement as Kevin finished his deadly pirouette in a lunge, tagging Oscar a second time. Off balance, there was nothing Oscar could do: Kevin's lance neatly tapped his chest plate, dead center. He rocketed off his feet and cannonballed across the synthetic turf. If the field had been made from the real deal, he would have left a flaming furrow in the earth.

Mid-leap, I had no way to arrest my trajectory. Kevin slid to a halt at the end of his lunge, gathered his feet under him, and sprang upward. His force-lance flashed toward me like a shooting star. I slashed downward in a wild overhand chop, praying for contact. There was the thrum and crackle of the two lances' kinetic fields and a brilliant blue flash. I pinwheeled straight up, toward the arena ceiling. The field and the stands whirled end over end in a dizzying blur. I caught a distinct glimpse of Amyati, Sarah, and Susie on their feet as they zipped past below me. Susie was alight with sororal joy, cheering wordlessly for her brother's success. Amyati, like most of the crowd, was screaming savagely right along with her. Sarah, shocked out of her passive state by the sudden violence of the game, stood with her hands clapped over her mouth, worried eyes as big as saucers as they traced the path of my flight.

Just for an instant, our eyes met. Time slowed to a crawl. The thrum of connection suddenly hummed between us, drowning out the roar of the crowd. Between one terrified beat of my heart and the next, her senses became mine. For a suspended moment—though it seemed more like an eternity—I felt her heart hammering in my chest. I felt her fear welling up from my belly, her urge to scream my name pushing up my throat. I was still tumbling through the air, but the Powerball field was no longer below me. Her irises had expanded, a pair of luminous green rings marking the edges of bottomless black pits. I spun dizzily into her eyes, and they swallowed me whole. I felt as though I raced along a branching highway that dropped toward a convoluted maze. I had a single glimpse of it, laid out before me, infinite and labyrinthine, before the walls surrounded me. I instantly lost all sense of direction. It wasn't a maze of corridors and crossing hallways. It was a series of chambers, each connected to a hundred others. The gaps between them were bridges of electric light that snapped into being only long enough for me to pass from one space to the next. I leapt like a spark from ledge to ledge, veered and spun, careening from room to room, disoriented by the whirling passage. For one endless instant, I traveled this bewildering path, then arrived back at myself. I hung in the center of the maze, suspended in time, frozen in the act of cartwheeling through the air, while in the stands below a thousand motionless Powerball fans roared and cheered.

Momentum carried me over backward, and Sarah was snatched from my line of sight. I came down hard near where I had started, with the action of the game having moved on beyond me. Barely a second had passed. Kevin, in dealing with me, Oscar, and Eddy at once, had left Jake an opening to charge past on the right. Juggling the ball with strikes of his right knee and elbow, occasionally using a hip-check, he bounced the ball off the wall of the Gauntlet back to himself in a desperate bid for the goal zone. His progress was too slow. Alan moved in with Tanis and Griffin to surround him.

I pushed myself up to my knees, groaning. *What just happened?* I could hear the thunder of half a dozen heavily armored Powerballers charging past me. I shook my head groggily. From the corner of my eye, I saw Jake launch the ball high and make a mighty push to batter through his opponents. It was no good. He hit the turf as Alan crashed into him. Tanis neatly intercepted the ball as it descended. It bounced between her and Griffin. Casually, while Alan wrestled to keep Jake pinned, the two bashed the ball back and forth across the Gauntlet. A handful of bonus points richer, they made their way back to our end of the field. Kevin shadowed them to the goal zone just in case Oscar, Eddy, or I recovered fast enough to try making a charge. But there was no hope of that. Oscar and Eddy were already trudging back to the starting line, knowing a lost cause when they saw one. Within moments of the game's start, Alan's team was up five-nothing, tossing the ball to Jake for our second attempt.

I tottered to my feet. Heaving bodies in the stands moved like waves on the ocean. It was a sickening blur of color and motion. I couldn't pick Sarah from the uproarious crowd. But I could *feel* her. I knew she was still there. I could almost hear Amyati shouting in her ear, asking her if she was okay. She was nodding her head, pushing at words as heavy as boulders. Trying to say, "I'm fine, I'm fine," and managing only to mumble. I could still see the pathways I'd traveled through her mind, branching like rivers. The network of semi-organic wires in her brain that made her eyes work. I could still see how they'd grown out of control, how they interfered with her ability to speak.

A wave of nausea passed over me. I staggered and sat down, hard. Jetman was suddenly there, Jake close behind him. They pulled off my helmet. A horn sounded, signaling a time out. Kevin appeared, removing a gauntlet to place his palm on my sweaty forehead.

"Rattled your can, did I?" He waved Jetman and Jake away. "He's fine. No injuries I can see. Just a little surprised, I think."

I forced myself to nod. "You can say that again. Those lances pack a punch." My smile was more grimace than grin. I didn't feel like explaining what had really happened.

Jetman helped me to my feet. "You want to sit this one out?"

"And let down my team? It'll take more than a little tumble to keep me down." No way was I going to be able to get Sarah alone to discuss what had happened, not while she was stuck in the stands watching the game. I ground my teeth in frustration.

Jetman took it for determination, maybe. He clapped me on the back. "Good man. Get back in there." It spoke volumes for my state of mind that the encouragement from my childhood hero hardly even registered. He lofted over the field as I jogged back to the starting line, refastening my helmet as I went. Jake double-checked my suit was in order and signaled the start of the second match.

It went much like the first, and no surprise, as I couldn't focus. Sarah's feelings kept rising like a tide inside me. I struggled to stay afloat, to sort out where I ended and she began. I felt like I was drowning.

Something slammed into me. The world tilted. I found myself helmet to helmet with Tanis, her manic grin only inches from my face. She rolled off me as the rest of her team pelted past. I made a grab for her ankle and brought her down hard enough to make her bounce off her kinetic shields. The crowd howled. Dirty play, but not illegal. The ball was changing hands, then changing hands again. I tracked it, trying to get my head in the game. I had to pay attention to what was going on around me, or I was going to get hurt.

Kevin's force-lance described a wide zone of control midfield. He was fending off Oscar and Eddy with ease. I blinked—clamped down on a choking sense of anxiety that wasn't mine—and scrambled to my feet. Maybe I could get at him before he took them down. I poured on all the speed the suit could give me. He maneuvered the force-lance like it was a part of him, keeping my teammates off balance. I saw my moment, drove my shoulder into his side, and lashed out with my lance. He twisted and let it fly wide. Our kinetic shields sparked, and we glanced off each other, spinning drunkenly. Instinct made me duck. His force-lance whirred over my head. I enjoyed a split second of elation that I'd evaded his attack before the lance came at me again.

I back-pedaled desperately, trying to get my guard up, Kevin bearing down on me. Oscar had the ball now, and I was supposed to be keeping Kevin away from him. He couldn't risk dodging past me until I'd engaged, and Kevin had caught me wrong-footed, driving me backward into Oscar, forcing him to give ground. Alan and Tanis were approaching fast, and I was losing my window of opportunity to get through Kevin's guard.

Panicking, I swung my force-lance around in a wide arc and let it fly. It was a last-ditch effort to fend him off, but to my surprise, it worked like a charm. Force-lances are powered by the suits; throwing them isn't technically illegal, but since the kinetic field making them strike with such entertaining results shuts off the moment the lance leaves your hand, all you usually get for your efforts is a thunderclap of energy dissipating harmlessly into the air and strange looks from the stands. Kevin never saw it coming, though. I don't know, maybe he expected more gentlemanly conduct. Or maybe he never would have considered such an unorthodox maneuver. My force-lance whirled low over the ground, tangled with Kevin's feet, and he went down in a heap, his own force-lance flying from his hand. Before he could recover, I ran over, snatched up both lances, and took off as fast as my suit could power me, giggling like an idiot.

The crowd went nuts. There I was, armed to the teeth with two force-lances, running in apparent pants-wetting terror from an unarmed guy half my size, our arms and legs pumping furiously. The rest of the game was forgotten. I was laughing so hard my legs felt like jelly. I had to stumble to a halt. I tossed the lances away just as Kevin tackled me from behind, and then we were rolling on the ground. We hit the wall of the Gauntlet and flew apart, coming to rest with a few meters between us. I clutched my stomach and laughed so hard my ribs ached. Or maybe that was from getting knocked around so much. When I finally managed to regain control of myself, I was gasping for air. My eyes were streaming with tears.

Kevin rolled to his hands and knees. "What the heck was that?" he demanded, but there was amusement in his voice.

I propped myself on my elbows. "You're a bloody menace," I gasped. "Nobody should give you a force-lance, ever."

The crowd bellowed in approbation. I looked over at the score-board. Twelve to one! Someone on my team had made it through! I pointed and whooped.

Kevin chuckled and pulled his helmet off. Sweaty hair was plastered to his forehead. He wiped it away with a gauntleted forearm. "Want to know a secret?" he asked. There was a mischievous look on his face.

I lifted a shoulder. "Sure."

He leaned toward me and lowered his voice. "I don't even like Powerball. I just enjoy knocking Alan and Jake around with the force-lance."

The look on my face must have been priceless.

He cackled, grinning, then clambered to his feet. "It's good for them. Keeps them humble. I like to think of it as a public service."

I let him haul me up after him, then stooped to retrieve his helmet. By the time I'd double-checked to be sure it was properly secured, Jetman had joined us. He handed us our force-lances. Kevin looked at the weapon for a moment, then saluted me with it. Handing it back to Jetman, he said, "Let's play some Powerball."

Tossing my own lance back to Jetman, I followed Kevin back onto the field. *If I'm going to get trounced,* I thought, *I might as well get trounced fairly.* But I resolved to make them work for it.

Without the whack-sticks, the rest of the second match went a lot better than the first. They still wrecked us, of course, but if entertaining the crowd was the goal, we certainly achieved that much. The Riot was slated for best of five, so there was at least one more game to lose before I could get off the field. To be fair, I didn't intentionally throw the match—I wasn't skilled enough at the game to have that much influence over the outcome, anyway—but neither did I put my best foot forward, despite my best intentions. I was hyperaware of Sarah, keenly cognizant of her attention both externally and internally. She had even less of an idea what to make of our reforged bond than I did, and she didn't have any way to manipulate it. But that didn't stop her from trying, and I could feel her attempts to interact with me through our link like being poked in the mental ribs. With grim determination, I clamped down on the flow of information coming down the line. Sarah would have to wait. I wasn't going to find the necessary peace and quiet to experiment with our bond while surrounded by a thousand screaming Powerball fans, that much was certain.

In the locker room after the match, Jetman had some choice words for our performance. "You call that Powerball?" he fumed. "I call it a travesty! A disaster! An unmitigated farce!" He rounded on the others. "Have any of you even played Powerball before?"

I grimaced, but Alan laughed. "Not me. Jake?"

"Never," said Jake. "How about you, Eddy?"

"Is that what we were supposed to be doing? Powerball? Aw, man, I wish I'd known in advance. I've actually played a few times." He shook his head in exaggerated chagrin.

Oscar stretched and headed for the showers. "Wasn't my fault! My suit was on the fritz!"

Jetman looked at each of us in turn, mock serious, but the flippant comments kept coming. I was beginning to see that he already had a relationship with these guys. The banter between them seemed more like a post-game ritual than a serious effort at coaching. He gave everyone plenty of time to talk back and crack jokes. I held back, uncertain of where the lines were drawn. Eventually, the group calmed down.

Jetman leaned back against a locker. "I'm glad y'all enjoyed yourselves out there. I won't lie; being on the field again brought back some fond memories of my days back at U of East C." He paused, eyes distant. Then he gave his head a little shake and refocused on the present. "I won't bore you with nostalgia. Y'all know my qualifications. PA has asked me to sort out a real Powerball team, and from what I saw today, y'all got the heart, if not the experience. What do you say?"

"Seriously?" I asked. "I thought this was a one-off, some kind of promotional stunt."

"Nah," said Eddy. "Mr. Wallace has been here over a month now. This is just the first time PA made it public."

Mr. Wallace? Come to think of it, I'd heard his name on the news before. What was it, again? Basil? No . . . Ba-something. Baxter? Yeah, Baxter Wallace.

Jetman was nodding. "Could have been a one-time gig, but Project Arete made an offer I can't refuse. Besides, I'm slowing down in my old age. Been thinking of retiring from the Super-hero life anyway. Powerball has always been my first love."

Up close, I could see his closely cropped hair was more gray than black. Still, his arms seemed as solid with muscle as they'd ever been. What did "slowing down" mean for a Super like Baxter Wallace? Did he max out at Mach 4 or 5, now? Was he losing his reflexes? His invulnerability at speed?

Jetman let the chorus of questions and babbled comments subside before he addressed us again. His deep voice boomed in the echoing confines of the locker room. "I'll make some time to answer any questions y'all might have later. There will be some official tryouts, soon. PA is looking to recruit a full roster and field a team or three, if you're interested. Have y'all been into Powerball the whole time you've been here?"

"Uh, no," I admitted, "not me. I'm fairly new to PA, and this was my first game with these guys."

"Really?" He cocked an eyebrow. "I had no idea."

"Ouch." But his grin took the sting from his words.

"Relax, son. You've got potential. We'll make a Powerballer out of you, yet."

Was that what I wanted? I'd had fun despite everything going on. For a while, I'd even forgotten about Simantha, which had been the whole point of getting out to the Gymnasium in the first place. I shook my head. Simantha hardly seemed to matter in light of the day's developments, but it seemed I was helpless to stop thinking about her. My first sight of her wasn't something I could simply un-see, and Dawn's team *had* asked me to escort her around PA. I couldn't believe I'd actually agreed to it. In hindsight, it seemed pretty foolish. And yet . . . I couldn't deny I was looking forward to it. I didn't really believe she was dangerous, that she was some kind of weapon. I couldn't say why, exactly, but I felt weirdly certain we would become friends.

Jetman took Kevin aside and began speaking to him earnestly in a low voice. No doubt he was keen to keep Kevin interested. The studious young man had pro enforcer written all over him. I got up off the bench and headed for the showers. I rinsed off quickly, then went looking for my street clothes. Which locker had been mine? I was exhausted, but the stimulants the Powerball suit had provided weren't going to let me sleep for a while yet, and I didn't feel like counteracting them with a nano-dose designed to slow me down. I knew I'd be sore the next day, but right at that moment, I was feeling oddly self-satisfied. There was nothing like the burn of physical exercise to make one's worries fall by the wayside. And now that the initial shock had passed, I was certain my connection to Sarah was stronger this time. If I tuned out the noise around me, I could still sense her. It was a vague and distant plucking at my consciousness, but it was still there. The intensity had passed, and in its wake was a strangely comfortable sense of awareness. How long would it last this time?

I'd seen evidence in that endless split second that Sarah might actually care about me. I had a vivid and very pleasant memory of her distress when I'd been knocked into the air. She'd feared for my safety. She'd even wanted to call out my name. For some reason, it made all the bruises and rattling of my brains worth it. It seemed like whenever I had glanced up at the stands to see if my sense of her location was accurate, she'd been looking back at me every time, like she couldn't take her eyes off me. I certainly hadn't needed the green glow of her eyes to spot her in the crowd. Even here, in the locker room, I felt like I could close my eyes and point her out.

Jake interrupted my thoughts. "Post-game plans?" Behind him, Alan was already on his way out. There was no sign of Jetman.

I pulled my hoodie over my head. "Nah," I grunted.

Kevin leaned around a corner. "Neon?"

"Great minds," confirmed Jake.

Alan called over his shoulder, "Meet you guys there. Going to see if any of the girls want to join us." The door closed behind him.

Jake smirked. I heard Kevin making a comment to Eddy and Oscar, who chortled.

"What's Neon?" I asked.

"Best club in PA. I'm not into dancing, but their food can't be beat, and there's usually a live band or a DJ." Jake slung his gear bag over his shoulder and headed for the door. "Second level, off the main connector. Ask your Map!"

Oscar and Eddy began singing an off-key duet in the shower. I grimaced and hurried after Jake, Kevin only a stride behind me.

XIII

We parted ways in the busy corridors outside the Gymnasium. Kevin wanted to stop by the Greenhouse before heading to Neon. Jake had another class to attend before he'd be free to join us there. Now that I was off the field, I didn't want to put it off any longer: I needed to find Sarah. There were too many unanswered questions. I couldn't just keep stumbling blindly into situations that triggered my abilities. I needed to know what caused these moments of melding. The first time, I hadn't been in a fit state to appreciate what was happening. I hadn't been able to hold on to it. I'd been hurt pretty badly and passed out almost immediately. This time, I'd been conscious but also keyed up by the rush of the game. My adrenaline had been flowing. The stimulants provided by the Powerball armor had likely enhanced the clarity of the visions even further. The experience had been both mental and emotional, a visual hallucination coupled with strong empathic sensations. I had felt what she felt! Was my ability some sort of telepathy? Was I looking inside her mind when our eyes met? I couldn't be sure. But I felt a growing excitement: a new awareness seemed to be unfolding within me, a way of perceiving the world that had nothing to do with my other senses. I found I could maintain my link to Sarah with a little mental effort and feed it energy to keep it active. It was a little like refocusing my attention, but in an entirely different direction I hadn't been aware existed before now. Was my exhaustion simply a product of the late night with Cory followed by the physical demands of the game? Or was the link to Sarah draining my reserves in some way?

One way or another, I wanted to find out. I intended to hold onto it as long as I could.

Her Map had her listed as available, and her location was flagged. I concentrated until a ghostly line overlaid my field of vision, guiding the way. Like her eyes, it glowed neon green. I frowned and rubbed my chin as I considered the color of the route. Coincidence? Or were my feelings for her so obvious that even my Map couldn't refrain from commenting? I peered suspiciously at the device for a moment, wondering what kind of programming made it work. Did it have a personality it chose not to reveal?

I sighed and set out. Useless to ask. I'd adopted the alien technology in a hurry, despite my earlier misgivings. It was too convenient not to. As long as it led me to Sarah and kept most of its opinions to itself, I couldn't be bothered to care. There was enough on my plate already.

My eagerness to see Sarah and talk to her was somewhat overshadowed by my knowledge of Simantha's presence somewhere beneath my feet in the CSD labs. Even now, I found my thoughts being dragged back toward her. The perfection of her body, the sound of her voice . . . the way she moved with such grace and confidence. I tried to picture Sarah stepping out even half so confidently, but I couldn't do it. She was too timid and meek. But with the insight of my recent vision, I thought I might have an idea why.

When I finally caught up to her, she was sitting on a bench overlooking a multi-level atrium. The vaulted hall was full of tall, dark marble columns ribboned with veins of gold. They floated freely in a ponderous and stately dance, suspended by some kind of maglev or anti-grav device hidden from sight, tracing unhurried arabesques through the open space beyond the balustrade. People filled the surrounding balconies, working with their heads bent over data devices or sharing food and conversation.

I approached slowly, feeling like I'd cornered a frightened Anymal, though I could sense she'd had time to focus on her breathing and relax. I marveled at the clarity of it. She currently felt self-possessed and calm despite the sound of my approaching footsteps causing her heart rate to speed up slightly. She didn't look up as I sat next to her. Her mechanical gaze was fixed on the hovering columns that swung from nothing in front of us. The low babble of voices around us ebbed and flowed like a tide.

I hesitated to break the silence. A keen awareness of her was rising from within. Coupled with her physical nearness, the sight and sound and smell of her, it was almost overwhelming. She was sitting small and still next to me; had in fact been waiting for me to find her, knowing I would. But she might as well have been ten meters tall. Something had passed between us in the arena, and it hadn't been the first time. Our original connection had been reopened and reinforced. I felt her presence in an indescribably powerful way, as though her body were a shade placed over a very bright light. Her inner fire might be hidden from sight, but I could still feel its heat.

I swallowed. My mouth felt dry. It was all I could do to say her name. "Sarah." It came out as little more than a whisper. Who was having trouble with words, now?

I felt her fingers graze mine, like a falling leaf touched in passing. Her confidence faltered. I felt it as if my own courage were failing.

"I feel your unease," I said, wondering at the sensation even as I said it. "I can feel how hard you're trying to find the words."

She bit her lip and stared straight ahead.

"You feel trapped. Locked behind your own lips."

She made a sound then, something between a gasp and a whimper. A single tear trembled at the corner of her eye, glimmering neon green in the glow of her irises—frustration and helplessness rising behind a dam of stubborn determination to overcome her handicap. My heart nearly burst in my chest. She was an isolated warrior, and for so long, she'd been fighting her war in silence. I found I had to force my next words past a constriction in my throat.

"I saw the wires behind your eyes."

She turned her mechanical gaze upon me then, brows drawn down in a quizzical frown. For a moment, I was afraid I would fall into her eyes again. She looked away, and the moment passed.

"Th-they . . ."

I waited, knowing precisely how difficult it was for her to push the words past her stubborn tongue. Faulty bio-mechanical connections were multiplying in her brain, growing far beyond their original programming. I could sense the links between disparate parts of her mind that never should have been directly connected. When she spoke, the signals seemed to be split between the visual cortex and speech center of her brain. Did her words trigger visual distortions? Did she see half of the things she said without ever giving voice to them? What other functions did the wires interfere with?

"They're nuh . . . nuh . . . not real."

The visions I'd seen? *No . . . something else.* I stared at her profile, unsure of her meaning. Her attention remained fixed on the hanging columns. I turned to inspect them more closely. "Holographs?" I asked.

She nodded. I whistled in appreciation. Not even a flicker betrayed their illusory quality. I would've sworn they were solid stone. Indeed, I had assumed they were massive blocks of marble being levitated by some kind of technology. A holograph was a much simpler explanation. Still, there was a sense of weight to them, a solid certainty. It seemed inevitable they would eventually crash to the ground, falling from their dignified flight just as soon as they realized they were impossible.

"Muh . . . me," whispered Sarah. "Mmmy wuh . . . wuh . . . words." I could feel her struggling to express herself. I sensed the outline of her ideas but couldn't see the details. She gestured helplessly at her mouth. The tear fell, sparkling. Irritated, she dashed the moisture from her face with the back of her sleeve, then pulled her Map from her pocket.

My Map pinged. *"What is wrong with me? What did you see?"*

"I'm not . . ." I paused. I'd been about to say, "I'm not entirely sure," but that wasn't true. I *was* sure, even though I had no way to know if I was right. But did I need to know? My intuition had been right before. Just how far could I trust my power? "Not sure" wasn't what she needed to hear right now. She needed certainty. She needed a way out. I thought about Miguel's schematic. About Simantha and Cory. About making connections. Heart hammering, I took her hand in both of mine. "Sarah, will you trust me?"

I'm not sure what she sensed in that moment. Did something of what I felt pass down the link to her, or was it only one way? Her eyes grew wide as she searched my face. I think my emotions must have been written plainly there, even without our connection. I was falling in love with her, though I hardly even knew her. I couldn't help it. She seemed so frail and frightened, but looking deeper had shown me she was precisely the opposite. Stronger than anyone I'd ever met, bearing up under a burden that might easily crush others. I saw now why Amyati and Sarah were friends. They were both fierce, in their own ways. But Amyati wasn't held back by a glitch in her brain.

I'd never felt this sense of connection with anyone else. Even my connection to Cory couldn't compare. My link with him was fraught with difficulty and struggle. It was uncertain and subject to the whims of his power. But this . . . it was growing stronger by the moment, and if I concentrated . . .

Yes . . . Yes, she did. She felt it, too.

She bit her lip and nodded, a short, sharp movement of the head—afraid of what it might mean, but even more afraid of being trapped inside herself, alone. I took a deep breath and closed my eyes. Cautiously, I slid inside her. But no, that's not quite right. That makes it sound physical. Outside, physically, nothing had changed. I was still sitting next to her, holding her hand in mine. But within, I felt her unfolding. The blaze of her inner light opened to embrace me. Simultaneously terrified and elated, I let go of myself. I drifted from my body, trading my awareness for hers.

It was too much. It may not have been physical, but it *was* incredibly intimate. All at once, she curled in on herself, rejecting my presence. I snapped back to myself, feeling out of alignment in my own body. Some moments passed while my racing heart calmed, and my breathing slowed. Gradually, the sensation of being Sarah-sized inside my much-larger frame diminished. I became aware I was squeezing my eyes shut. I opened them uncertainly, feeling like I'd been in a trance. Had I spoken out loud? Explained what I'd seen? I couldn't be sure. For a moment, I'd been completely outside of myself.

Sarah was standing at the rail, her back to me. She was breathing in short, sharp gasps. Her field of view was superimposed over my own. To her multi-layered mechanical gaze, the floating pillars seemed hazy, insubstantial. They drifted like forlorn spirits, the collective ghost of a ruined temple. I blinked, and her unusual perspective vanished.

"When did it start?" I asked.

She gave the barest of shrugs.

"It can't have been immediate, or you would have known it was the eyes causing your issues. When were they replaced?"

"Th-they . . . they've always . . . always b-been like th-this."

"Always?" It was hard to keep the disbelief from my voice.

She nodded.

"You were born blind?"

Another nod.

How had that happened? Another mech-womb glitch, like Susie's? What were the odds of two such cases ending up here at Project Arete? Slim to none, unless PA specifically sought out people who suffered from such defects—which they would probably do. How else to study the phenomenon, find the causes? PA's mission statement was nothing short of the perfection of humanity, and the mech-wombs were deeply tied to the increase in Super-births over the past few decades.

But I was getting sidetracked. Her eyes had originally been replaced in infancy. They would have been replaced a few times since then as she outgrew them. What about the wires behind them? Too problematic to remove them and regrow them. They would still be the originals, growing with her. A quick diagnostic while connecting them to each new set of eyes, and that's it.

"When was the last time your eyes were replaced?"

She turned from the atrium and leaned back against the railing. One eye dilated as she zoomed in on my face. The other flickered briefly. Checking data logs in a heads-up display?

"Ff . . . four y-years uh . . . ago."

Four years ago, the optic nerves were working perfectly, or well within parameters, at least. They may have already begun to grow in unusual ways by then, but if no warnings were triggered at the time of her last replacement, they'd have had the last four years to spread through her brain, linking things in odd ways. The shift would have been gradual—a slow degradation of her ability to communicate. Why would anyone think her eyes might be responsible for her speech defect? Maybe, in a few more years, once the visual distortions became noticeable enough, they'd start to connect the dots. What else would she have lost by then? Would she even be able to make her condition known? Left unchecked, her optic nerves would continue to grow unnecessary connections, creeping like a cancer through her mind.

"How long have you been having difficulty speaking?"

"A . . . y-year . . . or . . . s-s-so." She always spoke slowly, deliberately, trying to minimize the problem. But it seemed so obvious to me now. Her shyness was just a natural reaction to the embarrassment the stuttering had caused her. She'd become introverted, withdrawn from social interaction to avoid the shame and pain. Had she been bullied before arriving at PA? Was she here in the hopes of finding an answer to the problem? I wondered if they could even fix it, if the bio-wires that made her eyes work could even be removed. They'd integrated with her brain and become a part of it by now. Nanos might be precise enough to perform the delicate surgery, I supposed, assuming they were of high enough quality, but it was a sketchy proposition to unleash a swarm of nanos into the brain. Their programming had better be faultless if you didn't want to cause more problems than you solved.

"Sarah, you need to talk to PA about this. I think your eyes have begun to rewire your brain, and it's not going to stop on its own. If it were me, I'd go right to the top. Beg Ms. Ruiz to find a solution. If anyone can, it's her."

Sarah returned to the bench and sat down heavily. A moment passed while her mechanical eyes whirred and refocused, slowly coming to rest on mine. For the first time, we shared a long, unbroken look without her blushing, turning away, or hiding her face behind her hair. She was pale as a ghost. I could see it slowly dawning on her as she searched my face: I was telling the truth.

Somewhere inside her, a dam broke. Great wracking sobs shook her whole body. Grief? Or relief at finally having an answer? It didn't really matter. She collapsed onto the bench, and I moved to put my arms around her. Tentatively at first, then with more certainty as she reached out and clung to me, bawling and hiccupping. Awkwardly, I crouched next to the bench, rubbing her back in small circles, murmuring soothing nonsense. Had I been hoping for answers to my own questions? It seemed that wasn't the way my power worked. I sighed and set it aside. I would figure it out eventually.

I gathered Sarah close. For two minutes, maybe three, we stayed that way. She recovered herself quickly but made no move to pull away.

"D . . . David?"

Slowly, I turned my face toward hers. "Mm?" Her lips were inches from mine. I sensed her heart begin to pound in tandem with mine.

"Thank . . . th-thank you," she whispered. "I . . ." She lifted her chin slightly, then blushed.

The invitation was plain. I leaned down.

"Well, isn't this sweet?"

I jerked back as if burned. Sarah sat up more slowly, hunched and unwilling to face the accusation in Amyati's tone.

"Why are you crying?" Amyati demanded.

Sarah dragged a sleeve over her face. She remained mute.

"Shall I guess, then?" She took a step toward me. I stood up and turned to face her. The aura of menace radiating from her was palpable. Why was she so angry? And why did I feel so guilty for comforting a friend? I had nothing to be ashamed of!

"Relax, I was just trying to . . ."

Maybe it was my defensive tone. Maybe it was telling her to relax. Amyati bristled. "You know what, David? I don't care." She gestured imperiously. "Leave. You're upsetting my friend."

"H-he . . . he was . . . wasnuhh . . ." Sarah *was* upset, and embarrassed besides. It always made her stuttering worse. Her protests weren't going to arrive fast enough.

"Amyati, wait. Listen!"

But she wasn't listening. "I said leave!" she barked. Her out-flung arm and finger still pointed the way.

People were turning to stare. Still, I hesitated. Amyati, however, did not. She stalked toward me with steady steps, dark eyes blazing.

I felt myself lifted and swept backward on a wave of pressure that advanced before her. She forced me away from the overlook and dumped me unceremoniously through an archway into a connecting hall.

Seriously? Some kind of force-field? I was too stunned to react. She spun a one-eighty and stomped away. I raised my voice to call after her. "Amyati, please! Sarah needs our help! I'm trying to *help* her!"

She whirled. "Your help looks suspiciously like a predatory male making moves on a vulnerable female," she spat. "Keep your filthy hands off her!"

"What?!" I couldn't believe what I was hearing. "Amyati, I . . ."

"Stow it," she interrupted. "She deserves better than you."

My protests died in my throat. She glared down on me in silence for a moment before storming off. I just shook my head. What was the point? She wasn't hearing anything I said. I couldn't fathom why she hated me so much; there didn't seem to be any reason behind it! What had I ever done to her?

Picking myself up, I trudged back to my dorm, feeling distinctly aggrieved. Sarah hadn't been able to speak up in my defense, but that was understandable. It bothered me far less than Amyati's vile accusations. I just had to hope Sarah would eventually be able to disabuse her friend of such nasty assumptions. It was obvious Amyati wouldn't be swayed by anything I said.

Resigned, I went to Neon to meet the team as planned, but I remained irritable, unable to shake off the unpleasant encounter with Amyati. For a moment, I had thought Sarah would kiss me, or at least let me kiss her, but even that pleasant thought couldn't dispel the dark cloud that hung over me. Kevin did his best to cheer me up, and for his sake, I put a brave face on it, but it was obvious my heart wasn't in it. I picked at my meal and watched Alan flirt with a variety of attractive girls, wondering how he made it seem so easy. I listened with half an ear while Tanis and Jake discussed a tricky physics problem that was likely to be on an upcoming test. Eddy and Oscar were dancing together, lost in their own little world, somehow making it seem like the music was stubbornly refusing to match their rhythm rather than the other way around. Griffin hadn't bothered to show up. Unsurprisingly, neither had Sarah or Amyati.

"*Go home and get some sleep, David,*" Susie signed. "*You look rough.*"

Kevin put a hand on my shoulder. "She's right, David. You could use a good night's rest."

"Is that your professional opinion?"

"Would it encourage you to listen if it was?"

I sighed and answered them both in sign, "*You're probably right. The Riot really took it out of me today.*"

Susie gave me a sympathetic smile. "*You're a good sport, letting my brother beat up on you like that. Will you be playing again?*"

"*Yeah, I think so.*" I glanced at Kevin and smirked at his expression of wounded innocence. "*I'm used to getting beat up, but now that I'm here at PA, I don't get as many opportunities.*"

Susie giggled.

"*Will I see you in art class tomorrow?*" I asked her.

She nodded. "*I'm nearly done your portrait. Think you might actually sit still this time?*"

I shrugged and levered myself to my feet. "*No promises.*"

"*Fine, but if your face looks crooked, it won't be my fault.*" She spread her hands helplessly.

"Go on, take off," said Kevin. "We'll pass on your regrets." We bumped knuckles.

Susie seemed immensely pleased to be offered the same parting gesture. Her tiny fist was dwarfed by mine, but nothing could diminish her smile.

It wasn't until I was drifting off to sleep that evening that I realized Project Arete *did*, in fact, have a way to correct Sarah's problem.
Simantha. She was a fully synthetic human. Her bio-mechanical eyes
and nano-network integration were far more advanced than Sarah's
robotic devices. Sarah's eyes were almost entirely robotic, only uti-
lizing bio-mechanics for the optic nerve. The unwieldy growth of
that optic nerve was the crux of the problem. But a nano-net like
Simantha's, AI driven, could safely dismantle Sarah's errant connections. Unlike a pre-programmed nano-surgery, an AI could react
in the moment to ensure the best outcome, with a much greater
degree of certainty and success than a human surgeon. If left in place
with the right program, over time such a nano-net could replace the
defunct bio-wires with a more holistic bio-mechanical system that
was seamlessly integrated into her brain. Eventually, Sarah's robotic
eyes might even be swapped for some that were almost fully organic.
Likely, they could be grown from her own genetic material. They'd
be nearly an exact match for the eyes she'd never had.

Would they still be green? I wondered. I lay awake, staring into
the darkness, trying to visualize how it might work. Did it need
to happen this way, or were there other options available? If it was
necessary, would Sarah agree to it? Would Simantha consent to share
her inner workings? Who else would need to be involved to make it
happen? How could we convince them to make the attempt? It was a
lot to ask, entrusting such a delicate operation to an AI derived from
the nano-network underlying Simantha's consciousness. So much of
it seemed to pivot on faith, on my intuition telling me it would
work. Why should any of them believe me? For that matter, why did
I believe it?

Once again, it seemed to circle back to the first time I'd met
Dawn, Francis, and Miguel. By making Simantha possible, I had set
in motion a chain of events that was still revealing itself. A seemingly
innocuous meeting might now make a solution to Sarah's problem

possible. What else might it be connected to? And where would it end?

Despite my whirling thoughts, sleep did eventually arrive. I surrendered gratefully, and hardly stirred until morning.

XIV

Over breakfast the following morning, I caught up on messages. Most of it had to do with my evolving schedule, which would now include physical education, weight training, Powerball practice, and martial arts. Powerball enforcers don't just throw their lances around, you know! Duels between top players are demanding tests of speed and skill. I wasn't entirely sure I wanted to end up being an enforcer for the team—the aggressive role didn't seem to suit me—but I was willing to give it my best shot.

I let my mind wander, munching my breakfast. Unsurprisingly, my thoughts kept returning to Sarah. My first meeting with her, the sense of sudden knowing, and the way I'd connected with her yesterday had left me with more questions than answers. With an inadvertent application of my power at the docks, I'd made a connection to a total stranger. It had happened again at the game. And then, afterward, I'd actually managed to make it happen on purpose. Sarah had been frightened by the intimacy, and I had to admit, so had I. The intensity of the connection, the way it laid us both bare to the other's scrutiny . . . it was a lot to handle all at once. I had the feeling it would be wise to slow down a bit and find a way to work on my control. I didn't want to scare Sarah away.

Connections. Upon reflection, my power had always been about connections. But I'd never considered it in a spiritual light. It had always been a physical thing. That was how it all started: shoelaces; practicing knots; tangling and untangling things. The first real exception had been that strange moment with Sarah at the docks, but I hadn't really been aware of it then. It had taken some time for me to realize that moment had been a result of my own power. Really, if I had to pinpoint when I began to wonder, it would be with the diagram for Dawn's project. That hadn't been a physical, hands-on application of my ability. I hadn't tied the chart in a bow or anything like that. But it had looked exactly like a big tangle of loose strings to me. Pointing out the parts in the jumble that need to be tackled first had been instinctive. If it *had* been a pile of string, those were the places I would've started untangling to avoid making the knots worse. Still, even then, I hadn't really considered it. It had been too weird, too different from my usual shoelace manipulation. Even Francis's comment, at the time—"*Strings are David's thing*"—hadn't really sunk in.

Then there was the Quantum Cube with Cory, that weird moment of being spread across every dimension. But no, wait . . . that hadn't been the next thing. It had been in Mr. Gold's classroom before the Abeyant Vector test, when I saw Cory for the first time. The way I'd suddenly realized he'd been sitting there the whole time, that humming sense of being *linked*, had been almost identical to my first connection to Sarah—an overwhelming sense of awareness. Too much other stuff had occupied my attention right then for me to focus on it, and because of Cory's power, I'd simply forgotten about it. But it had felt like . . . well, like fate, I guess. Sounds weird to say it now, but I'd known in that moment the two of us were tangled up together somehow. A couple of beat-up old shoelaces knotted up so tightly that even I couldn't figure out how to pull them apart.

That had led to Cory pinging my Map out in the hall. I'd received just enough confirmation from Mr. Gold for Cory to risk jumping in the cube with me. That was, in truth, the only time we'd been totally connected, every single dimension collapsing into this one. We'd remained connected since, just not to the same degree. Still, it was better than it had been. I was mostly aware of him now. Some kind of residual link remained between us, something left over from all the different Corys, all the different Davids. A sort of tension. I could feel it right that moment, now that I was thinking about it, like he was tied to me with a piece of string.

Had my second experience with Sarah, on the field, somehow strengthened my connection to Cory? Actively using my power to reconnect to Sarah in the atrium after the game had definitely opened some kind of inner door. Maybe I was becoming more instinctively aware of my powers and what they could do. There was no denying how keenly I felt Cory's presence despite the fact that he wasn't in the room.

Maybe it was stupid, but I couldn't help myself. I'd spent my whole life believing real Super-powers were beyond my grasp. But I'd scored an 83 AV! Now that the tantalizing possibility of powerful abilities was within reach, I wanted to know what I could do. I *needed* to know. For better or for worse, I was tied to Cory.

I took a deep breath and closed my eyes. Then I reached out and gave the string between us a tug.

I watch as Simantha, behind the force-field in Dawn's lab, trails her finger over the glowing blue barrier. A faint crackle of energy sizzles from her fingertip, leaves an incandescent afterimage hanging in the air. She uses this luminous line to draw ghostly people, fanciful buildings, and childlike impressions of Anymals. She pauses and draws a glowing heart.

My own heart hammers in my chest. Is she trying to tell me she feels the way I feel? She is laughing, and it makes my spirit soar to hear her happiness, to know that spending time with me brings her such joy. She taps the barrier again and watches the sparkles that crawl across its surface, fading as they escape from beneath her fingertip. She giggles.

"It tickles," she says.

I reach up to touch her fingertip with mine. In an instant, I'm punched across the lab, knocking over a bookcase on the way. Books and flimsies, smart-glass tablets, and file folders full of loose diagrams explode into the air. A fluttering cloud of papers slowly drifts down to settle on me where I lay, stunned, staring at the cream tile ceiling.

Simantha is frantic. "Cory? Cory!" She screams my name, over and over. "Cory! Cory, wake up! Cory!"

I hear the crackling impacts as she beats against the force-field, trying to get to me. Inside, I smile. She really does care! I lay there a moment longer, savoring her distress, reveling in the realization of her love. Then I take pity on her. I groan and try to rise.

Now it's my turn to panic. I can't move. I . . . I can't move! I'm paralyzed! The energy in the barrier . . . it did something to me! I can't feel anything! My whole body is numb!

Struggling desperately, I strain to wiggle even one finger. Nothing. There are voices approaching. Someone heard me crashing around. Someone is coming to investigate.

I snapped back to myself. My bowl of cereal had gone soggy. My spoon was frozen in the air, halfway to my mouth.

Cory! I lurched to my feet, but my knees had turned to jelly. I found myself leaning hard against the wall, gasping for breath. A horrendous sense of guilt assaulted me. I could barely think straight. I had a sudden, vivid recollection of Cory, that first day we'd met, talking about meeting a Cupid. I remembered considering how weird and creepy it must have been to have one push images and feelings into your head. How . . . *invasive.* Had he noticed me there, in his head, bearing witness to his private moment with Simantha?

Queasy, I pushed off the wall and staggered through my apartment. I didn't waste any time debating with myself. I had no doubt what I had witnessed was the real thing; it was happening right that moment. I had to get there and make sure Cory was all right. Who else could? I would worry about the intrusive nature of my abilities after I knew he was okay.

I cursed myself as I ran. I knew! I *knew,* even as I'd said it, that encouraging Simantha and Cory to spend time together was a mistake. Worse, I'd suggested they keep their friendship a secret, so Simantha wouldn't be seen talking to empty air, assumed to be mal-functioning. Because of me, Cory had been hurt in the lab. Simantha had no way to get past the barrier to assist him, and whoever he had heard, they might not be coming to investigate. They might just be passing by in the hall outside. Even if they did enter Dawn's lab, they might not notice Cory laying there, with his powers in full Forget-Me mode. I was the only one who knew he was there and could actually reach him.

My footsteps pounded in the corridors. Startled people jumped aside as I hurtled around corners and through doorways. I drew numerous stares and quite a few acerbic comments about my heed-less pace. I barely noticed. My thoughts kept circling back to what I had been considering over breakfast: my power was starting to mature. It kept reaching out to make connections. I had connected Dawn's team to a solution. Simantha was now awake and function-ing as a direct result of making that connection. While I was sure they would've figured out a way to reactivate Simantha eventually without my help, it hadn't been them who connected Simantha to Cory despite their own misgivings. That was all me.

It was worrisome. How much of my group of friends coming together was a result of me, of my power, pulling the strings in some way? Were the connections between us even real? Or were they forced into place against everyone's natural inclinations? Amyati certainly wouldn't spend any time with me if she had a choice about it. And Cory . . . even before we'd connected in the Quantum Cube, I had somehow seen through his memory-blanking power to notice him in the classroom. We had already begun to connect before I'd ever been aware of him! How much control over this did I really have? Was it really me, reaching out to Sarah and Cory? Or was I just along for the ride, believing I had some agency over my own fate? My power might simply be using me to make opportunistic links whenever it pleased! There were no guarantees these connections were even a good thing. How much did my intentions matter when I wasn't always in control? What if I only ended up accidentally hurting people? Or worse . . .

I staggered and leaned against a wall. I felt sick. I couldn't believe I was even thinking such a thing. It seemed crazy. Was it even possible? The implications were terrifying. Cory was hurt, right now, because of me. But what if he had died? How could I live with myself if my power could derail people's lives that way? How could I continue just walking around, letting my ability reach out to tie people's fates together in random combinations, never knowing what the consequences would be? How could I predict the results? How could I *control* it?

I shoved the idea away. *Later.* Head pounding, heart assailed by guilt, I rushed to the CSD labs to find Cory.

Predictably, Cory was nowhere to be found. The lab was in total disarray, and it didn't appear like anyone had come to investigate. Simantha spotted me the moment I walked in.

"David! Did you see Cory in the hall?" Simantha had been seated on the bench in the cell when I entered. She stood hurriedly.

I ignored her and walked over to where Cory must have fallen. Nothing. I couldn't be certain I wasn't staring right at him and forgetting he was there. But I didn't think so.

"David? Once again, you do not speak to me. Please answer my question!"

I turned to look at her. Just like in my vision, she was wearing a high-necked body sheathe of soft gray material with darker blue panels at the sides. The overall effect accentuated her height and athletic slimness. The jumpsuit covered her from wrists to ankles, lovingly hugged her body. As she moved to the force-field, standing as close as she could without actually touching it, I could easily watch the play of muscles in her legs and stomach. Her hair fell loose about her shoulders in bouncing ringlets.

I was afraid to even talk to her. I didn't want to make any more inadvertent connections, but her eyes were worried, imploring me silently. If she was simply mimicking human emotions, I couldn't tell the difference. And I couldn't just walk away.

"Simantha, what happened?"

"You must already know, or you would not be here looking at the floor exactly there, where he lay. You came to find Cory. You knew he was hurt."

"Yes," I admitted.

"Then you waste time asking me to tell you what you already know. I will instead tell you what you must not know, since you came here rather than wherever Cory is. He left the lab shortly after the accident. He would not speak to me! I believe he was embarrassed. The energy field overloaded his nervous system, particularly his motor control functions, and this caused him to soil himself. But the paralysis was only temporary. His Map is there, by the file cabinet. He could not locate it under the scattered papers, and I did not think to detect it until after he left without it."

I looked where she indicated. Flimsies crunched under my feet as I bent to retrieve Cory's Map. The durable percipient plastic was intact. It glowed faintly at my touch but remained blank. It knew I wasn't Cory. It would be logging my contact and would allow the use of basic functionality, but that was it. Accessing Cory's personal files to see if there was some clue as to where he might go to lay low wasn't an option. Maps bind with a person's unique energy signature. Simple, effective security.

"He loves you, you know," I said to the Map in my hand.

"I know," said Simantha. I looked over at her and saw her move away from the force-field to stand pensively in the center of the cell. Her hands clasped her elbows close to her body, and her shoulders were drawn in. She was looking at the floor. I waited for her to say more, to tell me she loved Cory, too, or that she would be careful with his heart.

Simantha said nothing.

I left her that way, furious with her for leading Cory on. But my traitorous heart had started racing as her silence stretched out. Because if she didn't love Cory . . .

I rejected the thought before I'd completed it. What was it about her that made me desire her? I understood Cory's obsession, but did she have the same effect on everyone? Or was she subtly manipulating the two of us, somehow, because we were both impressionable teenage boys and she might be able to use us to secure her freedom? I had already agreed to escort her around PA once she was cleared for release, against my better judgment.

Pushing Simantha from my thoughts, I wracked my brain, trying to think of some way to locate Cory. It was an insoluble problem. Without his Map, I couldn't simply ping him. And with his powers, if he didn't want to be found, he simply wouldn't be. *Unless* . . .

I turned my steps and hurried to the Quantum Lab.

Ralph was in, running some basic calibrations of the system, tinkering with the parameters, trying to improve performance. A group of potential Supers had just come through, and the readings had been lackluster. Nothing unusual in that, as most people rated fairly low, but Ralph seemed to take it personally, as though everyone had powers and it was up to him and his machine to suss them out. He was a bit of a worry wart, despite the way he goofed around with Gavin and Moses. He was probably just trying to satisfy himself that nothing obvious had been missed.

I would've felt more comfortable asking Gavin or Moses. They were more easy-going. Ralph had a tendency to do things by the book, citing PA rules and regulations to dissuade any funny business. Still. *Nothing ventured, nothing gained,* I told myself. Taking a deep breath, I made my request. Carefully, without mentioning Cory, I explained a bit about my first experience in the Quantum Cube, the way I had seen myself in different realities. I pointed out that it had been drastically different from the second time through. I told Ralph that I hadn't had much luck, since then, in unlocking my Super-powers. Did he have access to the results? No? Well, I had rated really high. Like, really, *really* high. With no real manifestation of my powers beyond the shoelace thing (and here I mentally nudged my laces for emphasis), I couldn't shake the feeling my power was somehow connected with the whole multiple-dimensions thing. What else could account for that bizarre vision the first time through? And so, I wanted to take another ride in the box. If he didn't mind, that is. Think that would be cool?

"Sure," said Ralph. I slowly let out my breath. I hadn't realized I'd been holding it. *Well, that was easy.* I had expected some kind of resistance, maybe an application through official channels or something, but Ralph simply took my rambling explanation at face value and started spinning up the machine.

"I'll have to call in Moses and Gav, just to make sure I've got enough pairs of hands in case the Goat starts eating the Meanstreak's tail," said Ralph, pushing an amber button. "But the cube has been used thousands of times, and it's safe enough. We don't usually take it out for joyrides—the Bearcat, and all that—but your hypothesis is certainly interesting." He flipped a few more switches and twisted a dial sharply. The wheels on his office chair hummed as he slid down to the far end of the panel, then toggled more doodads.

"Uh, sure. Bearcat. That's the one that sits around eating leaves all day, right?" Ralph nodded. "So . . ." I hesitated. I didn't want to seem pushy. "This might take a while? Should I come back later?"

"No, no. Just be a few minutes. Ah, here they are."

Gavin and Moses appeared. They weren't in lab coats, but otherwise, they looked much as they had the last time I saw them.

"Hey, Dave."

"David."

We bumped knuckles. I was struggling to remain calm, but inside I was seething with impatience. "Hey, Gavin. Moses. Thanks for doing this."

"No worries, kid," said Gavin. "If the perceptions of the trip weren't so subjective, I'd say take a camera with you."

"We'll settle for a thousand-word essay instead," Moses put in.

Ralph stood. "Ready?"

We descended the ramp into the hangar. The Quantum Cube split along the dividing yellow line and opened wide. Fog machines hissed as blue lights strobed.

"For science!" cried the Quantum Crew in unison, palms raised in mock worship of the cube.

I stepped through the mist into . . . everywhere.

"Cory?"

The space around me had gone dark, save only the tiny stars of the sensors. As I watched, the walls receded into infinite distance, linked to me by chains of myself. The chains divided, spread, then split again. Davids that were, that are, that would be.

"Cory?" My voice seemed to echo in the void. He wasn't anywhere to be seen. Just me, alone again, feeling isolated, adrift in a sea of myself.

The floor fell away, and I looked down. I stood on my shoulders, and I stood on my shoulders below that, on and on again, down into the infinite depths. Looking up, I saw more of the same: Davids stacked above me as far as I could see. David, David, David, David. But no Cory.

Had I been wrong?

"Cory? Answer me!" I pleaded. Where on Earth could he have gone?

"CORY!" I screamed. I was beginning to panic. I didn't know how long I had left in the cube. I knew my time inside seemed longer than it actually was. Had minutes passed, or only a few heartbeats?

There was no one but me inside the cube. Hopelessly, I sank to my knees. Davids all around me did likewise, dropping to their knees amid a throng of those who remained standing. It was the clue I needed.

I leapt back to my feet. He must be here somewhere! Only some of the Davids were giving in to despair. Only some of them . . . only some of *me* were displaying the same emotions I was feeling. That meant that some of us didn't feel lost. They didn't have to, because I hadn't lost Cory in their world. . .

My head was spinning. I was having difficulty figuring out how to think about this. Me, them, us. I looked around, feeling dizzy, and picked out a couple versions of myself who seemed confident, standing tall. What did they know that I didn't? What was different in their world? *If only I could see through their eyes!*

I didn't feel the shift, but my perspective seemed to change from one moment to the next. I was in a different part of the crowd. I had switched positions with one of the other Davids.

Oh no . . . Did I just jump between dimensions? How would I even know? And how would I find my way back? But I couldn't stop now. I had to find Cory.

I shifted again, picking another David at random. Then again. I tried to pick Davids who seemed to know what was going on, but how to tell? There were just so many! An infinite ocean of myself that stretched out in all directions. Hopping through the crowd, blinking from one point in the lattice to another from moment to moment, I swapped places with myself over and over, scanned around desperately, and called Cory's name. I reached inside myself and felt for that humming vibration, that link between us. I pulled on it, shouted for him, and switched places with still more Davids. I teleported wildly through the crowd.

Suddenly, I felt the connection twitch. How to even describe that sensation? Like holding the opposite end of a rope as someone flicks their end. A ripple passed down the line and into me, then traveled back, like a wave washing up against the shore, then retreating. I chased after it, wading deeper into the sea of me.

There was a fog growing all around me now. A rising mist. The furthest Davids were no longer visible. Those in the middle distance were slowly fading, lost in the fog. The horizon was closing in as the haze thickened.

Soon, I couldn't see anything beyond the reach of my own hands. I was completely alone in a gray limbo. There were no more Davids to jump to. The place I had come from was lost somewhere behind me, but I could feel Cory now, a sense of reaching from somewhere in the fog just beyond my vision. He was right there! And he was hurt, upset, confused. But where was he? Where was *I*?

"Cory? Cory!" I called.

A dim shape solidified. It seemed the mist condensed and thickened into a tall, distorted smear, vaguely man-like in appearance, without real edges, impossible to focus on.

A Cupid.

Oh. Oh no.

Alien images and feelings assaulted my senses.

<bewildering variety of arches and domes>
<triumph, long anticipated>

My mind reeled. Sweat prickled my skin. Nausea gripped me, making my stomach heave. I swallowed back a flood of saliva.

<fish, flopping helplessly on dry land>
<distinct sense of belonging somewhere else>

I struggled to make sense of the concepts as they rushed through me. The pictures flickered past too fast to grasp them. Not just one fish, gasping out its dying breath, but thousands, each one distinct, each setting different, each moment concrete and separate from the others, yet all of them linked. Identical in theme. The fish weren't synthetic; they were natural—precursors, actual fish! I focused on that one detail and clung to it like a drowning man clings to a buoy. The images heaved like a sea, threatening to pull me under.

<men pushing boulders up steep hills>
<exhaustion, fear of what is to come>

The emotional undercurrents of the mental images exploded inside me: huge feelings too big to contain. They wracked me and turned me inside out. My own thoughts and feelings were shoved aside. There was no space for them. Swept under by a wave of dizziness, I cowered away, but in the fog, there was no direction, no up or down, just me spinning helplessly, terrified of the next deluge, knowing I had to endure it, uncertain I could.

"Please!" I begged the Cupid. "Please help me!"

The thing hovered in the fog, silently watching me struggle for something to anchor myself to. An eternity of worry stretched within that single moment. The dread it had instilled in me closed my throat. The certainty of a terrible doom approaching wrung a forlorn sob from my battered soul. I had nothing else to give. I was merely human, only seventeen years old. I didn't have the years of experience required to appreciate the staggering expanses of time it had endured. I didn't have the capacity to encompass the unending emotional distress it had attempted to share with me.

Perhaps it realized as much. After ages or mere moments—I couldn't be sure which—it relented.

<hands offering water>
<terrible pity>

My relief was immense, every bit as overwhelming as my terror had been. As quickly as it had come, the Cupid vanished.

I felt the electric hum of the link to Cory snap into razor focus. Shivering convulsively, I cast about me, searching for some sign of him. From the corner of my eye, I saw a silver cord that passed from me to a nearby David, through him to a David beyond. Link by link, it disappeared into dark distances, a shining thread leading home. Back to my own reality. Instinct? Or alien assistance? At the moment, I didn't really care. I just wanted to get back to where I'd started.

"Cory, where are you?"

He slowly gathered color as the obscuring fog withdrew. I knew this was not my Cory, just a version of him. A thought or a memory—knowledge possessed by some other version of me. Another David was looking at Cory while I looked through his eyes. This Cory belonged in a different dimension. But this was what I had come to find: when he got scared, he probably ran to the same place my Cory did.

"Where have you hidden?" I asked him.

He looked at me, mouth opening, then hesitated in confusion. He seemed to struggle, trying to focus on me. I had my foot in the door, but was it enough? I reached across the barriers that separated our worlds, and I willed him to hear me. To *answer*.

"*Cory!* Tell me *where!*"

"Restoration Point Church," he said uncertainly. "Who . . .?"

But I was already racing back down the chain, leaping from David to David, swapping positions as rapidly as I could. Each step took me closer to home, to my own reality. I felt horrendous pressure, a sense of urgency so powerful I began to weep, terrified I wouldn't make it in time. The walls of the cube had reappeared, still so very far away but closing in fast. David after David was winking out of existence.

A glowing yellow line encircled me, delineating the distant horizon. Like a lasso, it was cinching rapidly tighter as the walls collapsed toward the center. The radius of existence was shrinking, and it was moving much faster than I could go.

With a defiant scream, I made one final effort and leapt for home.

XV

Now might be a good time to discuss our uninvited guests. I'm sure you've been wondering.

They revealed themselves on Christmas Eve in December of 2270, and they came bearing gifts of advanced technology, science, and mathematics. With these gifts the aliens rapidly established a firm grip on the hearts and minds of the intellectual community and were almost universally hailed by them as the saviors of humanity.

With the benevolent hand of the aliens hanging protectively over them, the world's scientists, artists, inventors, and other creative types had free reign and nearly unlimited resources to pursue their visions. The aliens made it clear, despite the language barrier, they would only contribute to those efforts that were intended to advance the progress of humanity as a whole—and Super-humanity in particular—with one proviso: the aliens would severely curtail any and all scientific and cultural activity they deemed "atavistic," as the translator put it.

The world had, by then, descended into an appalling tangle of miniature wars, border strife, political coups, hostile corporate takeovers, mercenary activity, terrorism, protests, and riots. While nuclear armaments had been mercifully abolished and systematically dismantled over seven decades earlier by the unprecedented One World Treaty of 2193, the return to "safer" non-nuclear warfare had emboldened tyrants and power-hungry madmen the world over. When the final signature was affixed to the armistice documents, the carefully maintained balance of mutually assured destruction tottered, tipped, and fell to pieces practically overnight. As the wealthy elite struggled to protect their assets, gathering mercenary armies to defend their corporate interests and establishing areas of absolute control, influential politicians used the tried-and-true combination of lobbying, glad-handing, and misinformation to pit rivals against each other and eke out their own little kingdoms amid the turmoil. Gangs flourished, battling with police forces as they rose to power. Vast tracts of real estate were walled off, becoming anarchist enclaves or surveillance states.

Advances in high-density nutritious food production, coupled with sustainable energy in the form of efficient, environmentally friendly photosynthetic building materials perfected in the late 2090s, had led to a population explosion, and by the time the aliens arrived, humanity was already well on its way to paving the globe. In 2270, probably eighty percent of Earth's landmasses were citified, and perhaps twenty-five percent of our oceans supported floating extensions of the City as well.

The ice caps had been melting for centuries, so in 2201, we tapped what was left of them for water and began applying experimental weather control devices to the problems of the ozone and drastic climate change. Eventually, after a series of horrendous, man-made, *un*-natural disasters had wiped out nearly two million people and inspired God-fearing cults the world over to rise and murder thousands more scientists, a balance was found in 2255. Weather control devices, at long last, had been honed and calibrated to a point where they began to work as desired. The weather calmed, and climate change was reversed, or at least arrested. The summers were still hotter everywhere, the winters uniformly more extreme, but as the years went by things were resetting to a more natural rhythm. Not that anyone could remember what a natural rhythm was anymore. Most plants and Anymals that had survived to that point were either carefully husbanded in small numbers to be cloned at need or had been genetically modified so drastically they were no longer recognizable in their original forms.

In 2271, shortly after their arrival, the aliens introduced their version of nano-technology, a thing we already had here on Earth but had never truly mastered. No longer solely the province of the excessively wealthy few, nano-technology became nearly ubiquitous, though the tiny devices varied wildly in quality, reliability, effectiveness, and longevity. Still, the overall result was improved health, extended lifespans, cleaner air and water, and further improvements in food production and nutrition. The new nano-technology also revolutionized recycling, turning demolition and construction into simultaneous parts of the City's ongoing expansion. The population exploded again: people were healthier, better able to produce more children more often, and didn't die nearly as young. As icing on the cake, the City was now able to grow rapidly to keep pace with the population boom. Abandoned and decrepit districts were efficiently cannibalized by nano-machines and reassembled into shiny new enclaves of smart-glass and photosynthetic plastics. Generating their own energy in the sunshine that was now allowed to shine on a strict schedule, most buildings were self-contained little cities in their own right. The City continued to grow upward and outward. By 2312, most of the remaining dry land was slowly being devoured by the City, and the oceans were vanishing underneath the leading edges as the City expanded.

During all this unexpected extraterrestrial generosity, the aliens had never specifically told us who they were or what they wanted with us. Though it was common knowledge they had an interest in working to advance humanity's burgeoning Super-powered community, exactly why this concerned them remained a mystery. Any alien who was asked was liable to give a different collage of imagery weighted with subjective truckloads of emotional freight. For every alien, the very concept of identity seemed to be different. There were bound to be some similarities in their ideas of race and purpose, but by and large, they were as individualistic as humans. There are people who think of humans as a virus, or a cancer, rapidly killing Mother Earth, and still others who view us as being made in the image of a benevolent creator, inheritors of the kingdom of Heaven—just two examples of what I mean. The aliens were no different.

Speaking of Heaven, it was only a matter of time before someone began comparing our new friends to angels. They had already been hailed as saviors by certain segments of Earth's population. Comparing benevolent aliens, who descended from the sky, with angelic beings from religious writings didn't take a huge stretch of the imagination. The fact that a lot of old religious artwork depicts angels in a distorted, hazy, or indistinctly glowing way was no doubt a contributing factor to the sudden popularity of this notion, considering the appearance of the aliens themselves. Two or three hundred years ago, we might have thought this art was simply poorly rendered, made with shoddy materials, or damaged by time and neglect, thus difficult to see clearly. But once the aliens revealed themselves, it didn't take long for people to wonder: What if the artwork was perfect? What if it was actually an exact rendering of alien beings that had descended from the sky? Fuzzy outlines and all, a lot of it looked just like them.

Such theories were quick to gain traction. The aliens had, in fact, been here for millennia, inspiring our religions, watching and even guiding our development until we were ready to meet them in person. Indeed, this was Dawn and Miguel's take on things. Working on Simantha had only served to reinforce their view since she was a superior piece of artificially intelligent technology that had originally been constructed something like three thousand years earlier. The aliens themselves didn't exactly admit to it, but through early interactions, their longevity became common knowledge. A lot of connections were drawn between them and humanity's early advancements. Many very intelligent people thought the Egyptians had help building the pyramids, for example; Stonehenge was either built by giants or people who had assistance; some of the columns in old Greek temples had capstones that weighed twenty-three tons. It's hard to imagine, with the limited engineering technology of the time, how people could have lifted those stones into place on their own. There are even stories, written around the time those temples were built, that claim the gods themselves descended to assist with the construction. Similarly, the Nazca Lines in Peru had been built on such a massive scale that they can only truly be appreciated in all their grandeur from a good height above. People certainly didn't fly back then, but perhaps their intended audience did? Some of those images depict elongated human forms, alien-looking beings with glowing auras. Coincidence? People had begun to wonder.

Were they aliens or angels? Either way, some opinionated pundit on a popular syndicated talk show wound up comparing our alien visitors to *Kheruvim*, the angels described in Hebrew religious works. The interviewer was baffled by the obscure reference and had asked for clarification. The speaker informed him that "*Kheruvim*" is the word we derive "cherubim" from. The cherubim were angels who served at the throne of God. They were typically represented as having multiple pairs of wings, sometimes even lion faces, but despite this discrepancy, a lot of the artwork did resemble the weird aliens with their hazy, vaguely human appearance. Besides, argued the guest speaker, the aliens spoke in images. It would not be far-fetched to assume some of the artwork was a combination of their actual form with imagery taken from the things they had said to the people of the time.

By the time of that widely viewed conversation, we had been talking to the aliens for quite some time, mostly through computers, but also through a few rare individuals with exceptional gifts for interpretation—people like Susie. The aliens no longer prevaricated;

their primary intent was to guide us toward genetic perfection and the next stage of our evolution: the Super-human. Super-powers had already begun to appear around the world, sporadically, for well over a century—possibly even millennia, at various intervals throughout history—but the aliens insisted the time had come to accelerate the process. They urged us to start breeding selectively to encourage our development. And they would be happy to guide our choices . . .

In 2275, the aliens introduced their mechanical womb, a wonder of technology that had been in development for thousands of years. Now the breeding could begin in earnest.

Well, what were we to think of that? It *was* like playing match-maker, I suppose. If it seemed strange that aliens had appeared out of nowhere simply to give us great dating advice, it was also easy to ignore; they didn't make any overt efforts to prevent us from mixing and matching in whatever ways we chose. They might decree, for example, that Scientist A, who had developed Super-intellect, must provide genetic material for experimental combination with Athlete B, whose range of Super-athletic abilities might prove an effective match. Once the genetic material was secured, Scientist A could continue pursuing whomever he liked, and Athlete B could do the same. The actual combination would take place in a mechani-cal womb, so it hardly inconvenienced anyone. Letting them play matchmaker seemed such a small price to pay for all the benefits the aliens provided. Human greed was only too happy to make apologies for the rare alien demand.

I assume someone who watched the syndicated program where the *Kheruvim* connection was made took this matchmaker idea one step further, making the leap from cherubim to cherubs, those chubby little angel babies seen flitting about in so much ancient artwork. From there, it was only a small step to a particular and more contemporary cherub who tended to pop up with a bow and arrow around Valentine's Day, back when that ancient custom had been observed: Cupid, the angelic matchmaker. The name got trotted out in reference to the aliens on a couple different talk shows, and before anyone realized it, it was in our everyday vernacular.

The intellectuals of the world rejoiced. The Cupids would lead us to the next stage of our evolution. From the tone of their support, they were already in love, no matchmaking required. Super-powers were a much-studied phenomenon by then, but now we knew that the Cupids had had a hand in the origins of our burgeoning abilities. This meant we could get *our* hands on the wealth of genetic research they had collected, to streamline our own efforts.

It certainly did seem, to those in the know, that the Cupids had been carefully maneuvering key individuals since time immemorial, experimenting with different genetic lines, slowly working their way toward combinations that would prove more and more likely to create Super-humans. They had an incredible amount of data on the intricate inner workings of our DNA. It could only have been gathered over a vast period of time, unless, as some scientists believed, it had been gathered over multiple short periods of time *simultaneously*, which is to say, in multiple different realities that were . . . advancing in parallel, I guess. This was a theory much scoffed at, rarely advanced in serious circles, though my experiences in the Quantum Cube sometimes made me wonder. At any rate, now that Super-powers were becoming more common, the Cupids had revealed themselves, admitted to their experimenting, and requested willing human involvement.

"No more alien kidnappings or unwanted probing," joked one comedian. "Now we can *volunteer* for the probe! I sure hope that old saying about Cupid never missing is true!"

Supporters of this vision of the future—humans and aliens working together for the greater good of humanity—formed the backbone of a new echelon in human society. With direct links to our alien benefactors, access to technology the Cupids had so far withheld was granted. Scientists the world over got a leg up on the competition. Groups like Project Arete flourished, though often in secret.

Religious fundamentalists, anthropocentric elitists, even military groups hoping to score some sweet tech, all targeted the Neo-Intelligentsia, with mixed results. Some Cupid technology was captured, studied, and even replicated. Other things were either impossible to comprehend or couldn't be fabricated with our current technology and understanding. Still other bits of alien gadgetry were swiftly and severely recovered by the Cupids, who gave no explanations nor apologies for their surgically precise reprisals. We learned very quickly that certain things were off-limits. The Cupids, for their part, never took it beyond what was necessary to make their point. Sometimes, they even responded lethargically, or not at all, and stolen technology was allowed to disseminate. There was never any need for them to make a regular example out of anyone. Occasional demonstrations of their superiority were enough. Nobody wanted to risk making them angry; at best, they would withdraw, leaving humanity to its own devices; at worst, they would wipe the planet clean and start over, using genetic material from their vast library of human DNA. The Cupids would supply us with what we needed when we needed it, and we would simply have to accept it.

One would think the Cupids would have tried to guide us toward repairing the badly wrinkled and often violently torn social fabric of our world in order to free more of humanity to bend its efforts toward their goals, but they showed no interest in our politics whatsoever, nor in the elevation of humanity as a whole. Earlier alien comments about the advancement of humanity in its entirety (and the punishment of so-called "atavistic" pursuits) notwithstanding, they focused primarily on their desire to increase the prevalence of Super-powers in each new generation. The development of the *Übermensch* was their one true goal, whatever sugar-coating they or their translators might apply to make the idea palatable. The only time the Cupids paid any attention to our internecine violence was when some ill-considered attack was launched at them directly, or indirectly by targeting the scientific bodies working under them. Anyone so foolhardy as to assault the Cupids or their mission was disciplined with de facto authority.

Thus, a new status quo was reached. On the ground floor: warring factions, politicians, police forces, gangs, companies, military and mercenary groups, and everyone else caught up in the mix—a great writhing sea of Normal humanity. Rising from this: the Super-humans, a rapidly growing percentage—still so very human, still hopelessly connected to all of the striving and competition that has defined humanity for our entire existence. And above the Supers, urging them on: the Neo-Intelligentsia—those scientists, teachers, creative thinkers, and visionaries (many of whom had unusual abilities themselves) who saw the vaunted goal of Super-powers for all and were charting a path toward it.

Above them: the Cupids. Otherworldly. Unknowable. Alien. Watching us all.

XVI

"There you go, Davy. Hot cocoa with exactly nine little marshmallows."

My mother placed the heavy ceramic mug in front of me, then gave my shoulder a squeeze before resuming her seat across the kitchen table. Outside, the sky had been overcast and slightly muggy, but the clouds were beginning to break up. Bright silver light filtered through the glass, which tinted itself to an appropriate level of safety against the sun.

Silhouetted by the luminous square of window behind her, my mother's face had fallen into shadow. But I could still see her small smile of satisfaction as I took my first sip. My mom had always taken a peculiar pleasure in catering to my strange childhood whims. I couldn't really remember the day I'd decided eight marshmallows were too few and ten were too many. It had likely been during some childish tantrum, an effort to exert control over an environment that had grown increasingly beyond my abilities to manage as I grew older.

Not that my parents hadn't tried to do right by me. It's just that I'd been frustrated by schoolwork that seemed pointless, since I hadn't been allowed to actually go to school. I'd felt certain that schoolwork belonged in schools. The fact that it had followed me home after I'd been rejected from those hallowed educational precincts was insult on top of injury. Stuck at home all the time, I'd been sure I should be *playing*.

Frustratingly, the playing part had eluded me, too. More often than not, I'd watched other kids at the playground, unwilling to risk joining in for fear of being shoved and punched until I fell down. Despite this, I hadn't been totally willing to leave others to their play. Street games had slowly migrated away from me while I followed along disconsolately. I had been desperately lonely.

Angry and frustrated all the time, that was me. I guess I'd acted out at home because I'd just wanted one place where I could make the rules. *Nine* marshmallows, Mom! *Nine!*

My other protests fell on deaf ears, however. I'd been forced to slog through my education, regardless of my opinion on the matter, by a father whose temper had grown shorter right alongside mine. He had always been slightly more stubborn than I was, and he'd insisted I needed to learn if I was going to make something of myself.

I never could figure out what he meant by that. I was David. His son. I had already been made! My parents had done the real work of making me, choosing traits like eye color and hair type at the gene-bank, selecting a decent midrange nano-package offering a good mix of immunities and disease resistances to give me a shot at a long and healthy life. They couldn't afford a real custom kid, not on my dad's salary, so certain things would have to be left to fate, but they had scrimped and saved for almost a decade. They were going to make me right, even if they had to donate the majority of the genetic material themselves.

The actual process is something I'm not terribly familiar with; I haven't ever really considered being a father. But I know the gist of it, and it's nothing terribly fancy. My parents did the usual thing: go in, chat with some doctors and nurses, fill out some forms, and give a blood sample or a little scraping of skin. A natal farm does the rest, with its technicians and nano-machines and bio-mechanical wombs that are a thousand times safer and more efficient than the real thing. The idea that I might have more work to do to "make something" of myself seemed pretty far-fetched back then. What had all those people and machines been *doing* if not making me perfect, just the way I am?

Kids, eh? So certain of everything. Well, you live and learn. Most of the time, anyway. I knew now that I still had plenty of work to do. A *lot* of growing up. That, in essence, was why I was here, visiting my mother. She had always been the one to give me the perfect advice I needed whenever I found myself in a jam. But to be perfectly candid, running home to my mother hadn't been my first choice. I had started out chasing Cory, sprinting full tilt at my problems, as always. I'd hit a wall, though, and in the dazed aftermath, I'd realized the wall looked a lot like me. Maybe if I had gone home first, sought advice sooner, some of the pain and confusion could have been avoided.

After emerging from the Quantum Cube, thoroughly shaken by my encounter with the Cupid but more determined than ever to find Cory, I had stumbled up the ramp into the control room expecting solicitous concern for my clearly frazzled state. The Quantum Crew had elicited no hint they had any notion what had just transpired. To them, I was just an overly sweaty teenager emerging from a routine run through the cube. Did I look a little pale and dizzy? They didn't comment if I did.

Ralph glanced over from the computer displays. "Hey, how'd it go, kid?"

"Uh, hypothesis confirmed, I think."

He grinned and gave me a thumbs up. "Hear that, Gav? We got some kind of dimension-hopping wizard, here, just like in that stupid card game you play."

"It's not stupid, Ralph, it's classic, from before the turn of the millennium. Just because you don't understand it doesn't mean . . ."

"Yeah, yeah," Moses interrupted their argument. I had the distinct impression it wasn't the first time he'd done so. "You can enlighten us on game night. Right now, I need you to hop in the pit with the Danger Noodles and pull some fangs. I'll handle the tail end."

"Nullifidians . . . it's *classic*," muttered Gavin. He moved to a locker and pulled out a radiation suit.

Ralph sighed. "You better scramjet," he said. "Gots us some work t'be did."

"Sorry," I told him. But I didn't hang around. I was itching to get to the church and find Cory.

Now that I knew where Cory had likely gone to hide, it seemed obvious. It was where he had spent a lot of his time growing up, where he would go for food, sleep, even a semblance of company when he felt particularly lonely. He had confided that he would sometimes sit and listen in at Sunday Mass, or during other gatherings when guest speakers visited. Cory had taken some comfort in the idea of a Heavenly Father looking down upon him, loving him unconditionally, even if He never came down to offer a hug when things were tough.

I didn't think a remote God was what Cory needed, right then. In my mind, an older brother—someone who was actually present, who recognized him, who could tend to any injuries he had sustained—seemed of greater benefit.

I left the Project Arete facilities and made my way through the mall topside. It was unusually crowded, compared to the usual lazy activity, but judging by the signage, there was some sort of sale underway. Either it was the actual businesses in the mall trying to drum up some hype, or PA was doing some casual fundraising. Director Ruiz had her finger in about a million pies, pulling in income from all over the City to fund the massive and ambitious Project Arete.

I took a service tunnel under the street, rather than contend with the insanity of City traffic, and emerged a block from the Restoration Point Church. Approaching the building, I got the sense of a very old structure, lovingly restored until it had nearly fallen down despite the best efforts of the faithful who worshipped there. Then, with the advent of nano-machines, this building, along with much of the neighborhood, had received a long-overdue facelift. While it still resembled an old-fashioned church of timber and fieldstone, it was most likely made of photosynthetic plastics, polymer resins, and good old reliable concrete.

The beauty of this kind of construction was that, on the strictly regulated schedule of sunlight the City now enjoyed, most buildings generated their own power supply, with excess going to a storage battery for backup or sale to those who didn't generate enough energy for themselves. The system was a staggeringly complex network made up of relatively simple individual cells. The City, in some ways, was a lot like a living body.

I realized, after a moment, that I was simply standing on the walkway fronting the church, contemplating the building. Hadn't I come here for something more important than sightseeing? It *was* a nice building, but I had never had much of a passion for architecture. I scratched my head, befuddled. Well, whatever, I was here now. A quick glance at my Map showed me that my schedule had been cleared—by me, in some haste—less than an hour ago. I knew it must be important if I was dodging classes to come here. But why a church? I had never really had any interest in them before.

My Map chimed in. "*You are displaying signs of confusion and uncertainty. As instructed by you, this reminder has been activated to assist you in recovering your focus and agency. Please take three deep breaths, counting slowly backward from ten. Try to clear your mind of distractions. Further instructions to follow.*"

What on Earth? I set this up?

My Map insisted. "*Focus, David. All will become clear if you follow these instructions.*"

More bewildered than ever, I closed my eyes and took a deep breath. As I let it out, I started counting. A second breath, and I began to feel . . . something. Encouraged, I took a third deep breath and held it for a moment. As I exhaled, I relaxed, trying to let go of my spinning thoughts. Whatever was going on, I had obviously planned for it. Might as well go with the flow.

The Map pinged. "*Cory*," it said.

Everything came back with a snap. Images and sensations slammed into me. I had a visceral reaction, recoiling on the sidewalk and bumping into someone who was passing behind me.

"Easy, pal. I'm walkin' here."

"Sorry," I muttered. But I was furious. *Cory!* I shouted internally, pushing my anger down the link we shared. *Are you fuzzing me?* Incensed, I strode into the church, determined to corner him and get to the bottom of this. Didn't he realize I was here to help him? I'd been so worried about him!

The Restoration Point Church, as Cory had described, operated an outreach program for less fortunate citizens. While public replicators existed and had originally been installed throughout the City in an effort to end hunger, they were often poorly maintained, lacking in the essential nutrients needed to build healthy meals. Worse, they were sometimes hacked by malicious pranksters, producing vile flavors or even dangerous variations of requested items. Those in reasonable repair were often controlled by gang toughs who restricted their use to a select in-crowd or sold what was supposed to be free. In response to this, many groups in the City had decided to take the same approach, strictly controlling their own replicators for those who were willing to abide by their rules. As a recruiting tactic, it worked well. Not only gangs, but companies, political parties, Super-groups, and mercenary outfits all offered food and clothing to those in need. Thinking about it, Project Arete had essentially done the same thing for me. Practically every place of worship in the City did so as well, and the Restoration Point Church was no exception. Beyond meals, they also offered shelter, connections to education, employment, and, of course, spiritual guidance. The main difference here was that their meals were cooked in an old-fashioned kitchen, made from raw ingredients sourced from a replicator, rather than replicated ready to eat. Many believed the time and effort involved, the care required, somehow made the food more nutritious. I wasn't so sure about that, but there was something to be said for the sense of community in places like this.

Once in the main vestibule, I followed the delicious smells coming from the kitchen, making my way through a side door and down a long hallway. This led into a dining hall, half filled with long tables, behind which volunteers in aprons were busily putting together plates of food for a lineup of respectfully patient people. The low hum of voices was frequently punctuated by laughter. People arriving were warmly embraced with hugs and friendly greetings. Smiles were everywhere. I could see why Cory might keep returning here.

I spotted Cory just before he spotted me, standing in a lineup across the hall. He was serving himself something to eat while everyone around him carried on as if he wasn't there. He had become adept at slipping among strangers who weren't aware of him, avoiding collisions, constantly aware of his surroundings.

He saw me in the next instant. His eyes flew wide. Hesitating only briefly, he slapped his plate of food onto the back of the careworn older gentleman standing next to him, then swayed aside as the man turned in surprise to scan the room behind him. He saw me standing there, staring, and jumped to the obvious conclusion as the people around him clucked and muttered angrily about the mess on his nice coat. How ungrateful, to throw this nice food across the room like that.

The old man was moving purposefully toward me, saying something like, "Now see here, young man," while stripping off his soiled overcoat. I had the ludicrous notion that he was going to give me the option to make things right by laundering the coat for him, but

I didn't really have time for that conversation. What was going on with Cory? Why was he avoiding me?

"Your shoelace is untied, sir," I said. Despite his anger, he instinctively glanced down, and so it was. In fact, his laces were busily securing his feet together. His eyes shot back to me, the look on his face suddenly wary. I ducked aside and followed Cory out of the hall while the old man stood there, seething. There were voices raised in anger behind me, but I ignored them.

In the kitchen, the mouth-watering smells of home-cooked food distracted me. I stood stupidly for a moment, trying to remember what I was supposed to be doing. Someone barked at me to stir the rice. *Oh, right.* I took up a large synth-wood spoon and moved to comply when my Map pinged. This time, I didn't need to read the reminder. I dropped the spoon with a clatter and raced out the other end of the kitchen, leaving a rising babble of concerned voices in my wake. Cory had exited the church and was running across the yard, making his way for the Skyway station. He glanced back to see me leap down the back steps and sprint in pursuit.

"Leave me alone!" he shouted.

"Don't make me tie your freakin' shoelaces together, dude! Stop!"

Through our connection, I felt him focus his power, shape it into a club. The unfamiliar sensation wasn't nearly enough warning. He whirled as I caught up to him and smote my brain with it. My eyes crossed and I stumbled. Dizziness forced me to my hands and knees. I heard his hurried footsteps slapping the pavement, but I didn't bother trying my threatened shoelace trick. I wasn't sure I could focus enough to make it happen, and besides, he had taken me seriously enough to kick off his shoes. I was still staring at them, trying to figure out who they belonged to, when members of the Restoration Point Church congregation caught up to me.

They were upset, of course, but it seemed Cory had taken pity on me, and they didn't entirely remember why. It was evident I was in some distress, however. I was helped gingerly to my feet, the people around me trying in vain to piece together their various versions of the last few minutes to make some sense of why we were all out in the yard.

My Map was pinging relentlessly. *Yeah, I know,* I told it. *Shut up.* My memories were coming back. Only now, I didn't want them. I couldn't help it. I broke down and cried. Then I felt stupid for crying. Wasn't I angry with him for running away? Why had he messed with my head like that? Why was he avoiding me? I consoled myself with the knowledge that he was at least well enough to run away. I guess he didn't need me to treat any injuries from the force-field incident.

There was a woman sitting on the back steps of the church next to me. She had her graying brown hair pulled back in a loose pony-tail, and her face, though traced with fine lines around her eyes and mouth, was smooth and slightly tanned. She had her eyes closed and her chin lifted, enjoying the warmth of the washed-out sunlight as it filtered through machine-made clouds. She was simply dressed in brown slacks, a plain forest-green blouse, and ratty sneakers. She held a cup of tea in her hands. I sniffled, catching a whiff of synthe-sized jasmine, something citrusy.

"You okay?" she asked.

"No." I sighed. "Not really."

"Want to talk about it?"

I did, I realized. Just not with her. I didn't have a clue who she was.

"Uh, no thanks." I stood to go. "Hey, listen. Um . . ."

She opened her eyes and looked up at me. They were a startlingly clear gray. I opened and closed my mouth a few times, but nothing came out. I had been about to ask her to keep an eye out for Cory, to be kind to him if she saw him again, but it was a waste of breath. I felt certain she wouldn't know him if she met him. The woman closed her eyes and turned her face back toward the sun. I stood there for a moment, looking down at her, knowing there was some-thing I was forgetting, but not at all certain I wanted to remember.

I shook my head and walked away. I felt oddly bereft. If he pushed me away, what was left for him? Nothing. And where did that leave me? I had become used to the feeling of being important to somebody. Of being needed. But I was beginning to realize how much I needed him, too. He gave me purpose. Defined me, in a way. I felt like I didn't know who I was. I had been trying so hard to play the older brother, but somewhere along the line, I had gotten side-tracked, started pursuing my other friendships. I'd been caught up in the excitement of finally being accepted, being a part of something.

No wonder Cory was upset with me. I'd been neglecting him, and naturally, he'd turned to the one person who would always remember him. Simantha might not be human, but maybe that was the attraction; she wouldn't make human mistakes. She wouldn't get distracted. She wouldn't *forget*.

Reflecting on my relationships made me realize how slack I had been when it came to my parents. I had called over a month ago and found out they had gone to Tahiti—one of the rare places on Earth still separate from the rest of the City, though it was growing rapidly across the surrounding waves—and then I'd been so caught up in everything at Project Arete that I hadn't followed up when they got back. My mom had called and left a message two days ago. I had meant to get back to her, but . . .

No time like the present, I told myself. It was time to stop taking these things for granted. Besides, I could really use her advice. I turned my steps for home.

And that's basically how I wound up sitting in the kitchen at my parent's place, drinking hot cocoa with exactly nine little marshmal-lows in it. I was so choked up with jumbled emotions, I didn't know where to begin. I wanted to tell her that I didn't actually care how many marshmallows were in it—what mattered was that she had made it herself, just for me. She had remembered I liked hot cocoa with marshmallows. She had sat me down at the kitchen table and put the cocoa in front of me and asked me how I was doing. No guilt trip about being gone for the last couple years, about never calling her back. No recriminations or judgments. Just her gentle care and concern, her genuine interest in my life. My mother loved me, simply and completely. I could see that sometimes she felt hopeless about ever really understanding me. She tried, though, and I wasn't so sure I deserved it. I'd spent most of my life hardly noticing the efforts she made. But I couldn't bring myself to say any of these things. Instead, I told myself I would try to be worthy of her. Better late than never, I guess.

So, we talked. She told me about their trip, the way it had reignited a spark between her and my father that hadn't really been missing, exactly, but hadn't been the fire it used to be. Coals can smolder for a long time, though. They had rediscovered their passion for each other, for adventure, and they had made the most of it, exploring their exotic locale with a sense of discovery and joy. She could see I was somewhat embarrassed and uncomfortable with the topic, despite my best efforts to show an interest. She didn't dwell on it, but she smirked a bit. Her look said, *One day you'll understand.*

I thought about Simantha, three thousand years old or more. What would it be like for her, rediscovering a lost love? Like the Cupids, she had existed for so long, had experienced so much, it was hard for someone like me to fathom the depth of her emotions. Perhaps I could forgive her for not returning Cory's affections in quite the way he had hoped. It was a bit of a relief, actually, to realize that she couldn't love either of us the way we loved her. It would make it easier for me to let go and move on. I could see, now, that was what I had to do. Quite aside from the fact that I didn't want to compete with my adopted brother for her affections, part of me knew I didn't really have a clue what I felt for her anyway. Was it really love, or just infatuation for something interesting and exotic?

All this, and my mom hadn't even started giving me advice yet. I found myself feeling profoundly grateful for the effect she had on me. I'd been running away from my problems for so long, I'd forgotten she was such a positive and calming influence.

I told her a little bit about Project Arete: how I had ended up there, the things I had been learning. I told her about the friends I had made. Even Cory, and how complicated *that* could be. I saw how it made her light up with pride, and yes, maybe a little relief. Her little outcast was finally starting to fit in. Is there a word for taking pleasure in someone else's success? If there isn't, there should be. She radiated satisfaction, and it gave me a little more of the confidence I needed to face my fears—which brought us around to discussing my Super-power, and the way it had been awakening. I admitted that I was terrified of talking to people now, more than I'd ever been. Not because I worried that I couldn't make a connection, like when I was a little kid, but because I was worried *I would*. It seemed monstrously unfair to me that now, when I was finally coming into my own, growing in confidence, finding friendships, I'd been burdened by this incredible weight of responsibility, the knowledge that the things I said and did might lead to horrible pain or even death. It was too much for me to handle. I didn't know what was right and what was wrong anymore. I practically begged her for her insight and advice.

My mom stirred her cocoa as she thought about what I'd told her. She always left the spoon in when she drank cocoa. She never drank it quickly, complaining that the chocolate settled to the bottom before she could finish. I, on the other hand, had gulped it down the moment it had cooled enough not to burn my face off; my own mug had been empty for a while. I got up to heat some more water, then started rooting through the cupboards for the cocoa supplies.

"Let me see if I've got this straight, Davy. You're beginning to think your power has something to do with . . . what? Manipulating fate? Tying the threads of destiny together somehow? And you're worried that anything you might try to do could turn out . . . poorly?"

"Not just poorly, Mom. Disastrous! Cory was hurt because of me, and it could have been a lot worse. Those shields can paralyze your lungs if you're not lucky. Probably the only reason he didn't end up choking to death is because Simantha was touching the other side of the shield. Some of that energy went into her." I paused, suddenly uncertain. Simantha could clearly handle a lot more energy than a mere human. Had she been using Cory to figure out just how strong the shield was? The thought made me feel sick, but not because it was entirely possible. Rather, I didn't want to believe it. I wanted Simantha to match my fantasies. I desperately wanted her to be something pure and good and kind. I wanted her to be my *friend*. But how much did I know about her, really? She could be deadly dangerous, and soon, she was going to be wandering around Project Arete, with only me to keep her in line. What had I gotten myself into?

I leaned on the counter and put my head in my hands. My voice was subdued as I said, "I couldn't handle it if someone died because of something I put into motion."

"Step back a bit, honey. Nobody has died," replied my mother. Then she lapsed into silence, slowly stirring her cocoa. I waited, knowing that she would explain what was on her mind once she found the words to express it. I reached for the kettle. Hot water joined the cocoa powder, cream, and sugar in my mug. The spoon rattled as I stirred. Then, one by one, I tossed tiny marshmallows to their doom. In my mind, they had the names of my friends as they fell to their fate: *Sarah, Jake, Alan.* I hesitated a moment. Tossed in Amyati. *She's connected to all this,* I thought. Then *Kevin, Susie, Cory. Simantha.* And the final marshmallow for me. *David. Headstrong son and poor excuse for an older brother. Drowned beneath the flood of connections he could no longer control.* With my spoon, I pushed the little marshmallow I'd named after myself under and watched the way some of the others stuck and went under with it.

Man, I was feeling morbid. I heaved a sigh and returned to my seat at the table.

My mother reached across and put her hand over mine. Her fingers were warm from her cocoa mug. "You know," she said reasonably, "doing nothing is also a choice that has consequences."

That put things into a different perspective. I frowned, thinking it through. She was absolutely right: I couldn't just curl up in a ball, refuse to engage with the world, and hope that would be the end of it. My absence would cause changes just as much as my presence would. I couldn't just give in to fear and live a timid life trying to avoid trouble. There were absolutely no guarantees that would work. Life was uncertain. I had to accept that uncertainty and make the best choices I could with the information I had. How could anyone hope to do more than that?

"Thanks, Mom." I gave her fingers a squeeze. She smiled and reached up to touch my cheek, then returned her attention to her cocoa. We sat in companionable silence, each of us thinking our own thoughts. There was so much more to be said, and yet, somehow, there was no need to say any of it. It was clear, if this was the only time she got to spend with me, she intended to enjoy it. I smiled ruefully. Making amends with my father probably wasn't going to be so easy. I found myself feeling relieved that he wasn't around, then immediately felt guilty for it.

When my cocoa was finished, I stood up and headed for the door, stepping into my shoes on the way through the foyer. My mother leaned against the doorframe, second mug of cocoa in hand, watching me cross the yard toward the Skyway as I shrugged into my jacket. My laces snugged themselves up as I went. Behind me, my mother nodded to herself. Then she went back into the house.

In the kitchen, at the bottom of the mug I had left on the table, were nine tiny marshmallows. A little worse for their ordeal, perhaps, but still recognizably nine little marshmallows, even if their edges had blurred somewhat as they melted together.

XVII

I would love to tell you things went back to normal after that. In swooped the Super-hero David with a newfound sense of purpose to put everything right again, wouldn't that be nice? I could wrap up this little memoir of mine, sign off with a comfortable happy ending, and put a tidy little pink bow on it.

Unfortunately, even the best advice is useless without actions that fall into alignment. I went back to Project Arete with the best of intentions, but let's be honest: I had always been better at tangling things up than undoing the knots afterward. Well, no, that's not entirely accurate; I could undo knots just fine. It was just that I tended to create more knots before I got the first ones fully undone. When I was younger, this sometimes led to me simply grabbing a knife and slicing through whatever had become tangled, like Alexander the Great with the fabled Gordian Knot. Problem solved, right?

Once again, the days blurred together, and that's only partly because there were so many things for me to juggle. Some of my distraction was because Cory continued avoiding me, fuzzing my mind if I got too close to cornering him. I don't know what he was dreading. I only wanted to talk, to let him know I was sorry.

My Map consistently reminded me of Cory's existence, so he couldn't simply blank my brain and walk away. Once I recovered my wits, I always managed to dredge up the memories from somewhere. I sometimes wondered if I was stealing them from other Davids in other realities, but I decided I couldn't afford to go down that particular path just then. It would drive me crazy, thinking about it. The main thing was the Map reminders worked.

I slowly came to the realization that I couldn't force Cory to deal with me. I'd sent him more than enough messages, and I knew he got them because I'd turned his Map in to the PA Lost and Found first thing when I got back. Later, when I checked in, I was told he must have come to pick it up because the device wasn't there anymore. A Map was no good to someone who didn't own it, and while they can be rekeyed, with a little effort, it was usually easier to connect to a new one than to go through the hassle. A new Map would simply fetch your data from your old one once it had verified your identity, then trigger a reset of the old device so that someone else could be keyed to it. Doubtless Cory had his old Map, or one that was functionally identical. He was getting my messages; he simply wasn't responding.

Fine. I had more than enough on my plate without worrying about him.

As much as I was able, I threw myself into my classes. Power and politics, ethics, and philosophy were all with Mr. Gold. Electronics, computer technology, robotics, cybernetics—these classes had a variety of teachers, but Francis put in an occasional appearance for nano-technology discussions as well as a few programming classes. This stuff was largely optional, just something I had a vague interest in since meeting Simantha. After talking with my mother, I had resolved to forget about the simulant girl, but the classes were fascinating, so I stuck with them.

A lot of my physical training fell under the direction of Jetman, who also coached us at Powerball practice and loudly despaired of ever making a respectable team out of us. But you could tell he was pleased, despite his ability to find fault in the tiniest things we did.

"He yells because he cares," Jake told me solemnly one day. He tried his best to say it with a straight face, but he couldn't do it. We both split our sides laughing. It was funny mostly because it was true. Jetman did care, and it was because of that we could put up with his ranting exuberance. He was just doing his best to hammer us into an effective team. His bluster was easy to see through anyway. I caught him wiping a tear with the back of his hand the first time I bested Kevin in a head-to-head force-lance duel on the field. When I asked if he was okay, he made me call for a medic, who arrived promptly and failed to find anything in his eye. Jetman cussed the medic out of the locker room, but the point had been made: he was proud of us, and he'd be damned if he'd ever admit it. Somehow, this made us try that much harder to impress him. It was something of a badge of honor to break past Baxter Wallace's gruff exterior and get him to evince some real emotion.

Martial arts and weapons training—and by extension, force-lance practice—fell under the auspices of Doctor Kernshaw, a sour little lemon of a man who said little to nothing, behaving as if his students ought to know what was expected of them. I struggled to keep up with the others in his classes, and if I learned anything at all there, it was that my stubbornness itself could be a weapon. There were matches I shouldn't have won that I bulled through by dint of sheer bloody-minded determination, refusing to lose rather than pursuing any clear idea of how I might effectively win. I also gained a great deal of hard-won experience sparring with Kevin, who had been involved in martial arts of one form or another since he was a toddler. Sometimes, too, we'd watch matches between Alan and Jake, trying to pick apart their duels. A three-minute fight between those two, in slow motion replay, was like watching an hour-long battle between two Normal combatants. Their efforts to outdo each other led to incredible and bewildering exchanges, full of surprising maneuvers and unexpected reversals. A lot of what they did couldn't be replicated by someone like me, but there was still a great deal to be learned from their clashes.

My favorite classes, though, were the ones I shared with Sarah: sculpting, pottery, drawing, painting, and—best of all—music.

There were, as with many of the classes at Project Arete, a variety of teachers who came and went. None really stick in my mind as being particularly gifted with the ability to impart their skills. In truth, I learned from Sarah in those classes. Mostly by watching her work, but sometimes, she would talk quietly of her thought process while daubing paint on a canvas or experimenting with an instrument, though never to anyone but me. She continued struggling to express herself—Director Ruiz was still in conversation with the medical and nano-tech departments regarding her case—but she wasn't embarrassed about her disability around me anymore. She knew I knew it wasn't something wrong with *her*; it was the wiring of her eyes. I think it helped that I didn't insist on having conversations with her. The more time we spent together, the more she seemed to relax in my quiet presence. Sometimes, it was as though she forgot to be afraid. This was especially true when she was caught up in the creative process. It was like watching a flower bloom beneath the sun. These were my favorite moments with her.

I hadn't taken any formal music instruction before those classes, but in my isolation as a child, I had come up with a guitar somewhere. I had figured out how to play it moderately well, even if I do say so myself. I was no rock star, but I could strum a good tune, and I had a knack for making the guitar express what I was feeling. My Super-power likely had a lot to do with it. String thing? That's got David written all over it. I was encouraged, while at PA, to focus on music as a method of honing control of my abilities. Over time, I managed to play a few basic melodies without touching the strings at all. With two guitars, I could accompany myself with a bass line or play harmonies. The concentration this required was definitely good practice. My power would still act up occasionally, but I was getting better at reining it in.

I didn't sing unless I was alone, though. It always embarrassed me when I tried to perform for others. My throat closed up, and I'd get all squeaky. Sarah, though . . .

I'd added the music curriculum to my schedule mostly because I'd experimented with guitar throughout my life, and I had this vague notion I might eventually become good at it. I have to admit, too, a part of me was hoping it would help fill time while I waited for Cory to make his next appearance. Sarah, on the other hand, played piano like she'd been born to it. She attended music classes because it was a part of her, as necessary as breathing. I remember arriving late for my first class, standing in the doorway, uncertain where to go. The auditorium was packed, and I couldn't see any free seats. Awkwardly, I had hovered in the aisle at the back of the room while the teacher of the moment made some flowery statements about the importance of balancing technical skill with the reason for learning that technique in the first place: beautiful and artistic expression of emotions and ideas.

When she wound down her presentation, she left the stage, and the lights went down. A curtain rose to reveal an ancient grand piano, a truly priceless instrument, made of real wood. And who should be seated there except Sarah? I stood dumbstruck by the jarring image of this painfully shy girl sitting alone on stage, the focal point of a crowded theater. I simply couldn't imagine what she might be doing there.

She had her eyes closed. Idly, I wondered if she was trying to minimize their interference. Her difficulties with speech had taught her to shy away from public attention, and she couldn't have been comfortable, sitting there with a hundred pairs of eyes on her. I'm sure I wasn't the only one in the auditorium who noticed the subtle shaking of her fingers as she fought bravely to keep her uncertainties at bay. The expectant hush that had fallen over the room as the curtains rose had arrested me instantly. It seemed nobody breathed.

Then she touched the keys. Just barely, at first, a feather light ripple of sound that stilled the last restless members of the audience, making everyone pause so they wouldn't miss the next subtle notes. Sarah let the silence stretch a moment. Then, when the tension felt like it couldn't be drawn any tighter without breaking, she let it unwind, gently weaving a sweet melancholy into the room and wrapping it carefully around our shoulders. When she had settled this new musical shawl about us, given us just enough time to become familiar with its weight, she added another layer, then another, and another—each layer a little heavier than the last, each allowed to settle a little less, the melodies never quite becoming comfortable or familiar before a new burden of notes was woven in.

Just as it began to feel onerous, she lifted her voice, high and forlorn, a breathy counterpoint to the deeper, darker landscape described by the keys. I was shocked and nearly cried out in my surprise. This girl who could barely string two words together was singing! My mind raced, trying to come up with an explanation for what seemed to be impossible. Was this form of expression channeled through a part of her brain that wasn't yet touched? Was this pure muscle memory, something her eyes couldn't affect? I couldn't concentrate on my thoughts. Her song was pulling me out of myself, taking me with her as she flew through a grim landscape of wild invention. The melody rippled, coiled around itself, broke into cascades of running notes, then fell momentarily still. I felt as though I was standing on a sharp border, caught between high mountain passes covered in ice and low, scorching deserts bereft of refuge—a choice that was not a choice, as both routes lead to death.

Her finale was an agitated, anguished hammering of the keys, the sound of birds beating their wings against the bars of a cage, or maybe of angels pounding on the gates, trying to get back into Heaven. The staccato rhythm petered out, becoming a faint echo of itself, before it collapsed. The music was exhausted. Only Sarah's voice remained: a single note, pure and sustained, a final bright slash to the heart that cut off abruptly. It was like a question mark at the end of a sentence, when one knows there is no answer forthcoming. Sarah hung her head, breathing heavily, shaking hands squeezed tightly in her lap. Then, to uproarious applause, she stood and stiffly left the stage. Her face was a mask.

I circled the back of the auditorium, made my way down the narrow side aisle, and slipped through a door into the backstage area. I heard lonely, broken weeping echoing faintly from down the hall. Following the sound, I pushed through a dressing room door.

I froze. Sarah, looking tiny and hopeless, clung to Amyati's waist, shaking with the force of her grief. The taller girl had her arms wrapped around Sarah's shoulders. She whispered softly between gentle kisses placed on the crown of Sarah's head. Together, they rocked slowly to the ebb and flow of Sarah's passion and pain. She held so much within, and so little of it was ever released! Only in music could she properly express herself. Once again, I resolved to find a way to fix the issue with her eyes. I'd seen the solution, and I knew it could be done.

Amyati's dark eyes had locked on mine the moment I pushed open the door. Her whispered reassurances ceased, but she offered me nothing. Her look said more than enough. I wasn't welcome here. Carefully, I stepped into the room anyway. I was Sarah's friend, too, whether Amyati liked it or not.

Amyati narrowed her eyes as I put my arms around Sarah from the other side. I felt as though I approached a dangerous Anymal. Almost nose to nose, I stared at Amyati defiantly, daring her to deny the comfort I was offering our mutual friend. Sarah, pressed between us, seemed the only source of warmth in that frigid silence.

For Sarah, I mouthed silently at Amyati. *Please.*

A tense moment passed. At last, Amyati relented. She turned her face resolutely aside. I sighed in relief. I had been banking on the idea that Sarah had somehow managed to explain the scene Amyati had interrupted in the atrium, and that she wouldn't want to pick a fight with me while Sarah was so distraught. It was a relief to know she could bend that much, at least.

Cautiously, heart pounding, I wrapped my arms tighter around Sarah, offering my strength and solidity as a shield, hoping I could be of some use in keeping her anguish at bay, though I knew what I was offering wasn't much—not when held up in the face of the overwhelming emotions she'd just revealed during her performance.

There aren't many decisions in my life I can be so certain were correct, but that was one of them. The soft pressure of Sarah's fingers as she squeezed my hand was all the reassurance I needed. I knew Amyati didn't truly understand what Sarah was battling, but I had been inside Sarah's mind; I had traveled the pathways behind her eyes. I had wandered, stumbling from one dead end to another, through the maze of her synapses. Just like her voice, I had struggled to find a way out. To some small degree, at least, I understood Sarah's forlorn bewilderment. I felt it myself. I knew I had to support and encourage her until the problem was fixed. It was like my mother had said: doing nothing was a choice that carried consequences, too. Left alone, Sarah's problem would only get worse. What would happen to her when even music offered no release? I dreaded to think.

During that time, when Cory was avoiding me, one of Mr. Gold's classes stands out in my mind, in part because it was the first time I'd seen Cory in any of my classes without him actively fuzzing my recollection of his presence. Quite aside from that, I often found myself returning to the lesson, reflecting on the ideas Mr. Gold presented, and thinking about how my fellow students had reacted.

By this time, I was no longer surprised to find most of my friends attending the same classes. It seemed to be PA policy to organize schedules around peer groups rather than around the teachers or the topics themselves.

Mr. Gold was wearing a black T-shirt that appeared to have been dipped in blood. I couldn't be sure, but I thought the logo for the metal band read "grim gore guts." It might have been "grim-gorgeous" or even "gargantuan," though. I snapped a photo with my Map and ran a search, but the Map couldn't be sure either. It tentatively offered the profile of a performance artist calling herself "Gamma Glow." She lived somewhere in the Antarctic area of the City, did awful things to genetically altered reptiles, and called it art. Anymal rights activists were in an uproar over her abuses, but she claimed the Anymals wouldn't exist without her growing them in the first place, so they were hers to do with as she pleased. Technically true, perhaps. It still seemed wrong, somehow.

"So," Mr. Gold was saying, rubbing his hands together as he warmed to his topic, "we have a man who has miraculously discovered an untouched piece of land in some obscure corner of the Earth. No one has ever lived there. He is the first to ever visit it. He finds that it is beautiful, and it has many resources. So, he claims the land for his own. Does he have any right to say it belongs to him?"

"Sure," said Alan.

"Just like that?" asked Mr. Gold, with a raised eyebrow.

"Yeah, why not?" insisted Alan. "Nobody else lives there. He's the first, like you said."

"True," agreed Mr. Gold. "In this context, the question of ownership is very simple. But what if there were people who lived nearby, and he just happened to be the first to find this place?"

"Well," put in Jake, "that still seems okay. But what's he doing with the land?"

"A key point, Jake. What if I said, 'Nothing'?"

"Seems like a waste, if he could be growing things, or building houses or something."

Mr. Gold nodded and smiled. Jake was consistently thoughtful and conscientious, unlike his headstrong, irascible brother. "I like where you're going with this, Jake, so let's follow the idea a little further. What if half a dozen people from the nearby village came along and demanded the man clear out? They have plans to build homes and start farms to help feed their people. Do they have a right to evict him? He was there first, after all. Does he have a responsibility to make efficient use of the land? Or is that responsibility being imposed on him by a group of people who don't own it? And if they have a right to make such an imposition, does he really own it or do they?"

Jake frowned. "Well, I mean, if it's for food . . . people shouldn't go hungry."

"You're absolutely right." Mr. Gold let his eyes rove over the group. Then he stood and began pacing. "Jake sides with the villagers for the greater good—an admirable choice. Anyone else have any thoughts?"

I thought about Gamma Glow torturing lizards in the frozen south. I found it disgusting, but did I have a right to decide what she did with her lizards? Did the lizards have any rights or freedoms? The protesters certainly thought so. But it seemed odd because we grew the same kind of reptiles as food Anymals in some parts of the City. They were just being raised for eventual slaughter, and nobody seemed to be fighting against that. People had to eat, like Jake said. The argument seemed to hinge on priorities. Food security is a pretty big deal, and so maybe we're willing to do bad things to secure food sources. On the other hand, killing for artistic reasons seemed selfish, barbaric, and cruel.

I said as much.

"Interesting, isn't it?" asked Mr. Gold. He stopped pacing, leaned back against his desk, and spread his arms to both sides to indicate everyone. The City. "Suddenly, we're in a moral gray area, and so far, we've only involved a few villagers."

"You're saying adding more people to the scenario will complicate things," said Amyati; it was a statement not a question.

"Unequivocally. Think about it: The six villagers take over, but they can't work the land themselves. They're too few. So, they bring people from the nearby villages to start building new homes, working the fields. They grow lots of food, and they have plenty to share. The new homes are spacious, and the prosperous villagers are able to start producing new children with the certainty that they will be able to provide." Mr. Gold paused to look around the class. His eyes lingered on Sarah for a while, but she had her head down. Her fingers tapped quietly on a smart-glass tablet while she took notes.

"Any of you ever been hungry?" Mr. Gold asked. "I don't mean just for a few hours while you wait for a lunch break. For days?"

Cory raised his hand. I winced. It was the first time I could remember seeing him in almost a week, and he hadn't acknowledged me beyond a perfunctory nod. I was glad he was there, anyhow. He seemed to like Mr. Gold's talks, even if he couldn't directly participate. Mr. Gold ignored him, of course.

"I'm hungry now," quipped Alan. Mr. Gold smirked but said nothing. Nobody else indicated familiarity with chronic hunger.

"So, let's add another village to the scenario. They live across the valley, and their end of the land is rocky, with poor soil. They haven't had quite so much luck growing food, and half of them are starving. Those who work the unproductive fields need to stay healthy so they're able to produce what little they can. The villagers have agreed that most of the food produced should go to the workers. Nevertheless, the workers are slowly wasting away, and they're watching their loved ones sicken and die much quicker.

"The people of this second village are growing desperate. All their work isn't enough, and they know it. Then news reaches them: across the valley is a place much more bountiful than their own home, full of good land and good food, with plenty of space to build homes.

Off they go to investigate. How do you suppose the prosperous villagers receive these newcomers?"

"With open arms," stated Jake. "It's the right thing to do."

"C'mon, bro," Alan groaned. "You can't be that naive!"

"What? I'd feed *you* if you were hungry. These poor villagers probably wouldn't eat half as much!"

"Are you calling me fat?"

"No, but your butt looks big in those slacks."

Susie had been following this exchange, watching their lips closely. She snickered, covering her mouth to hide her smile. Jake grinned at her. Mr. Gold patted the air with his hands and the twins subsided. He addressed Jake as he continued.

"Maybe the wealthy villagers welcome them in, as you say. If they do, they must consider that their resources will no longer stretch quite so far. On the other hand, by feeding the newcomers, they will gain workers and become even more productive. Space will be less readily available, but you can build up as well as out, so they can manage. In an ideal world, this would be what happens. But you know as well as I do that greed is a very real thing, and maybe, just like that original landowner, the prosperous village doesn't want to share what they have. Why should they? They did the work in the fields to grow the food. They built the homes to shelter their loved ones. Who are these others, and why should they care about them at all?

"Now, altruism is just as real as greed, so in any such scenario, both generosity and selfishness are likely going to happen together. Rather than swing to one extreme or another, the prosperous villagers will fall all along the spectrum. The most likely result is actually that they will be *divided* on how to respond. Once again, we find ourselves in a murky gray area, with no clear answer as to what is best. On the one hand, by sharing, they may become more prosperous than ever. But there are no guarantees, and they may just be inviting disaster. Indeed, by showing generosity, they advertise to others who are lacking that here is a place where one can find relief. Perhaps more poor villagers will come, demanding handouts. Where do they draw the line?

"If they turn the poor villagers away, they're no better than the original landowner who protested the theft of his land. They stole it on what they believed were valid moral grounds, as it wasn't being used for the greater good. Now they defend the land by turning that same argument on its head, applying the greater good only to their own people. These others will have to fend for themselves.

"Which brings me to my final thought exercise: What if the poor villagers decide they will steal the good things the prosperous villagers have grown and made? In their desperation, are they justified in doing so for the sake of survival? They'd really be no different than the prosperous villagers who took the land from the man who found it—arguably better, since they only steal because they must. And if the prosperous villagers defend their land, their food, their homes, what are they really defending?"

Kevin furrowed his brow. Silent until now, he asked what everyone was thinking: "What do you mean?"

"Ownership," said Mr. Gold. "They are not just defending land, food, homes; they are defending the idea that they own these things. Ownership implies a right to make unilateral decisions with regards to your property, regardless of the benefit or harm it may have on others. But owning a thing requires agreement from everyone else. They must agree to respect your ownership, or it is meaningless.

"By making his original claim, the man imposed on those around him to agree to his ownership. Nothing as formal as asking them; he simply said, 'This land is mine. I intend to do nothing with it.' Those around him suddenly found themselves in a strange position. Either they must respect his claim to ownership, thereby supporting it, or they must ignore it, invalidating it. By what right did the man push such a responsibility onto them? He was the one making the claim! And yet it falls to others to defend his right to ownership.

"This idea of social agreement was immediately discovered: the lone man found himself powerless to stop others from claiming his land. They had the numbers to enforce their view of things, so he couldn't own the land without their agreement. He couldn't keep it all to himself. Of course, others could have stepped forward and said, 'No, that is wrong. He owns that land, and you cannot take it.' Thus, society itself supports the idea of ownership, even private ownership, such as whose Map is whose, or which vehicle belongs to me. One man makes the claim; society supports or denies his claim by their response.

"I want you to think about that as you go about your daily business, because ownership feels individual when it is not. Everything you claim to be your own potentially belongs to someone else, or to no one at all. More importantly, what you own, or think you own, might suddenly change in the blink of an eye if society changes around you and the unspoken agreement shifts. Everything you own can be taken from you without warning, and you may find yourself powerless to stop it if others agree that it doesn't belong to you. Out there, in the City, this happens daily.

"This is important because all of you are Supers. Indeed, you have all rated higher, on average, than any class I've ever taught. You have abilities that others do not, and your powers will allow you to influence the world around you to a much greater degree than Normals. All of you, at some time or another, will find yourselves in a position to influence the thinking and beliefs of those around you. By doing so, you will shift the agreements of the people who make up society here in the City.

"It is vitally important, then, that you consider the responsibility such power gives you. I might write letters to protest hostile corporate takeovers or speak to others about how we might defend against the gangs encroaching on our residential neighborhoods, and my effectiveness will be determined largely by how many other people I can convince to side with me. But some of you will be able to go out and actually change these things, individually helping or hindering them as your consciences dictate.

"Consider your choices wisely. The consequences of your actions have the potential to reach much, much further than the actions of others."

Mr. Gold fell silent, watching as we tried to process what he was saying. As always, he didn't exactly tell us what was right and what was wrong. He just invited us to think about it, decide for ourselves. I glanced over at Cory, who had stolen his Map from a box of unkeyed units. Ownership claimed, just like that. Harmless, and since nobody could really protest, his claim was essentially legitimate, however shady.

Sarah, sitting to my right, was frowning as she mulled over Mr. Gold's words. She had rated higher than anyone, with an Abeyant Vector of eighty-five. I suppose if anyone needed to take his words seriously, it was her and I. I'd rated eighty-three. In theory, if I ever figured out my powers, I'd be in a position to enforce my opinions whether people liked it or not. Maybe I was already doing so. This was, more or less, what had me worried when I'd gone to talk to my mother. Maybe by making constant subtle connections, shifting ideas and opinions, I was weaving the social fabric around me into a new configuration. My powers did seem extremely powerful, possibly even dangerous, when considered in that light, but I sure didn't *feel* powerful.

Amyati, seated on Sarah's other side, was watching me watch Sarah. Her dark-brown eyes were appraising as our eyes met. With her exotic beauty, she was rather imposing in her severity. I had always found it difficult to match her gaze, but since the group hug in the dressing room, I felt that I had at least established myself as someone worthy of her respect. We could at least agree that Sarah was someone worth protecting. Amyati hadn't exactly warmed up to me, but she didn't actively push me away anymore. I counted that as progress. A tentative agreement about who had a right to Sarah's attention? The thought made me pause.

The twins, along with Kevin, were discussing the ideas Mr. Gold had put forth in low tones. Susie put in the occasional comment through her brother, with a quick flash of her fingers. Jake and Alan, with their 27 and 28 AV, were much faster, stronger, and more durable than any Normal. They could pretty much do whatever they liked.

Consider: They wore exoskeletons during Powerball games *to slow them down,* to resist their massive strength and speed so the rest of us would have a chance. Even without the kinetic shielding offered by the Powerball armor, they were hard to hurt. I'd watched the twins sparring in martial arts classes. It was incredible the kind of beatings they could endure. Looking at them, I realized that Mr. Gold was absolutely right. Those two would one day be able to walk into almost any area of the City and simply claim it, and few people would be able to stop them.

The City was so huge, if they didn't get too greedy, there'd be no reason for any other authority to bother stopping them. Provided they didn't commit any egregious atrocities, ran their little district with a modicum of efficiency, they'd probably get away with it. Their assertion of ownership would be backed up by their Super-powers. They wouldn't even require the agreement of everyone around them, really, just the agreement of those who had the power to stop them. People with higher AVs, like me, Sarah, and Amyati. But for the life of me, I couldn't think of any way I could stand up against them if they decided to become Super-powered tyrants.

All this made me realize what Mr. Gold was really talking about. Ownership didn't just apply to things, but to people, ideas, and freedoms. Morality. What was right and what was wrong when Supers acted without concern for those who couldn't hope to stand in their way? If the people in power killed without compunction, how would people living under their leadership behave?

Further consideration on the use and abuse of power was cut short when my Map pinged. I glanced from the message to Cory, who was just leaving the classroom. Gathering my things, I hurried after him, nodding to Mr. Gold on my way out.

Catching up to Cory a little way down the hall, I said, "Dawn just messaged. They're letting Simantha out of the cage. I wouldn't feel right going to show her around the facility without you along."

We walked side by side in uneasy silence for a hundred meters. When he turned into a side hall that would lead us toward the CSD labs, I said a quiet thank-you to whatever gods were listening.

Then Cory said, "It's because you were in my head . . . looking through my eyes."

The unexpected admission startled me. I had been trying to figure out how to broach the subject. My steps slowed as I tried to formulate a reply.

"You . . . you were aware of that?"

He glanced over his shoulder and shrugged. I hurried to catch up.

"Not at first," said Cory. "At the time, I was too caught up in *her.*" No need to ask who he meant. "But touching the force-field paralyzed me for a few minutes, and I had this paranoid feeling my idiocy had been witnessed. Not by her, but by someone else, someone who would judge me for it." The sideways look he gave me left me no room to mistake who he meant.

Did I really judge him like that? Make him feel stupid?

"Being laid out helpless like that had me trying like crazy to fuzz everyone in the area. But when the people out in the hall passed by and I realized I was still being watched despite how hard I was blanketing the area in a mind-fog, it seemed obvious. I reached inside myself and followed the thread."

His pause was significant. He took my silence for acknowledgement; I knew the thread he meant.

"So yeah. I knew you were watching."

"I'm sorry," I said lamely.

"Whatever. It's fine."

But it wasn't. He didn't seem fine at all. I felt like he could barely tolerate my presence.

"Cory, you have to believe me. I wasn't watching on purpose. I was eating breakfast and thinking about you, and somehow, I just . . . I don't know. I pulled on our connection and there I was, looking through your eyes. I didn't even know what was happening at first."

He stopped walking, and I bumped into him. He turned and gave me a shove, then advanced a step, ready to push me again. I backed away hastily, and he stopped advancing. "You weren't just watching," he accused me.

"What? What do you mean?" I felt totally flummoxed. He was so *angry*, and I couldn't figure out why.

Cory stepped in to shove me again. I let him. "You weren't just looking through my eyes, David. You were *feeling what I was feeling*. You were *thinking my thoughts*. You invaded my privacy and never stopped to consider how that might make me feel!"

"Cory, it was an accident! I didn't know what I was doing!" I refrained from pointing out that he was *constantly* invading people's minds.

"That doesn't make it right, man! It made me feel so . . . so . . ." Words failed him. He pushed his hands into his hair and squeezed his intense gray eyes shut. His jaw worked as he ground his teeth.

I held up both hands, trying for a cease-fire. "Look, Cory. You're right. It wasn't intentional, but it still hurt you, and I'm sorry. I . . . I just wish there was something I could say that didn't sound like an excuse. But it happened, okay? I saw what I saw. Once I realized you were hurt, everything else went out of my head. All I could think about was that you were lying there, unable to move, and Simantha couldn't get out of the cell to help you. Nobody who came in would even know you were there. I came as quickly as I could to find you, to *help* you, but you were already gone."

Cory remained mute, silently seething. Confronted by the depth of his anger, I had to face the truth: I had stolen something from him that didn't belong to me. It hadn't been intentional, but then, was it intentional when a vehicle lost control of itself due to some glitch in its programming and killed a pedestrian? Accident or not, the damage was done. How do you go back to the way things were after something like that? Not to put too fine a point on it, but I had essentially raped him. I had violated the sanctity of his secret inner life.

The realization left me feeling stained. I had become something monstrous in his eyes. How could I expect him to trust me now? If I had done it on purpose, that would be one thing; I could agree not to do it again. He might even learn to trust in that choice if my actions admirably demonstrated my intentions. But it had been entirely out of my hands. Neither of us had any way of knowing if it would happen again. I simply couldn't guarantee that kind of control over my abilities. I couldn't promise him that it would never happen again. Not yet anyway.

Just one more reason to get a handle on my Super-powers. But what about right now? I still wanted to be his friend. I still wanted to protect him, to be there for him. I still wanted to be his big brother, to make sure that he would never be forgotten again. I wanted to make things right. And he couldn't even look at me.

"Cory, I'm so sorry." What else could I say?

He spun on his heel and walked away. Feeling lower than dirt, I trailed after him. I would take Simantha out for a tour of the

Project Arete facilities, as Dawn had requested, if only so Cory could be with her without a force-field between them. I owed him that much, at least. But I couldn't help feeling that I was putting myself in the position of voyeur all over again. I couldn't see how it would fix anything.

Somewhere deep down, there was a slow-burning ember of anger and resentment, too. He had no way of knowing it, but I had risked my life in the Quantum Cube to find him. I'd faced down a Cupid, for crying out loud, and I had the distinct impression I could have been lost forever, trapped in another dimension, some other David stranded here in my place. Would he even have noticed? Or would he have carried on ignoring the other version of me and mooning over Simantha?

Surly now, on top of remorseful, I stalked after him. I admit it, I was not at my best to make a good impression on Simantha just then. But I had my doubts about her, too, and I wasn't sure I cared anymore.

XVIII

Despite my mood, it lifted my heart to enter the CSD labs and see Simantha light up with joy at the prospect of freedom. It wasn't really me she was excited to see, I told myself. It was what I represented. Even so, it was hard to hold onto my misgivings when she smiled at me with such warmth and appreciation. She might be a gigantic and potentially very dangerous question mark, but she was so disarmingly genuine! *All I can do is try my best to be on my guard,* I told myself.

Cory glared jealously, knowing he had no way to influence proceedings until I had taken responsibility for the simulant girl. I made a point of inclining my head toward him, tipping her a wink. If anything, her grin widened as she made eye contact with Cory. Her silver eyes sparkled in genuine pleasure, and I got the impression her growing enthusiasm for the coming adventure was now only barely held in check.

Cory seemed somewhat mollified by her obvious delight at his presence, so it was with the air of a calm amidst the storm that the three of us left the CSD labs and began our explorations—but not before Francis took me aside for a stern word.

"David, you're an intelligent kid with a good head on your shoulders, and I've had a few glimpses of what might transpire, so I will be blunt. Simantha's programming appears to be functioning optimally, and there is no reason to believe she is a risk to herself or others. However, she is not entirely herself; a lot of her memories have not been recovered, and there is evidence they are still there. They appear to have been buried by some kind of malicious code, intentionally locked away from her. So, who she is right now is not necessarily who she always was. We don't currently see any way to remove the code to restore her memories without damaging her personality, nor can we find any obvious mechanism by which the process might be triggered. But that doesn't mean it won't happen. So take this." He handed me the kill switch. "Be willing to use it if she shows any signs of abnormal behavior. It is better to err on the side of caution."

I took the small rectangle of plastic Francis pressed into my hand, looking at it with some trepidation. A small button, like a bubble in the plastic, made a little bump on the otherwise smooth bluish surface. I wasn't so sure I wanted the responsibility. Francis indicated that all I needed to do was hold the button down for a few seconds. The delay was to ensure I didn't inadvertently push the button and fry Simantha's brains accidentally. Nervously, I slipped the device into my pocket.

Truthfully, I didn't think of Simantha as a robot, as some kind of program. She was clearly sentient; she had thoughts and feelings. Synthetic or not, she was a person. I wasn't sure I could push the button to cut off the flow of information in her neural pathways, even if I needed to. They said it would put her into a temporary coma, allowing them to assess her systems and reboot once any problems were fixed, but it felt an awful lot like holding a gun to Simantha's head.

Maybe Francis could read the look on my face. Or maybe he'd had a glimpse of the future and had more faith in my ruthlessness than I did. He said, "Don't worry about it too much. We have no reason to believe there will be any issues. This is simply a precaution necessitated by the fact that she's much faster and stronger than most people here in the facility. I'm sure you can imagine the harm a rogue simulant might do. PA simply can't take the risk. However, we want her to feel like a valuable member of our little society, and we can't achieve that if she stays locked up here. She's been a model of patience and understanding, but I can't help wondering how long we could hold her here before she began to question our treatment of her. She is very intelligent and very self-aware, as I'm sure you've noticed."

I had, but that wasn't what I was thinking about just then. Either Francis was lying to me about why this precaution was being taken or he was being a hypocrite. Alan, Jake, Jetman, and plenty of others here in the facility were Super-fast and Super-strong. Every one of them was potentially deadly. *They* didn't walk around with bombs in their cerebral cortexes. Why? Because they were human. What kind of message were we sending to Simantha? Assuming Dawn's team had bothered to make her aware of the nasty little surprise they'd buried in her brain. She may have volunteered for it, in an effort to allay their fears, but that didn't necessarily mean they had informed her when they followed through.

"Now, then," said Francis. "Plan B is that station over there." He pointed to a computer that had been set up on his desk. "It will display readouts from Simantha's internal systems and trigger an alarm to warn me of anomalies. If I see anything of concern, I can trigger the kill switch from here."

I swallowed. *Wonderful. If she murders me and goes on a wild rampage, Francis can stop her remotely, provided he doesn't fall asleep or get up at the wrong moment to grab a coffee.* I shook my head at myself. What was with me, anyway? I'd become awfully morbid recently. Whatever Francis said, this was pretty much a date with the most attractive girl I'd ever met. I'd be a fool to get bogged down in a bunch of negative what-ifs and could-bes. Everything would be just fine.

Once we left the CSD labs, Simantha was free to speak openly to Cory, who took full advantage of her attention, babbling on about the classes he snuck into, the things he had discovered around the facility in his explorations, even a little bit about his abilities and how he was trying to learn to control them.

I rubbed my temple, remembering the mental clubbing he had given me behind the Restoration Point Church. I hadn't seen that coming. The boy would be a force to be reckoned with if he ever managed to reliably control his instinctive mind-fuzzing power. As it was, he was a nobody, a total cipher. With no real way to influence the world around him beyond what he could take from people, he could end up being a serious problem. In a way, he was dependent on people like me and Simantha, people who could remember him, to guide him as he grew up and help him form his ideas of right and wrong, teach him to make moral choices. I wondered if I was doing a good job of that. I had screwed up recently by demonstrating exactly the kind of behavior that I was hoping he wouldn't adopt. There was something intrinsically wrong with invading someone's mind. But surely, he was smart enough to see the bigger picture! I hadn't done it on purpose, and there were times when it was useful and good to enter someone's private domain, as when I'd explored Sarah's mind to help diagnose her problem. Surely, he could see that I was always trying to do the right thing! Isn't that what mattered?

Once again, I was brooding, worrying about the influence I might have. He was sure to learn a few things from me, for better or for worse. But how much control did I have over it, really? No doubt, he would turn out okay—*despite* me rather than because of me, most likely. I sighed and tried to focus on my companions' conversation. At that moment, we were passing an arcade, rows of open archways giving access to clothing boutiques, coffee shops, research kiosks, electronics stores, and even a theater. Cory was explaining that PA was a self-contained City in its own right, with everything one might need to pursue their wildest dreams. I watched him as he talked, and I could see he believed it. PA was a sanctuary for him, a place of safety and never-ending activity to keep him interested. There was always something new to learn, something fascinating to discover.

I watched Simantha smiling and laughing, nodding encouragingly at Cory's spate of words, and felt the way my heart flipped over. I could recognize Dawn's assistance in the simulant girl's elegant beauty; she must have sourced the outfit. Simantha's fiery copper curls were piled artlessly on top of her head. Dangling silver earrings trailed a scattering of stars and little crescent moons to brush her bare shoulders. She wore a simple flowing Mediterranean dress of royal blue that swayed gently as she walked and cork-wedge sandals that accentuated her height. She even carried a little clutch, blue like the dress, with a silver crescent moon buckle. Her appearance was striking, and it would be easy to assume that she was someone who had her life together, classes to attend, and a job to go to every day. She might have parents who cared for her, a brother or sister she doted on, and plenty of friends to gossip with.

Looks could be deceiving, I mused. Simantha, in truth, didn't have anything at all. I heard Mr. Gold's voice speaking of social agreements and wondered what responsibilities that might put on me, on Cory, on Dawn's team. What do we owe others who have nothing? What do they owe us? Dawn had shown nothing but kindness toward Simantha and had advocated for her earliest possible release. Would that constrain Simantha's future behavior in any way? Would she reciprocate the trust Dawn had shown her or break their unspoken agreement at the first opportunity to make a bid for freedom? I felt the hard plastic of the kill switch under my thumb and removed my hands from my pockets with a little frisson of anxiety.

After a few hours of touring around the Project Arete facilities, the three of us sat down at a café for an afternoon snack. We had visited labs, classrooms, philosophy debates, the Gymnasium, and even the ongoing spaceship restoration project that I had walked past during my first few days at PA. I was impressed by the progress they had made. Likely, before the year was out, they would have at least one working star-hopper. Cory had never been to this particular part of the facility before and had been full of questions, which Simantha and I helpfully asked on his behalf.

Apparently, the plan for the trio of starships was to take advantage of some kind of inter-dimensional technology to allow faster-than-light travel. I couldn't quite grasp how it worked and found myself thinking about my own inter-dimensional trips through the Quantum Cube. I shuddered. If that was how it worked, I'm not sure I would ever want to leave Earth.

Simantha seemed to follow the explanations well enough. We left the spaceship hangar with a number of bemused and thoroughly charmed technicians looking after us. Wherever we went, Simantha was equally wonderful, splitting her attention between her two chaperones effortlessly. She was curious, insightful, and humorous. If I didn't know any better, I would have said she was intentionally diffusing the tension between Cory and me, though she couldn't have had any notion of what had passed between us. Still, I got the feeling those shimmering silver eyes didn't miss much.

I was surprised when she ordered a Nu-berry scone and a cup of green tea at the café. She saw me watching her eat and said, "I suppose you assumed I must run on batteries or some kind of internal power plant?"

"Well, no, not exactly. I guess I just didn't expect robots to eat."

Simantha nibbled her scone, then sipped her tea. Cory had already polished off a massive slice of synthetic pumpkin pie and was considering stealing a second piece. I munched a Waldorf salad and a double portion of ham and cheese quiche. A tall cup of black coffee made a bitter counterpoint to the sweet and salty meal.

"I do have a miniature power cell," said Simantha, not bothering to correct the word *robot*. She tapped her heart with a glinting silver-nailed finger. "But I am also designed to derive energy from a variety of other sources: solar, through specialized photoelectric cells in my skin, though that has not been much use to me here . . . electricity, generated by friction from my movement; and also, food. I am, in most respects, built to mimic humanity—even your . . . less efficient functions." She quirked a strange smile, then leaned over with a napkin to wipe a stray bit of pie from the corner of Cory's mouth. I was struck by the tenderness of the gesture. It was so very human, something Cory's mother might once have done for him. He beamed at her.

"From what I can recall," Simantha resumed, "my creators assumed it was inevitable that I and others of my kind would eventually fall prey to accidents or violence, perhaps even the ravages of time. They built us to come apart in much the same way humans do. Most observers witnessing my dismemberment would not know the difference between my body and a Normal human's."

She was rather matter of fact about this revelation, but it still put me off my meal. I didn't really want to think about her demise, by gruesome dismemberment or otherwise. I groped for some way to change the topic.

"So, you sometimes have to eat for sustenance, just like we do. What's your favorite food?"

Simantha contemplated her scone, then said, "I feel I would adore some tagenites."

My Map suggested a near match to the traditional Greek breakfast: pancakes.

"Well, it may not be quite the same, but let's see what we can find," I suggested.

What followed was two more hours of wandering between the myriad Project Arete restaurants, sampling a huge variety of food, trying to determine Simantha's favorites. By her own admission, it had been so long since she had truly indulged in the pleasures of good food that she had forgotten how enjoyable it could be. In the process, I learned that Cory absolutely loved raspberry chocolates and that sushi was actually pretty good. Even the raw stuff. Cory made delightfully horrified faces when I sampled sashimi, flat out refusing to try it himself. Maybe that was part of why I liked it. Razzing him about being squeamish somehow brought us closer together than we'd been in a long time. He laughed at my immature gross-out antics, cringed at my equally immature and awkward flirtations with Simantha, and vied for her attention in his own charmingly boyish way. I suppose in Simantha's ancient silver eyes, there wasn't much difference between the two of us. Just children, with no idea what love truly was.

At some point, Cory asked Simantha what she would most like to do now that she had some freedom to explore.

"Oh, Cory," she said, with genuine feeling. "I desire very much to walk in the forest again . . . to roam tree-shadowed paths and feel the moss and leaf litter under my bare feet . . . to spot a dappled fawn pausing by a creek to drink . . . to hear the sweet songs of the winged creatures of the woods. I have been so long away from Mother Nature's tranquil embrace." She sighed, then finished quietly. "I do so miss the forest."

Cory and I looked at each other, bewildered. I don't think he had been expecting poetry.

"Forest?" I asked.

Simantha's silver eyes scanned my face for some sign of mockery.

"Yes. Have you no sacred groves here?" Her distress at the idea was evident.

"You mean like . . . where a bunch of trees grow together in the same place?" I was really reaching. She had mentioned Mother Nature. I was trying to dredge up what I knew of the natural world before the City had encroached on everything. It wasn't something

I'd ever really thought about. Natural wasn't a concept the world really understood anymore. Things were made or they didn't exist.

Her silver eyes jumped from Cory to me and back again. There was a growing fear written plainly on her face. "You have to ask? Where do you keep the animals?" The way she said it, "*animals*," was subtly different.

We led Simantha to an atrium, similar to the one I had passed through in my own early explorations. Three balcony levels overlooked what seemed to me a riot of unchecked plant growth. Ferns and exotic flowers of a dozen varieties crowded close around tall palms, ancient arbutus, and other, less readily identifiable trees. A graceful fall of water added its noise and moisture to the air. Colorful customized birds flitted in the shadowy spaces beyond the upper railing where we gathered to look down upon this fragrant, lively explosion of life. A Chamonkleon perched a few meters away, eyeing us warily. Its ruff of tawny fur bristled while the colors of its tiny scales shifted subtly. Its instincts warred between blending with the background and preening for our attention. Undecided, it bared its tiny fangs in a passable semblance of a human grin and shifted its sticky grip on the balcony railing. Simantha's unblinking stare eventually made it nervous, and it scampered away, vanishing with an impressive leap into the tangle of jungle below us.

"That was no natural beast," protested Simantha. "A chimera, if ever there was one!"

The jungle, too, did not satisfy her.

"This is not natural," Simantha said, with some distaste. "These trees would never grow next to each other in the wild. People have done this, forced these plants into proximity and encouraged their aberrant behavior. I do not understand this at all!"

She turned away from the rail and made a visible effort to regain her composure. I gestured for Cory to lead the way and he complied with characteristic eagerness, suggesting, as he guilelessly took her hand, that we visit a theater and watch a movie. Simantha, however, declined. She asked Cory to lead her back to Dawn's lab. Crestfallen, the boy made a token protest, but he could tell Simantha was upset. The pair left the atrium in subdued silence.

I stood for some time, staring down into that strange jungle, seeing it through new eyes. It suddenly seemed something alien and bizarre. Judging by Simantha's reaction, it was like no forest that had ever existed on Earth. I wasn't certain why she should care so much, but it was obvious she did—for there, on the sturdy resin railing, clearly imprinted by the strength of her grip, her finger-prints remained.

I fitted my own fingers to the marks she had left and shivered. I found my other hand had once again strayed to the kill switch in my pocket. To my shame, I was suddenly grateful for my guilty burden. With a grim sense of foreboding, I followed Cory and Simantha back to the lab.

Francis confirmed my fears: extremely elevated indicators of stress, anger, fear, and disgust. For whatever reason, Simantha saw our efforts to recreate a little bit of the world that had been lost beneath the City's expansion as a travesty. Rather than taking it as a celebration of life's past expressions, she had taken it for an offense against nature, a perverted attempt to reimagine something pure and holy as a twisted parody of itself.

Her concept of nature, however, was hard for us to grasp. It seemed, in ages long past, she had been imbued with a deep, abiding love for an archetypical mother figure, one who had in some way been manifested in the cycles of birth, death, and rebirth seen all around her as the seasons passed. Seeds were planted, good things grew, were harvested, died back to nourish the soil, left behind seeds, and were replanted. On and on, in every aspect of life, she saw repetitions of this same theme. There was a cycle to life, a rhythm.

That cycle had been upset, had ground to a halt. We started it and stopped it now at our leisure.

She was horrified. It could not last, she told me. It was not sustainable. She wept for us, for the things we had lost, and I was simultaneously disturbed and entranced by her tears; a simulant human, overcome by grief for the ones she had been built to emulate—the ones who, more callously than any mechanical thing, had reduced the world to a lifeless and arid reflection of themselves.

It was hard to deny. If mankind were to perish, very little would continue to grow for long. Practically everything in our lives was fabricated, synthetic, regulated. The most natural things we had were man-made replications using the original genetic building blocks, but of course, we weren't satisfied with the original blueprints. We tinkered with the patterns to improve on natural designs. It was something of a mania for humanity. But was it really an improvement? I hardly felt qualified to answer. If nature had died, humanity had at least survived. Arguably, we did more than that: we flourished. Then again, it wasn't our survival that she questioned. It was the cost.

All this came out over a series of discussions Simantha had with me, Cory, Dawn, Miguel, and Francis. She was still free to roam. She had displayed, even when terribly upset, an admirable grip on her self-control. Only I had seen any evidence to the contrary. The image of her fingerprints pressed into that railing was burned indelibly in my mind.

I didn't mention it, however. What was the point? Nanomachines would quickly find the divots and repair them. Ultimately, her little outburst, so exquisitely controlled, was harmless. Squeezing that railing had been a better alternative than squeezing the Chamonkleon until its weird little head had popped. To hear her tell it, she had made the choice to do minimal harm.

A convincing argument, and it allayed most of my worries about the threat she represented. It was no different from me punching the wall at home after a frustrating day. Admittedly not the most productive way to manage my anger, but a far cry better than punching Jake or Alan, or sour old Doctor Kernshaw. If anything, it made Simantha seem more human. She was passionate about something. She cared deeply about the world and the way it was treated. She managed her frustration and disappointment in much the same way everyone else did, by directing it in a way that wouldn't harm others.

Simantha was both much less and much more human than I had imagined her to be. It would have been wrong for me to implore Francis, Dawn, and Miguel to curtail her freedoms and restrict her contact with others on the strength of one incident. My mind circled back to Mr. Gold's talk about ownership and social agreements, and I realized that Simantha's freedom was essentially all she owned. If we took that from her, what was left? What kind of people would we be if we did that to her? Almost anyone, in the right (or wrong) circumstances, would be capable of causing great harm to others. Should everyone be locked away for safety's sake? I wouldn't want to live in a giant prison City, and I didn't think anyone else would either.

My sympathy and affection for her certainly swayed my thinking. Try as I might, the idea that I might be in love with her refused to die. But I was afraid of her, too. I didn't really understand who or what she was, and every time I looked in her eyes, I could see the truth of my ignorance staring back at me. Yet I remained stubbornly faithful to the notion that she was intrinsically human, that she was a good person.

I wasn't alone in my conclusions. As inclined as Francis was to an overabundance of caution, he could find no fault in her conduct. He even commented, somewhat wryly, that the world might be a better place if more *people* carried themselves with the same dignified comportment Simantha did.

His emphasis didn't pass unnoticed, but I refrained from picking a fight over it. Francis was a good man, but he had his opinions. I didn't have to agree with them. Besides, I didn't have the eloquence to express my conviction of Simantha's legitimate claim to personhood. I just knew that she deserved the benefit of the doubt.

Our outings continued sporadically over the following weeks. Simantha's free time was slowly filled by studies that caught her interest until, almost seamlessly, she had integrated into the Project Arete culture, becoming just another student. When she was free, I took every opportunity to spend time with her. She was monitored constantly by a sophisticated program of Francis's design that would alert him should an emergency arise, so I wasn't really needed, but I usually enjoyed her company.

Simantha, for her part, seemed to take some comfort from my presence. She often shared her thoughts and feelings with me, and I felt weirdly honored to enjoy her trust. Whenever I had pretty much given up on any ideas of romantic involvement, she would say or do something utterly charming, and I would fall in love with her all over again. The constant tug-of-war with myself was draining. Frankly, she made me nervous, and not because of her very obvious femininity (though I'll admit it continued to fluster me at awkward moments).

No, what held me back was more complicated than that. I could see she was deeply disturbed by the world around her. While she made every effort to maintain a cheerful and curious demeanor, to learn as much as she could about her new circumstances, there remained a knot of darkness within her. It wasn't something I could untie, even with my Super-powers. She genuinely engaged with me and with others around her, yet it sometimes seemed as if she was only half there. That metaphorical knot of darkness might have been rather literal, in fact. I remembered Francis mentioning some kind of malicious coding that kept portions of her memories locked up tight.

Will you think less of me if I admit that I continued to carry around the kill switch? Though I rarely thought about it, the little plastic rectangle could be a sobering comfort on occasion. Human as she was, Simantha was thousands of years old. Sometimes, I felt she was standing on the opposite edge of that yawning gulf of millennia, staring across the years at me. I couldn't begin to imagine what she saw when she looked at me that way. I could only shiver and look away and wait for the moment to pass.

It took some time for me to become comfortable enough with her to ask, but eventually, I took the plunge.

Simantha had been tapping away at a data device, researching a project for her engineering class. She paused, and her face became grave. I could tell she was giving my request the serious consideration it deserved.

Eventually she said, "Please allow me some time to consider the problem, David. I will help her if I am able."

I sagged with relief, though I wasn't entirely certain I hadn't just set in motion another disaster. "Thank you, Simantha."

She leaned forward to gently squeeze my knee. "Friends should help each other," she replied. "I know you value her, and that is enough for me."

It was embarrassing to hear it stated so plainly, though I couldn't have put my finger on quite why. Maybe it was because I still felt something for Simantha, too, and I was pretty sure she was aware of it. I remained silent.

Simantha said nothing further, turning her attention back to her research. Gratefully, I returned to my own studies.

XIX

"In 326 BC, shortly after conquering the Achaemenid Empire of Persia, Alexander the Great marched his armies into India by way of Pakistan. From there, he advanced into the Punjab region of Northern India, where he fought a pitched and deadly battle against an Indian king named Porus on the shores of the Hydaspes River."

Amyati paused to glare around the chamber. She needn't have bothered. She had everyone's undivided attention. Call it *schadenfreude* if you like, I was particularly enjoying her discomfort. I found it fascinating that this normally domineering and self-assured girl was uncomfortable with speaking in front of large groups. Judging by the rapt attention of everyone else, this glimpse of weakness in the seemingly impervious girl was just as surprising to them as it was to me.

We were seated haphazardly around an auditorium, a random scattering of a hundred some-odd students that included the group I had begun to think of as mine. It was a much nicer setup than Mr. Gold's usual cramped classroom space. Mrs. Blevins—a forty-something brunette who appeared to be decanted directly from the Scholar Archetype without noticeable modification—seemed to prefer teaching to large groups in PA's Grecian-styled amphitheater. Today, it was particularly apropos, considering the opening statements of Amyati's presentation.

The week before, Mrs. Blevins had assigned us a history research project, something she said all Supers being trained in the Project Arete facility were eventually asked to do. The idea was simple: dig into your family genetic history. Figure out where your Super-powers likely came from. If nothing else, it would give us a better concept of our own identity. In many cases, the research proved beneficial for another reason: for many of us, our ancestors had Super-abilities, or (further back) near-Super, so the stories of their greatness could inform our ideas of what good and evil were and help us to navigate the treacherous highways of right and wrong that crisscrossed the City.

Most of us had already presented our family histories in the form of a lecture to the rest of the class, at Mrs. Blevins's insistence. She could never resist an opportunity to combine lessons of different types, to help make us more "well-rounded" people, so a history research paper with elements of Super-genetic theory was now also an abject lesson in the horrors of public speaking. I smirked. It was evident Amyati was acutely aware that she was the current focus of attention. We might have been Supers, but we were still teenagers. We tripped over our own tongues and got flustered by things outside our comfort zones. I felt bad for Sarah, who hadn't presented her history yet, but she wasn't currently showing any signs of worry beyond the usual. Watching the shy girl write notes, it occurred to me that a little public speaking might not seem so bad to her. How was it any different from what she dealt with every day?

So, there I was, my own awkward embarrassment at the front of the class a few days earlier already forgotten, enjoying Amyati's turn in the spotlight. Credit where credit is due, to a casual observer she wouldn't have seemed too concerned. Despite the rest of us staring at her, Amyati's habitual armor of self-possession appeared brightly polished today. I thought to detect the hint of a crack in her fortress walls, though, a weakness in her ramparts. It seemed to me she was angrier than usual. Covering up her fear? Or just annoyed at being forced to engage with her inferiors in such a demeaning way?

Having reassured herself that she was receiving all due respect from her audience, Amyati continued.

"Impressed by Porus's conduct, both during the battle and afterward, Alexander left his former foe in charge of the kingdoms he had just conquered and marched east. There he came up against the Nanda Empire of the Magadha region of India." She touched her Map, which she had placed on the corner of the podium. A holographic projection appeared, floating in the air next to her. The globe. It expanded, the area of ancient India and its surroundings zooming closer. Amyati pointed to the eastern region of India she was referring to, situated along the Ganges River, south of the mountains of ancient Tibet.

"The Nanda were a foe so numerous they outnumbered Alexander's forces five to one," said Amyati. "His army, pining for home, worn out by the extended campaign, and having suffered grievous losses in the recent battle with Porus, were unwilling to face yet another deadly foe. They rebelled and would march no further."

Lines appeared on the map, charting the path of Alexander the Great's march through India. Amyati was warming to her topic now, but it seemed that Alexander was just the backdrop for her narrative. Historians had spent lifetimes studying him. She could have spoken of the great conqueror and his deeds for hours, embroidering her speech with endless details, but she was rushing him out of the picture, eager to get to the real revelations of her heritage.

"Alexander was forced to turn south, and eventually west, exiting India altogether, having made barely a dent in India as a whole. After his death, only a few years later in 323 BC, left in his wake in Northern India were several fractious Greek kingdoms, most notably the Empire of Seleucus."

Artistic depictions of Seleucus hovered over the desk, including bronze statues, stern profiles stamped on coins, and imaginative paintings.

"Seleucus," Amyati informed us, "was a Greek General who served under Alexander the Great. He became known as Seleucus the

Victor, because after Alexander's death, he fought with others who had been close to Alexander or served under him, and he eventually succeeded in taking control of the majority of the empire Alexander had built in ancient Asia. However, just like Alexander before him, Seleucus's attempts to expand further east were checked by a group out of the Magadha region of India."

Amyati grinned, a sudden fierce baring of her teeth. She wasn't giving me any satisfaction at all by actually enjoying the presentation! The aggravating girl was unflappable! But what on Earth was she grinning about?

"Not the Nanda, this time, but those who had since supplanted them: the Maurya Empire, which was destined to become one of the greatest empires in Indian history."

Maurya? I thought. *Isn't Amyati's last name . . . Mora?* Come to think of it, the name sounded awfully familiar. I asked my Map to put together a report of people in the City with the family name of Mora who might be connected to my adversarial peer. Then I settled back in my seat. Despite myself, I was getting caught up in the tale of her heritage.

"Chandragupta Maurya, taking advantage of the divisions left in Alexander's wake, had been rapidly expanding his empire and would eventually establish control over a huge area of India, creating a unified region that was arguably inspired, at least in part, by Greek methods and thinking. The cohesiveness of his rule unified the Indian kingdom like never before and paved the way for economic prosperity for the people he ruled."

I drummed my fingers on my leg. So much for seeing her get taken down a peg. But I couldn't be too upset about it. She had been attentive for my own presentation and had even asked questions, not that my history was terribly thrilling—a handful of Scottish barbarians and Scandinavian raiders, none of whom were terribly noble or notable. I was the first in my family to show evidence of

Super-powers. The most surprising thing my history research had uncovered was the fact that, as the first member of my genetic line to manifest abilities, 83 AV was some kind of record. Sarah, with her 85 AV, had told me she had three generations of Supers before her, each progressively stronger. Her father, apparently, was one of the most powerful healers in the world, and her mother hadn't been anything to sniff at, either, possessing a wide variety of tenuously related powers much like Sarah herself. But to come out of nowhere with an 83, like I had, was pretty much unheard of.

Amyati was still expanding on her family history. "Seleucus, the Greek general I mentioned—the one who took over in India after Alexander's death—fought Chandragupta Maurya for control of Eastern India." Amyati's holograph displayed scenes of battle, warriors riding into the fray on the backs of massive Anymals with great curving tusks, others charging astride sleek four-legged robots . . . or were those also Anymals of some kind wearing armor? It was a nicely rendered holo, if a bit fanciful. It couldn't have been all that accurate. Who had ever heard of Anymals so large? Even a Spikeface would cower in front of one of those gigantic, tusked things with the tails on both ends. What on Earth would such a beast eat? Children, perhaps?

"Seleucus was unable to defeat the Maurya," said Amyati triumphantly, "and in the end was forced to sign a treaty. Eastern India was given into the control of the Maurya Empire, firmly establishing their presence for continued expansion. But just to be sure Seleucus would stay friendly, Chandragupta Maurya himself married Seleucus's daughter."

At the back of the class, Mrs. Blevins cleared her throat. Looking at her uncertainly, Amyati faltered to a stop. *Ah! Here at last, the impervious armor cracks!* I glanced back at Mrs. Blevins, but she was taking a sip of water, making a *carry-on* gesture with one hand.

Amyati glanced at her Map, trying to figure out where she had been in her presentation before the interruption. Off her stride, now, she clenched her jaw, quietly seething. I sighed. It wasn't nearly as satisfying as I had hoped it would be. It made me feel petty. Sure, Amyati and I seemed to butt heads a lot. But she wasn't vindictive or cruel about it. She just didn't like me and seemed to assume the worst about me. I should probably try to get over myself, give her space, and let her have her opinion. Why did I care so much, anyway? Why did I want her to like me so badly? Did I really have to be friends with everyone? Frankly, it was hard enough just trying to be friends with Cory.

Amyati was still scanning her notes, looking flustered and a little embarrassed now as the silence drew out. Watching her, I realized that she and I would remain entrenched, staring across the battlefield at one another, unless one of us broke the stalemate and conceded the fight. I didn't even know what we were fighting about, really. Wasn't it Sarah's choice, whom she wanted to be friends with? Why couldn't we both hang out with her? Amyati was proud, and if I guessed correctly where her presentation was going, she had good reason. She probably came from a long line of nobility or something. Somehow, I doubted she'd be the first to stand down.

Well, my ancient kin wouldn't be rolling over in their graves if I waved a truce flag. There were plenty of other people to fight if my ancestors' ghosts rose up and insisted I had to die by the sword or something stupid like that.

"Seleucus's daughter," I offered. "The Maurya guy married her?"

Amyati glanced sharply in my direction. I gave her my most disarming smile. *See? I'm a nice guy. And I was listening, too.*

"Yes. Thank you, David." Amyati paused, taking a breath. "Seleucus's daughter. Well, let's see. Her name was Berenice. She was essentially a Greek princess, when one considers the status of her father and the expanse of the kingdom he controlled. Little else is known about her, as few Greek documents of the time concerned themselves with the doings of women. Still, we know this much: She bore Chandragupta Maurya a son, named Bindusara. Chandragupta ruled for sixty years, and his son ruled for another sixty after him. And Bindusara gave way to his own son, Ashoka."

I was rewarded with the barest nod as Amyati continued.

"Now, Ashoka is widely hailed as one of India's greatest rulers, and it's not hard to understand why. He aggressively expanded the rule of the Maurya Empire until it covered almost the entire Indian subcontinent, then—according to the tales he himself caused to be spread—repented of the violence and tragedy of war and converted to Buddhism. He was largely responsible for the spread of Buddhist teachings across most of ancient Asia, even—a little ironically— sending emissaries into the Mediterranean and converting Greeks, in a strange reversal of Alexander the Great's attempt to subdue India."

Amyati smiled, relaxing back into the task.

"The Greeks were once conquerors; now they were converts. History is full of things like this, circles turning through time to eventually close back on themselves right where they started." She looked around, seeing some of the others nodding. Their own research had unearthed similar things, I recalled. Amyati caught my eye for a moment. Then she looked over at Sarah, who still had her head down, focused on her notes.

"The point I'm driving at," said Amyati, "is that Ashoka himself was as much as half Greek, depending on who his mother is claimed to be. Regardless of his mother's ancestry, he was certainly no less than one quarter Greek since his grandfather Chandragupta had married the Greek princess, Berenice. Ashoka's father, Bindusara, was half Greek.

"In closing," said Amyati, "I am descended from the great Indian Emperor Ashoka himself. Through him, I am descended from royalty of both Greek and Indian genetics. Super-powers have popped up in the history of my family for centuries. In fact, the Mora clan, and before them the Maurya, might be one of the original Super-genetic lines. There are historical documents that reference Ashoka's miraculous powers of healing, his great strength and stamina, his ability to charm even his most hateful foes. It was said he was able to hear the thoughts of his subjects and send soldiers to areas of unrest before the unrest even began. These things go back to 300 BC, perhaps even earlier. Hinduism is full of stories of people, demons, gods, and demigods, all of whom display abilities remarkably similar to those of modern-day Supers. It's entirely possible Super-powers contributed to the building of the great Maurya Empire.

"It's a similar story on the Greek side of things. If you read Homer's Iliad, not to mention a lot of other Greek hero tales like the story of Hercules, you'll find accounts of men and monsters who performed incredible feats beyond the abilities of Normals. Those stories go back even further, to approximately 1800 BC, perhaps beyond. Who knows? Maybe the gods worshipped by the ancient people were the original Supers. Maybe the Mora genetics can actually be traced back to the Titans of ancient Greek mythology."

"Or the *jötunn* of Norse myth," said Alan, whose own ancestry, like mine, was primarily of barbarian stock. I could see he was enthused by the idea. Why settle for captain of the Powerball team when you could be descended from a god?

It was an interesting thought, but I had a sneaking suspicion Amyati wasn't quite correct. And there was someone I could ask who might remember the truth. Simantha had been alive back then, hadn't she? I resolved to broach the topic with her when an opportunity presented itself.

The class broke up after a few more presentations, and I spent the remainder of the afternoon at the climbing gym, striving to conquer a 5.9 route that consistently had me losing my grip only a few meters from the top. I was an average climber, at best. I didn't spend enough time at it to master the more technical aspects of the sport, but I found it strangely calming. Just me and my tenuous connection to the wall. My Super-power didn't matter here; either I had the strength, the skill, and the endurance, or I didn't. I was perversely cheered by my routine failure to reach the top. Each time I fell, I would lean back on my elbows and contemplate the route while I rested, then lever myself to my feet and try again. It didn't seem to matter how I approached the route; I couldn't see the trick to that final five meters. The only solution I could see was to keep chipping away at it and hope that I finally figured it out.

In a way, the climbing route was a lot like my relationship with Amyati, or with Cory: consistency was key. I couldn't make them like me, but I could at least demonstrate through my actions that I could be relied on to keep trying, even when the going got tough. I wasn't going to abandon my hopes for more amicable interactions, and I wasn't going to give up on the idea that we could find common ground. I'd settle for respect if I couldn't have genuine goodwill. It seemed like a very steep climb, sometimes, staring up at the lofty heights where Amyati looked down upon the rest of us, but if I fell along the way, I'd simply have to pick myself up and try again. As for Cory, well . . . I knew I wouldn't always remember the route, but that didn't mean I shouldn't keep looking for it. I knew it must be there, somewhere. I'd seen how close the two of us could become, that first time through the cube.

I paused on the wall just below the problematic traverse, trying to catch my breath. Sticking close to the vertical surface, I supported my weight on my legs and hung from one hand while I shook the other out, then switched hands. Fifty meters off the ground, and

I might as well have been back in the cube, floating in the darkness: I'd also seen how often Cory and I could become enemies. I
couldn't deny the possibility that there was no coming back from my
mistake. I hated to admit it, but the visions in the cube had stuck
with me. I couldn't un-see them, however hard I might try to ignore
them. Lately, they seemed to be coming back with more and more
persistence, as if I were approaching a crucial crossroads. Soon, I felt,
I'd have to make a hard decision and live with the consequences.

I grimaced. How on Earth did Francis deal with this kind of
thing? Hints and intimations of things to come and no way to know
if what you were sensing was a glimpse afforded by your power or
just wishful thinking—it was so frustrating!

I grunted and lunged for the next handhold, skipping the one
that always defeated me. For a moment, I clung by my fingertips to
the barest ledge that protruded above it, struggling to get my feet
back in contact with a suitable foothold. My right toe jammed in
a narrow gap. The barest improvement of stability, but my fingers
were slipping. I scrabbled with my left foot to find some place to
anchor it. I needed to take the weight off my hands so I could adjust
my grip.

My toe kicked a protrusion. I stepped onto it, shifting my weight
to my feet. A triumphant sense of elation filled me. I was going to do
it! I was going to conquer this wall!

And then I slipped. My left foot wasn't as securely anchored as I'd
thought. As it took more of my weight, my leg shot out from under
me, and my fingers lost their grip. I slapped into the wall, catching
my chin on the knob my left foot had only just vacated. I swung out
into open air as the safety harness took my weight, arresting my fall.
I drifted slowly toward the ground, face throbbing.

"Too bad, man. I thought you had it that time."

I touched down to find one of the climbing coaches standing
nearby, helping a first-time climber into a harness. I shrugged

ruefully and began to unstrap myself. "Bit of an idiot maneuver at the end there," I admitted, mumbling a bit.

"Nah. Sometimes, you gotta take a risk to make progress."

"Maybe in the climbing gym," I said. I worked my jaw, but there didn't seem to be any real damage. "Falling isn't quite so dangerous here as it would be in the real world."

"Fair point." He turned back to his client.

I left the climbing gym feeling weirdly reassured. To extend the climbing metaphor, I had just taken a gamble that didn't pay off, but I hadn't unduly suffered for the attempt. Maybe I was blowing everything out of proportion, and things with Cory and Amyati would work out fine. Maybe the risk I was running, encouraging Simantha to get involved with Sarah's problematic eyes, were risks that Sarah would eventually have to face on her own anyway. At least this way she had support, people around her who cared. What if we'd never become friends, and a few years down the road, she found herself isolated inside her own head, unable to express herself in any meaningful way? Would she even have the chance I was offering her?

It was a moot point, anyway. There were no guarantees Director Ruiz or the medical faculty would countenance my crazy idea or allow a simulant like Simantha to get involved.

Back in my flat, I showered and ate a simple meal, then requested a cup of strong coffee from the fabricator. I kicked my feet up on the coffee table and leaned back on the sofa with my Map. Time to see what Amyati was all about. I hadn't forgotten our encounter at the pier, and if she was going to continue being antagonistic, I should probably know more about what I was up against. Mora was a familiar name to me, and I wanted to know why.

I spent close to an hour reading what the Map had dug up with increasing concern. When I simply couldn't take any more, I pinged Sarah.

"*What's up, David?*"

How to begin? After a few moments of consideration, I opted for honesty. *"I'm curious about Amyati,"* I sent. *"Her family history today was interesting, and I found the name Mora ringing some bells. So, I did a little research, and now I'm wondering why I hadn't realized it before. Her aunt is Rana Mora, isn't she? The leader of NE?"*

"Yes," Sarah confirmed. *"Amyati was raised by her* mausi.*"*

"Her what?"

"Sorry. It's a Hindi word. It means her mother's sister. Her mother died in a really bad multi-vehicle accident when Amyati was quite small. Cyber-terrorists hacked the traffic system, which caused the vehicle network to make totally arbitrary risk assessments. It was awful."

It was enough info to rapidly locate an article on the death of Amyati's mother, Sunita Mora. Emergency crews had found Amyati without a scratch on her in the back of the smashed car. She was laying quietly in a perfectly spherical pocket of empty space. The plastic and polymer of the vehicle had been smashed inward on all sides but had inexplicably halted before crushing her. She'd instinctively manifested a kinetic force bubble to protect herself. At two years old!

It was obvious to the emergency team on the scene that she was a Super, and a strong one. In a perfect world, she would have been placed into social services. Her area of the City had been well managed enough to support that kind of thing, apparently. In a best-case scenario, surviving relatives would be located and she'd be handed off. Failing that, she'd be filtered through official channels into some kind of government or corporate Super-training facility. Unfortunately, the City isn't perfect. Instead, Amyati had been sold. A corrupt bureaucrat offered her to black-market gene-rippers to line his own pockets.

I was horrified. Supers were good money, if you could get your hands on one when they were young enough to be manageable. Cupid-led scientific groups weren't the only ones trying to crack the genetic code to produce custom Supers. It's a sad testament to human heartlessness: Emergency crews on the scene couldn't be bothered to fill out the paperwork necessary to track down Amyati's relatives. Overwhelmed by the number of casualties at the accident, it was easier for them to simply call in an unclaimed infant. The lack of proper diligence gave an opportunistic social services worker his chance. The emergency crews probably knew what the likely result would be but handed her off anyway. It might have been the last anyone ever heard of her, had it not been for her aunt.

Sarah confirmed it. "*Rana Mora spotted her sister's death on the news. One of the syndicates had broadcast an image of the inexplicable zone of safety within the vehicle and speculated on the missing child. NE mobilized fast.*"

NE had been funded from its inception by Sunita Mora, who was the de facto queen of a massive textile and clothing empire before her untimely demise, so it's no wonder Rana Mora's ears perked up when she heard of her sister's death. Maybe you've heard of Sunny brand? Even if you haven't, you're probably wearing something they made, or at least something that was produced using synthetic fabrics woven in their factories. Rana was still comptroller of the entire Sunny fortune until Amyati came of age, which was, what, another year or two away?

"*Being hunted by NE is a frightening thought.*" My Map passed the sentiment along to Sarah, who readily agreed.

NE, or Normal Eyes (an intentional play on "Normalize"), was a paramilitary group created with the express intent of defending Normal rights against the potential of Super-tyranny—violently, if necessary. Over the years, they'd made quite a name for themselves as an effective group of high-tech warriors. They'd made big news only six months ago with the triple assassination of the Super-villains known as Dark Father, Fortress, and Killbuck. Despite their methods, most Supers tolerated and even openly supported NE; the

Supers they eliminated were typically a menace to the entire City. In a way, other Supers (by virtue of staying off NE's radar) were lent a certain legitimacy; maybe they weren't exactly good guys, but they also weren't villainous enough to draw NE's ire.

Sarah had more to add. *"When Amyati's* mausi *made inquiries to see if Amyati had been found at the scene of the accident, she was told Amyati had vanished. Rana put two and two together. Amyati practically worships her* mausi, *but if you ask me, she's a scary woman. Her response was to publicly mobilize NE forces, then release a statement on almost every news channel in the City, demanding Amyati's return. We're talking a full-day takeover of the news syndicates within hours of finding out Amyati had been kidnapped. She pulled strings, made threats, who knows what else? She outright purchased smaller stations that hesitated to waste the necessary airtime. When the bigger broadcasters got wind of it, they took up the story just to cash in on the hype. The countdown was overlaid with talking heads giving updates, regular news, all that, but she got the message out."*

"I remember watching that," I told Sarah. "That must be why her name seemed so familiar."

"What?" Sarah protested. *"How old are you? You would have been two or three years old when it happened!"*

I laughed out loud, despite Sarah not being in the room with me. *"My dad's a historian. Whenever he's working on a restoration from a new part of the City, he starts at the present and works his way backward, trying to get familiar with local power and politics before he does a deep dive into the area's history. I was probably fourteen when I saw the broadcast. Just one more bit of folklore from a place I'd never heard of, but I remember him frowning over the event, telling me that it was deplorable what people will do to each other for money."*

"He sounds like a good man," Sarah commented, a trifle wistfully, perhaps. She never spoke of her own father, and I knew very little about him beyond what she'd shared in her own ancestry project:

head of an anti-tech Super-enclave somewhere to the north, tucked away in the gulf islands of erstwhile Canada's rugged west coast. Given Sarah's robotic eyes, it was maybe no surprise that she and her father were estranged.

"*He is,*" I admitted, somewhat grudgingly. "*But we tended to butt heads a lot. Both too stubborn, I guess.*"

"*You? Stubborn? Get out of the City!*"

"*Har-har,*" I replied, but her teasing made me smile.

My mind circled back to the reason I'd contacted Sarah in the first place. Amyati had stolen an alien laser rifle from some gang-controlled lab and passed it off to her aunt's people on the barge. Had Rana Mora's influence really stretched so far across the City? Amyati and Rana were both from the other side of the globe, some-where in or around the Indian subcontinent. That was an awfully long reach. Had they relocated? Or simply opened new branches wherever the political climate was forgiving enough? When Sunita Mora died, Rana would no longer have been dependent on her sister for an allowance. With the wealth of the Sunny empire under her control, she would have been able to expand NE aggressively. She wouldn't have much trouble recruiting with that kind of wealth. No wonder the people on the barge hadn't felt the need to fly their colors. They were backed by NE!

Amyati had let me watch the handoff, probably to show me she had friends in high places and to warn me off interfering with her. I had to laugh. I was a little slow on the uptake, but better late than never. Message received! I'd have to be very careful around her, going forward. It was probably a good thing that lately we seemed to be finding—if not mutual respect—at least a mutual understanding.

I stifled a yawn. "*Thanks for the insight, Sarah. I'm going to bed.*"

"*Okay. See you in music class tomorrow.*"

I couldn't be bothered to head to my room. I stretched out on the couch instead and watched the broadcast I'd seen around three years ago. Rana Mora, an athletic and severely handsome woman wearing full tactical combat gear, silver-shot black hair cropped short, stood at a podium with NE's sun-haloed staring eye emblazoned in gold on a black flag behind her. Her combat helmet was placed to one side of the podium. In brisk, matter-of-fact tones, she laid down her ultimatum. No notes. No teleprompter. Just a fixed stare that pinioned every single viewer with the conviction of her purpose.

"To those who took custody of the infant Super-girl found in the wreck at Noorpath and Jain, you have twenty-four hours to turn the child over to NE forces at any NE branch, no questions asked. You will return her in the exact condition she was found, healthy and intact, without injury or evidence of gene-ripping of any kind. Failure to comply will result in NE's forces being deployed throughout the City to recover her by every means at our disposal. We will pursue with extreme prejudice anyone involved in her abduction to the exclusion of all other activities. Those found responsible will be held to account by our own tribunal and can expect no leniency. Their holdings will be systematically dismantled and redistributed at our discretion. Any affiliate discovered to have aided or abetted the culprits in any way during the perpetration of this crime will receive similar consideration.

"The twenty-four hours begins now. *Vigilantes sumus.*" NE's motto: *We are watching.*

Rana Mora gave the NE salute—right fist over the heart—then left the stage. The broadcast ended with a ticking clock, counting down the promised span.

It was easy enough to find follow-up reports; the broadcast had been tantamount to a declaration of war. Amyati had been returned only three hours later, unhurt, by a woman who claimed she'd been handed the baby and a fat stack of credits by a bunch of men in an unmarked black vehicle. The gene-rippers hadn't been able to get anything from Amyati because of her force-screens. The human-interest angle told the heart-wrenching story: her father had been a heavy drinker, abusive toward her mother. Amyati had learned to distrust men when she was just an infant, instinctually shielding up whenever men were around. The gene-rippers could've easily taken what they wanted if they'd just put her in a room alone with a female med-tech, but they hadn't known enough to realize it.

My eyes were drooping. I yawned hugely, turning the whole sorry affair over in my mind. I found I could sympathize with Amyati. Her attitude toward me was a little more understandable, at least. Would we ever be friends? Doubtful. But my father had been right: knowing the past helps us plan for the future.

I drifted into dreams full of shadowy figures, like murky past horrors returning to haunt the present. By morning, however, my thoughts were blessedly free of worries. Any presentiments I might have had during the night had vanished along with my dreams.

L ate in the summer, as Simantha and I wandered around the facility prior to her first official introduction to my circle of friends, we stumbled across the Greenhouse. I'm not sure why I'd never taken Kevin up on his offer to visit him there, but now that we were looking at the sign on the wall, directing us down a wide, brightly lit hall lined with unusual ferns, I realized I was uncomfortable with the idea of interrupting him at work. He wasn't just a student at PA; he was also an employee. The more I thought about it, the more I realized that fact had made me a little more aloof with him than I was with the others. He'd never been anything but friendly toward me, but I'd kept him at arm's length, restricting our time together to classes and Powerball practice.

Simantha noted my frown. "Something troubling you?" she asked.

Lost in my own thoughts, her question jerked me back to the present moment. "Uh, no. Not really. I was just thinking that I've never dropped in on Kevin while he was at work. I don't know if he's on shift right now, but if he is, he might be willing to give us a tour. What do you think?"

Simantha clasped her hands together, pressing her thumbs to her lips. Her eyes flicked back and forth, taking in the ferns decorating the entry. For a moment, I thought she might express disgust at the unnatural plants, as she'd done before. But her face broke into a rapturous smile. Whatever the difference was—between the plants being grown here in the Greenhouse entry hall and the plants in the atriums—I couldn't see it. As we wandered deeper into the Greenhouse precincts, her growing enthusiasm became increasingly odd to me because most of the plants in the Greenhouse were individually sealed, each beneath its own little dome. This wasn't a forest, as she had described it; it was a cold and clinical nursery, where every precaution was taken to prevent cross-contamination, where germination and pollination were strictly monitored and controlled. The technicians in the Greenhouse raised the plants in carefully programmed miniature biomes, mimicking as closely as possible the conditions the plants had evolved to take advantage of.

As luck would have it, Kevin was available. He spent most of his free time here, and he offered to show us around without any prompting from me. Botany was his passion, and nurturing plants was the most developed aspect of his healing power. I remembered him telling me when he'd first healed me that he was much more adept at assisting plants than people. Human bodies were too messy and complicated.

Kevin laughed at my confusion over the difference between the plants all around us and the synthetic varieties everywhere else. "The plants here," he said, "are near-perfect replicas of natural plants, things that evolved in the world hundreds, even thousands of years ago before the interference of humanity. PA has been painstakingly reconstructing them from genetic material, partial bits of DNA, blueprints cobbled together by best guesses in a lot of cases. A lot of the technical and physical necessities were supplied by the Cupids, from samples they've collected ever since arriving at Earth something like five thousand years ago."

I was stunned. That was a timeline a great deal longer than I had expected. Dawn and her team had proposed something like 3000 to 3500 years. I watched Simantha with new eyes as Kevin continued.

"The goal here is to eventually reintroduce natural flora in carefully controlled environments carved out of the City until the plants can begin doing what they used to do, spreading themselves around, competing with other species, living or dying by natural selection.

It's fascinating work, and you'd be surprised how much we're learning about the synthetic and genetically modified breeds by looking at their antecedents. Sometimes, getting back to basics requires reverse engineering from something a little more complicated that may not even resemble the original."

He had been guiding Simantha and I between the rows of computer-controlled environment capsules, showing us a variety of plants, describing the way they might fit into a larger ecosystem, and detailing the more interesting aspects of things that, to me, were green and sticky oddities that wasted a lot of their energy growing stems, leaves, and flowers, without producing a whole lot you could actually eat or use.

Simantha, however, was enchanted. She was quick to point out that ancient peoples all over the world had long used plants for their natural power to heal or to harm. Most of the synthetic chemicals and medicines we now used, in fact, were originally derived from plants. Often, if the plants were rare, they were hard to source, so we had turned more and more to synthetics to simplify acquisition and increase access to necessary ingredients.

This was the window of opportunity I had been waiting for since Amyati had proposed the idea that the gods of ancient peoples had, in fact, been Supers. I had a growing certainty the gods had actually been simulants, like Simantha. She didn't tend to talk about her past in anything except the vaguest terms. I usually assumed it was a result of her buried memories. Who knew how much she even remembered of the thousands of years she had lived? But she had just made a clear reference to ancient people and their habits as if from firsthand experience. She had made similar odd comments from the day I met her. My curiosity burned within me.

As casually as I could, I said, "A while ago, Amyati and I were discussing something similar. Her ancient ancestor, Ashoka, one of India's great emperors, supposedly had the power to heal people.

Do you suppose he did it with the power of plants, or with Super-powers, as Amyati suggested?"

"I do not know," said Simantha, absently. "I have never met him."

The reason for her distraction was obvious. Kevin had stopped by one of the biomes and was now demonstrating the very Super-power in question. Reaching into a canister by way of heavy gloves built into the side of the dome, so he wouldn't compromise the carefully regulated environment within, he took a wilting specimen in hand. Gently, he stroked its leaves, lifted the drooping flowers, and lovingly coaxed it back to life. Even as we watched, life flowed through the multitude of stems. Browning leaves uncurled and regained their healthy color. Wilted petals freshened, growing full and plump. Within moments, he was holding the near side of a spectacular shrub full of roses, pale cream in color, with large, multi-layered blossoms. Though he had only touched the near side, the entire plant had benefited from his attention.

Simantha's hands, upon seeing the rosebush restored, flew up to cover her mouth. Her eyes grew damp. Kevin, his back to her, was oblivious. "Unfortunately, it can take some trial and error to get the exact balance of each plant's environment right," he said, withdrawing his hands from the gloves. "My job is to maintain their health until we hit on the winning combination. In between rounds, I try to get my fingers into the actual work of gene-splicing, seeding, and so on. I can't think of a more worthy pursuit." He paused, admiring the refreshed flowers for a moment. "Artemis roses," he said. "Lovely things."

The worshipful look of adoration Simantha bestowed upon Kevin as he turned from his contemplation of the newly invigorated rosebush was enough to make the normally serene teen swallow nervously.

"Apollo's gift," Simantha breathed, eyes shining. "Son of the Sun."

He glanced at me uncertainly. I shrugged.

Uncomfortably, Kevin continued our tour. He regained a measure of his natural aplomb by the time we had circled back to the Greenhouse entrance, then lost it again when Simantha told him she would volunteer at the Greenhouse so he could teach her everything he knew about modern plants.

"I desire to assist your efforts to restore the natural world," she insisted. Since she wouldn't take no for an answer, Kevin perforce said yes. He promised to send Simantha a schedule so that he could begin showing her the ropes.

We exited, turning left from the Greenhouse entrance, and negotiated a crowded corridor. Simantha was grinning, so plainly suffused with joy that it was hard not to smile with her. But I had an odd, queasy sensation in my stomach, as if I'd just swallowed something rotten. As we navigated the crowd, I tried to draw Simantha out on what she had meant by her strange comment to Kevin.

"Who is Apollo?"

Her brows drew down and she frowned. "I . . . I am not sure. I felt as though I knew him for a moment, watching Kevin heal the roses in the Greenhouse. Whoever Apollo was, I feel we were quite close."

We sidestepped a rambunctious party of students playing keep-away. One of their number ran back and forth across the hall, trying to retrieve her Map as the others tossed it back and forth over her head. Catcalls and good-natured jeers accompanied her scrambling efforts and vociferous complaints.

Simantha looked thoughtful. "Dawn said another of the simulants found in the bay looked much like me. She suggested we may have been twins. Many of his parts were salvaged to complete my reconstruction since they were a near match to my own. Perhaps he was my brother?"

My Map said: "*Apollo; ancient Greek god of the sun, archery, healing, truth, prophecy [list continues . . .]*

"*Most beautiful of the Greek gods, matched only by his twin sister, Artemis. He was the patron of the Oracle of Delphi and seen as a representation of the ideal Greek youth.*"

There was more, but I could read it later. I reached out and touched Simantha's shoulder. She paused to allow me to draw her to the side of the corridor.

"Simantha, Apollo was one of the ancient Greek gods, worshipped thousands of years ago by the people of Earth who lived in that area. If he was your brother, then you were Artemis, goddess of the moon." I nodded as her fingers reflexively touched her stomach, where her opalescent tattoo resided. "The huntress. Protector of the innocent. Kevin reminded you of Apollo because Apollo was a healer, too. The roses Kevin restored, he said they were called Artemis roses. To have both reminders happen at the same time like that must have triggered one of your memories." What were the odds?

"Is any of this sounding familiar?"

She was looking at me, perplexed. It was apparent none of this made sense to her. *But maybe if . . .*

"Should we go back to the Greenhouse? See if we can trigger more memories there? Talk to Kevin a bit, see some more nature?"

She shook her head, a single sharp negation. "No. Thank you, David, but I am distressed by this. I feel I need time to consider the implications."

I relented. "Right, of course. Um . . ." I looked around. The corridor had cleared out some. "Let's carry on. You can meet the others. There'll be plenty of time to think about all this stuff later."

Simantha nodded unsteadily. I forced myself to think cheerful thoughts as I took her hand and led her into the plaza. The touch of her warm fingers in mine was unnerving. With her percipient plastic skin, I never knew how much she might detect of my thoughts, and just then, my thoughts were awhirl with the possibility that she might be a goddess, someone who had been worshipped by the ancient Greeks as a divine being.

As we entered an open plaza, surrounded on all sides by shops and eateries, I caught sight of Sarah and Susie. They'd been seated at a table on the level above us. Simantha followed me quietly. A moment ago, she'd been full to bursting with the thought of beginning her new work at the Greenhouse. Now she was pensive, unsure of herself.

Susie, catching sight of us as we ascended an escalator, produced one of her infectious giggles, accompanied by a cheerful grin and an enthusiastic wave. She tapped Sarah's shoulder to get her attention, then pointed our way. Simantha seemed to set aside her concerns; it was time to make some new friends.

Sarah turned and gave me a grave nod. I could see her growing nervous as she took in my traveling companion's beauty and poise. It wasn't the first time she and Simantha had interacted—they shared some classes together—but it was the first time I had seen the two side by side. It was odd to watch Sarah, shyly greeting Simantha, and realize I found her every bit as attractive as the simulant girl. She didn't have the same polished beauty-by-design that Simantha had, true. She was more waifish than curvaceous, and her hair was an unruly chestnut-colored cloudburst. But her skin was clear. Her robotic eyes were a perceptive, luminous green. She had a sharp-featured, intelligent face, and her voice was musical to me, even when she stuttered. It echoed the time I'd heard her sing. Her fingers could tease heart-breaking music from the inert keys of a piano or evoke raw emotion with nothing more than paint and canvas. She was creative, talented, sensitive, observant, and funny.

Seeing her in this new light felt like watching the sun emerge from behind the clouds. My perspective changed, and I felt suddenly sure that what I felt for Sarah was genuine. By contrast, my feelings for Simantha were confused and uncertain, forever in flux. I never quite knew where I stood with her. How could that be love?

Sarah, by this time, had slowly turned inward, sitting almost paralyzed, while Susie made much of Simantha's outfit and hair, using gestures even I could follow. Simantha seemed pleased by the attention, instantly catching on that Susie was deaf, and the two were soon communicating rapidly in sign language. It was nice to see the warmth of Susie's response.

Relieved to see Simantha recovering from her uncertainty so quickly, I pulled a chair close to Sarah and seated myself with a sigh. Simantha and I had been on our feet most of the day. I was pooped.

"Where are the others?" I asked.

Sarah shrugged. "H-held up, I . . . I guess."

To my surprise, she reached out and took my hand. After I had just watched her withdraw inside her shell, it was startling—just about the last thing I would have expected. Had she sensed my thoughts and feelings as I'd arrived? So close on the heels of my realization of how attractive I found her, the touch of her fingers was overwhelming. My heart lurched in my chest and began to race. A traitorous part of my mind whispered, *Using your powers to force the connection, David? That's not exactly ethical.* It was a worrying thought, but I was afraid to move. It was as if a bird had unexpectedly perched on my fingers: I didn't want to scare it away. My hands grew sweaty, and that made me worry she might notice and be grossed out. I fought the urge to wipe my palms on my slacks, sitting as still as I could.

We stayed like that for some time, quietly watching Susie and Simantha get to know one another. I tried to play it cool, interject the occasional joking comment, but I was too focused on the feeling of Sarah's hand in mine. Likely, I came across as awkward and uncomfortable.

Simantha had discovered Susie was Kevin's sister and was now telling the Korean girl how wonderful her brother was while Susie rolled her eyes and interrupted Simantha's effusiveness with embarrassing stories of Kevin's essential and unfortunate boy-ness.

Sarah's Map chimed. Wordlessly, she tipped the screen so that I could see. The message from Amyati read: "*Delayed. Be there in 5. Love you.*"

I don't know why I did it, but I reached into my pocket with my free hand and touched my Map. Quick as thinking, a second message flashed onto Sarah's device. "*I love you, too.*"

She blushed outrageously and turned her face away, hiding behind a fall of her hair, but she didn't take her hand away. I sank into the moment, feeling happier than I had in a long time.

Then Amyati arrived, and everything spiraled out of control.

XXI

Amyati stepped off the escalator, following the railing around the balcony toward where we were seated at the table overlooking the plaza. Simantha didn't see her until she was quite close, maybe ten meters away. Sarah and I had our backs to Amyati's approach, so our first indication that something was wrong was when Simantha, seated across from us, broke off from her silent conversation with Susie and stood bolt upright. Her chair clattered over behind her. Susie, startled, clapped her talkative hands over her silent mouth.

Simantha wasn't paying attention to Susie anymore. She was staring over our heads at Amyati. Sarah and I, still holding hands, turned toward each other in unison, sharing a brief look of concern as we pivoted to look in the direction of Simantha's gaze.

"It *can't* be . . ." Simantha whispered.

Amyati had stopped, sensing some threat in Simantha's sudden movement, the way the simulant girl's opalescent silver eyes were locked on Amyati's face, unblinking. A direct stare is a challenge, and Amyati wasn't one to shy from a challenge. She stared right back, trying to assess just what was going on.

I turned back to Simantha. She had begun to move, the slow steps of a sleepwalker taking her toward Amyati in a daze. The pair never broke eye contact. I rose to my feet and reached for the simulant girl's arm. Sarah, frightened by the sudden unpredictable tension in the air, clung to my hand, holding me back.

"Simantha, what's going on?" I asked.

Almost at the same moment, Amyati spoke. "Who are you?"

"You don't recognize me?" Simantha's voice broke on the question. She stifled a very human sob, shoulders shaking with the effort. Her chest heaved as she gulped in a shaky breath.

Amyati remained mute.

"Iphigenia, my love," breathed Simantha, "it's *me*. Artemis."

What? I was right?

The simulant girl made to advance. Amyati splayed a hand in her direction with an angry push, the universal gesture for "stop." A shimmering wall of distorted air appeared between them. "Stay back," she demanded. "Who are you? What are you talking about?"

"Simantha?" I called. "Simantha, maybe we should just sit down and talk about this! I'm sure we can figure it out."

"This does not concern you, David. Be silent." The snap of command in her voice shocked me, and I subsided, watching warily. My heart hammered for an entirely different reason now, adrenaline surging through me. Something was very, very wrong here.

Simantha continued advancing until she was pressed against the force-field Amyati had summoned. She placed her palms flat against it and looked through the rippling distortion.

"You are Iphigenia," she said with conviction. "I know you are. I recognize you. I remember . . . everything." She applied pressure to the force-field, experimentally. It resisted her. "Please, just let me touch you. All will be made clear."

"No," said Amyati. A flat denial.

"Please," begged Simantha, her voice rising. "Please, my love, listen to me. You are Iphigenia. I can show you the truth. You must believe me!" Her voice was edged with something sharp, a hysteria barely held in check. She could see that Amyati was not interested in what she had to say.

Amyati didn't bother to deny her a second time. She simply turned and walked away.

With a cry of despair, Simantha leapt the hovering force-field. She pivoted smoothly in the air, flipped gracefully through a ten-meter arc, and came to rest in front of Amyati, who recoiled in surprise; she hadn't been aware she faced an artificial human.

Simantha reached for Amyati while she was momentarily taken aback. She almost touched her, too. Without knowing why, I found myself assuming it would be a bad thing if Simantha succeeded. But in all honesty, I didn't have a clue what might happen if she did. Things were happening too fast for me to figure them out. I didn't know what to do.

Amyati, however, had rapidly revised her original estimate of her opponent. Realizing she was dealing with perhaps a mechanically enhanced human, a Super, or someone of other unknown potential, she marshaled her focus and decided to attack. The best defense was a good offense, at least in Amyati's view, and the faster she took this girl down, the faster she could make good her escape.

Energy flashed. Simantha was shoved away by a rolling wave of force. It quickly dissipated as it moved past her, but not before doing some collateral damage. Simantha crashed down amid toppled chairs, cracked tables, and unfortunate diners. A rising babble of voices was starting to fill the mezzanine, cries of concern mingled with shouts of outrage.

Despite the distance Amyati had managed to create between them, Simantha was incredibly strong and fast. She flipped to her feet and lunged at Amyati, a blur my eye had trouble following. "Please!" she cried.

Her hand slapped into Amyati's oldest instinctive defense: a bubble of force like a swirling blue marble. The strike sent the force bubble—and Amyati held in its center by a cushion of kinetic energy—skittering across the mezzanine, straight back in our direction. I had no time to help Susie. It was all I could do to get my arms around Sarah and topple us both over the balcony railing.

Amyati, wrapped in her bubble of force, smashed the table and chairs we'd just vacated like a bowling ball and tore through the railing beyond, spreading a sparkling spray of glass like shooting stars into the air. She dropped out of sight to the sound of screams as glass rained down on the level below. I heard the piercing shriek of an alarm bell. Someone had tripped an emergency signal, summoning security. But I couldn't focus on Amyati's problem, just then. I had my own problems to deal with.

I'd managed to arrest our fall by using my shoelaces. They whipped outward, lashing themselves to the railing before my feet got more than ten centimeters into open air. I gritted my teeth, concentrating fiercely to keep my shoes painfully tight on my feet. My synthetic leather belt, the cord from my hooded sweatshirt, and Sarah's shoelaces all supported the strength of my arms by tying Sarah to me even as I clutched her tightly. We slapped upside down into the resin panel below the rail, dangling above the escalator. I watched helplessly as my Map and the kill switch tumbled from my pocket and clattered onto the moving staircase below.

Thankfully, since I was closer to the railing when I grabbed her, Sarah had come down on the outside, my body cushioning the blow, though it knocked the wind out of me and wasted precious moments while I fought for air. Her back was pressed to me, and she was curiously still, but I didn't stop to consider it. I knew my laces would hold; they were practically indestructible. But this wasn't a comfortable position to be in, and if my shoes slipped off, we'd both be in trouble. Whispering in Sarah's ear, I managed to grunt out between gasps, "Hold on . . . I'm going to . . . untie you. Lower you down."

Gripping each other's forearms, I managed to accomplish the maneuver without incident, flipping Sarah over until she dangled beneath me with only a short drop to the escalator. As soon as she touched down, I whipped my belt around the nearest balcony post, letting it wrap around my wrist. My shoelaces let go and I flipped over in a barely controlled fall, crashing painfully onto the escalator right where Sarah had landed a few moments before. Luckily, the stairs had carried her upward. I narrowly missed flattening her more by good fortune than by design.

Shins screaming in agony, left knee protesting with every step, elbows scraped raw from my landing, I lunged past Sarah and dove for my Map and the kill switch just as they reached the top of the escalator. My frantic grab knocked the Map skittering past the gap onto the mezzanine floor. The kill switch dropped into the narrow space at the top of the escalator and vanished from sight.

Rolling to my feet, I grabbed my Map and ordered it to call Francis. Sarah stepped off the escalator and hurried to join me as Francis's voice spoke in my ear.

"David, what's going on? Simantha's readings are . . ."

"Hit the kill switch!" I yelled over him. "Do it right now!"

"Done," he said. I could hear Dawn's voice in the background, raised in concern, Miguel saying something in Spanish. I ran to the railing and scanned the space below for some sign of Amyati and Simantha, but their struggle had carried on beyond the plaza.

"I'll call you back. Get Dawn and Miguel on my signal and keep watching Simantha's readouts. Coordinate with the security teams heading to Plaza 3B. I'm going to track down our rogue simulant."

I pocketed the Map. Sarah was looking at me as though seeing me for the first time. She'd frozen in panic, the sudden eruption of violence catching her off guard, whereas my time on the streets had conditioned me to act without thinking. I knew from experience what she must be feeling now. I'd felt it myself, the first time I'd stood helpless in an emergency.

I took Sarah's hands. "I have to find Simantha," I told her. "Make sure she didn't hurt Amyati. You don't have to come with me, but I know what you can do. I'd feel safer if you were backing me up."

It was a relief to admit it. I was scared, and the kind of firepower Sarah was packing with her 85 AV would go a long way to calming my nerves. Besides, she was Amyati's best friend. Timorous as she could be, I didn't think she would want to carry around the regret of doing nothing while her best friend was in danger, especially if something bad happened to Amyati. I had seen Sarah play the piano and sing in front of a crowd; I knew there was a core of strength and bravery inside her.

Sarah's lower lip quivered, but she nodded.

"Thank you. I will do my best to keep you safe if you promise to do the same for me."

Another nod, firmer this time.

"Okay." I took a deep breath, then buckled my belt. Sarah's shoe-laces snaked back into her shoes and tied themselves snugly. My own followed suit. "Let's do this."

Sarah used her tele-K to fish the kill switch from beneath the escalator, and I tucked it back in my pocket. I rushed down the up escalator, taking the steps as fast as I could. Sarah simply jumped, floating a meter above the stairs and touching down gently just behind me as I reached the lower level. As we hit the plaza floor, I saw Susie stretched out on the ground below where Amyati's force bubble had burst through the rail. The twisted wreckage of the chair she'd been sitting on was lying in a heap a little way beyond. Her right leg was badly twisted in a direction it shouldn't have been able to go, and her face was a rictus of pain. My stomach lurched with nausea. I felt shaky and clammy with sudden sweat. I reached for Sarah's hand.

Replaying the scene in my head, I saw Amyati had been facing Simantha with her back to Susie when the frictionless force-bubble went flying. Simantha's touch shouldn't have been enough to produce that kind of result. Amyati must have taken advantage of the force of the slap, multiplied it with her Super-power, and used it to escape.

She'd blasted through the rail so fast, she probably didn't have any idea Susie was in the way, couldn't have reacted in time even if she'd known. *Or she simply didn't care*, said a merciless part of me.

Kevin knelt over his sister, hands on the sides of her head, doing his best to heal her injuries. He must have come running from the Greenhouse when he heard the alarms. But he was only 18 AV: he probably wouldn't be able to do anything about the broken leg until medics arrived to straighten it properly. Still, he could deal with any other damage from the fall and make sure she didn't have any serious internal injuries or a concussion. Once she was comfortable, he could heal any cuts and bruises the bystanders had sustained.

He looked up at me as I approached with Sarah, his face giving away nothing, withdrawing behind a mask, holding it all in. Maybe later, when Susie was safe, he'd freak out. He had to be sick with worry for his sister.

"Hall C," said Kevin, divining our intentions. "I think I heard the elevator to the Gymnasium singing that stupid welcoming tune it loves so much. It would let Amyati run anywhere in the facility if that's where she went."

I nodded. As Sarah and I hurried away, Kevin called back over his shoulder, "David! Hit the locker room and gear up. Find Jake and Alan, Jetman if you can!"

I knew what he was thinking: berserk simulant. Jetman, though? Was it really that serious? I sure hoped not.

We found Simantha as soon as we stepped out of the elevator. The ride down a dozen levels to the Gymnasium had passed mostly in silence until the lift had begun to slow its descent. Just before the doors opened, Sarah whispered, "Iph . . . Iphigenia. I f-feel like I . . . like I know that, that, that name."

I felt the same, but racking my brains had turned up nothing. I gave up trying to figure it out. There was no time. The doors slid open, and we heard a concerned voice saying, "Miss? Miss?"

Stepping into the hall, we saw a thirty-something man wearing grubby brown overalls crouched by Simantha's inert form. She had just exited the elevator and started down the hall toward the Gymnasium when Francis activated the kill switch. She had fallen facedown, one arm flung out over her head, the other folded beneath her stomach. Her hair was a riot of flame-colored curls that tumbled over her face, spilling across the floor. The mechanic, if that's what he was, was gently shaking her shoulder as he fumbled in his breast pocket for his Map to call emergency services. He looked up at us as we emerged from the elevator.

I said, "Oh, good. It worked." I knelt across from the mechanic, giving him an apologetic smile. "Simantha's had a rough day. The lab-techs are coming to collect her. She'll be fine once they figure out what went wrong with her programming."

He looked at me blankly for a moment, finally connected the dots. "A robot girl?" he stammered. He looked back down at her inert form in disbelief.

I nodded. *Close enough.*

"Huh. Could've fooled me." He took his hand from her shoulder. "She has a pulse, but it's a bit weak."

"She was designed to imitate humans almost exactly. Cupids made her, if you can believe that. We still don't fully understand how she works."

The mechanic looked doubtful.

Tentatively, Sarah said, "D . . . Dawn's here."

Dawn hurried up and crouched next to Simantha. "Thanks for helping us find her, David. We'll take it from here."

Miguel, only a few seconds behind Dawn, was hastily unfolding a portable gurney, struggling to snap the telescoping sides into position. As he raised it upright, letting the wheeled legs drop to the floor, I moved my hands in the air like I was securing the crisscrossing straps that would support Simantha's body. They jumped at my mental nudge and lashed themselves into position.

The mechanic, watching suspiciously from a few steps away, gave an involuntary grunt of surprise at this display. A Normal, I guessed. He seemed to realize he didn't have any leverage to protest the doings of Supers. With a shake of his head, he walked away.

Cory popped around the corner at a dead run, knocking the man in overalls into the wall. There was a brief struggle while Cory disentangled himself. After a moment, he sidestepped the confused mechanic and sprinted toward us as Miguel and Dawn lifted Simantha onto the gurney.

"What happened?" he asked. He grabbed Simantha's hand without thinking.

Dawn and Miguel jumped back in alarm as Simantha's arm moved. Forgetting Cory was there, they must have thought she was suddenly reviving.

I pulled him away from the gurney and pried his fingers off of Simantha's. His clear gray eyes were stricken, but he didn't struggle. He watched as Dawn and Miguel, encouraged when Simantha's arm dropped limply back to her side, wheeled the simulant girl toward the far end of the hall. They disappeared through a door and were gone.

Giddy with relief, I slumped against the wall and closed my eyes. Unaware of Cory, Sarah spoke up with little of her usual shyness, though her hesitant phrasing was still pronounced.

"Amyati's not too . . . far away," she said. "She m-must have done . . . something to her Map. To short out its reg . . . regular ping. But I have her lo . . . lo . . . location n-now." She stepped close hurriedly, as if she might lose her nerve, and lifted onto her toes to give me a lingering kiss on the cheek.

I held my hand over the warm spot her lips left behind as she ran off.

"What happened?" repeated Cory, annoyed by my distracted state. Alone now, I finally turned to face him. He stood in an attitude of impatience, arms crossed, glaring at me. His look was accusing. "Simantha pinged my Map to tell me she needed help."

"It wasn't me," I said. "Francis hit the kill switch."

He narrowed his eyes.

"It needed to be done," I insisted. "She was going nuts!"

"Why? What did you do?"

"*Me?* Why me? You need to quit with this jealous rival crap! Didn't you see Sarah kiss me just now?"

Oh man, Sarah had *kissed* me! My heart skipped a beat, and a slow smile started to spread across my face as I recalled every detail of that delicious feeling. The way her lips were so soft against my cheek . . . the smell of her shampoo as her hair tickled my nose . . .

Cory slugged my arm, and I snapped back to attention. *Bloody mind-fuzz.* I shook my head, trying to focus.

"Look, we were just hanging out. I introduced Simantha to Sarah and Susie. Everything was fine until Amyati showed up. Then Simantha started acting like she knew her or something. From a long time ago. Kept insisting that she had to touch her. It didn't make any sense! Then when Amyati refused to let her get close, they started fighting. Well, not fighting, exactly. But Simantha kept trying to touch Amyati, and Amyati used her force-field powers to fend her off. It was a mess."

Now *there* was an understatement! That little fracas had nearly killed Susie. Me and Sarah, too! My legs felt suddenly shaky as I realized just how close it had been. I let myself slide down the wall until I was sitting on the floor.

My explanation seemed to take the wind out of Cory. He had been keyed up to get into a scrap with me over Simantha, my use of the kill switch. My recap of events, while terse, was true, and he knew it. It was hard to lie to each other with our connection. I hadn't used the kill switch, and I hadn't started . . . whatever was going on.

I frowned. Or had I? In the Greenhouse, with Kevin, her mention of Apollo, me bullying for answers out in the hall . . . I had insisted she was the goddess Artemis, and not ten minutes after I'd said it, Amyati walked in. Suddenly, Simantha recalled herself and started accusing Amyati of being this . . . this Iphigenia person.

I passed a hand over my face. What the heck was going on? Cory was watching me. I think he could see I was every bit as bewildered and upset as he was. Maybe our connection helped with that, too. I tried to push sincerity through the channel as I levered back to my feet and took him by the shoulders.

"Cory, please believe me. I don't want Simantha to get hurt or taken apart any more than you do. There has to be some kind of explanation for this! I don't believe Simantha is some kind of evil killer simulant. Not for a second!"

He hunched his shoulders. The love of his life had just been wheeled away on a gurney. Without his anger to sustain him, the poor kid looked miserable.

"She's in the best possible hands now, man. Dawn and her team will fix her up. I'm sure of it."

He looked doubtful and seemed on the verge of running after them. Probably not wise. Cory's presence would just make their job that much harder to focus on.

"Come with me," I begged him. "We'll go find Amyati and Sarah and talk it over. Maybe if we put our heads together, we can come up with some clues or something. Figure out what happened."

Cory hesitated, looking in the direction Simantha had gone. Then he seemed to deflate. Disconsolately, he trudged after me as I followed Sarah, calling up her position on my Map.

Half an hour later, Amyati started killing Cupids.

XXII

It only took a few minutes to catch up to Sarah and Amyati. They were sitting on the bleachers in the mostly empty Powerball arena, talking quietly. Sarah was leaning into Amyati, her arms about the taller girl's waist. Amyati, who might normally have returned her best friend's affection, sat stiffly, staring sightlessly at the field below. Her jaw was tightly clenched. As we approached, Sarah sighed and sat up, disengaging from Amyati. She gave me a solemn nod, unaware of Cory's presence.

I stopped and stood on the level below them so that we were eye to eye. Amyati glanced over, worked her jaw. "Thank you," she said stiffly. "Sarah told me you got it shut down."

"Her."

It was a stupid thing to say. Amyati's eyes stabbed me like knives. But even then, I felt like it was all a misunderstanding of some kind. I'd spent more time with Simantha than almost anyone else, except maybe Dawn's team and Cory, and I knew she was as human as the rest of us. I couldn't say how I knew, but she wasn't a killer. Whatever had set her off, it couldn't be that simple.

Amyati stood to go. As hard as I had tried to earn her respect, she barely tolerated me at the best of times. Clearly, she didn't have the patience for me now. Well, whatever. Amyati could choke on her righteous indignation, for all I cared. I was done playing nice.

"What's your deal, *princess?*" I sneered the royal title, mocking her lineage. "Why do you hate me so much?"

Amyati stared down at me, standing on the tier above. With a sort of wonder, I realized it didn't bother me anymore. She was always looking down at me. She was always looking down at everyone, except maybe Sarah. I doubted it even had anything to do with me. She just had a massive chip on her shoulder for some reason, and I was a convenient target because I never fought back.

"Puh . . . puh . . . please don't f-fight," Sarah whispered in a tiny voice.

Amyati ignored her. "Do you *really* want to know?" Amyati bit off every word, voice venomous.

"Actually, no. Forget I asked. It's really not that important." I said it as casually as I could. I dismissed her. Dismissed her concerns. Dismissed her feelings. Just like she always did to me. It was the cruelest thing I could think of doing. See how she liked it, for a change.

Petty? Yes. Satisfying? Absolutely. And absolutely disastrous.

Amyati flung me away. The force wave lifted me and tumbled me down the bleachers like a rag doll.

That could have been the end of it. Broken neck. Game over. Except Sarah was sitting right there. She screamed my name, flinging out a hand, fingers spread wide. Her tele-K caught me before I hit the turf, left me spinning end over end in the air. Another gesture, and I floated back up into the stands. When I drifted to a halt, Sarah spun me upright to face them. Amyati, bubbled up in her forcesphere, was hanging helplessly in the air a few meters away from me. Her wide eyes were fixed on Sarah. I almost laughed out loud. It was the first time I'd ever seen Amyati look scared.

Sarah's hair crackled with static electricity, standing up in all directions. Little arcs of energy snapped in the air, leaping from her body to ground out in the bleachers. Her eyes blazed. "You. Will. Be. *Kind* to each other!" she informed us. "N-now . . . apolo . . . apologize!"

I opened my mouth to shout a warning, but I remembered too late.

"Let him go!" Cory shrieked, and clubbed Sarah down with a heavy Powerball helmet someone had left lying in the stands. The light in her eyes went out like a switch had been flipped. Amyati and I dropped like rocks.

Amyati reacted to Cory's presence faster than I did, since I had further to drop. I came down badly among the bleachers, wrenching my left knee again. Pain shot up my leg as I struggled to stand. When I looked up, Amyati was lunging at Cory. She had been aware of him as he struck, if only briefly. Perhaps his mind-fuzzing power wavered momentarily as he focused his attention on Sarah. Probably Amyati was already forgetting him even as she leapt to the attack.

All she knew was that she was furious. Sarah had been bludgeoned to the ground by an unknown assailant. For just an instant, all her rage at me was redirected at Cory. Amyati eschewed the use of her Super-powers in favor of tearing him apart with her bare hands. Then, mid-leap, she forgot what she was doing and who she was intending to do it to. Dazed, Amyati failed to execute anything even remotely resembling a proper strike. She went loose. They collided and tumbled in a flailing tangle of limbs.

I scrambled to mount the bleachers, crashing down hard when my knee folded under me. I heard Cory shouting, the slap of his small fists as he pummeled Amyati's dead weight.

I regained my feet. Amyati had risen, swaying slightly. Her long black hair was disheveled, her lip split and bleeding. Her eyes were totally unfocused. Cory scuttled backward, breath rasping in his throat, my broken ion-blade clutched in one hand. I'd completely forgotten I'd gone to the pier to retrieve it! When had he stolen it, I wondered? The blade was shockingly red under the stadium lights. The shallow wound in Amyati's side slowly seeped blood, staining her shirt, but Amyati was a million miles away.

My leg shrieked in protest as I tried to get closer. Heavily, I sat down, two tiers below, grimacing in pain. As Amyati's eyes slowly regained their focus, I urged Cory to move away with a terse gesture. He did so, with alacrity.

Amyati seemed to come back to herself. A sweep of her dark eyes took me in, then shifted to Sarah's crumpled form. "See to the girl," she said, and strode away. Her voice was the same, yet her inflections, her tone—it was unrecognizable.

"What? Amyati!"

She reached the field, kept walking.

"Amyati!"

But she was gone.

When Kevin arrived, I made him check Sarah first. I cast about for Cory, but he, too, had vanished.

Ten minutes later, the security bulletin flashed on our Maps. Hearing my Map give the security tone at the same time as Kevin's and Sarah's was disconcerting, to say the least. But there was a fourth Map making the noise, too. I got up and limped over to where Amyati had fallen. I read the security bulletin off her Map.

SECURITY ALERT / THREAT LEVEL YELLOW
Amyati Mora {photo} 68 AV [Defensive/Offensive Kinetic Force; Kinetic Friction Regulation; Potential Other (Certain)] At [y2312.m08.d18.16:37:17] Amyati Mora entered Security Station Gym4, subduing 2 security personnel on duty, injuring 1 other citizen present. She is attempting to gain access . . .

Even as I read the security alert, the threat level was updated to "ORANGE" and "*is attempting to gain access*" suddenly read "*has gained access.*"

Only a few minutes ago, Amyati had forced open the Security Station weapon lockers, stolen a Hazer, a pair of high-output machine guns known as Chatterboxes, and—most frightening—a

Sunlance, the kind of mega-powered photon-cannon used to slag mechs and carve open bunkers. It was a versatile arsenal, allowing for targeted non-lethal disruption, lethal and non-lethal crowd control (if the Chatterboxes carried different types of ammunition), and maximum stopping power.

She is armed and considered extremely dangerous. If seen, do not approach under any circumstances. Respond to related Security Bulletins with message "sighting" to send coordinates to PASec and exit area if safe to do so.

Uncertainty and dread shadowed Sarah's gaze. Neither of us could understand what had come over Amyati. But I had heard the change in her voice. I felt sure that whatever was walking around in her body, stealing weapons, it wasn't the girl we knew.

It had to be connected to Simantha. This had all started the moment the two girls had met, when Simantha started trying to touch Amyati. Simantha hadn't been successful, though! So how . . . ?

Cory? Or me?

He'd grabbed Simantha's hand in the hallway before Dawn and Miguel had taken her away. I'd pried his hand loose from hers. Simantha must have transferred nano-machines onto our hands. I hadn't touched Amyati, so . . . when Amyati jumped on Cory . . . but how? Simantha's nanos should have been paralyzed. Francis had hit the kill switch!

I fumbled Maps, switched to my own, cleared the security alert, then called Francis. I got no answer, signed off, and tried Dawn.

Nothing. I was starting to get very worried. I called Miguel, fearing the worst.

"Little busy, David. Make it quick."

Relief flooded me. "Miguel! Where's Simantha?"

"Never got this far. She jumped off the stretcher halfway back to CSD. Apologized for the inconvenience, then ran off. Scared us half to death. Hang on . . ." Miguel spoke to someone else in the room. "Francis wants to know if you still have the kill switch."

"Yeah." I held the Map to my ear with my shoulder to take the little rectangle of plastic out of my pocket.

"Fire it off, will you?"

I stared at the kill switch. Was Simantha really the problem here? Or was she the solution? I didn't know enough about the situation to decide. If my guess about the nano-machines was correct, then I might need Simantha to undo whatever had been done to Amyati.

"David?"

"Yeah, I'm here. Isn't it working?" I hadn't hit the button yet.

"No, nothing."

Francis, in the background, shouted something angrily.

Miguel said, "She must have found a work-around, or it just doesn't have the kind of duration we hoped for. Hold onto the switch in case Francis can get it back online. And if you see Simantha, steer clear. I know you think you're friends, or whatever, but she's dangerous. You hear me?"

I disconnected.

Simantha (*Artemis!*) was active and undoubtedly seeking Amyati. *Or was it Iphigenia now?* What would happen when the two met? And why did Iphigenia want weapons?

Kevin was watching me closely. Sarah, still looking a little groggy from her knock on the head, was seated in front of him. He gently inspected her scalp. I knelt in front of her and took her hands in mine. She gave me a shaky smile, then squeezed my fingers.

"I promise I will do everything I can to help Amyati," I told her.

"Whatever you're thinking of doing," interjected Kevin, "forget it. It's too dangerous. Let the pros handle it."

RETURN

"I can't. They'll just cut her down, Kev! Rogue Super. They can't take the chance of trying to capture her alive. And that puts PA in a bad position because Amyati's aunt is the leader of NE. How long do you think PA would survive if NE decided to level this place?"

Kevin scowled.

"You know it's true! But I might be able to stop her before that happens."

I made to rise, but Sarah captured my hand. "There's . . . there's s-something you sh-should . . . nnn . . . know," she whispered.

"What?" I crouched down, knee throbbing. Kevin had given it a quick pass with his healing power, but it still ached like mad. Sarah held my fingers tightly.

"Amyati . . . she's . . ." Sarah swallowed. "She's vuh, vuh . . . very d-dangerous."

"Dangerous? How? The weapons she stole?"

"N-no, not j-just that," stuttered Sarah. "She . . . she knows how . . . hhhow to use them . . . t-too."

I stared at her.

Sarah struggled to push the words out, forcing them past the stubborn resistance of her disobedient tongue. Was she nervous about betraying her friend's confidence? Or anxious for me because I intended to go after Amyati? I could feel her pulse racing under my fingers. Squeezing her eyes shut, she took rapid little gasps of air, then tried again. "Sh-she . . ." But whatever she was trying to say, it wouldn't come out.

Sarah shoved my hands away to dig shaking fingers into her pocket and pull out her Map. Messages started appearing on my Map faster than I could read them. I gave her knee a squeeze before limping toward the field below, heading for the locker rooms.

"When you're done with Sarah, suit up and follow my signal!" I called over my shoulder. "Bring a force-lance!"

I didn't wait around to see if Kevin would agree. Pocketing Amyati's Map, I headed across the field toward the locker rooms, scanning Sarah's messages as I went.

"*Amyati grew up as a sort of mascot for NE, David. Her* mausi—*the whole group—doted on her. You heard Amyati's family history in Mrs. Blevins's class. She was raised to believe she's a queen in all but title. She's been training with NE forces since before she could walk. She's even joined them in the field since she was 14. She hasn't confirmed it, but I'm certain she was involved in the assassination of Killbuck, in a supporting role at least, possibly even the one who pulled the trigger. Her* mausi *has been grooming her for leadership for years. A Super fighting for Normal rights would be a major coup, from NE's point of view. Other Supers would soon join the cause.*"

"*So?*" I interjected. City politics had very little to do with what was going down, right here in PA, right now.

"*Amyati is every bit as dangerous as Rana Mora, David. You can't just chase her down and confront her. Whatever she's doing, she knows how to do it, and she won't let you stand in her way. You don't know enough about your powers to use them effectively if it comes to a fight. For that matter, neither do I! We're still in training, David! But Amyati has combat experience and has been using her powers all her life. She's a born talent, someone who's never had to think about it. And even if you could rely on them, your powers aren't really meant for combat anyway.*"

She had me there. That was why I was going to borrow a Powerball suit. Enhanced speed, strength, and reaction times certainly couldn't hurt if it came to a fight. But I was hoping to avoid all that. I didn't really want to see Amyati get hurt, and there was something bigger going on here. I just didn't know what, nor did I have a clue how I could explain it to Sarah.

I changed tack. Now that it had been pointed out, it was obvious, and I had to wonder. Why was Amyati at PA if she didn't really need training? I asked Sarah.

"*She's ostensibly here for Super-training, but she's really just a spy for NE. PA knows it, but they're cozying up to NE for some reason, so Amyati gets to stay. It's all a big joke to her. She knows PA is just going to feed her whatever info they want NE to have. I don't know what it's all about. Amyati won't tell me everything. But I think they have plans to recruit Supers through PA's training programs. Amyati's also been keeping an eye on Simantha. You know fully sentient AI would be a huge benefit for any group who could make effective use of it. NE would kill for that kind of tech. But she's been avoiding meeting Simantha directly because you were always around.*"

I frowned. "*Me? Why should Amyati avoid Simantha because of me? I know she doesn't like me, but is that enough reason to—*"

"*Oh, David, you can be such a dummy. You don't even know what you do to people, do you?*"

"*What do you mean by that?*"

"*If you don't know, I'm not going to tell you! It's not all the time, and it's better if you don't do it on purpose anyway. I love you, okay? Please . . . just be careful. I don't think she really hates you, but she sees you as a rival. So long as that's the case, you'll be okay. It's when she starts seeing you as an obstacle that you need to worry.*"

Well, great. That was just great. It was time to track down a heavily armed Super-powered *rival* who, if her history was any indication, particularly hated men. I was in way over my head, and if I'd been able to pretend that wasn't the case before, I certainly knew it now. I almost wished Sarah hadn't said anything.

Still, if I didn't try to protect Amyati, who would? There was too much at stake. I didn't think I could live with myself if she were executed by PASec, especially if that precipitated an all-out war with NE. City justice tended to be of the "shoot first, ask questions later" variety. But my instincts told me she was as much a victim in all of this as anyone else. There had to be an explanation for what was going on, and I seemed to be the only one who knew there was more to it than meets the eye.

"*I'm sorry, Sarah. Like it or not, I'm involved. And doing nothing is a choice that has consequences, too. I think in this case, the results would be worse if I simply watched from the sidelines.*"

She didn't respond, and I'd reached the locker room. "*I'll be careful,*" I promised her, then turned to focus on the task at hand.

XXIII

My father made his living restoring old artwork and mold-ering documents for museums and wealthy collectors. Occasionally, some dusty layer of the City would cough up forgot-ten treasures. Among the relics might be bits of paper, scraps of old books, and my personal favorite: comics.

Shipped to him in hermetically sealed resin cubes, with built-in gloves for handling the contents (much like Kevin's bio-domes in the Greenhouse), these ancient treasures had to be restored with meticulous care. Each artifact cube, aside from the document or bit of artwork itself, housed a side chamber with all the tools he might need for the job. The side chamber worked like an airlock; if any-thing needed to be added to the box to complete the task, it could be tossed inside, sealed, then accessed from within the cube through the gloves.

A lot of the work was done with specially programmed nano-machines. Bit by minuscule bit, using the image-enhancing smart-glass screen built into the top of the box, my father would scratch away at the contents, painstakingly restructuring the underlying material, until it would no longer crumble at the slightest touch.

Then, when it was safe to remove the item from the box, he would begin the work of restoring the pigments. Those colors that remained relatively intact could be refreshed by nano-machines. For others, the exact color first had to be determined. With knowledge, care, and a little luck, such information could be extrapolated from the residue of broken-down pigment molecules that still remained. For the very worst damage, my father's artistic skills came into play.

He would sit, for hours at a time, sketching, re-sketching, painting, and directing his little nano-servants in restoring the faint details each lost document presented.

Once finished, these priceless remnants of antiquity would be shipped back to the museum or collector who had commissioned my father to do the work. My father's workshop was strictly off-limits, due to the inestimable value of some of the things he restored. But one of the perks of the job, to me at least, were the resin flimsies he made, perfect copies of each document captured in thin, durable synthetic pages, something an unruly child with an untrustworthy Super-power couldn't carelessly destroy—something I was free to get my grubby little hands on and peruse at my leisure. Indeed, I was encouraged to! I didn't take to reading right away, like some kids, but my father insisted. One of the ways he captured my attention and got me hooked on reading was through comics.

While Sarah had been messaging me, I'd limped out of the stands and across the field. I definitely wasn't moving as quickly as Amyati had been. Once inside the locker room, I began pulling Powerball gear from my locker. As I worked, I kept turning those two names around in my head, examining them from all angles. Over and over: *Artemis and Iphigenia. Iphigenia and Artemis.* Why did I know those names?

I'd looked up Apollo after Simantha had mentioned him in relation to Kevin's healing power, stumbling across the bit about Artemis being Apollo's twin sister. Artemis was goddess of the moon, and Simantha had a moon tattoo on her stomach. It fit. She'd confirmed it only moments later, when meeting Amyati had caused her memories to resurface, yet I felt like I'd already known who Artemis was. I'd heard of Artemis and Iphigenia before. Sarah had said she'd recognized the name Iphigenia, too. But how would Sarah know it? She was an avid reader, adored mythology and fantasy stories. I was beginning to think I must have read them somewhere, too. For me that meant an old comic book, something my dad had restored.

I continued to mull it over while I pulled on the padding that goes under the Powerball armor and started strapping into the exoskeleton. Once done, I began equipping the kinetic armor. It wouldn't do me a bit of good against the Sunlance Amyati had stolen, but the shields should deflect the hail of bullets from a Chatterbox. As for the Hazer . . . I'd just have to hope she wouldn't frazzle my brain.

A Hazer was a stun-gun that worked by shorting out the cerebellum and primary motor cortex in the brain. This cut off a person's ability to control movement, and ruined balance and coordination to boot. Hazers were finely calibrated to avoid shorting out the medulla oblongata in the back of the brain, which controlled involuntary muscle action like breathing, heartbeat, that sort of thing. The goal was to paralyze, not kill, though most people who became familiar with the weapon knew you could overload them, draining the entire power cell for a single deadly shot. It wasn't a done thing, really. Aside from the obvious moral problems most citizens would have with such a thing, the overload typically ruined the weapon. But on reflection, after what Sarah had just told me, Amyati wasn't most citizens. She was a highly trained mercenary assassin and spy. I'd best keep my wits about me if I didn't want my brain to get fried.

Both Alan and Jake had told me what getting tagged with a Hazer was like. They were taking security training as part of their PA curriculum, and one of the requirements of PASec enforcement was knowing what the weapons you used did to the people you used them on. It made sense. Sec'ers (that is, *sec*urity offic*ers*) would be less likely to engage in unnecessary brutality if they had some empathy for the people they were trying to control. The twins had compared the stun-hangover a Hazer leaves behind to Godzilla stomping through the City. The City in question would be my brain. I'd seen Godzilla LXVIII with my dad as a child, in the Ravenswood

Theater across the bay. I knew exactly what the twins had meant by
the comparison.

I was halfway through suiting up when the security alert was
updated again. "*THREAT LEVEL RED.*"

Oh no. Amyati!

She had just murdered someone. No, not Amyati—*Iphigenia.*
Amyati was a hostage in all this, I was certain of it. I hurried to finish
pulling on the kinetic armor, using my power to snug hard-to-reach
straps. Kevin hurried in from the field.

"Did you see the security update?"

"Yeah." I kept working.

Kevin watched me for a moment. I could see him struggling with
his conscience.

"A milligram of prevention," I grunted. *Is worth a kilogram of
cure.* The end of the statement hung unspoken in the air between us.

Kevin threw his hands in the air. "By that logic, I should grab
a force-lance and knock you out right now!" he exclaimed. But he
helped me finish getting into my Powerball gear.

Once I was suited up, the pair of us got Kevin equipped in far
less time. We locked our helmets in place. I held up four fingers,
and Kevin switched to the same channel. His voice crackled over the
suit-radio. "Read?"

"Loud and clear. I'm going to patch my Map into my suit's
heads-up display, use PANet to get Amyati's location if I can. Call
Alan and Jake. They might be involved already if they were in Sec
training when things went south. If they're not involved, they should
be. Their powers would be extremely useful right about now."

I sent out a ping with my Map and got immediate feedback:
Amyati was in the locker room with us. I nearly jumped out of my
Powerball armor before I remembered I was carrying her Map.

Crap. No luck there. *So what next?*

If Jake and Alan were part of the PASec detail, they'd get in serious trouble for passing anything on to me. PASec forces would lock me out of their intel, so I couldn't just call them and ask where she'd gone.

Kevin handed me a force-lance. I checked the connection and felt the vibration as I gripped the haft. Kevin did the same. Satisfied, he gave me an ironic salute. I led the way out of the locker room.

Security updates were feeding Amyati's suspected coordinates to everyone's Maps so they could steer clear of her. It wasn't perfectly accurate, but anytime she was spotted, or someone *thought* they spotted her, an update would get sent out. Our Maps filtered out any egregious anomalies—simultaneous sightings on opposite sides of the facility would be analyzed, and the more likely sighting, based on her most recently known whereabouts, would be used—so from a series of sightings, I was able to project a few possible routes.

Trusting my intuition, I angled across the facility in a direction I hoped would help us catch up to her, taking side corridors and cutting through empty classrooms whenever possible. There were few people around, most members of PA having retired immediately to their apartments the moment it was known a murderer was on the loose. Best to steer clear and let PASec do their job. As more updates came in, I adjusted my course: Amyati's options were slowly narrowing. She appeared to be heading for the Deep Labs, the lowest floors of the PA facility. They were out of the way by design, since that was where most of the high-risk testing of experimental tech occurred. Was that what she was after? Some fancy new gadget? Was she out to steal another alien weapon for her *mausi?* Assuming she stayed on her current route, we wouldn't be able to cut her off before she got there.

While we jogged in pursuit, I called home. My mother answered.

"Hi, Mom. Is Dad around?"

"Sure, Davy. Hang on a sec."

My father picked up and said hello in that way dads do that makes it sound like, "Yellow?"

"Haven't red that one yet." My traditional response.

"Aw, ya blue it," said my father, but without his usual chuckle. It had been a while since we'd bantered, and I knew I'd have to make amends with him soon.

"Nice of you to finally check in," he said, his deep voice reserved.

I took a steadying breath. "Dad, let me level with you. I want to come home and see you some time soon, and we're going to talk this out, okay? It's a conversation I very much want to have. I've done a lot of growing up over the last few years, and I'm beginning to realize just how much I owe you and Mom."

From the heavy silence on the other end of the line, I sensed he was caught off guard by my directness.

"Dad?"

He sighed. "I've waited this long, I suppose. I can wait a little while longer. I take it you need something?"

I pushed down my feelings of guilt and forged ahead, pathetically grateful for his uncharacteristic forbearance. "I'm trying to figure out where I heard a couple of weird names, and I'm pretty sure it was in one of those comic books you restored ages ago."

"That's not quite what I expected." His tone said, *"And this matters, why?"*

"Artemis and Iphigenia."

"Oh, that's obscure!" The history buff in him perked up immediately. "They feature in Euripedes's final play, if I recall correctly. A little tragedy on the way to the Trojan War before all the stuff covered by Homer's Iliad."

"Sooo . . ." I tried to draw out my father's memories, like I drew out the word. Kevin and I had slowed as we crossed a dripping, shady jungle plaza, scanning for PASec forces. I wasn't sure what they'd do if they spotted a couple teens running around in Powerball armor waving force-lances, but *react well* probably wasn't it. My father rambled on while I listened with half an ear.

"Let me think. The Sunset Archaeological Society unearthed an old bookstore that had mostly burned down in the early 2100s. Galaxy Comics, something like that. I guess the floor safe had never been discovered, and there were a bunch of things lost under future developments until the Washout in 2220 pretty much drowned the entire Sunset area. That whole section of the City was condemned until after the Introduction in 2270 . . . basically became a giant lake for the Sunset University kids to party on. But when the Qs gave us the trick of reliable nanos, the SAS started rebuilding. Dredged that whole area from the muck. Among the antiquities was Galaxy's lost safe. A lot of goodies in there! Including a graphic novel treatment of Euripedes's play. We're talking ancient history. Originally written by Euripedes in 400 BC or so, referring to a time eight hundred years further back. Comic was done much later, of course."

Count on my father to forget everything else when history was being discussed. My relief was a palpable thing. I egged him on. "What was it about?"

"Hm? Oh, your typical Greek tragedy: gods and people disagreeing, sacrifices, that kind of thing. It was a beauty to work on, all right. Originally printed in 2051, I think . . . over two hundred and fifty years old when I got my mitts on it! I finished it in, oh . . . 2306, maybe oh-seven."

Vague details were floating back to me, but it wasn't enough to work with. I needed to know more. Kevin and I dropped from a balcony, plummeting three floors to the bottom of another atrium. Instinctively, I had aimed for the water feature, unnecessarily trying to reduce impact. The exoskeleton absorbed the fall effortlessly, but my knee still gave a twinge. A wall of water shot up in all directions from my landing. To my right, the wave bent and twisted around

Kevin's kinetic armor, flying off in spiraling rockets of spray. A Chamonkleon shrieked in outrage somewhere in the trees.

I tried to cajole my dad into grabbing the flimsy and giving me a quick rundown of Iphigenia's story. We were closing in on Amyati's last known whereabouts. I was getting impatient and trying hard not to come across as pushy. My father was indulging me, for now, but I knew he was still angry with me for walking out on them.

"Hang on a moment," said my father. I heard him get up and set down a cup of coffee before walking across the kitchen into the den. The door to the study creaked. He muttered softly to himself as he rifled through flimsies on the shelf. "Why the sudden interest?"

"I remember reading it when I was eleven or twelve. And my, uh . . . my girlfriend, Sarah . . . she mentioned it." I heard Kevin, listening in on his suit-radio, make a strangled sound as he choked back his surprise.

My father didn't seem to notice my awkward stumble. "Well, here it is. Not much to tell, really. The pictures pretty much say it all. A king gathers an army, camps out on the doorstep of some temple, offends the goddess who lives there, kills her pet goat or something . . . I'm not sure what kind of Anymal that's supposed to be, but it has horns."

He was in full historian mode now. "A goddess is a mystical being with great power, by the way. People of the time believed they controlled things in the world around them. Anyway, this king makes the goddess angry, so she demands the death of his oldest daughter in payment for being a jerk. Seems extreme, but she controls the winds and the waves. He can't sail on to do battle unless he makes her happy. So, the daughter gets the knife." He chuckled. "End of story." It seemed an inappropriate moment for laughter, to me, but my dad had always found odd things funny.

"And the daughter is . . . Iphigenia?"

"Yup."

"So, Artemis is the goddess. The one who wants the king's daughter."

"You got it, Dave."

"Thanks, Dad. Sorry to bother you."

"No bother, son. Though it would be nice," he continued ponderously, "if you called every now and then just to catch up, rather than leaving your mother to worry herself sick over you." I smiled at that. *Mom* was worried. He'd never admit he'd been concerned, too. Some things would never change, I supposed.

"I will," I told him, and was surprised to discover just how much I meant it. I had to force the words past a lump in my throat.

My father pretended he didn't hear the emotion in my voice. "Oh, and hey . . . not that my opinion is worth a wise man's toot . . . but if this Sarah girl reads this old stuff, she's probably a keeper." He chuckled again.

Awkwardly, I agreed. I was about to disconnect when he piped up unexpectedly.

"Hang on a sec, Dave; there's an afterword. Says that in some versions, the king isn't able to sacrifice his daughter. The goddess saves her at the last second, puts an Anymal in her place, and whisks her away to become a high priestess at some temple or other."

"What's a high priestess?" I asked. The elevator we were in hummed quietly as Kevin and I descended. Five floors, and then we'd be almost on top of Amyati. Either she'd be waiting for us, or we'd have to start hunting. I shifted from one foot to another, adjusting my grip on the force-lance.

"Sort of like . . . well, the goddess's favorite worshipper, perhaps. Maybe even her voice on Earth. Her chief servant. She gets to boss around all the other worshippers, take the pick of the sacrificial offerings, that kind of thing. Hope all that helps."

"Yeah. Thanks." I signed off, with more questions than ever.

We had reached Amyati's last known whereabouts. Security forces had moved on, and further updates were not forthcoming. But we no longer needed them; Amyati had left a glaringly obvious clue, and recently.

Alan and Jake were lounging against the opposite wall when Kevin and I exited the elevator. They stepped forward as we moved to join them, partially blocking our way. Judging by the massive hole that had been melted in the cargo lift doors, the twins had been tasked with playing guard-drone for PASec, preventing anyone else from gaining access. As far as I knew, the cargo lift went down. Like, *way* down, to the Deep Labs. It was one of the rare areas of PA that was totally off-limits to all but the highest security clearance. Now I knew why Amyati had snagged a Sunlance.

"Yo," said Alan. He looked us up and down, brawny arms folded across his chest. "What's with the rig?"

I gave him a brief rundown. He already knew from the security updates Amyati was on the warpath, but I was able to fill in some of the gaps, citing when it had all started and who else was involved. I finished with what Sarah had told me about Amyati's skillset and my guess about the nano-machine takeover of Amyati's mind.

"Iphigenia was a servant to Simantha, way, way back when Simantha was Artemis and the people worshipped her as a . . . well, as a Super-hero of some kind, I guess. My theory is that Simantha's nano-machines somehow took over and turned Amyati into this high priestess lady, so now she has to do Simantha's bidding."

They looked at me like I was a little bit nuts. Maybe I was. I sure felt crazy because what I was about to say didn't make a lot of sense, given everything we knew.

"So, we need to help Simantha do whatever she's recruited Amyati to do."

They immediately erupted in protest. Kevin demanded to know why he shouldn't just knock me out right then and there. Alan was accusing me of being obsessed with Simantha, not thinking clearly.

Jake shouted them down. "At least, hear him out!" he said reasonably.

"Look, I know it sounds insane, and maybe it is! But I have a hunch that . . ."

"A *hunch*?" exploded Alan. "Dude, you're *nuts*. You can't go running into a firefight with a trained killer on a hunch! Amyati friggin' murdered *a Cupid!*" He pointed a beefy finger at a patch of bluish-gray dust spread across the floor in front of the melted cargo lift doors. I swallowed hard. That . . . that had been a Cupid?

Alan saw my uncertainty, and he was relentless. "Cupids are mostly energy. Whatever physical stuff they're made of, it's like a fizz of atoms held in an energy net. That *dust* over there"—he jabbed his finger again—"is what's left when someone like Amyati spins a kinetic field around a Cupid and then *yanks* on it. All the energy of the Cupid passes right through the field, but the physical stuff doesn't. Whiff, just like that! Dust, separated from spirit. *That* is what we're dealing with here."

Jake frowned, shaking his head. "I hope you have something better than a hunch, David, or I'll just sit on you until all this blows over."

I called Simantha.

Simantha's skin, real as it seemed, was a form of percipient plastic, and her internal nano-network allowed her to operate more or less like a Map, in addition to everything else she could do. Unlike a Map, her own sentience clouded her perception of another person's thoughts. Still, I had always been a bit leery of touching her because she could read something of what I was thinking whenever we made contact. Reaching out to her now, Map to mind, was more like a normal call with any other person. Because of the way my Map was personally encoded, I was banking on the idea that she wouldn't be able to pick up any of the thoughts my Map was tapping into.

To my relief, and somewhat to my surprise, Simantha actually answered. I flipped on my external speakers.

"Hello, David." Her voice was normally inflected, neutral—totally unexcited by what was going on. Either she was truly nothing more than a very sophisticated bio-mechanical robot, or she was in complete command of herself at that moment.

I held up a hand to forestall any protest from the guys, hoping they'd stay quiet. "Simantha! Thank you for answering." Kevin and Jake glowered, and Alan opened his mouth, but I kept my hand up, raising it a little higher. I patted the air, begging them to wait a moment. "Tell me how I can help," I said.

The line went quiet. Was she considering my offer? Or had she heard the guys around me and cut me off? I was about to say more when her location suddenly appeared on my heads-up display.

"Did you get it?" she asked. Now there was excitement in her voice. She thought she had an ally. I hoped I was making the right choice.

"I see you," I said.

"Good. Iphigenia is descending to the lower levels. She has been executing Cupids. I am on my way to intersect her projected path."

"Cupids?" I asked, pretending ignorance, hoping she wouldn't hear the lie in my voice.

Threat Level Red. Call me heartless, but I was thankful it had been Cupids and not some poor Sec'ers just trying to do their job. I'd encountered a Cupid and talked to one. Or been *talked at* by one, anyway. Whatever they had done for humanity, I didn't believe the bizarre aliens were our friends. They did not care about us. Simply talking to us required them to run roughshod over our sanity. Maybe what had happened to me was biasing my opinion, but everyone seemed to forget that they were selectively *breeding* us, working to unlock Super-powers in as much of humanity as they could. Why would they do that if they didn't have some ulterior motive? I didn't believe for a second it was altruism. All the shiny new tech they had gifted humanity couldn't hide the fact there was something bigger going on. I just didn't see how Artemis and Iphigenia fit into the picture.

Simantha and Amyati, I reminded myself. My friends were wrapped up in this, too.

"Why intercept Amyati if she plans on killing Cupids?" I asked innocently. "Why not just let her work?"

Simantha's reply was instantaneous, smoldering with conviction. "David! That is an appalling attitude. Life is sacred! But we will have to discuss your views on the Cupids at another juncture. Rest assured that Iphigenia is working under a misapprehension. She believes the Cupids to be responsible for her present predicament. That is . . . not the case. I have neither the time nor the inclination to go into it now. Will you help me stop her or not?"

I raised an eyebrow at Alan, Jake, and Kevin. Simantha had explicitly stated her intention to stop Amyati from killing more Cupids. Or rather, Iphigenia; she'd called her Iphigenia twice, even after I'd referred to her as Amyati. That pretty much confirmed my theory. At the very least, it confirmed Simantha was operating on the same assumption I was: Amyati's body had been co-opted by the nano-tech personality of Iphigenia.

And Simantha would know. She'd likely triggered the takeover. But I still couldn't shake the feeling that she was just as bewildered by this turn of events as I was. Whatever else the Iphigenia program had been intended to do, murdering Cupids hadn't been in the plan.

The guys looked back and forth between themselves. Then, as one, they turned back to me and nodded. A sudden chill prickled my skin. Were they choosing to support me because they'd been convinced? Or was my power subtly influencing their thinking without any of us knowing?

I took a leap of faith. "Not just me," I told her. "All of us." And I fed her our coordinates.

 XXIV

Normally, we wouldn't have had access to the cargo lift that was right in front of us, but Amyati had conveniently melted a hole for herself. Alan informed me that she had blocked the hole behind her with a force-field, preventing anyone from coming after her until PASec forces with appropriate clearance could be marshaled to open the lift. By the time they'd arrived, the force-field had already flickered out.

PASec had descended, only a couple minutes behind Amyati, keen to stop her before any more Cupids were killed. As I'd feared, the PASec troops had been authorized to use lethal force. The moment Amyati had murdered the first Cupid, all bets were off. *Threat Level Red* meant she had to be stopped, at any cost.

Leaning into the hole now, I saw the open shaft descended like a steep hill, down and away from me at a forty-five degree angle. The cargo lift itself, riding an electrified rail, had halted about three hundred meters below. It was simply a large open platform with a control box at the right-hand end, perhaps twenty meters by thirty. It took up only half the space in the shaft, allowing room for tall stacks of equipment to remain well clear of the ceiling, but unlike a normal elevator, there were no walls separating those riding the lift from the sides of the shaft or the drop beyond the edge. Instead, there were sturdy resin rails that could be raised or lowered at the front and back for loading and unloading. Scattered around on the platform, which was secured at the lower docking bay, were the half-dozen members of the high-clearance PASec team who had followed Amyati. From my vantage point, they looked like discarded action figures. Two of them were only now beginning to roll around, emitting faint groans, clutching at their heads. From the looks of things, Amyati had tagged them all with the Hazer.

Every thirty meters or so, the shaft was punctuated by well-lit recessed nooks holding security-scanning equipment married to gas-bombs, brain-breakers, and EMP devices. Anyone riding the platform could look over the rails to see the entire length of the shaft above and below, but they had best be carrying the appropriate clearance badges, or a variety of responses would automatically eliminate potential security threats. Non-lethal options, mostly, but I noted rail guns that likely fired armor-piercing flechettes, as well as high-powered laser cannons. The only areas that weren't covered by the security grid were the entrance to the shaft, at this end, and the platform where the lift stopped, down below. Everything in between was scanned constantly.

Whatever went on in the Deep Labs, it was strictly on a need-to-know basis. This wasn't something we could just drop into. The rail guns alone would punch right through our suits; they fired their armor-piercing barbs at incredible velocities. I had to wonder how Amyati had managed it. Would her force-fields have protected her from all that? The security update had said she could create kinetic fields, so they would only protect her from physical harm. Unless she had some hidden powers, she couldn't stop energy weapons. Her shields wouldn't protect her from the lasers, and definitely wouldn't help against the brain-breakers, which were sonic weapons, as far as I knew. Maybe she had used her force-fields to mess with the scanning devices somehow? I couldn't see how that would have worked. Again, they scanned with energy: lasers, infrared, ultraviolet, X-ray, that kind of thing—nothing her kinetic shields would have blocked.

I heard a loud groan and glanced back down the shaft. A third guard was beginning to come to. Now that I had started watching them, I noticed the way the guards were scattered across the platform. The first two to recover had been on the left. They had moved around a bit, but they had been lying face down when I'd first looked. The third one in from the left had also been face down. Just then he was trying to get his arms under himself to push himself up. Had he been a little bit on his left side? The fourth one *was* lying on his left. Same with the fifth. The sixth was lying on his back, right arm flung across his chest, gripping the butt of his rifle. Almost as if he had been in the middle of turning around and raising the gun when he went down.

They would probably regain consciousness in the same order they had been shot. Left to right. I scanned across their ranks again, picturing the sequence of events in my mind. *Take out three before they notice. They fall face down. The others start to turn, all in the same direction. Training. Minimize interference with each other's weapons; avoid friendly fire. She takes out two more. They collapse to their sides.* The last one, lying mostly face up, laser rifle in hand, had been about to fire back up the shaft. I'd have bet my laces on it.

I looked above me. A ventilation tube entered the lift shaft about five meters up. The grate covering the end had been carved open and pushed inward. I looked back down at the platform again. A fourth guard was coming to. I whistled in appreciation and new respect. Amyati had expertly shot six moving targets in the head with a Hazer from, what? One hundred and fifty, maybe two hundred meters away? If she had waited until they were halfway down the shaft before opening fire, that would be about right. How long did it take a man to recognize a threat and spin to face it? A second? Maybe two?

No matter how you looked at it, it was incredible. Nano-machine enhancement from whatever had taken over her mind? Or was this the training Sarah had warned me about? Whenever they'd popped up on the news, I'd never seriously considered what Normal Eyes might be capable of. They weren't fronted by Supers, so I'd never really paid attention. Matter of fact, Amyati might be the only Super currently on their roster. Sarah had hinted as much. They didn't have a big, splashy public image. But this . . . this was Elite Task Force level stuff. Better, maybe. ETF relied on their Super-powers more than their equipment. I seriously doubted ETF could have trained a sixteen-year-old girl to do something like this.

I backed out of the hole in the lift doors. "I think after she got in, she blocked the hole behind her so she could climb up and camp out in the air vent," I told the guys. "Waited for Sec to start riding down, then ambushed them with the Hazer. After that she could've used a little force bubble to steal one of their Sec badges and scoot it up the shaft to where she could get at it. Her force-fields wouldn't have protected her from the electricity in the lift track, but if she was careful, she could have managed the descent."

"So, how do we get down?" asked Kevin.

"I don't know. Sec is down at the bottom, and some of them are starting to come around. Maybe they'll loan us a badge?"

"Ha!" scoffed Jake. "Make sure you say 'please'!"

I shrugged, looked at Alan.

"Far as I know, the badges that give access to the restricted areas work on proximity. If they're down at the bottom, they won't stop any of the security measures at the top of the shaft from taking us out. We'd have to drop most of the way down before we were safe."

"Too risky," I said. "What happens if we get a weapon and shoot the scanners?"

"Probably set them all off and get fried. Don't think that will help."

I frowned. Even if I had enough shoelaces, three hundred meters was way too far for me to control them and fish up a badge.

Unexpectedly, Cory tapped me on the shoulder. On his outstretched palm lay a PASec high-clearance badge. I took it, astonished, but before I could open my mouth to ask him where he'd found it, a reckless burst of his power wiped the event from my mind. Jake, Alan, and Kevin were all staring at the security badge on my palm with open mouths. All of us, me included, couldn't explain its magical appearance any more than we could have explained a Spikeface prancing through the hall in a Sec'er uniform with the badge skewered on the end of its horn.

A loud clanking snapped me back to reality. The safety rails on the cargo platform at the bottom of the shaft were being levered into an upright position. Those rails would have dropped automatically when the lift reached the bottom of the shaft so that passengers could exit and unload cargo. Pulling them back up could only mean one thing: the dazed PASec team was aborting their mission and about to ascend.

Clutching my inexplicable new PASec badge tightly, I dove into the hole, shouting in a voice amplified by my Powerball armor, "STOP! AT LEAST ONE OF YOU DOESN'T HAVE A BADGE!"

The platform shuddered and began to rise. Even as I hit the slope and began to slide downward, the security guards were rising to meet me. They had heard me, and they were shakily checking pockets, trying to figure out who had the badges and who didn't. The one who had activated the lift had lost his balance when it started to rise and was now crawling toward the control box, trying to hit the emergency stop.

He wasn't going to make it in time. As they approached the thirty-meter mark where the first scanning devices would decide their fate, the Sec'ers started scrambling to leap clear of the rising platform. They were all Hazered, dizzy, and stumbling too slowly. The sixth member of their team hadn't even woken up yet.

Sparks flew from my boots as I rushed pell-mell down the shaft. Gyro stabilizers in the exoskeleton helped me stay upright, but it wasn't a given; extra strength and speed meant one wrong twitch would send me cartwheeling in an instant.

I watched in horror as three of them made clumsy armor-assisted leaps over the rail, flopping awkwardly onto the lower landing and stumbling through the open door at the bottom of the shaft where they tumbled like dominoes. The fourth missed his footing, flipped as if boneless over the rail, and crunched down to land in a heap like a rag doll. He fetched up against the heavy resin barricade meant to stop the lift platform. Woozily, he tried to regain his feet.

The fifth security officer was struggling to get his helmet off. Getting Hazered, standing up, falling down, trying to stand up again—it was all too much for him. No sooner had the helmet come off than he was emptying his guts noisily over the edge with a white-knuckle grip on the railing to keep himself from falling.

Sliding precariously down the slope in a series of barely controlled leaping strides, pinwheeling my arms for balance, I had already covered over two hundred meters, but I was getting ever closer to the electrified track that carried the platform. As it loomed near, I pushed off as hard as I could. My frantic leap carried me out and down. I hit the slowly rising platform with an echoing crash just as the scanners focused their attention on the two Sec'ers who were still aboard. My knee screamed in protest.

I ignored it, made a split-second decision, and hauled up the guard who was still unconscious. The other would have to fend for himself. My exoskeleton had mostly absorbed the brutal impacts of my rapid descent, but I had one more jump to make. I could only hope my knee could take it.

The scanner, oblivious to my presence because of the PASec badge still clutched in my fist, had decided the unconscious interloper in my arms was a minor threat. It launched a gas canister the moment I cleared the railing. I twisted in the air at the woofing sound of the cannon. The canister whined off the kinetic shielding of my shoulder, then ricocheted into the wall of the shaft. A sickly yellow cloudburst unfolded above my head as I dropped the final thirty meters to the hall below, landing at a sideways tilt. Hugging the security guard to my chest, I locked my arms in place and prayed. We caromed off a wall and barely missed stepping on his comrades, finally fetching up in the middle of the hall.

Unfolding my arms, I pushed him off me, then checked him over. He was breathing steadily. He had slept through the whole thing.

The solitary guard left on the platform flopped onto his back and passed through the disorienting yellow fumes. The scanners ignored him; he still had his badge. Now, on top of everything else, the poor schmuck was huffing a compound that would make him giddy and agreeable, rendering him totally pliable to the coercion of any security forces trying to stop him, had he been an unauthorized visitor. Or, in this case, to Jake, who remembered to say "please" when he asked for the officer's security badge. The platform locked into place at the top of the shaft, and the railing folded out of the way. Solemnly, as if performing a sacred duty, the PASec man walked stiffly out into the hall and handed over his badge. Then he burped before collapsing in a fit of giggles.

With only one security badge, Jake rode the cargo lift back down alone. By the time he reached me, I had pulled the security guard who had fallen to the bottom of the shaft out of the path of the descending platform. Spikes of pain hammered into my abused knee the whole time, but I couldn't just leave him to be crushed.

The five officers in the Deep Labs with us were in no shape to resist someone with Jake's Super-speed and strength, even if their own gear gave them a boost. They were simply too dazed, only barely conscious. He sat them all against the wall of the corridor, tossed their badges onto the cargo lift, and sent it back up the shaft.

When Alan and Kevin snagged two of the badges and descended to join us, they were unaware of Cory quietly riding with them, a third high-clearance badge tucked securely in his pocket. Nursing my injured knee when the platform arrived, I didn't notice him either.

XXV

Amyati was somewhere in the Deep Labs with us, but there was no way to know precisely where in the warren of interconnecting passages and chambers she might be. Simantha—according to my heads-up—had found an entrance to the Deep Labs through another elevator shaft at the far end of the PA complex and was moving toward the tunnel that gave access to the seafloor under the bay.

Wait a minute, that tunnel is down here? Cory had been down in the Deep Labs when he met the Cupid! How on Earth had he gained access back then?

I shook my head. It hardly mattered. I hadn't seen him since Amyati had attacked him at the Powerball field. I doubted he had come down here chasing her. From the look on his face after she had tried to tackle him, he'd rather be anywhere other than where she was. If there was some escape route other than the pair we knew about, I could call him later to tell me where it was if I needed it.

Alan seemed inclined to grab one of the Sec'ers' laser rifles, but I shook my head. We didn't want to kill Amyati or scare her and make her think she needed to kill us. *Rivals, not obstacles.* I pointed to the EMP grenades on the bandolier about the guard's chest. Maybe if we could pop one of those off near Amyati, it would short out the nano-machines that were controlling her. It was our best bet. Alan unstrapped the bandolier and looped it over his shoulder. Flashbangs, stun grenades, smoke bombs, frags, EMPs—these PASec guys hadn't been playing around. Unfortunately, neither was Amyati.

Kevin took a moment to ease the pain in my knee. Then, with an open connection to Simantha to coordinate our movements, we began systematically searching the labs.

We found the remnants of a second dead Cupid five minutes later. The halls had been eerily quiet as we moved from room to room. Personnel had been evacuated—scientists, technicians, even custodial staff—removed via the nearest exit in a quick, calm, efficient manner.

The high clearance security badge gave me access to the Deep Lab schematics. As we moved, I looked over the network of corridors and chambers on my heads-up display, trying to get a feel for the labyrinth. It was a huge area, covering over three-square kilometers, roughly arranged in a radial pattern, like five nearly concentric wheels of varying sizes. Hallways like radiating spokes sliced the curving corridors into a tangled mess of sectioned wedges. Curiously, some of the spokes extended out of the nested circles, connecting to other similar yet smaller sunbursts of radially arranged rooms linked by gently curving halls. Smaller PA controlled facilities, maybe.

We had entered by the southeast elevator, Simantha via the northwest, both located on the middle ring of the complex, maybe a kilometer and a half apart. If we headed inward, access points to deeper levels of the facility were labeled on the map. Outward, there were at least four other possible entrances that I could see, and it didn't look as if they'd lead back to the Project Arete facility that I was familiar with. Different entrances to the Deep Labs, scattered around the surrounding neighborhoods of the City above.

We almost missed the next corpse. Amyati's force-field had torn the Cupid's physical essence free of its moorings, splashing it against the curving wall of the corridor. It was like lavender chalk dust, the vaguest indication of an elongated man-shape. A smell like ozone in the air made me wonder if I was breathing the remnants of the Cupid's life force. I nearly got sick inside my helmet at the thought and had to turn away and move a few steps down the hall. I concentrated on inhaling slowly and deeply for a few moments.

Simantha contacted my Map less than a minute later. Her voice came through on the suit-radio as if she were standing right next to me. "I believe I have found the remains of a Cupid. There is the feel of static in the air. It cannot have died more than a few moments ago."

"Yeah, us too. This kill is probably less recent. She was heading your way. Any idea where she might have gone?"

"Yes. The tunnel under the bay. I suspect Iphigenia may have gone there to verify who I am, and . . . for other reasons."

"Why should she doubt you?" I asked.

Simantha was silent for a time. We jogged steadily down the main corridors, my knee throbbing with every step. I gritted my teeth, trying to ignore it. We were only a few minutes away from joining up with her. I had just signaled the guys to duck down a cross corridor when Simantha spoke again.

"Because," admitted Simantha. Her voice was soft. Regretful. "Artemis would not have betrayed her as I did."

My team shared a look. None of us had any response to that. I had so many questions I wanted to ask her, like: *How will the tunnel under the bay confirm your identity?* Or: *How did Amyati/Iphigenia even know about the tunnel?* More importantly: *What else is down there?* But just then, we had to halt, pressing ourselves flat against the inner curve of the hall. A troop of half a dozen Sec'ers loped past along the next cross corridor, looking intent. They were heading precisely the wrong way, but I wasn't about to enlighten them. We still had a chance if we could just find Amyati first.

I suspected the high-security badges we carried informed them of our presence, but since they didn't make visual contact, they assumed we were another team, working our own section of the Deep Lab maze. I'd figured out how to call up the Deep Lab blueprints, but I didn't know how to access telemetry for the PASec teams that had been deployed. There was no way to know how many of them were down here with us. We'd been fortunate, thus far, not to run into anybody else.

When we finally worked our way to the western end of the Deep Labs, we were just in time to see Simantha step into the tunnel, vanishing into dim blue shadows. Our company was of uniformly grim countenance as we slowed to a cautious walk and followed her out under the bay.

XXVI

The sense of déjà vu I felt as we entered the tunnel added a dark layer of foreboding to that eerie excursion. I'm sure my link to Cory had something to do with it, a layer of his memories that percolated through my own experience: dim light filtering down through the water above; the spooky blue glow of the low lighting, which seemed to create more shadows than it banished. Gloomy shapes loomed in the murk outside the glass tunnel walls.

Walking down that submerged corridor, I felt a dreadful certainty that I would see a Cupid floating off to my left in the water, just as Cory had. Things had come full circle—here, at last, was an end to events that had begun millennia before—but I didn't foresee any joy waiting at the terminus of that dismal tunnel. What had my father said? *Your typical Greek tragedy.* I suppressed a shiver of fear and forced myself to put one foot in front of the other.

Simantha had slowed her stride, perhaps feeling some of the same uncertainty I was. We matched her pace, continuing in silence. I was relieved to finally have her at my side. Whatever was waiting for us, we would face it together. That was how friends did things.

The tunnel went on and on, extending into the bay for three kilometers. After fifteen minutes, our pace slowed slightly by my sore knee, I looked sideways at the goddess who padded quietly to my left. *Artemis.* I still couldn't quite believe it.

"Why is Iphigenia killing Cupids?" I asked her. "You said she blamed them. For what?"

Simantha continued walking in silence for a time. Our footsteps echoed weirdly ahead and behind. Alan, Jake, and Kevin fell back a few paces, but it was only a respectful nod to privacy, not enough to actually cut them out of the conversation. Squaring her shoulders, Simantha began to speak.

"Iphigenia did not fall prey to her father's blade. My masters were breeding for Super-powers, and it was my role to secure ideal genetic candidates for this purpose. I had been ordered to separate Iphigenia from her family. The girl's genetic traits would lend themselves perfectly to the Cupids' aims.

"My anger over the buck in the sacred grove was real enough— life is sacred to me—but my anger alone was no justification for demanding the death of Agamemnon's eldest daughter. Fortunately, men did not often question the whims of the gods in those times. It was the perfect opportunity, and I took it, playing the role of the incensed goddess to the hilt.

"Nano-inspired dreams had the king's seer, Calchas, encouraging Agamemnon to make the sacrifice. For certainty's sake, a bout of uneasiness, easily triggered by nano-induced hormone release, caused the king's brother, Menelaus, and many of the soldiers, to insist on the path Calchas the Seer suggested. With weather and waves becalmed by the Cupids' weather-control machines, Agamemnon had little choice. I almost felt bad for him.

"Iphigenia was brought to my temple at Aulis. My brother Apollo would later call it fate, for the name Iphigenia means 'from whom strength is born.' Even without him saying it in that moment, I could easily see it for myself. Iphigenia displayed an intense strength of will, powerful faith, and unfailing love for her father. Even as he raised the knife, she accepted that her death would serve him, and embraced her fate. The girl's beauty had intrigued me before; seeing her face her death so bravely, I was totally smitten. I wanted to possess her for myself.

"I had already stepped from the shadowy recesses of the temple as Agamemnon approached the altar with his daughter, the silvery light of the moon warping around me, only the faintest etching of my form visible in the flickering light of the torches and lanterns held by the soldiers. All eyes were on the drama at the altar, so few, if any, noticed my presence as I quietly slipped through the struggling throng of priestesses who held the queen and came to stand behind the king. A handful of soldiers must have seen me, but if they did, they made no sound; the goddess Artemis herself had appeared, in this, her sacred temple at Aulis. One did not interfere with such things. Awe stilled their tongues, bound their hands. Many pressed their faces to the floor in abject fear.

"I waited while Agamemnon raised the silver knife. I witnessed Iphigenia's stoicism with wonder in my heart. When, with a despairing yet determined cry, her father struck, fully prepared to finish what he had begun, I was satisfied by the depth of his intent to make reparations for his crime. Only then did my hand flash forth, a silver blur in the moonlight, to catch the king's wrist. Even as I moved, I was revealed. The cloak of moonlight fell away from me. To them, it was the sudden manifestation of the divine. There stood a young woman with flashing silver eyes, skin as pale as the moon, hair the exotic, flaming red that could only belong to a divine being.

"I stood as still as the statue carved in my likeness that loomed above us. Compared to Agamemnon, my strength was the strength of the mighty lowland oaks. The king was held immobile by my grip. Only my toga and my hair, rippling in the breeze, indicated that I was not made of stone.

"When the proud king at last dropped his gaze, I released him. Slowly, he lowered his knife. Slower still, he knelt, pressing his forehead into the cold flagstones of the temple floor. Eyes downcast, he awaited my decree.

"I caused a deer to be laid in Iphigenia's place. When King Agamemnon next raised his eyes, both the goddess Artemis and his daughter Iphigenia were gone.

"Rising, the king took up the sacrificial dagger and completed the sacrifice."

There was no sound in the underwater tunnel beyond the echo of our own footsteps. I was having difficulty processing everything she'd just told us. Euripedes's play was *true?* And this girl next to me had *actually been there!* Never in my life had I felt so tiny and insignificant. Somehow, we were caught up in events so immense, it was almost impossible to fathom.

"I imagine Agamemnon rejoiced," said Simantha, after a time. "Iphigenia had been spared. I wonder if he would feel the same if he knew what she had been spared for."

She sighed. It was poignant, in its total insufficiency. I recalled the overwhelming feelings the Cupid had pushed into me. Thousands of years of loneliness, regret, and despair. I doubted any sound could encompass such a thing.

"I fell helplessly in love with Iphigenia from the moment I met her. Fortune blessed me; she returned my love in kind. For love of me, she embraced her new role. She became the mother of nations."

Simantha's steps faltered to a halt. She placed a hand on the glass wall of the tunnel. Her unfocused gaze looked out into the murky waters of the bay, looked through them, into the lightless past.

"My Cupid masters would determine a suitable match. I would arrange the tryst and bless the union." In the reflection of Simantha's face, a small silver glimmer appeared in the corner of her eye. "Iphigenia never took a man to her bed unless I first warmed it," she admitted. She blinked and the shimmering tear dropped into darkness.

A shooting star, I thought. *Make a wish.* If only it could be so easy.

"After each match, Iphigenia would carry the child until it could safely be removed from her womb and put into a mechanical incubator to finish growing. At that time, the robotic wombs the Cupids would later share with humanity were not perfected. They were unreliable if used to grow children who had not first developed five or six months naturally. It was hard on Iphigenia, even with the nano-machines to repair her and prepare her for the next birth."

Simantha turned from the glass. Her silver eyes were luminous in the dimness of the tunnel. I met her gaze as steadily as I could while Kevin and the twins looked on in silence.

"More than three hundred years passed in this way. More than five hundred children." I was astonished. Almost two pregnancies every year, each carried halfway to term before being removed to the mechanical wombs. A brief period of nano-assisted rest and recovery before it began again. Simantha held my eyes a moment longer, then turned away.

Following her lead, we began walking again. The tunnel slowly resolved from gloomy obscurity ahead.

"Iphigenia grew tired. One day, she asked to die. She had served faithfully, and more than her body had been used up. Her spirit was exhausted. She wished to pass on to the next world, to await me in the soft repose of Elysium. But I knew, even if Iphigenia did not, that there was no such place where I might choose to visit her after her demise."

Walking down that dark tunnel, footsteps echoing, I might have been walking into the Underworld. Had Iphigenia's ghost drifted past the window, I doubt I would have been surprised. But I knew the ghost of Iphigenia was actually somewhere up ahead, inside Amyati—the spirit of a woman dead three thousand years and more. How did one reason with something like that?

"I could not bring myself to reprogram the nano-machines," Simantha whispered, "to let her die. I could not bear the thought of being without her. I refused to grant her final request. But I was a coward! I blamed the Cupids, told her they would not allow her Super-genetics to go to waste. When the mechanical wombs were perfected, I said, then she would be free to die. Then, her body would no longer be required. Only her genetic material, which they could replicate from her remains."

She clenched her fists in anguish. I held my peace. Words seemed so totally inadequate. What could I possibly say to ease the burden she was carrying?

"Dear, faithful Iphigenia! So loving! So trusting! She *believed* me, and I watched. As the years went by and she slowly withered in torment, I *watched*. I watched as she was hollowed out, drained of the last remnants of her vitality, and still she offered herself on the altar!

"Finally, when I could bear to witness it no longer, when the sight of the torture I had inflicted upon her grew more horrifying than the fear of losing her, when my guilt at last outweighed my grief, I relented. I granted her wish. I reprogrammed the nano-machines within her, and I allowed her to die."

Tears coursed freely down Simantha's face. She held her head high, eyes straight ahead, ashamed of the truth but relieved to be unburdening herself at last. Somehow, the four of us had become confessors to a goddess. It was surreal. I knew there was nothing at all we could say to ease her pain. She would have to learn to live with the burden of her choices. But Simantha wasn't finished.

"Even then I was a coward," she continued, voice low. "I introduced the lethal nano-machines as her final pregnancy drew to a close. I also introduced others, which stole her thoughts, her memories, and took them into the unborn child. When the Cupids removed the infant and placed it in the robotic womb, the baby girl took her mother with her, nestled in the infant's own developing womb. The child grew up strong, healthy, and beautiful. As a woman, she was much desired. Iphigenia's genetics were powerfully expressed in her. When she bore daughters, they too carried Iphigenia, hidden dormant within them. On and on through the generations, in every daughter since."

The circular airlock at the terminus of the tunnel loomed out of the gloom ahead. It coalesced from the dark like a ghost manifesting. To either side of the airlock, through the resin windows of the tunnel, I could discern the curving face of a massive dome, a hulking, oppressive curtain of resin-reinforced fabric soon lost to sight in undersea shadows. A bright yellow logo, a meter high and depicting a cheerily smiling sun, was plainly visible on the left-hand stretch of dome. *Sunny brand.* They'd made my nearly indestructible shoelaces. A quality dome, then. How reassuring.

Propped against the airlock door, clutching his stomach, was a man in diving gear. His mask had been pulled free and discarded on the floor. Water puddled around him. A slow trickle of blood, like leaking ink in the dim blue light, seeped from beneath his fingers.

Kevin moved quickly to his side and applied his healing gift. The man, face pale, opened his eyes and took us in. As his strength slowly returned, he coughed, then turned his head to spit up a dark gob of blood-tinged phlegm.

"Thank you," he said on a shuddering breath. He wiped his arm across his mouth, smearing shadowy liquid through his salt-and-pepper beard. His eyes were unfocused.

"The girl who did this to you," guessed Alan, "she went in there?" He indicated the airlock.

"Yuh," grunted the man. He winced as Kevin's power began to knit the wound. "Said . . . said she had to . . . make a sacrifice."

I raised my eyes to Simantha. Her face was carved of stone. Somehow, I knew this was what she had been dreading.

"What's in there?" I asked.

"A temple," he said. Simantha answered simultaneously, a quiet echo of the man's words.

"A temple?" asked Jake.

"Yes," she said. "My temple." Simantha turned to meet my gaze. Her opalescent silver eyes had always fascinated me, but in that moment, they were utterly alien. The eyes of the goddess Artemis. I felt she looked straight through me, sifted my soul. Then she said, "Iphigenia seeks death. This is where it was promised to her. This is where that promise was broken, where her death was denied."

"Is that why you tried to touch her?" I asked.

"Yes. I recognized Iphigenia in Amyati. Darker skin and hair, perhaps, but her eyes are the same. Seeing her triggered a cascade of memories. I realized that Amyati was descended from Iphigenia. I hoped to use my nano-machines to awaken the dormant Iphigenia program, to apologize. To beg her forgiveness, before I let her go."

"One of us woke her instead," I said, voicing my earlier guess.

She nodded.

"If she wants to die, why hasn't she simply committed suicide in Amyati's body?" I asked.

"Amyati is Iphigenia's hostage, and you are correct, Amyati's death is the threat," admitted Simantha. "But like me, Iphigenia views human life as sacred. I am saddened to discover this reverence does not extend to the Cupids." Simantha looked down at the scuba diver, who was following the conversation with some difficulty. He likely had Iphigenia's supposed reverence for life to thank for the fact he was still alive.

"She would want to avoid killing her host, if at all possible," continued Simantha. "By programming the location of the temple into the nano-machines I passed to Cory, I hoped to appeal to Iphigenia's strong sense of justice. She awoke with the knowledge of the temple's location waiting for her. Think of it as a peace offering—my signal to her that I will do what is required. Here, where it all began, with Amyati's life held in the balance, Iphigenia knows she can force me to do what I failed to, so long ago."

Simantha spun the airlock wheel, then pushed the door wide.

Within was a large chamber with a similar door on the far side. Two smaller portals at either hand gave access to the bay. A line of lockers to the left likely housed scuba gear. Judging by the toolkit sitting in a puddle of water, the diver had been outside the dome, attending to some repairs, before he had the misfortune of coming inside and running into Iphigenia.

Had she been caught off guard when the airlock cycled, when water swept in to fill the chamber? Would Amyati's kinetic fields have protected her from the deluge, allowing her to create a little bubble of air until the chamber drained? Or had she floundered and struggled to hold her breath while the pumps did their thing?

Despite Simantha's insistence that her high priestess held life to be sacred, Iphigenia had shot the scuba diver ruthlessly, at point-blank, with a Chatterbox. From a gun that could spray hundreds of bullets in mere seconds, it *had* only been one, a disabling wound that would be slow to kill him, but also an excruciatingly painful one. Had she hoped he would live long enough to receive help? Or had she simply wanted to prevent him from pursuing her? I had to wonder if I was searching for some sign of humanity that was already long gone, submerged beneath the ancient ghost of Iphigenia. After so much time, it was highly likely she was no longer the same person Simantha thought she was.

The Sunlance and the Hazer were laying in the corner. The saltwater soak hadn't done the photon-cannon any good. Powerful as they were, Sunlances were finicky pieces of equipment. She'd abandoned it, and the Hazer, too. The Hazer's power cell must have been nearly drained by her encounter with the PASec team in the elevator shaft. Maybe she'd tried the Hazer first, then shot the scuba diver with one of the Chatterboxes when she realized the stun gun was out of juice.

Lucky him. Kevin would have his bullet wound patched up soon. A Hazer hangover could last for days.

Simantha had crossed to the far side of the airlock. A green light glowed next to the door; the dome within was pressurized, full of air. She spun the wheel and hauled the door open.

"I must atone," she said, and stepped through the portal.
Somewhere within, Iphigenia awaited us at the Temple of Artemis.

XXVII

Kevin hung back to tend to the diver, Jake standing guard, while Simantha, Alan, and I stepped through into a substantial space of misty air, easily two hundred meters in diameter, perhaps twenty-five to thirty meters high. The bay had been dredged much deeper than it used to be before the Washout, but even so, the top of the dome must have been halfway to the surface. Within, it smelled richly of rotting seafloor detritus and brine. Bright lights suspended from the dome illuminated the space, harshly glaring, haloed by rainbows in the moist atmosphere. Shadows crawled and flickered everywhere. The deep hum of pumps thrummed constantly from somewhere out of sight.

The ground was thick with silty mud, and the underlying stone was roughly hacked into a jumble of broken and eroded plateaus. The area to our right was noticeably higher, on average, and a path had been carved through the muck, curving off in that direction. The path was marked with posts supporting lengths of drooping synthetic cord and little flags of white fabric. It mounted a series of short rises, culminating on the high ground to our right at the front steps of a temple in the old Greek style.

Simantha hadn't been joking. There was an ancient Greek temple. Here. Beneath the bay.

The pillars were tilted and laced with cracks. Massive lintel stones had fallen. Entire sections of the roof had caved in or were subsiding dangerously. I could see scaffolding had been set up to support the worst of the damage, but there were still sections I wouldn't want to walk near. A gravity conveyor sat powered down by the steps to the temple, tilted at an angle, some of its weighty load of blocks fallen in heap.

I took it all in, absorbing every detail, in a state very much akin to awe. I was at a loss. I couldn't imagine how it had come to rest here, at the bottom of the bay. Eleven thousand kilometers, give or take, from the part of the City that had once been ancient Greece. Some of those columns and capstones must weigh tons. Shifting the temple piece by piece would have taken . . . forever. And all at once? I tried and failed to wrap my mind around it. What on Earth was it doing *here*, of all places?

Amyati stepped from the shadowed portico of the temple and stood framed by the leaning pillars at the top of the steps.

"Artemis!" she called, and it was Iphigenia's voice, full of grief. Amyati's long black hair had come loose from its customary braid. It flowed in midnight waves over Iphigenia's shoulders and brushed her hips. Her eyes were shadowed sockets in the dome's glaring light. A single Chatterbox dangled loosely from her right hand. Evidently, she had abandoned the other gun, for her left hand was clutched tightly to her heart, as though enclosing something precious.

"So, you found it," said Simantha quietly to herself. She took a shaky breath, then squared her shoulders and raised her voice. "I had hoped to have a chance to explain before you made this discovery," she called.

With a shriek, Iphigenia flung the object in her hand. It sailed through the air, glittering like a shooting star, before splattering into the muck at Simantha's feet.

"How *could* you?" Iphigenia screamed. Emotion choked her voice. Rage, anguish, betrayal . . . and, horribly, love. A terrible, passionate love, utterly hopeless, incapable of hating her betrayer despite the pain she had caused.

Simantha stooped to pluck the object from the mud. A little silver emblem: a crescent moon. She wiped her thumb across its face and watched the nacreous glimmer pass over it. It was twin to the crescent moon tattooed on Simantha's stomach, though smaller. She closed her hand around it.

"Iphigenia, I . . ."

"You *swore!*" Iphigenia shouted, anguished. "You promised me *death!*" She looked toward the sky, beseeching the gods, but found only the dome. Her eyes blazed in the harsh lights, and she tore at her hair as she began stumbling down the temple steps. "Instead, you condemned me to *this!*" She waved the Chatterbox wildly, a gesture to encompass everything, even life itself. "After all I have done for you, for your masters, the *legions* I have produced . . . I deserve to *rest!* I deserve *peace!* But *this* . . . this is not death. This is not even *life*. You have made a *monster* of me . . . a hollow *thing!*"

Simantha stood frozen, watching Iphigenia's raving approach with such pity in her eyes, I thought she might fold under the weight of her emotions and begin to weep. Quietly, she said, "I loved you too much!" Her eyes hardened. "But this is not what I intended."

Iphigenia heard none of it. She pointed the Chatterbox at Simantha as she neared, a vicious jab. "*You* did this. You! Now you must undo it. You must let me go!" She raised the gun to her own head, pressed the barrel to her temple. *Amyati's* temple.

Simantha took a quick step forward. "I will," she said, raising her voice. "Yes, of course, I will. I know I must." She began walking toward Iphigenia.

That's when the Cupid appeared.

It faded into view, drawing its physical substance to itself, displacing a patch of rainbow-misted air. Iphigenia stumbled backward at the sight of it and slipped in the mud, clutching at the rope rail of the path for balance. Simantha crouched, her posture suddenly feral, like an Anymal about to pounce. I could see her calculating how long it might take to reach Iphigenia, whether she could prevent another murder.

The Cupid hung in the air between them. I couldn't tell which way it was facing. But when it spoke, I knew it had singled me out.

<*detailed views of arches*>
<urgent dismissal>

I reeled, clutching my head. The Powerball armor suddenly seemed confining, the helmet much too close. I couldn't breathe. I fumbled with the straps of my helmet before hauling it free, only to suck in damp, rotten air.

The images flooding my mind were like the pictures the other Cupid had shown me, but different in detail. Arches, again, thousands of them, but each image focused on the arch's upper curve. Simultaneously, my heart raced with the need to leave immediately. I was not wanted here—no, that wasn't quite it. The Cupid was *afraid*—worried!—for *my* safety!

I fought the alien emotions as I took a step forward. A thunderous staccato hammering split the air; Iphigenia was unloading the Chatterbox at the Cupid. Tendrils of bluish mist were plucked loose from its spectral form, spooling out behind it: miniature eruptions as each bullet passed through it. The Cupid's surface roiled, outlines blurring as it moved, spinning to face its assailant.

A dozen flows of water began to bubble and spill down the inner surface of the dome. They gained pressure as I watched, trickles becoming streams that arced out and down, splashing into the mud below.

I heard squelching footsteps behind me, then muffled shouting. I risked a look over my shoulder. The commotion had brought Jake and Kevin running. Jake outpaced Kevin, despite the Powerball armor the healer wore, but a shimmering wall of force appeared across the airlock door, blocking access. Only Alan was on this side with me and Simantha.

Jake looked like he was about to bash his way through the wall of the dome instead. "Stop!" I barked. But I'd taken my helmet off. My voice was lost in the hum of the generators and the roar of the cascading water. I waved my force-lance over my head to get Jake's attention while making a frantic *abort* gesture across my throat with the other, then pointed at the water that was already spilling into the enclosure. Jake turned to look and vanished from sight. Over the noise of the water, the thrumming of the pumps, I thought I heard him calling to Kevin, ordering him to close the airlock door. Cut off by Iphigenia's force-field, Kevin watched helplessly for a moment. Then he pushed the airlock door closed. The wheel spun as he locked it in place.

There was a crackling sound. My hair stood on end. Turning, I saw the Cupid encased in a glowing ball of force. The alien was helpless as the force-field shrank, squeezing its physical body into a smaller and smaller area, tearing atoms from its energy matrix. Tendrils of lightning arced from the force-field to the ground, snapping loudly.

"No!" I shouted. I raced around the maelstrom, circling to the right, hoping to reach Iphigenia before she killed again. Simantha cried out and tried to time a leap beneath the struggling Cupid but was struck by a blaze of lightning as the Cupid came apart.

<blacksmiths, masons, carpenters>
<acceptance>

Blinded by the flash, my disorientation was compounded by the Cupid's dying thoughts and feelings. I slipped in the muck, feeling my knee give out with a sickening crunch. I hit thick slime and rolled, spitting out a mouthful of gritty mud. Cupid dust drifted down and coated my face. I blinked stinging eyes and watched the colors of the world slowly go awry.

Cupids, as it turned out, were hallucinogenic.

Pushing up onto my elbows, I looked about blearily, trying to find Iphigenia. She had vanished off the edge of the path. I saw Alan approaching the place she had been, the bandolier of grenades held in one hand, an EMP armed in the other.

The Chatterbox spoke again. Alan was punched off his feet, flung away by multiple impacts. Even as he tumbled through the air, he threw the EMP, a whip-snapping sidearm that buried the grenade in the muck where he guessed her to be.

Waves of kinetic force pulled inward, piling silt a meter deep. There was a muffled thump. The EMP's electromagnetic charge was grounded. As she rose, dripping from the mud at the side of the path, Iphigenia was clearly still in control of Amyati's body.

Rainbow haloes hanging from the lights above smeared crazily when I moved. I groaned, squeezing my eyes shut. Motes of electric light whirled and danced behind my eyelids. I felt sick to my stomach.

Drawn by my noise, Iphigenia turned to face me where I struggled in the muck and pointed the Chatterbox at my unprotected face. Before she could pull the trigger, a small shape flew at her, shoving hard. She tripped over the rope railing and splashed onto the path. Cory dropped on top of her, pummeling furiously with both hands. I felt the familiar wave of "*forget me, forget me, forget me*" roll outward.

Too late. The nano-machines in control of Amyati's body made full use of her senses. *They* didn't forget, even if Amyati did. The Chatterbox erupted, loudly knocking five times before clicking rapidly. Cory's small body lifted into the air, jerked and danced, then fell limply. The wave of forgetfulness rolled over me. I realized I was screaming in anguish and choked to a stop, bewildered. Smoke coiled lazily from the barrel of Iphigenia's gun, painting watercolor arabesques on the stark geometric background of the temple. She tossed the weapon away.

My head spun like the gun, landing in the muck. My arms and legs felt tingly and numb.

Alan hurtled out of the jumbled boulders beside the path. His PASec armor was shredded, his ribs and chest a welter of black and blue, but the bullets had bounced off his Super-durable frame. A wave of giddy relief crashed over me, washing away coherent thought. I paddled mentally and surfaced to see Alan deflected by a wall of energy. He bounced at speed off the temple steps, then came charging back. This time, the wall of force launched him upward. His momentum was turned against him; Iphigenia guided his trajectory with successive bumpers of kinetic energy. Like a pinball, he rebounded helplessly from one to another, then shot at a low angle across the muddy path. Skipping through the muck, he slapped into the fabric of the dome. A bubble of force sealed him in place.

Suddenly, I was alone with Amyati/Iphigenia. Simantha was lying face down in the muck, utterly motionless. The Cupid had been destroyed; what little remained of it was at work on my mind. My helmet was off, and I had no idea where my force-lance had ended up.

My knee screamed in protest as I struggled to my feet. The exoskeleton supported my weight, but the pain was relentless. In a way, it was a good thing. The agony anchored me to reality. I hopped toward Simantha, slipping awkwardly in the technicolor slime of the seafloor. Water was pouring in torrents from the holes Iphigenia had punched in the dome with the Chatterbox. It didn't look like I had much time left to figure out a solution, but my sense of urgency was disfigured, distant. I felt I was wading in rising, weirdly bulging, distorted emotions. The thought of a mundane drowning in everyday water didn't seem much of a threat, by comparison.

I knelt clumsily by Simantha, left leg stuck out straight to the side. My knee hurt anyway, making me gasp. Tears stung my eyes. *She's so beautiful.* My heart ached at the sight of her. I felt like I might split open, spill my gigantic feelings everywhere. Dizzily, I pried Simantha's hand open and picked up the little crescent moon.

"Iphigenia," I called, and my voice was firm. I was so proud of myself, I nearly burst. I held out the emblem. "You dropped this."

She whirled to face me. Behind her, I caught a glimpse of a pathetic, huddled shape. *Is that . . .?* A terrifying realization loomed, too gargantuan to comprehend. I looked away hurriedly; now was not the time for distractions. Instead, I focused on her face, looking for Amyati, trapped somewhere behind her own eyes. But they were also Iphigenia's eyes, like holes into the distant past. I saw no recognition there; if Iphigenia had access to Amyati's knowledge of who I was, she gave no sign of it.

Upon foggy consideration, I realized that might be a good thing. Amyati and I hadn't gotten on so well. Yet here I was, risking my life— and everyone else's!—in this desperate effort to save her from . . . from what, exactly? Nano-machines carrying Iphigenia's memories?

I couldn't find a line of thought that didn't wriggle and squirm in the grip of my attention. Thoughts twisted from my mental fingers, splashed into the mud. *I think . . . I think with my hands?* No, that wasn't right. My head was pounding. Dizziness twisted my stomach, and the pain in my knee distracted me. I fought for clarity.

What was all this about? She'd said she had been promised *death*. And I thought *I* was morbid, sometimes! But if she wanted death, why the fierce struggle to stop us?

The Cupid? When it arrived, Iphigenia had freaked out. Clearly, Iphigenia hated Cupids. Blamed them? Is that what Simantha had said? Or were they simply a scapegoat for the anger she couldn't take out on Simantha because of the love they shared? I couldn't recall if Simantha had managed to explain all this to Iphigenia before . . . before the Cupid turned into a storm.

It was no use. My thoughts darted away, scattered like schools of little synthetic fish.

I offered the silver moon again. It seemed huge and heavy in my hand, as if I hefted the actual moon.

"You are Iphigenia," I said. "But you are in the body of my friend." That much, at least, I knew to be true.

Iphigenia stared at me. She was no longer armed. Amyati had been uncertain of what I could do with my 83 AV. Maybe that was why Iphigenia hesitated now. Maybe she was no longer certain she could stop me if I attacked her. Besides, all she had to do now was wait. Wait . . . and drown. Water was splashing behind me to my left, echoing loudly under the dome. Laid over the hum of the pumps, it had a musical cadence. I had to raise my voice to be heard.

"You want to die," I told her. "I'm sure Amyati wants to live. These two things . . . they're the same. But you can't find release if you kill the one person who can help you." I gestured at Simantha's inert form. "You're in every female descendant of your line. The body you're wearing is only one of them. You could kill yourself, but that wouldn't be the end of it."

I lifted Simantha's limp body in my arms. *Now* I was lifting the moon. I fought back an unseemly giggle as I cradled Simantha's head on my armored shoulder.

Cold water was rising around my ankles as I tried to stand. My knee objected mightily. But have I mentioned I'm stubborn? I forced myself upright, then tried for dignified as I said, "It's time to end this. To make it right."

I took a tentative step toward her. Iphigenia watched my slow approach: shaky step with the right, slow drag with the left, knee locked in place by the exoskeleton. Step, slide, step, slide.

When I reached her, I held out the emblem again. Slowly, Iphigenia reached out with Amyati's graceful hand and touched the cool silver on the open palm of my glove. She lifted it reverently, raising it to her lips. Her eyes closed with some overwhelming passion, struggling to hold it inside. Tears leaked from beneath her eyelids and formed trails down her mud-spattered face, Amyati's mascara drawing lines that couldn't begin to describe someone else's ancient sorrow.

Like the girl who normally inhabited the body she wore, Iphigenia was strong. Noble. She steeled herself and opened her eyes. My imagination balked at what she must be feeling in that moment. Even in my addled state, I could only wonder at the expanses of her soul. I hoped, fervently, that I would never live so long. Seventeen years of emotional confusion had already been plenty, thank you very much. I still had another 150 years ahead of me if I was lucky. But thousands? *Gods spare me.*

I had no idea how to address a high priestess. *Respectfully*, I guessed. "My lady?" I offered her an arm, shifting Simantha over my shoulder. The simulant girl's weight was negligible in the Powerball armor.

Iphigenia accepted my proffered support, wrapping Amyati's slender hand around my upper arm, leaning on me for balance as we negotiated the slippery path. Solemnly, we limped our way to the temple, passing under the shadowed portico.

Bright light flooded through gaps in the roof, lanced between the pillars forming the open walls, drew stark lines that crisscrossed the open space. I felt like I was moving between worlds as each bar of darkness gave way to light. In the center stood a large block of stone, pitted with age and slimed with algae: an ancient altar. Broken in pieces all around it was the great statue of the goddess Artemis that had once stood there, chunks of white marble streaked with grime. I recognized Simantha's face staring sightlessly from the floor. She watched with empty eyes as I carried her living counterpart across the open space, passing from light to dark and back again. Olympus to Hades, Hades to Olympus. My feet alternately echoed and scraped.

The sound of shouting outside the temple failed to divert my attention: Alan and Kevin exclaiming over something they had found. Some part of my mind registered that the force-fields holding them must have fallen, and I wondered where Jake had gone. But the Cupid dust had me now. I was adrift on a river of time, caught in the final act of a drama thousands of years old. I must play my part.

At the altar, I could see a space beneath had been excavated. The interior had remained inviolate all this time. The dry smell of antiquity, like dust, issued from the gap. The altar sat mostly astride it, but the great stone had recently been heaved aside, moved enough to allow access at one corner. Amyati's ability to control kinetic friction and force would have made it easy, even without power-armor. No resistance at all.

I could see, cradled in a hollow very much like a coffin, a collection of musty bones wrapped in pale cloth that might once have been a toga. Long hair, curly and dark, formed a nest for the skull.

With Amyati's eyes, Iphigenia gazed upon her own remains for a long moment, mutely considering all that had led her to this place. Then she lay down on the great altar stone. "Set me free," she whispered. "Please."

I placed Simantha next to her. Iphigenia took her goddess's hand and kissed her palm. Then she placed the crescent moon on Simantha's forehead.

Artemis awoke.

I suspect it was nano-machines within the emblem, seeking out and rapidly repairing the damage done by the Cupid's electric death. Perhaps Simantha had been steadily repairing for the past few minutes. Either way, her awareness slowly returned, and she took in her surroundings somewhat dreamily before her eyes snagged on

Iphigenia's gaze. She looked wonderingly at Amyati's face, so like Iphigenia's, yet so different.

Amyati leaned in and pressed her forehead to Simantha's. Three thousand years ago, maybe more, Iphigenia leaned in and pressed her forehead to Artemis's. Past and present, linked. The circle complete. The lovers reunited across the gulfs of time.

They stayed that way a long while, sharing a quiet moment. Then, ever so gently, Simantha reached up and touched Amyati's face. Artemis touched Iphigenia for the last time. They kissed.

So much passed between them in that simple touch, in the pressure of their lips, in the taste of their mingled tears. Love and sorrow. Forgiveness. And perhaps, some measure of relief. When they separated, a silver crescent moon was imprinted on Amyati's forehead, a mirror to the goddess's crest. It slowly dissolved, nano-machines sinking through her skin to begin the work of un-writing Iphigenia from existence, following the trail from the present back into the past, sweeping it free of the debris of ages.

I stepped back from the altar and turned away, offering them privacy for this final moment—a small measure of dignity for Iphigenia's death. I heard Artemis murmuring to her lover as I walked away.

". . . you were my soul. How could I let my own humanity die? I needed to know some part of you would remain. . ."

It was over. Artemis had at last released her high priestess into oblivion. Piece by piece, Simantha's nano-machines were erasing the programming that trapped Iphigenia inside Amyati. I found myself hoping Amyati would eventually be herself again, even if that meant we fought bitterly over Sarah's attention.

The realization of why Amyati despised me was unexpected, but it fit. I stepped out onto the temple's front porch, weighing the notion. Yes. Sarah had as much as told me. I was Amyati's rival. Her protectiveness toward Sarah, her physical affection—she must've felt

I had stolen Sarah's love away from her. I had no idea how I would navigate those troubled waters, but it was a problem for another time. Just then, I was deeply relieved Amyati would still be around to be jealous and judgmental, find fault in everything I did. I could accept it. It seemed better than losing her.

I felt like I had been chasing headlong after this forever, but . . . in amazement, I realized it couldn't have been more than two hours, maybe two and a half, since that fateful meeting at the mezzanine.

And Simantha . . .

Simantha would survive. She had been without Iphigenia for thousands of years. Yes, I felt certain she would survive. Because she must. For love of Iphigenia, she had finally let her go, but she would very likely mourn for a long, long time.

I fervently wished—as I watched Alan and Kevin splashing through the rising water—that Simantha would come to me if she ever needed a friend. So strange, to think I had befriended a girl who had once played the role of goddess to the people of ancient Greece. I would need to take a refresher course on mythology. Maybe Sarah could help with that. . .

Alan and Kevin were waving at me. What was it they were carrying? Was that a *body?*

The fog of forgetfulness was suddenly torn away. Memories came flooding back, rising like the waters all around me.

All at once, I was drowning in the awful realization of Cory's death.

XXVIII

Jake, I would later discover, had rummaged through the lockers at the dome's entrance until he found some scuba gear of an appropriate size. Donning it hastily, he had exited the airlock while Kevin waited with the diver in the tunnel. A patch kit in the diver's tool bag allowed Jake to slow the flow of water into the dome. It wouldn't have been possible for a Normal to accomplish quickly, but the resin-reinforced fabric was tough stuff. Despite the massive pressure of the water, it resisted tearing, and the slowly widening holes held, with Jake's Super-powered help, until a full repair crew arrived to restore the dome's integrity. He had managed to buy us the time we needed.

The fact that Amyati's father had named the Sunny brand after the wife he had abused seems like kismet to me. After his death— Amyati once confided to Sarah that she believed her mother had arranged her father's disappearance with the assistance of her aunt— Sunita Mora wound up with everything he had built. There's plenty of information available on Sunita and the jet-setting lifestyle she had enjoyed. I gather she took full advantage of her late husband's empire before meeting her sad end, and she didn't even have to change the name.

I'm tickled by the notion that Sunita Mora posthumously saved her daughter's life. I'd noticed the Sunny brand logo on the fabric of the dome on our way in. It was this excellent synthetic fabric that allowed Jake's attempts to slow the flow of water into the dome to have any chance of success at all. Had Sunita Mora not been so insistent on producing a quality product, none of us would have made it out of there alive.

But while Jake worked with grim determination in the chilly waters of the bay to save his friends trapped in the flooding dome, I found myself trapped beneath my own dome of misery and desolation. My only company was Cory's corpse, a mute testament of my failure to be his friend and protector.

His body was a sad, punctured husk. With so much of his blood drained into the muck, he looked so pale. So small and empty. I took him from Alan's arms and cradled him to my chest, folding myself around him. I thumped to my knees in the mud, heedless of the physical pain of my injury. The pain of Cory's loss blotted out all else, unfolding endlessly within me until it became everything. I fell into a bottomless ocean of grief, vanishing like a stone dropped into dark waters.

The remnants of the Cupid's corpse had dusted me like icing sugar—getting into my eyes, into my blood—and had gone to work on my soul. I don't know if it made what happened next possible. I don't know if I would have been able to do what I did if my spiritual barriers hadn't already been swept aside by the immensity of the dead Cupid's emotional landscape. But as I screamed out my anguish, as I begged and pleaded the universe to have mercy, to take it all back, to make Cory whole again, I heard an echo: an electric hum, like a power chord being strummed.

My connection to Cory was still there.

I didn't stop to think. I grabbed it.

And I *pulled.*

The infinite void opens up around me. It is an emptiness so vast, so ineffable, I feel less than a speck of dust. Cory, cradled in my arms, is less even than I am. At least I am alive.

Never have I felt such loneliness. This is not as simple as me experiencing a great emptiness. This is a great emptiness briefly experiencing me and caring not at all. I am but fleeting. Like all else, I manifest only to sparkle one terrible, intense instant, then cease. There is nothing here, nothing to soothe my aching heart. If Cory ever filled this place with his laughter, with his hopes and dreams, all of it has drained away with his life's blood, leaving nothing. There is only the weight of the empty clay I hold in my arms.

I hear the humming connection, like a high-tension wire keening in a heavy wind. I followed it here. But where is here? *Is this Cory? Is this his death? It is an unmitigated, relentless absence, a hollow cavity that can never be filled. Is this all that remains of him?*

No, there is something else . . . I can feel it: the link between us leads further. I can feel it pulling in so many directions. In all *directions. It goes everywhere. And I think . . . I think I understand.*

This is a gateway.

This is only one reality, one manifestation of Cory. It has ended, but it is only one possibility among many. The Cory that was here no longer is, but I am connected to all of him. In every dimension, in every existence, the two of us are linked, for good or ill.

Carrying Cory, I follow the hum.

I wade through corpses. Cory after Cory, dead: Cory shot full of holes; Cory crushed beneath massive temple stones; Cory drowned in the dome's collapse . . .

I pull on our bond and haul myself through a whirling blur of hollow spaces. Each is another death. Each is achingly empty, another outline of another horror. Cory, electrocuted. Cory, horribly burned.

Each void is the cored remnant of what once was, vast abandoned shells on a string of possibilities: the empty corpses of a vibrant, active boy; the myriad deaths of a curious, lonely child trapped in the cage of his own Super-power, shackled by the forgetfulness that wiped him from the minds of everyone around him. Cory, overwhelmed by a Cupid; Cory, a suicide.

Everywhere I turn, every path I follow, Cory is gone. Infinities flash past me, and with each possibility snuffed out, with each young life ended so tragically, I feel my grief swell.

When we were first connected in the cube, I was overwhelmed by possibilities, and while many of them were full of joy and laughter, I knew then that many of them would also end in grief. But I didn't expect this! I didn't expect him to be wiped from existence entirely—every possible path truncated brutally, abruptly—leaving no hope that he might live on somewhere, somehow! It was as if, by joining myself to him, by putting an end to his isolation, I had chained him to his fate. I had constrained his possible futures.

Could this really be my doing? Is this all my fault? Would he still be alive if it weren't for my influence?

I feel a spreading stain within, a dark mirror to my surroundings. Guilt. Like my despair, it, too, is growing. For a moment, it is all I can do to keep moving, to keep searching. There is so much death and pain here, and it is overwhelming me. Almost, I begin to wish for death myself. To be hollowed out and empty, like Cory. Anything but feel this awful loss!

But I have always been stubborn. I can't believe it could be so definite. So final. I have seen realities in which the two of us never meet! I know there must be a version of him that still lives. Somewhere, he is laughing, talking, mooning over Simantha! Somewhere, he draws breath, knows his parents. Somewhere, his parents know him and love him!

Maybe . . . maybe these empty vistas are merely the realities that exist near my own. Maybe these are the realities I once moved through, and they break away from the path I follow with every choice I make. Maybe the deaths now splitting from my own existence are simply the fates closest to me in the ever-branching flow of time. Maybe I'm not looking far enough.

I pull on the link again. Tentatively, at first, and then with growing resolve. Resolve becomes anger, and anger quickly becomes fury, and before I have time to consider what I am doing I am raging at the emptiness all around me.

I will not . . . let . . . you . . . DIE.

I pull on the link and leap further into the darkness.

Further and faster, racing now, flashing past hollow spaces, tumbling past the empty husks of Cory, past Cory's so injured I know they, too, will die. I deny them. They are not true. Cory is not dead. I haul on the link savagely, furious with the world for stealing my friend away. Furious with myself for allowing it to happen. I scream Cory's name . . .

And I hear him answer.

Hope chokes me, makes my heart leap painfully in my chest. I am getting closer; I can feel it. Some of these Cory's yet live. Some may even recover. I must keep searching.

A feeling of imminence is growing within me, propelling me. I feel the weight of my momentum, all the realities I pass through trailing behind me like a wave, piling higher and higher.

Now Cory's injuries are less brutal. Cory hangs back, unsure if he should follow us into the tunnel. Cory has lost track of Amyati, is unaware of what is happening in the Deep Labs down below. Cory does not witness when Amyati and I argue. Cory has never met Simantha. Cory and I are fast friends. Cory and I occasionally hang out after class. Cory vaguely puts a name to my face. Cory doesn't know me at all.

I cast about, fly off at tangents. Have I gone too far? The sense of urgency is towering now. I need to find the right one, a Cory who knows me, but who isn't hurt, one who . . .

. . . who doesn't have Super-powers.

I halt to stare wonderingly at the space all around me. I am surrounded by him.

Cory.

Alive.

Whole.

Normal.

But something makes me hesitate. Now that I am here, now that I have found him, now that I know he is alive . . . I do not know if this is the right thing to do.

Carefully, I lay Cory's corpse at my feet. Gently, I close his sightless, empty eyes, still so startlingly clear and gray. Softly, I kiss him goodbye. My tears dampen his cheeks. Grief threatens to overwhelm me again.

I don't want to think about it. I know I would miss him too much.

Standing, I reach out for the Cory I have found. He is all around me, yet I find I can wrap my arms around him and hold him close. Relief floods me as my sorrow gives way to joy. I hug him tightly, crying out my love for him, and let it wash away my fear, my uncertainty. I let it fill the void of Cory's absence. I will take this one back with me. Everything will be okay.

Behind me, the rising wave of offended realities crests.

There is a moment of stillness. I feel Cory reaching toward me, tentative, curious.

David?

The wave breaks.

Crashes down.

Like a wave flung against the shore by the tide, I have beached in a new existence, another dimension, some distant channel of the branching river of choices. Like a wave, I am helplessly hauled back out to sea, but as I am pulled back to my own reality, I cling to Cory. I refuse to let him go. I bend all my stubbornness to the task and lash him to me with every fiber of my being, with every string of words he and I have ever spoken, with every promise like knots in the rope of our friendship, with every bond of love, I bind him. I tear him from that shore like an undertow and I drag him out to sea with me.

The current tumbles us back, faster and faster, images flashing past, moments unstuck from history, reality outraged, pelting us with undeniable facts—he is dead, he is dead, he is dead, dead, DEAD—digging insistent fingers between us, threatening to pry him from my grasp, and still I hold him close. I look reality in its screaming, livid face, and I deny it. Cory is mine.

Returning to my body feels like slamming into a wall. I have an inkling of what Jetman must feel striking a target at Mach 6.

Everything goes black.

XXIX

Director Ruiz's office had no door. Ostensibly, this was a physical demonstration of her policy of being available to every member of PA, whatever the concern might be. In practice, however, reaching the director's open doorway required navigating the outer precincts of the Project Arete administrative offices. In most cases, this would necessitate a number of lengthy bureaucratic maneuvers, any of which could bog down a prospective supplicant with background checks, endless data forms, or even mind-scanning by trusted Super-powered aides. Actually seeing Mercedes Helena Cantero Ruiz without her express permission was unlikely, given how busy she was.

Unless, of course, she had taken an interest in you.

I was fully prepared for this to be my last day at PA. Yesterday's events had led to the deaths of numerous Cupids, not to mention Sarah and Susie's injuries, the injuries of numerous bystanders in the cafe, the wounding by gunshot of the scuba diver, and Cory's bizarre death/not-death. Amyati had been stabbed, mentally enslaved, and suffered the trauma of Iphigenia's mental and emotional instability for a prolonged period—never mind Iphigenia's ancient and endless grief—no doubt leaving her in need of some serious therapy.

If that alone didn't condemn me, I had casually flouted PASec orders and followed Amyati through the breach into the Deep Labs, where I had absolutely no business being. That had been flagrantly delinquent enough, but I'd also managed to convince Kevin and the twins to do it, too. Compromising my own integrity was one thing, but the three of them, up until that point, had been model members of PA. My influence had been enough to tarnish them all in the director's eyes, possibly without hope of ever polishing their reputations. If Director Ruiz decided I was a security risk, due to the strange influence my power exerted over those around me, I wasn't going to make excuses.

But I wasn't going to let her kick me out without pleading Sarah's case a final time. Her speech malfunction was a serious problem that might eventually lead to a complete incapacity to communicate, and the only other solution I could see involved blinding her and hoping the malignant growth of the wires could be arrested somehow. I felt very strongly the fix I'd conceived was the best course of action, and I needed to impress upon the director that the idea wasn't just me grasping at straws. I'd had a Super-powered glimpse of the best possible future for Sarah. If convincing the director of my ability to intuit possible connections and outcomes required damning myself with a detailed account of my activities over the last few months— and how my influence had culminated in yesterday's fiasco—then so be it. I would happily take whatever was coming to me, if it meant Sarah would have a chance.

I stepped through the open doorframe into the director's office. I had expected to be interviewed alone, as I had been when I'd first arrived at PA, but to my surprise, I was not the only one invited. In fact, it seemed I was the last to arrive.

The director sat at a large console equipped with numerous smart-glass screens and communication devices. Stationed all around the room were the usual aides and assistants who attended to the director's daily business. For a change, they were at rest, waiting in patient silence, their devices stowed or held at their sides. Only one woman moved when I entered, tapping briefly on her data-pad with a manicured finger to log my arrival.

To my left, Sarah, Susie, Kevin, and the twins sat in stiff-backed resin chairs in various states of squeamish uncertainty. Sarah looked about as unhappy as I'd ever seen her, and only briefly lifted her eyes as I entered. Next to her, Susie's broken leg was encased in a slim exoskeletal support, which would take the majority of her weight until she was fully healed. She smiled wanly and lifted her fingers in a brief wave, but even she seemed less than customarily cheerful to be there. No doubt she had no idea why she'd been involved—she was peripheral to the whole thing—but she could at least corroborate the altercation between Simantha and Amyati at the cafe. Kevin offered me a solemn nod, but his focus was plainly inward. He was holding Susie's hand, channeling his power to speed her recovery. The twins, on the other hand, simply stared straight ahead, falling back on military discipline in their uncertainty as they awaited their turn in proceedings.

To my right, Amyati stood defiantly. She glared at me the moment I entered, most likely for the incredible inconvenience I had caused her, but it didn't have the intended effect; I grinned warmly in response. Her antipathy toward me was well worn and comfortable, by now, and I was honestly relieved to see her outwardly unchanged by her recent experiences. Surprised by the genuine feeling of my response, Amyati pursed her lips. Her irritation transformed into a thoughtful look of appraisal.

Next to her, at parade rest, was none other than her *mausi*, Rana Mora, the leader of NE. She appeared relaxed, but there was steel in her gaze as she looked me over. The smile fell from my face, and I swallowed nervously, but I managed to meet her eyes. She gave me a cool nod and turned her attention back to Ms. Ruiz.

The director made a shooing gesture, and her aides hastily departed the room, including the grizzled military man who had been watching from the hall outside my hospital room the day the director had first introduced herself. Inexplicably, he paused next to me long enough to drop a heavy hand on my shoulder and give me a brief squeeze. Our eyes met for a moment before he moved on, but I couldn't decipher what I saw there. Sympathy, perhaps, and . . . was that pride? I suppose he might have made the same decisions I had, rushing in without hesitation to help his friends. Then again, being a military man, he might have followed orders, and PASec had been clear: Stay away from Amyati, and don't get involved.

I didn't have time to consider it further. The man took up a position blocking the doorway, and the director cleared her throat. All eyes swiveled to her.

Mr. Ruiz rose from her seat and walked around the desk to lean against its front edge. Her suit was severely tailored, today, and her hair was pulled back in a tight bun. She looked every inch the disciplinarian as she crossed her arms and simply stared at me for an uncomfortably long period of time. The others in the room began to fidget or look back and forth between me and the director, wondering who was going to speak first.

I couldn't take it anymore. "Ms. Ruiz," I began, but she held up an imperious hand.

"Don't say a word, Mr. North." Her voice was clipped, impatient. Safe to say she wasn't very happy with me. Injunction in place, she resumed staring at me.

My skin prickled with sweat. I was becoming increasingly uncomfortable. Now everyone was watching me closely, wondering how I would react, and the tension in the room was becoming palpable. Bad enough that the director of PA was drilling a hole into me with her eyes, but Rana Mora's weighty gaze was clearly measuring me, too, and my friends were no longer sure what to make of me in light of the director's continued disapproving silence. Had I done wrong in my attempts to rescue Amyati? Had *they*, as a result of befriending and supporting me? I didn't think so . . . at least, I was certain my intentions had been good, but . . . what did it matter, when the results had been so awful? I had to wonder just how much she knew of it. And then another thought intruded: *Where is Cory?*

I glanced around the room, suddenly afraid. He wasn't hiding; the Cory I'd brought back didn't have any powers. Had PA taken him away for questioning? Were they interrogating him, or . . . or worse?

I felt my power building inside me, responding to my racing heart, to the claustrophobic sense of being cornered. My shoelaces waved about uncertainly, and I realized I'd taken a backward step towards the open doorway when I bumped into the military man standing firmly behind me.

"That's enough of that," he growled, but I couldn't tell if he was talking to me or to the director.

Ms. Ruiz abruptly sighed and stood. She began pacing the room.

"I told you it wouldn't work," Rana Mora said.

I couldn't restrain myself any longer. "What's going on here?" I demanded. "What are you trying to do to me?" But I had a sneaking suspicion I knew.

"Take a seat, David." Ms. Ruiz sounded more tired than angry.

I took a step toward her anyway. I was suddenly furious. Everything I had done had been to protect people, to protect Project Arete.

"No," I said. "I won't sit, and I won't be intimidated. You're trying to trigger my fight or flight response, make my powers activate on their own. Why? Explain yourself, or I walk out of here and never come back."

A heavy hand landed on my shoulder. "Take a seat, son," advised the military man. His voice was low and reasonable, but I had no doubt he could make me do it if I chose to ignore him.

All at once I deflated. It was too much! I'd only been trying to help, and now I was about to lose everything! It seemed like such an injustice to have landed in a place like PA, a place beyond my wildest dreams, only to have it all get snatched away just when I needed it most. It was obvious they'd already discussed the situation and decided their course of action in my absence. I wasn't even going to be allowed to speak up in my own defense! I slumped into a chair and stared at my shoelaces. They trailed loosely across the floor, limp and defeated.

To my surprise, it was Rana Mora who spoke next. Her voice was hard, but not without sympathy. "David, your time at Project Arete has come to an end. You are . . ." She paused, considering her words, then opted for the truth. "You are a liability. They can't afford to keep you here any longer."

I stared bleakly at my laces, only half listening. I'd known this was coming. I should have just walked away, left PA of my own volition, spared myself and everyone else the trouble of going through all this. It didn't help that she was *right*.

Rana Mora continued. "You have rated unusually high on the AV scale, but unlike Supers such as Sarah, or my niece, your powers are largely unknown. What is known of them, however, suggests that your continued presence here will serve only to create further disruption. Whatever influence you exert on those around you, it is subtle and unpredictable. And in a facility like PA, law and order are integral to progress."

That got my attention. I lifted my head and narrowed my eyes at her. Was I imagining things, or was there was as much meaning *between* her words as actually in them? Was she suggesting a facility other than PA might be less bothered by the uncertainty my powers created? Given who she was, there was only one place she could possibly mean.

"Are you serious?" I asked. I tried to catch Amyati's eye, but her expression had turned sour, and she was pointedly looking away. It was all the confirmation I needed.

I stood and turned toward the open doorway.

Behind me, Director Ruiz spoke in a deceptively mild tone. "You'd be wise to consider her offer, David. Not to put too fine a point on it, but your power has influenced everyone in this room, and others besides. If I let you walk away, everyone here becomes a liability as well. I won't be able to trust them, knowing they're too closely involved with you. I can offer them valuable and productive lives here, but I must have absolute faith in their loyalty in exchange.

"Go with Rana, David. Join NE. You will have nearly the same opportunities there as you would here, and with Rana keeping an eye on you, I will be willing to give your friends the benefit of the doubt. Otherwise . . ."

She didn't need to say more. Kevin was smart and gifted with the power to heal. He would be able to find a place for himself almost anywhere. Susie had already been accepted by the CSS. Project Arete could stop her from going to Luna and assisting with the efforts to further understand the Cupids, but why would they want to? They worked with the aliens and stood to benefit from Susie's involvement. Jake and Alan would be invaluable to any outfit that took them in, and they were perfectly capable of striking out on their own if the idea of working for others didn't appeal to them. Of all of us, their powers gave them the best shot at surviving out in the City.

But Sarah? It didn't matter how powerful she was. If she couldn't speak, if her eyes failed her . . . the City would eat her alive.

Slowly, I turned back to face Director Ruiz. I looked at her for a long time, wondering at the utter ruthlessness she had just revealed. It was disconcerting to realize I couldn't trust her, after all. That PA wasn't quite so wonderful a place as I'd come to believe. But what did it matter, really? I'd already known my fate was tied to Sarah's. I'd known it from the moment I'd met her. This wasn't how I'd seen my influence helping her, but if this was what it took to make sure she received the care she needed . . .

I looked at each of my friends in turn. They remained silent, worry etched onto their faces. Their futures were at stake, because of me. None of them would beg me to decide in their favor—they all had too much integrity to try to influence my choice for selfish reasons—but it was plain they all wished to remain a part of PA, despite everything. There were simply too many opportunities here.

I looked back at Rana Mora, who was waiting patiently. She was doing an admirable job of concealing her triumph at removing this particular asset from PA's influence, but I could tell she was excited by the prospect of adding another powerful Super to her roster. I hated to simply accede to her wishes and let her win, but I couldn't see a graceful way out that would spare my friends. Briefly, I wondered how Rana Mora had convinced Ms. Ruiz that this was the best option. It seemed unlike the director to hand a possible advantage to a potential rival. Did the uncertainty I represented really scare her so much? Was I really so unpredictable, so dangerous?

The truth was, I really didn't know.

Slowly, I inclined my head. "I'll go," I said.

I felt a weight I hadn't realized I was carrying suddenly lift. If it helped Sarah, maybe it was for the best. Besides . . . I thought back to the display of Amyati's skill, Hazering six Sec'ers in rapid succession on her way to the Deep Labs. NE had taught her that. Certainly, there were things they could teach me, too.

And once I'd learned enough, I wouldn't need them any longer.

EPILOGUE

During the ancient past, in the centuries they were together, Iphigenia and Artemis traveled widely. With the technology of the Cupids, seen as the magic of the gods, Artemis could fly anywhere she chose, and she took Iphigenia along whenever she was able. There were periods of recovery between each of Iphigenia's pregnancies, and they liked to explore the world and visit remote locations. They loved the peace of living close to the land, and they never tired of discovering new vistas of natural beauty and wonder.

It was here, on the west coast of what was once called North America, that Iphigenia and Artemis discovered their favorite retreat. Simantha described the redwood forests with reverence and spoke of the open-hearted and generous tribal people who dwelt among those towering giants with admiration and respect.

They would spend endless days wandering the shores, watching storms roll in across the Pacific Ocean. It's hard to believe, but there was once a time you could stand on the western cliffs of Sunset and look across a vista of water that extended right to the edge of the world, sea and sky kissing on the horizon, without a single building in sight. Iphigenia and Artemis saw something of their own love in that distant meeting—the goddess of the sky descending to kiss the salt of the Earth. They returned there often.

After Iphigenia's death, Artemis recruited her brothers and sisters among the gods. They caused the temple at Aulis to be uprooted, spirited away to the other side of the world (a place that had so far seldom been visited by the Cupids, as they judged the primitive Western peoples were not yet ready to receive them). I'm unsure whether the gods had the power among them to affect the move themselves, or whether Simantha incited a small rebellion and stole the technology to make it happen. To her, that part wasn't important, and she didn't elaborate when I asked.

What mattered to her was that the temple came to rest on a promontory overlooking Iphigenia's favorite retreat, a little slice of paradise on the western shores of a pristine continent, wild and untamed by humanity—the largest sacred grove Iphigenia and Artemis had ever seen.

The Cupids discovered what their servants had done, of course. The vanishing of an entire temple and the sudden disappearance of the gods who had been so active in the lives of the ancient Greeks upset the careful balance which the Cupids had worked so hard to craft. Their breeding program was in jeopardy. And where was Iphigenia? They had found another potential match. Her womb was required.

Artemis broke. Her masters were so disconnected from the realities of their servants' lives that they might as well be vindictively cruel. The callousness of it all appalled her. She refused to assist them any further. Unsure quite what was happening but feeling solidarity for their sister, the other gods stood with her against the Cupids.

None of them truly believed they were slaves. They had never questioned their programming before. But maybe that was only because the Cupids had never given them reason to.

In punishment for resisting their imperatives, the Cupids took Artemis, along with those gods and goddesses who had had the temerity to assist her, and they forced them to watch as the temple that once stood at Aulis was cut free of the cliffs and dropped into the bay. Then they dismembered their wayward children, fused their nano-networks with powerful energy weapons, and scattered the pieces across those same waters. They hid everything beneath a self-sustaining nano-tech cloak of invisibility, tiny machines warping light, sinking the temple and everything around it into obscurity.

That nano-tech cloak eventually failed. I suspect it was industrialization that did it. All the effluvium of a continent caught firmly in the grip of progress, forcing the nano-machines to divide their energies between self-repair and maintaining the cloak of invisibility. Eventually, their systems were overwhelmed, and the network broke down. The temple was discovered, along with parts of ancient simulants that were nevertheless incredibly futuristic. Project Arete couldn't resist.

I'm not sure why the Cupids at Project Arete expressed urgency regarding Simantha's repair. Dawn had indicated that it was the Cupids who had originally discovered the simulants' resting place and brought the find to Project Arete's attention. Had the Cupids themselves forgotten what went on in the ancient past and been excited to discover this remnant of their own history? Or did those aliens who made the discovery have nothing at all to do with the original Cupids who punished their creations so severely?

Thinking about the Cupids raises more personal considerations, too. What on Earth were the Cupids trying to tell me with all those images of arches and domes? Was it simply a warning of the underwater dome I would eventually find myself in? Or are there details I missed?

Impossible to know. The pictures rushed by so fast, hundreds, even thousands at a time. If a picture is worth a thousand words, then it's no wonder most communication with Cupids happens through the medium of computers. Even then, it's a complicated, confusing, and difficult process.

It's a testament to the perseverance of those involved in human-Cupid relations that we've managed to work alongside them as well as we have. Human aggression has largely been met with a sort of long-suffering patience. The Cupids discipline us, then move on to more important things. The Cupids whom Iphigenia murdered aside, few attacks on them have been very successful.

Would things be different if we had managed to kill more of them in those early years after the Introduction? I don't know. But I will say this: it's not a huge leap from altruistic benefactor to stern overseer, or even tyrannical slaver.

Which leads me to my next question: Why are the Cupids breeding us? They've clearly been working since before most of recorded history to tilt our evolution toward Super-powers. To what end? I find it hard to believe they would do so just for our own benefit. I mean, is it really a benefit? Every year more Super-powers are discovered, and more people have them. It's only a matter of time before everyone does. The paradigm is shifting rapidly. Perhaps too rapidly for us to keep pace with it.

All it would take is a couple Supers with powers of a caliber similar to the Golden Knight's clashing over something, and *BOOM*. Suns explode. Poof. All done. Game over. As the old saying goes, great power confers great responsibility. But are we truly ready for that?

While I'm worrying about the future . . . I can't shake the feeling the last Cupid Iphigenia murdered was trying to tell me to get away before she killed me, too—as though it were worried about *me*, afraid *I* might die and be lost. I don't like that idea at all. Makes me wonder if the Cupids know something about my powers. Maybe they have some big plan for me. For all of humanity.

I'm afraid there are some questions I haven't yet found the answers to, but I'm still searching.

And then there's Cory.

At the time, I was simply relieved to have him back. Somehow, I had resurrected him. I had pulled on the strings of fate, and I had woven them into a new configuration. But nothing is ever so simple, is it?

In hindsight, I realized what I had done was *trade* him. My dead Cory, swapped for a living version from some other reality. I had leapt across dimensions, following our link, and I had made the switch. And I didn't ask Cory what he thought about it. I didn't stop and consult the David on the other side about it either. I certainly didn't want to consider what Cory's parents might think of it.

Like Simantha, I simply deferred payment, or, more accurately, foisted it off on someone else. I didn't want to deal with the loss, and so history repeats. This, despite the lesson that had just played out right in front of me.

That's what you get for sprinkling dead Cupid in your eyes, I guess. Nothing but bad decisions. Ah, but who am I fooling? I can't blame the strange effects of the Cupid dust. There was a moment there, standing on that far shore, when I paused. I hesitated over the action I was about to take. I had reservations, if only for a moment. But I did it anyway. *I* made the choice. No one else. Now I'll have to live with it. What scares me is that everyone else might have to live with that choice as well.

Because payment is coming. I know it, and so does Cory. We can feel it in our bones, in the humming of the wires stretched between us. There is a web of connections between all Corys, all Davids, and what I did will not pass unpunished. I have violated existence itself, and there will come a time when that transgression must be atoned. Like Agamemnon sacrificing his daughter in payment for what he stole from Artemis, I will one day be forced to make a sacrifice. Like Artemis, watching Iphigenia take Amyati hostage, I will one day find others held hostage by my choices.

I dread the future, but I will cross that bridge when I come to it. Call me selfish, I'm still glad to have Cory back.

❦

Oh, wait. There is one other thing.

On a warm autumn evening a couple months after all this went down, a day specifically chosen because the sun would be allowed to shine through the perpetual overcast for an extended period, I and my friends went to visit my parents to celebrate their thirtieth wedding anniversary. My parents had offered to host a barbecue, taking advantage of one of the last sunny days of the season.

The synthetic tree-lined avenue was a glorious riot of color. Say what you like about the clones, they do a commendable job of mimicking the beauty of the originals. Even Simantha was admiring their fiery crowns, so much like her own. I teased her, wondering aloud if maybe she was a tree in another life. She grew wistful and said, "Oh! That would be nice!"

If she was lamenting the loss of the forests that once grew here, it wasn't evident in her demeanor. Despite these momentary lapses, she smiled and laughed, behaving very much like a popular and attractive teenage girl. If she was sometimes a little aloof, if she sometimes paused for a moment and seemed to turn inward, well . . . we could all understand what she was going through well enough.

Kevin, too, was enjoying the beauty of his surroundings. My dad's employment had ensured that our family could afford to retire to a relatively stable and progressive neighborhood. There was an area not too far from here where Kevin and Simantha, along with others from the Greenhouse project at PA, would soon begin setting up a natural parkland. The ruinous swamp they would be terraforming wouldn't be missed, and if they were successful in restoring it to some version of its original state, they might earn funding for further efforts.

Kevin's sister, now walking without assistance, was enjoying a rare break from her training at the Center for Semiotic Studies on Luna and was her usual charming self. Susie's powers involved language, and she had been assigned to the project concerned with improving human-Cupid relations. Due to her deafness from infancy, Susie's main ways of learning about the world had been visual and tactile. From a very young age, she'd shown a facility for learning languages and deciphering scripts of all kinds with ease. By the time she was ten, she was fluent in over two dozen languages, though she was unable to actually speak any of them out loud. To her, language didn't have an audio component. It was a puzzle of ideas, of symbols. Now, with over a hundred languages in her repertoire, and more being added every day, Susie was on the fast track to becoming a liaison for the Cupids, whose visual communication was far less daunting to her than it was to others.

The emotional underpinnings of Cupid communication, however, were a dangerous current to navigate. Susie was naturally optimistic and cheerful, but I worried she might be overwhelmed by the constant assault on her emotions, just as I had been. Indeed, a stipulation of her training and ongoing employment in the capacity of translator for the Cupids would be daily psychotherapy sessions. It was a demanding role that had been assigned to her, but I suppose if anyone had the natural gifts to become an asset to the effort, it was Susie.

Kevin had confided his fears to me shortly after Susie had shared the news of her acceptance to the CSS. For him, the main concern was the risk of Susie's emotions being surgically removed if they proved to be an impediment to the task. While nano-lobotomies were fully capable of making a drone out of even the most off-kilter emotional basket case, Kevin couldn't bear the thought of his ever-cheerful little sister being hollowed out in such a way. I found the thought equally disturbing. Susie was an absolute joy to be around, and all the more wonderful for how rare it was these days. Her training and course load kept her busy and away from Earth most of the time. I decided I would make time, tonight, to reconnect with her. It might be the last time I saw her for an indefinite period.

Alan and Jake were their usual bantering selves. Alan had just unfavorably compared Jake's intelligence to a tractor's. Jake was defending tractor intelligence, saying farm equipment was actually quite high on the echelon of artificial intelligence. These days, tractors were required to make a massive number of production and logistics decisions by weighing and prioritizing a huge amount of variable data for optimal outputs. They were probably smarter than your average Powerball team captain, anyway.

Cory was egging them on, stirring the pot as always. He had, as it turned out, been held for questioning by PA, though they were gentle about it, and they'd made every effort to assist him in acclimating to his new environment. He'd been released shortly after my meeting in the director's office. What little he knew of me had been intuitively gleaned through our link, and it supported everyone else's versions of events. Since then, my friends had all more or less adopted Cory as the collective little brother of the group. My explanations of his appearance and inexplicable recovery from death were accepted at face value, more or less. Only Sarah really understood the full scope and implications of what had happened under the dome, and since she was always nervous, nobody but me really noticed the extra layer of fear she now carried.

I was sorry to do that to her, but in a strange way, she was my rock. Nobody understood my worries and fears quite like she did. If that was because she worried about practically everything herself, so be it, but I preferred to think it was because of the bond we shared. I did my best to reassure her, and she did the same for me. When we couldn't see a light shining anywhere, well, we simply held each other in the dark. If I had faith in anything, then, it was that Sarah would support me through thick and thin.

I squeezed her hand, enjoying her creeping blush and the furtive glances she gave me. I have to admit, it made me feel incredible to have that kind of effect on someone. It occurred to me her incurable shyness might actually be a benefit to our relationship. It was a constant reminder that I couldn't take her attention for granted. She might get nervous at any moment, turn inward and pull away. Besides, I saw her saw so rarely, now, and never for very long. My time belonged almost entirely to NE, these days.

I held out hope that the director would eventually consent to our plan to replace Sarah's eyes with bio-mechanical reproductions grown from her own genetic material. I was doing my best to honor the spirit of our agreement, and I told myself daily that if I just toed the line, PA would eventually allow Simantha to assist Francis and the medical team to rewire Sarah's optic pathways using the highest grade of nanos available: Simantha's own. Until then, I'd just have to clamp down on my impatience, and trust that even though the director might not have my best interests at heart, she at least had a vested interest in Sarah's well-being.

There was one member of our company, however, who was notable by her absence. I wasn't entirely sure what had become of Amyati, and I wasn't sure when, or if, I would ever see her again. She'd been alive and well at the meeting in Director Ruiz's office, but so far, my time at NE hadn't led us to cross paths. No doubt her *mausi* had her running around the City stealing alien technology or something like that.

Outside of my circle of friends, rumors of Amyati's whereabouts abounded: she was to be punished for the murders of the Cupids; she could not be punished for those murders, since it had been Iphigenia who had committed them; she must be hidden, since the Cupids would not understand the difference; the nano-machines that erased Iphigenia from Amyati's mind just kept erasing, and Amyati was now a vegetable in some psychiatric ward; she had left Project Arete in favor of the more welcoming climate of the Normal Eyes halls; she was still down in the Deep Labs, working on the temple project, assiduously avoiding us.

Amid all the swirl of speculation, another option occurred to me that I never put into circulation in the rumor mill: she was nursing a vendetta and would appear when I least expected it, defeat her rival, and steal Sarah away. With Amyati's skill set, it was enough to keep me awake some nights.

Not that I needed help losing sleep. I still had nightmares. I didn't know exactly what the Cupid dust had done to me, but the effects never entirely went away. It was as if it had widened the pathways along which my emotions flowed—trickles had become torrents. I had always been a kid who felt things in a big way, but now . . . sometimes I was overwhelmed by the most innocuous things.

Once, shortly after everything happened, I'd spotted a butterfly alighting on a sprig of lavender in the Greenhouse. I had gone there to invite Simantha and Kevin to this very dinner, in fact, but I had been overcome by the intense beauty of the butterfly, its connection to the flower, the web of life they were a part of. Or rather, the *absent* web of life they *once* were a part of. It wasn't even a real butterfly, just a tiny cybernetic pollinator doing its best to mimic what a real butterfly might do.

The lavender was real enough, though. Kevin told me so later, when I had recovered sufficiently in the hall to go back and actually extend the invitation. But at the time, I had broken down and wept like a baby. I couldn't even explain why. Something about the combined joy and sadness of it, the terrible absence of things lost juxtaposed with a glorious hope for the future.

Yet, in the nightmares, I am treading water in an ocean that reaches from horizon to horizon. All around me rise the remnants of a toppled temple begrimed by age. There's no land in sight, and beneath my feet, I feel things uncoiling. The waters bulge and rise, lifted by the leading pressure of something vast below me surfacing. Just as it reaches me, I awaken, sitting bolt upright in bed, cold and clammy with sweat. And I know, without knowing how, that the things rising from the depths are nothing more than feelings.

The knowledge is not a relief.

For all that, the transition from Project Arete to NE hadn't been as awful as I'd feared. So long as Rana Mora kept tabs on me and reported my activities to Director Ruiz, I was allowed free run of the City in the rare idle time my strictly regimented new life afforded me. I was even able to come and go at PA, though I was now a guest rather than a resident. They'd let me keep my Map, so I could communicate with my friends (and possibly so they could spy within NE's halls), but they'd done something to change the security clearance it offered. Most places within PA were off limits to me now. I now received my education and training from NE, and it had a decidedly more militant flavor. I'd miss Mr. Gold's talks, but it was a relief not to be cut off entirely. PA, it seemed, was content to keep me at arm's length, under the keen eye of NE. *Vigilantes sumus*, and all that. Likely, I was an ongoing experiment, and my brief visits to PA were monitored in an attempt to determine just what kind of influence I might be exerting over those I came into contact with.

At the party, my parents were the consummate hosts, alternately witty and serious by turns. They challenged our minds, drew us into lively debate on a variety of subjects, and deftly navigated the choppy emotional waters of recent events. My mother even managed, in that inexplicable way she has, to pull Sarah from her shell and make her feel at home. More at home, Sarah would later confide, than she had ever felt in her actual home, but that's a tale for another time.

No expense had been spared, and the coconut curry seafood dishes Sarah so loved as a result of Amyati's influence were available, along with the more traditional northwest steak and potatoes, steamed vegetables, barbecued ribs, roasted peppers. After the meal, there was hot cocoa, with little marshmallows, and the age-old tradition of embarrassing stories, mostly at my expense.

I think, in addition to celebrating their anniversary, my parents were tipping a nod to me, for finally managing to surround myself with good people. They could see the quality of the connections I had made.

That evening after the sun had gone down and the ever-present cloud cover had returned, I found a quiet moment and joined Simantha, where she sat on a bench beneath the spreading arms of a mostly denuded synthetic elm. Like many synthetic trees, it had erroneously decided a few days earlier that it was now winter and dropped its leaves almost entirely at once. The leaf litter was still browning underfoot and crackled as I sat down next to her.

"Hello, David." She offered me a wistful smile, breathing deeply of the cool night air. It had grown chilly, once the sun went down, but despite being clad in little more than an elegant white evening gown, Simantha didn't seem to notice.

Everyone had dressed up for the event—Jake and Alan were even wearing suits and ties—but nobody managed artless perfection in quite the same way Simantha did. Her only adornment was the glimmering silver crescent moon emblem, which she had taken to wearing on her forehead ever since the incident below the bay. I looked at it now, shimmering faintly in the dark, and wondered if she was punishing herself. Every time she looked in a mirror, it would remind her of what had been lost.

The crest had been a gift from Artemis to Iphigenia, in ages past. Artemis had caused a portion of her own moon emblem to pull free and transfer to Iphigenia's skin. Iphigenia, and all those who had witnessed the act, had seen it as the magic of the gods. Nothing but nanos, of course, but ignorant of how the magic was actually performed, Iphigenia was overwhelmed by the blessing. Forever after, she was marked as Artemis's favorite, as her high priestess. But only Artemis and Iphigenia knew what it really signified: they had been married. Through the nano-machines in the emblem, Iphigenia had been able to sense Artemis, to feel her love.

Simantha noted the direction of my gaze, perhaps divining something of my thoughts. She gestured to where the others were gathered, their voices and laughter filling the evening air. "Thank you for this, David. I feel it was precisely what I needed." She breathed deeply again and released a satisfied sigh.

It almost made me put off doing what I had planned. She seemed to have found some measure of peace. Who was I to ruin it with another reminder of what she had lost? But as human as she so often seemed, I suspected she might be engaging in that age-old human pastime: pretending she was okay when she was not.

I took a deep breath of my own and held out the rectangle of plastic.

She looked down in surprise. It was perhaps thirty centimeters by twenty and a centimeter thick. I had wrapped it in a thin resin-coating printed with a motif of stars and crescent moons.

"What is this?" she asked.

"A gift."

"A gift?" She glanced up, searching my face.

"Yes. Something to . . ." I swallowed, then forged ahead. "To remind you of her."

Simantha took the package and placed it on her lap. For a time, she simply looked down at it. I wondered if she would open it. I hoped she would. The gift felt appropriate, but perhaps it was too soon.

Squaring her shoulders, Simantha unwrapped it. The resin crackled beneath her fingers.

Within was a book. The title read *Iphigenia at Aulis*; beneath that: *Euripedes, circa 407 BC.* The cover art was a recreation of a painting by Bertholet Flemalle, originally created sometime in the 1600s. It depicted a man in golden hoplite armor, with that signature vertical crest on the helm, embracing a young woman in a dark-blue dress. She was being placed upon the altar even as he turned his face away, perhaps in shame or grief. Or maybe he was just looking for his sword in order to get the job over with. The blade was laying at his feet. A man in rosy robes in the left foreground was bowing in an attitude of worship, perhaps the seer, Calchas. Above him, a pair of soldiers covered their faces. Over it all, a pale blonde-haired maiden in gold-trimmed white robes reclined on a crescent moon, one arm flung over a terrified-looking horned creature—the Anymal Agamemnon slew in the sacred grove, I assume, with the goddess Artemis. In the image, she has a plump face and long limbs.

Simantha's eyes lingered on the cover for a time. A nostalgic smile quirked her lips. "This is horrendous," she said eventually. "It was nothing like this."

I was glad she could find some humor in it. I watched as she opened the book, then slowly turned the pages. Occasionally, she stopped to dwell upon one of the comic's panels. Her slender fingers traced an image of Iphigenia's face.

Carefully, Simantha closed the graphic novel. She held it pressed close to her chest for a moment, then set it aside on the bench. I looked up to find tears welling in her eyes. She dashed them away with the back of her hand and took a shaky breath.

"I'm sorry," I said sincerely. "I just thought . . ."

She stood and turned to pull me up after her. As I came to my feet, she embraced me. Awkwardly, I put my arms around her and patted her back. It was a clumsy business because of her height in heels. My nose pressed into her neck, the side of her jaw against my cheek.

"Thank you, David," she whispered. She held my face in both hands, then placed a kiss on my brow. The act had the feel of a ritual. Her eyes were once again dry. She disengaged and retrieved the graphic novel. Turning to leave by the garden gate, she paused with one hand on the latch, giving me a final, speculative look over her shoulder. Her eyes glimmered in the darkness as they searched my face. Then she was gone—the goddess of the moon vanishing into the evening twilight.

My girlfriend joined me, twining her arm about mine and leaning into my shoulder. "I suppose she's g-gone to finish what . . . what she s-started," said Sarah, with only a little of her usual hesitancy. "All those de . . . descendants. The d-daughters of the moon are s-still out there . . . s-somewhere."

Something about the way she said it made me uneasy.

I looked up at the moon. The silver crescent was riding high, its light mostly obscured by man-made clouds. I felt an upwelling of some unidentifiable emotion. Ruthlessly, I pushed it down. Tonight was a celebration, not a night to get bogged down in alien feelings. Arm in arm, we made our way back to the party.

But Sarah was right. Amyati was just one girl descended from Iphigenia. Beginning with Iphigenia's final pregnancy, sometime around 800 BC, the Iphigenia program had been propagating in the women of that line for more than three thousand years. The Mora women were but one small branch of a massive tree with its roots planted in far antiquity.

Simantha's tragedy had only just begun.

Afterword

Words alone cannot convey my overwhelming gratitude for everyone involved in this project, but I beg you to indulge my clumsy attempt.

First and foremost, to my wife, Shweta: I would never have finished this journey if you hadn't been there with me every step of the way. Thank you for your unstinting encouragement and support, for helping me back to my feet when I stumbled, for being the light to guide me when I lost my way in the dark.

To my mother: The list of gifts you have given me is too long to enumerate here, but it began early with inspiring my love of reading and writing. It has continued in myriad forms ever since. I owe you everything.

To the early readers of the very first (admittedly unpolished) version: Bryan Baker, Tiana Gordon, Martina Hinrichs, Shweta and Glenda Houston, Amber and Terry Hubley, Jennifer Orr, Kimberley Turner, Sarah Van Aken, Justin Wiseman, and anyone else I may have forgotten . . . your feedback and thoughtful criticism helped shape the story you now hold in your hands. If it is excellent, it is because of you. If it is terrible, that's entirely on me.

I'd also like to tip my hat to everyone at Friesen Press:

Jamie Ollivier, who set my feet on the path.

Erin Cutler, who kept them there.

Katie Heffring, for the insightful comments along the way.

And last, but certainly not least, Lissette Leivas, for capturing the essence of the adventure with her amazing cover art. You absolutely *nailed* it!

To all of the above, to anyone I've overlooked, and to my future readers, wherever this story may find you:

You're all Super-heroes to me!

About the Author

Ian Houston lives with his wife on Vancouver Island, off British Columbia's beautiful Sunshine Coast. He has been writing since he was in high school, and *Return* is his first published novel. You can connect with him @ianhouston626 on Instagram.

Printed in Canada